TALES OF A TRAVELER
BOOK TWO

Wolfsbane

N·J·LAYOUNI

Tales of a Traveler Book Two: Wolfsbane
Copyright © 2014 by N. J. Layouni. All rights reserved.
First Print Edition: September 2014

Edits suggested by Red Adept
Cover and Formatting: Streetlight Graphics

Connect with the Author:
Facebook:
https://www.facebook.com/pages/NJ-Layouni/405255156236485

Goodreads:
https://www.goodreads.com/author/show/8107337.N_J_Layouni

Twitter:
https://twitter.com/NJLayouni

Website:
http://njlayouni.blogspot.co.uk/

Dedicated to all those who dare to give life to a dream

chapter one

VADIM OPENED HIS EYES THEN groaned. His eyelids felt swollen and gritty, and his head pounded with the force of a hundred battering rams. Bile churned in his stomach, the slightest movement enhancing the unpleasant sensation.

Although he could not recall how he had gotten there, he lay stretched out upon the narrow cot in the hunting lodge. It must be evening, for shadows cast by the fire flickered and danced upon the wooden walls. With a growl of discomfort, he shielded his eyes. Even the darkness seemed too bright. *Erde!* How his head ached. The quiet murmurs of his comrades as they sat talking beside the fire made him hiss with discomfort.

Where was Martha?

As memory returned, a hot wave of shame washed over him. The way he had spoken to her earlier was unforgivable. How could he face her? 'Twas hardly the way a loving husband ought to speak to his new bride. What must she think of him?

Of course, Vadim knew the cause of his loutish behavior, the symptoms were all too familiar, but that did not make his guilt any easier to bear. Why, after such a long absence, had the malady of battle sickness returned to plague him? It had been several years since it had last visited him. Naively, perhaps, he had begun to think himself cured.

Now it was back, and the effects much worse than he had recalled. Perhaps his recent injury had somehow reawakened the inner beast. Whatever the reason, poor Martha had taken the brunt of his unmannerly behavior. He had to speak to her, to make amends if he could.

"Are you awake, m'lord?"

Vadim grunted in response, wishing Reynard's voice was less painful to his sensitive ears.

"Here." He heard the sound of something being placed on the floor beside the bed. "I have made up a batch of your usual infusion. It is your head that ails you, I take it?"

"Mmm." And not just his head. Even his teeth ached.

"I shall leave you to recover in peace."

Please do. But for the love of mercy, depart quietly.

Without bothering to open his eyes, Vadim stretched out his arm and tapped his fingertips over the wooden floor until he encountered a tall drinking vessel. He curled his fingers about the warm pot. Instantly, the sweet aroma of infused herbs assaulted his nostrils, reviving him even before the tankard touched his lips.

Thank the Spirits for Reynard and his remedy.

The effects of the herbal concoction were blessedly swift. Almost as he finished the last drop, Vadim felt the unyielding pressure behind his eyes begin to ease. Feeling a little more like himself, he sat up and swung his legs to the floor slowly, in order to avoid jarring his sensitive skull. He winced as the wooden bed creaked beneath him.

Reynard turned to look at him from his place by the hearth. "Excellent. There is life in you yet. Come over and sit by the fire, m'lord. Young Fergus has prepared a fine rabbit stew for supper."

Food? Vadim's stomach rebelled at the mere thought of it.

He shuffled over to where his friends sat by the fire, his legs wobbling beneath him like a newborn colt's while his head swayed painfully on its fragile stalk.

Fergus leapt up as Vadim approached, immediately surrendering his seat so that he could sit down. With a grateful sigh, Vadim crumpled onto the chair and leaned back, closing his eyes for a brief, blissful moment.

"Are you hungry, m'lord?" Fergus asked.

With great reluctance, Vadim forced his eyelids to open.

"Take this." Fergus thrust a wooden bowl at him, his gappy front teeth glinting red in the firelight. "A little food will do you a power of good."

Erde! Vadim recoiled, his spine pressing up hard against the chair's back. The bowl was filled to the brim with a steaming stew, but the lad might as well have presented him with dish of rotting entrails. A glistening, greasy slick floated on the watery surface of the stew, adding to its unwholesome look. A wave of nausea assaulted him, and hot bile flooded his throat. With effort, he managed to swallow it back down. He could not hurt the lad's feelings.

With as much grace as he could muster, he extended his trembling hand and took the bowl from Fergus. "Thank you," he murmured.

Reynard ruffled the lad's mop of carroty hair, smiling with affection. "Go and check outside, boy. I need to speak with Vadim for a moment."

"Yes, Father."

Vadim envied the lad his energy as he bounded away to do his father's bidding. He slammed the cabin door hard behind him.

As soon as Fergus was gone, Reynard took the bowl from Vadim's unresisting hand. "Let me take that for you." He emptied the bowl's contents back into the stewpot that hung beside the fire. The accompanying slopping noise sounded like the patter of falling vomit. "I had not the heart to tell him you would be unable to eat."

"Thank you, my friend." Vadim swallowed hard and took a deep breath. "The lad meant well. He was not to know."

"Rest easy for a while," Reynard said, settling back in his chair. "You will rally again soon enough."

Vadim sincerely hoped so. He had forgotten just how terrible a bout of battle sickness could be.

They both stared into the fire's swaying, crackling flames, but as the moments lengthened, Reynard's silence struck Vadim as peculiar. He darted a sideways glance at his friend. Why was he so unnaturally quiet? Was something amiss?

"How long has it been?" the older man asked at length, his gaze still fixed on the fire's dancing flames.

"Hmm?"

"Since you last suffered from battle sickness?"

Reynard's question took him by surprise. "A while," Vadim admitted. Why would he ask such a thing? Certain subjects were taboo, even between good friends. Was nothing sacred now?

Reynard fidgeted in his seat, appearing equally ill at ease. "Perhaps we might... talk about it?"

"What?" Vadim jerked upright in his chair, and a sudden bolt of bright pain flashed inside his aching skull, but he was too aghast to heed it. "Why in the name of the Great Spirit would we want to do that?"

Reynard stared determinedly into the fire. Beneath his neat gray beard, his skin appeared suspiciously red. "We might both... b-benefit from it."

Throbbing head dismissed, Vadim regarded Reynard with growing concern. "Have you taken a blow to the head, my friend? Indeed, I cannot imagine why—"

"Oh, forgive me, m'lord." At last, Reynard looked at him at last, his face stricken with shame. "I promised I would attempt to broach the subject with you, but I fear I must break my word."

Vadim smiled and relaxed back in his chair. Suddenly, Reynard's behavior made sense. "Martha, I take it?" His friend's unseemly breach of protocol reeked of his beloved wife's meddling. Nothing was beneath her notice—no subject too delicate to be tackled. And that was but one of the many things he loved about her. "Be at ease, my friend. You have done my lady's bidding. Let us leave this alone now."

Reynard sighed, but looked a good deal happier. "Your lady can be most persuasive," he said with a smile.

"Well do I know it, to my cost." A sound from outside drew his attention. Barking? That had to be Forge; the dog's booming bark was unmistakable. Vadim's smile faltered. "Did Martha leave Forge behind when she returned to Darumvale?" If so, it was most unusual.

"No, m'lord. He returned earlier, by himself."

A stab of ice pierced Vadim's heart. His blood chilled, flowing like water in his veins.

"We tied him outside so his whining would not disturb your rest," Reynard continued. "Fergus must have woken hi—"

"How long ago did he return?" Vadim battled to keep his voice calm as a fist of fear twisted his innards.

"Only a few hours—"

"A few hours?" Vadim leapt to his feet, clutching the back of the chair for support as the room pitched like a boat in a storm. *No. No. No!* Regaining his balance, he staggered for the door. "We must hasten to Darumvale." *Please let me not be too late.*

4

"Now? But you can barely stand, m'lord." Reynard hovered beside him like a mother hen, his face etched with concern.

Leaning his forehead against the wooden door, Vadim clenched his eyes tight, willing his body to serve him. "Do you not see, man?" he growled. "Martha and Forge are never apart. Not unless..." He could not say it, did not want to imagine it.

Unless. That one small word contained unthinkable sorrow. He clutched Reynard's arm. "Drag me there if you have to, but I must go to Darumvale." His voice betrayed his panic, but he did not care. "Now!"

The lights of the village came into view at last, and every hope in his heart died, withering and crumbling into dust like the last leaf of autumn.

"At least we will not have to waken them," Fergus remarked cheerfully as he drew his mask over his face. "The entire village is aglow."

"Aye." Reynard squeezed Vadim's shoulder in a futile attempt to comfort him. "And that should be a warning to you, lad."

No one should have been awake at that late hour.

Cursing violently, Vadim leaned heavily upon his staff. Even with the aid of his friends, it had taken them an age to descend the familiar trail to the village. Too long. He should have sent Reynard and Fergus on ahead. But in his heart, he knew it would not have made any difference.

He drew a deep breath. The village lights were certainly an ill omen. Even from where they stood, and hampered by the lingering effects of his weakness, Vadim scented trouble on the wind. Whatever the danger was, his instincts told him that it had now passed. For the villagers, at least.

Forge whined and bounded down the narrow path ahead of them. Without speaking to his companions, Vadim set out after him. The other men followed silently in his wake.

Swords drawn, they pushed open the doors of the Great Hall. Despite the late hour, Seth's home was full of people. Everyone turned, gaping at Vadim, his apparent resurrection soliciting many loud cries of shock and wonderment.

Ignoring them all, his eyes sought but one person in the oppressive sea of faces before him. Like a swarm of bees, the crowd enveloped him. Buzzing, unwelcome voices, all of them talking at once, each one competing to be the first heard. But, to him, their words were a mangled gibberish. He had not the will to translate the painful noise.

Be here, my love. Craning his neck, Vadim peered over the heads of the villagers, seeking Martha.

"Where is Seth?" Reynard shouted to be heard over the cacophony of excited voices. "Is Martha amongst you?"

Vadim replaced his sword. Weapons were of no use here. Not now. He was grateful for the company of his two friends. Their sturdy presence shielded him at either side from being jostled by the excited villagers.

"He took her—"

"The earl and Anselm—"

"—back along the North Road."

Only certain words penetrated Vadim's consciousness, but they confirmed all his fears in a sickening moment of clarity. Now he understood what had happened. The truth was stark and all too clear.

She is gone.

No longer did he search the crowd with hungry eyes. Instead, he leaned heavily upon his staff, suddenly sick and weary to his very soul.

"Vadim?" Seth pushed his way through the crush of villagers. "Please, friends," he cried, addressing them. "Step back. Let them breathe, at least."

Vadim met Seth's eyes. The sorrow on the older man's face almost exactly mirrored his own.

At the command of their chief, the villagers gradually quieted and then dispersed. Reynard and Fergus directed many of them in the direction of Seth's plentiful ale casks.

At last, Vadim could hear again. "Was she taken unharmed?" he asked Seth, inwardly flinching at the thought of Martha in pain.

"Aye. I believe so, lad."

Vadim arched his eyebrows. "You believe so?"

"They had me under guard at Mother Galrey's," Seth replied. "But Bren tells me..." Then he faltered and glanced at the ground.

"Go on." Vadim clenched his teeth, steeling himself to hear the worst.

"The earl...struck her. Only once, across her face," he added swiftly. "But your lady took the hit without making a sound."

That low growling noise, Vadim realized, was coming from his own throat. A fog of red rage engulfed him. No longer stooping and weary, he gripped his walking staff with both hands and bent it, imagining that it was the earl's scrawny neck. The wood gave a creak of protest, then splintered.

"He struck my woman?"

Seth blinked and took a step back. "But sh-she recovered, m'lord. By all accounts, the tongue lashing she gave Anselm and his master was—"

"Where is Bren?"

"At home. Now, Vadim." Seth circled around him as he cast down the broken pieces of his staff and marched for the door. "Her children are at home. If she sees you this way—"

"Bren has nothing to fear from me." He threw open the doors and stalked out into the night. The earl's safety, however, was another matter entirely.

I am sorry, Lissy, but I can no longer uphold my vow. Forgive me, my sister.

The current Earl of Edgeway's days were numbered. Come what may, only one of them would walk away from their next encounter. Vadim prayed that his sister would understand.

Despite the late hour, Bren answered her door swiftly. She was still dressed for the day.

"M'lord." She seemed unsurprised to see Vadim standing on her threshold. Her lips twitched as if she meant to smile then thought better of it. "It heartens me to see you alive and walking around again."

"Bren." Vadim battled to quell his impatience. The poor woman had suffered enough recently. "I was grieved to hear about Jared. He was a good man."

"Aye." The mention of her dead husband summoned a flash

of tears to her eyes, but just as quickly, they were gone. He could only admire Bren's strength.

He saw her two youngest children behind her, lying on their stomachs by the fire, while young Will reclined in a rocking chair. By the looks of it, the family had been sharing a late supper and playing a game of counters; he recognized the square-checked cloth and gaming pieces on the floor.

Bren turned her head, following his gaze. "They needed something to divert them before bed. Today has not been kind to any of us. Watch your brother and sister for me a moment, Will lad," she called, then stepped outside, gently pulling the door closed behind her. "What is it you need to know, m'lord?" she asked.

Anyone could have told him all that he wanted to know. But because Bren was Martha's friend, he especially valued her words.

The older woman's no-nonsense commentary was a sharp contrast to the excited gathering back at the Great Hall. In her usual blunt manner, Bren told him everything without embellishment.

Vadim listened without interrupting. His heart swelled with pride when he learned how Martha had taken the earl and Anselm to task. Despite his sorrow, he smiled when he heard all the terrible things she had said to them. Her capacity for such bravery he had never doubted.

But there was something he still did not understand. Why had she baited the earl so badly? Why go to such lengths to convince the earl and Anselm that Vadim was dead? By telling the truth, Martha might have spared herself a beating. Anyone foolish enough to venture into the hills would have been swiftly dealt with. There was no good reason for her not to reveal his hiding place. Why had she not done so?

He must have spoken his thoughts out loud, for he heard Bren's irritated tut.

"Why? To protect you, of course." Bren shook her head, obviously unimpressed with his lack of comprehension. "If you ask me, she would have gladly chosen death over betraying you, m'lord."

Vadim stared at Bren's lopsided head scarf, and the grizzled hair poking out from beneath its frayed edges, his mind gradually became acquainted with Martha's motives.

She did it for me? To protect me?

That was the reason for her boldness? Of course it was! Bold, stupid, incredible Martha. The earl should have killed her on the spot for the insults she had given him, and had it not been for Anselm's intervention, he might well have done so. Instead, they had done the next worst thing. They had taken her with them.

Vadim pressed a hand to his chest, his heart aching for what it had lost. What would become of her? Would the earl imprison her purely for the crime of marrying a wolfshead?

Or would he torture her? Vadim flinched from the sudden vivid images conjured by his imaginings, of all the ways in which Martha might now be suffering. Tormenting himself would not aid her. With effort, he closed and locked the doors to the darkest rooms of his mind. A method that had served him well enough in the past.

"Thank you, Bren." He placed a gentle hand on her shoulder. "You should return to your family." With that, he turned to walk away.

"What will you do, m'lord?" Bren's voice halted him before he had taken three paces. "The castle is a fortress. How can you hope to rescue her?"

"You forget, Bren. Edgeway was once my home too." His mouth formed a grim smile. "Whatever happens, trust in this: I will find her again. Come what may, I will bring Martha back home."

chapter two

S UBMERGED IN MISERY, MARTHA SAT within the circle of
Anselm's arms as the thundering horse train cantered
on through the night, carrying her closer and closer
to Edgeway.

Vadim. Vadim. Vadim. His name played in her head like a
heartbeat. Would she ever see him again?

They reached the outskirts of town, but the earl and his
men pressed on, barely slackening their pace as they negotiated the winding, narrow streets. Martha had never visited this
part of town during her stay in Edgeway. Her former landlady,
Mistress Weaver, had warned her against it. It was reputed to
be the haunt of thieves and drunkards, of ladies of the night
and cold-blooded murderers, all living together in the tangle of
stinking streets.

The horses cantered on. In the still of the night, their hooves
clattered noisily over the cobbles. Several late-night revelers
were forced to dive out of the way, pressing their backs against
the safety of the buildings as the earl's cavalcade swept by.
Dodgy part of town or not, no one shouted or swore at them.
The earl was apparently as much feared in Edgeway as he was
in Darumvale.

A few minutes later, the riders finally reined in their steaming, snorting mounts. A steep incline lay before them. In the
darkness, Martha made out the hulk of a hill, and the menacing
outline of a sprawling castle perched on top.

Any hopes she'd had of escaping died. *Shit!* It looked like Alcatraz. She'd never get out of there.

"I will do what I can for you," Anselm murmured, his breath brushing warmly against her ear. "But I fear you have angered his Lordship too greatly for my influence to hold much sway with him in this mood. Still, I will try."

For the first time since leaving Darumvale, Martha spoke. "Whatever." Her voice sounded husky. "I really don't care anymore."

Throughout the nightmare ride in the dark, she'd alternately cried then cursed herself for getting captured. Thinking about Vadim only increased her tears. Although she tried not to think about him, she couldn't erase him from her mind. As she stared up at Edgeway Castle, she felt the warmth of emotion drain from her body.

The present was bleak and empty. The future looked even worse.

Why am I still alive?

Back at the Great Hall, Martha hadn't believed she might still have a tomorrow. She hadn't banked on living. But now she was forced to consider a new reality, and in light of all the insults she'd hurled tonight, it looked pretty grim.

The horses moved off, taking a slow zigzagging path up the hill. Even in the dark, the animals' hooves never faltered. As they climbed higher, the castle vanished behind its immense outer walls.

Back in the twenty-first century, Martha had visited many ruined castles. Memories of sunny Sunday afternoons spent walking the foundation lines of long-since tumbled stones, trying to imagine what the castle must have looked like at the height of its glory days.

But nothing in her wildest dreams could have prepared her for this place. It was immense.

The horses' hooves made echoing *'thunk-a-thunk'* sounds as they crossed a wooden structure. This close to the castle walls, it could only be one thing: a drawbridge. They rode through a dark archway that momentarily blocked out the stars. The horses feet clattered and skittered over a cobbled surface.

Panic spiked in her heart. Did this place have a torture

chamber? Didn't all the best castles have one? *Oh, Jesus, Mary, and Joseph!*

As the last rider cleared the drawbridge, she heard a steady *tick-tick* sound followed by a soft *thump* as the drawbridge rose and then closed behind them with a deafening, squealing crash. She jumped in fright, and might have fallen from the saddle had Anselm not tightened his arm about her waist.

"Easy, sweeting. 'Twas only the portcullis being lowered for the night," he said softly against her ear.

Martha didn't reply. She was trapped. Sealed in. Cut off from everything familiar. From all that she knew and loved.

Her thoughts returned to Vadim, but his handsome face didn't comfort her, and only made her feel more wretched. Uncaring whether anyone noticed, she broke into hiccupping sobs.

The castle was in lockdown. *It's over. I'll never see him again.*

Her dreams were full of sunshine and laughter, a happy escape from the nightmare of now. Sleep was a golden ticket because it transported her back to Vadim.

Unfortunately, Martha couldn't dream forever.

Wincing at the burning, throbbing ache in her left hip, as she reluctantly opened her gritty eyes, the heaven of her dreams faded into the bleakness of her new reality: a narrow prison cell beneath Edgeway castle.

Physically weary and emotionally wrecked, she'd slept sitting up with her back propped against a damp wall. Fortunately, she still had Anselm's cloak. Huddling deeper into its woolen folds, she pulled it up to just beneath her nose. The fabric still smelled of him, but she was too miserable for principles, and much too cold to dump the garment.

Prisoner comfort wasn't a priority in Edgeway. She clenched her numb butt cheeks, her boots scuffing up the meager layer of straw that covered the packed-dirt floor. On the opposite wall, the rusting chains of a pair of manacles dripped down the stonework, hanging like a macabre Halloween decoration.

On the plus side—if there was one—her cell wasn't totally subterranean. A sullen sliver of daylight trickled through a narrow grill set high up on the wall. At least it provided her with a sense of day or night and, cold though it was, a little fresh air.

Although the grill was too high to peer out of, if she tilted her head back, she could see the sky. Well, a fragment of it, anyway. And standing sentry just outside the rectangular opening was a solitary weed, its small yellow head bobbing occasionally in the breeze.

In a few days' time, you'll have given it a name and be having conversations with it.

Martha looked around at her miserable little room. How might a real estate agent describe her current lodgings, she wondered.

A compact and bijou residence enjoying an isolated position in an enviable historic location. The property boasts cold running water, tasteful antique fixtures and fittings, and an excellent, if modest, view of the surrounding area.

She felt herself smile. Day one, and her brain was already starting to addle. The next month should be very interesting.

Then she heard chilling screams. *Mother of God!*

She wasn't alone in her tomb after all. The long, narrow passageways amplified the echoing cries of her fellow inmates. Clamping her hands over her ears, Martha screwed her eyes tight shut, willing the awful sounds away.

In a moment, I'll wake up. I'll be home again, safe and snug in my bed at Aunt Lulu's house.

But that would mean relegating Vadim to dream status, a subject to be related over the breakfast table.

Her vision shimmered with tears. No. Grim as this new reality was, she loved him too much to wish him away. Folding her arms about herself, she rocked slowly back and forth as if by doing so she could ease the pain of his absence.

Martha watched the ever changing strip of sky through the narrow wall grill, marking the passage of time.

Day two in isolation.

Although her accommodation wasn't exactly a des-res, at least the meals were regular. True, they were stale, rancid, and inedible, but mealtimes told her she wasn't completely forgotten. With the exception of her taciturn, skull-faced jailer, she hadn't seen another soul since she'd arrived.

What's keeping Anselm?

She hadn't yet given up on him, despise him though she did.

The night he'd escorted her to her cell, she'd sensed he genuinely wanted to help. He'd certainly told her as much, and for some reason she believed him. Why, though? A sick puppy like Anselm must have a very twisted reason indeed.

Was he still hunting her even though she was now incarcerated? Was he still trying to steal her away from Vadim? As sure as God made little green apples, it'd have something to do with Vadim.

Or maybe—just maybe—Anselm still had a shred of human decency left in him?

Martha dismissed that last thought.

With a sigh, she scrambled to her feet, her limbs stiff from cold and inactivity. She began pacing the tiny dimensions of her cell, carefully avoiding the bucket-toilet which stank only slightly worse than she did. Wrinkling her nose, she was just debating whether she dared to use it again when she heard footsteps in the world beyond her door.

Two people?

Straining her ears, she recognized the slithering footfalls of her jailer, but the other feet were louder, much more purposeful. Keys jangled, just like her nerves. She took a hasty step back from the door. A heavy key clanked in the lock, and the wooden door of her cell creaked open.

"Martha!"

Anselm. Her heart felt slightly less leaden. At least it wasn't the earl.

"Oh, this will not do." Anselm looked around, grimacing as if he'd never seen the inside of a prison cell before. "My poor sweet girl. How you must have suffered."

Martha stared. He was still trying to play the *friends* card? Really? She watched him in silence, not yet sure of the card she wanted to play.

He looked fresh and clean, all golden hair and shiny buckles.

"I have good news." Anselm's gray eyes shone like polished silver as he smiled at her. "My master has surrendered you to my care."

What? She took another step back.

Anslem's smile dimmed. "You do understand what that means, sweeting? You can leave this place. Now."

And exchange it for what? Martha shook her head, suddenly

reluctant to leave her little piece of hell. "I'm fine here, thanks all the same."

"You cannot mean it." Anselm frowned. "You would actually prefer to remain... here?" He glanced around, his distaste apparent.

"Oh, I don't know," she said. "It has a certain charm." She narrowed her eyes, all pretense of humor gone. "Unlike some people, at least my stinking cell wears its warts on the outside. Get real, Anselm. I don't want to be anywhere near you. Now feck off."

There followed a brief uncomfortable silence during which Anselm, Martha, and the jailer exchanged glances. Anselm was the first to speak.

"Let me put it another way, m'lady."

Martha smirked. *M'lady?* He was finally getting it.

"If you do not come with me, his lordship might proceed with his original plan."

"Death doesn't scare me, Anselm." It was the escape she'd been hoping for.

"I realize that. And, unfortunately for you, so does the earl."

Martha shivered as her *friend* suddenly forgot himself and momentarily de-cloaked, dropping his guard. When he smiled at her, she glimpsed a cold predator staring out through his merry eyes.

"For both our sakes, Martha, I beg you to reconsider. Lord Edgeway has a unique gift for torture. I should not enjoy seeing you... broken." He held out his hand to her. "Please."

Martha exhaled. Although Anselm's friendly mask was back in place, fear had transformed her insides to mush. "Just tell me why." Her voice trembled. "Vadim's dead. What do you want me for?"

Anselm shrugged, lowering the hand she'd refused to take. "My informant says otherwise, and she was most convincing."

Fecking Orla! "Your informant is a vindictive bitch out to cause trouble."

"Perhaps." Anselm smiled. "If so, she will be... punished. But if Vadim *is* alive, he will come to claim you. Just think of it," he said with a bright smile. "After all this time, he will finally come to us."

Martha's simmering temper flashed, overriding her fear.

"You're using me as bait to catch a ghost? Brilliant! And when Vadim doesn't come, what then, fuckwit? How long before you realize I'm telling you the truth and turn me loose, hmm?"

"By that time," he said gently, taking her by the arm, "you may want to stay." There was no mistaking the meaning in his eyes.

Her flesh crawled. "Oh, please tell me you're not thinking what I think you're thinking? I'd never—"

"Never is a long and lonely time away, m'lady," he said, leading her from the cell. "And, as you will discover, my dear, I am a very patient man."

Martha bit her lip. What was the point in hurling insults at him? Let Anselm believe what he wanted. She'd play along for a while. At least if she was out of here, she might find a way to escape or to send a message.

As much as she longed for Vadim, she hoped he wasn't planning a heroic, and ultimately suicidal, rescue attempt. If the earl ever got his evil hands on him—*No.* Vadim loved her, but he was much too wily for that. How else had he stayed alive for so long? Anselm wasn't the only one with a predator's blood flowing in his veins.

If the earl didn't kill her first, Vadim would eventually come for her. Until then, all she had to do was be patient. Even now, he'd probably be hatching some cunning plan or other to spring her from Castle Evil. In the meantime, she'd play the role of a wife in mourning, topped with a few sprinkles of madness. Starting now.

"Did I ever tell you I see dead people, Anselm?"

Anselm arched his eyebrows, but he didn't speak.

As they walked swiftly along the narrow, twisting passageway, Martha smiled to herself. By the time she was done, Anselm would be sorry he'd ever met her.

***

A stout-figured woman came into view, slowly puffing her way up the steep trail that led to the cave.

Finally. Vadim ceased his endless pacing and sprang down the slope to meet her, almost stumbling over Forge in his haste. The middle-aged matron was an unlikely looking angel.

"Well?" Vadim relieved the woman of her heavy hand basket. "Do you have news, Agatha?"

The woman held up her hand to ward off his words, her breathing much too labored for speech. Her cheeks were flushed with the exertion of her mountain walk. Sweat dripped in beads from the tip of her wide nose.

"At least give her time to catch her breath, m'lord." Reynard appeared at Vadim's side, his approach, as always, as stealthy as a mountain cat. "Greetings, sister," he said, addressing the red-faced woman.

Vadim cast an irritated glance at him. Only Reynard's vigilance had prevented him from hastening to Edgeway in search of Martha. The older man had become his constant shadow, from dawn until dusk, Vadim was aware of Reynard's watchful eyes on his back.

"Patience, my friend," Reynard was fond of saying. *"An early death will benefit neither you nor your lady wife."*

Patience. *'Tis too small a word to quell the hot tide within my breast.*

For now, Reynard was diverted by Agatha's hand basket, still balanced on the crook of Vadim's arm. "Let us see what little treats you have brought us today." He lifted the cover and began rifling through the contents. "Mmm... this bread looks delicious—"

"Get your... filthy hands out of there." Agatha recovered enough to swat Reynard's fingers. "You will wait for supper like everyone else."

Reynard chuckled. "Edgeway has not yet robbed you of your sweet disposition, I am glad to see." Agatha squeaked in protest as he hugged her, one arm about her plump shoulders.

Vadim forced a tight-lipped smile, though he had little patience for such horseplay. Agatha must have seen it and took pity on him.

"Your lady is alive and well, m'lord. Anselm removed her from the cells two days ago—"

Vadim exhaled and briefly closed his eyes. *Thank the Spirits!*

"Do not rejoice quite yet." Agatha's eyes flicked between Reynard and him. "He has installed her in his private chambers."

Vadim's jaw dropped, and a blast of jealous rage ripped

through him, urging him to punch something. *He shall not claim her for his own. Never!*

Or perhaps he already had?

The thought of Anselm despoiling Martha's exquisite body with his foul touch made Vadim feel sick to his stomach.

"I see." Not without difficulty, he managed to speak calmly, betraying none of the emotion that was tearing him apart on the inside. "And do you think he has..." He swallowed, unable to voice his fears out loud.

It was fortunate that Agatha understood him so well. "Oh, no, m'lord! No."

The speed of her denial enabled him to draw breath again. Vadim looked into the darkening sky so that his companions would not read the relief in his eyes. The low canopy of thick cloud held the promise of another downpour, and far off in the distance, a dancing ribbon of geese battled to stay in formation. Their melancholy calls were a poignant reminder of autumn's advance. But, for him, summer had already gone.

"By all accounts, young Anselm is behaving himself for once," Agatha continued. "Not that your lady pays him any notice beyond insults." She chuckled. "Her maid tells me she treats him worse than a cur."

By common accord, they set off walking back toward the cave and the comfort of its fire, Agatha leaning heavily on Reynard's arm.

After Martha had been taken, the outlaws abandoned Seth's hunting lodge, and moved on to another hideout. The change of location was merely a precaution. Vadim did not believe Anselm or the earl would come looking for him. He ground his teeth.

Why would they? They have my woman.

He swung Agatha's basket violently as they walked, consumed with thoughts of stealing Martha back from his foster brother. Although she was sheltered by Anselm's questionable protection for now, her situation could change in a heartbeat.

At that moment, Vadim truly envied Agatha. For all that she was slightly plump, and well past her bloom, the good woman had an ability he would give a great deal to possess: that of slipping back and forth between two worlds without rousing suspicion, and with all the stealth of a phantom. "Would you be able to get a message to her, Agatha?" he asked. Although Agatha spent much of her time in the castle's kitchens, he knew she was not always confined there.

"I will certainly try, m'lord," she replied. "What would you have me say?"

Vadim hardly knew. There was so much he wanted to say. How could he condense the contents of his heart into a few brief lines for Agatha to memorize? He had only a few hours in which to try.

chapter three

"I SAID NO." MARTHA SAT ON the window seat in Anselm's chambers, staring out of the mullioned window into the courtyard below. The small diamonds of thick, bubbled glass distorted her vision, reminding her of the House of Mirrors at a fun-fair.

"Please, sweeting?" Anselm stood at her side, attempting to wheedle her into submission. "The earl has a surprise for you."

"Yeah? Call me paranoid, but I don't think I'd enjoy his idea of a surprise." Martha alternately closed one eye and then the other, watching the riders in the courtyard *jump* from side to side.

"You might wear your new gown—"

"Are you deaf?" Finally, she turned to look at him, eyeing him with contempt. "No. No. No!"

Anselm's jaw tightened, a sure sign he was battling to keep hold of his temper. Again. She had to admit, albeit grudgingly, he was getting better at keeping a lid on it. So far, she'd given him plenty of opportunity to practice his self-control.

A week had passed since Martha first arrived at Edgeway castle. It felt like a decade. In all that time, she hadn't once ventured from Anselm's rooms. Every morning as he went out, he carefully locked the door behind him, imprisoning Martha and the young maid he'd supplied her with.

They didn't starve in his absence, though. One of the earl's brutish soldiers brought them food and drink at regular intervals throughout the day. For their added comfort, Anselm had supplied them with a medieval version of a portable toilet, which was just as gross as its modern-day counterpart.

If Martha had hoped to mug her maid for a spare key, she was to be disappointed; the girl didn't have one. While Anselm was away, young Effie was as much a prisoner as Martha was. The only difference was, when Anselm returned from whatever evil-sidekick business detained him, the maid was allowed to leave.

Martha bungeed from depressed to angry and back again, hitting every other mood swing on the way. Being parted from Vadim was a permanent unbearable ache in her heart. Although she refused to let Anselm see her tears, he must have heard her crying into her pillow at night.

At least she had her own bedroom. But her soft bed with its mountain of pillows might well have been a bed of nails. Without Vadim, there was no comfort in it.

She missed the way his long legs entwined with hers, the heat of his body, and the safety of his arms. The worst thing was she couldn't remember what his eyes looked like anymore. A symptom of her sorrow? Whatever it was, the more she concentrated, the further his face slipped away from her.

She glared at Anselm. *Bastard!* He was responsible for all of this. Him! But for Anselm's interference, the earl would've never given her a second glance back in Darumvale. And now he wanted her to go to some fecking party with him? No way.

Anselm took a deep breath. "Let me put it another way, m'lady—"

She liked when he called her that. It was an indication that he was about to be honest. The truth was much easier to stomach than his false friendship.

"—the invitation is not a request."

"Really?" She gave a tight-lipped smile. A command was a different matter. "Then why didn't you just say so?" She got up and swept past him on the way to her bedchamber. The last thing she needed was for Anselm to get the impression she was doing anything to please him. Only responding to direct orders was her small, if passive, act of rebellion.

"Where are you going?" he called after her.

"To change."

She reached the sanctuary of her bedroom and slammed

the door behind her. At least there was one place she could go to escape Anselm's foul company. She leaned back against the reassuring solidity of the oak door and closed her eyes for a moment.

How much longer will I be stuck here? Where are you, Vadim?

Tonight's supper invitation worried her. The earl must have got something nasty planned. Surely he hadn't captured Vadim. No. If that were true, His Evilness would've been unable to postpone his gloating.

With a sigh, she slid the door bolt then went over to the bed to look at the gown Anselm had bought for her. It was a frothy gold-and-cream affair, beautifully embroidered with tiny golden flowers and branching intertwining leaves. The low neckline and long sleeves were considered quite *de rigueur* by the noble ladies of Edgeway castle. It was beautiful. Perfect.

Martha hated it.

She would have much preferred to wear her old and battered gray dress—the one Vadim had brought for her so long ago—stained and worn though it was.

This dress looked like an invisible person lying there, splayed out on the bed. A ghost. She trailed her fingers over the cool, creamy silk. If she wore this thing, who would she become?

Stop it! She stalked away to the window and fixed her gaze on the horizon. The endless days of inactivity were getting to her. With only embroidery to distract her, she was slowly going out of her mind. Besides, she was useless with a needle. Even the ever-patient Effie had given up trying to teach her.

Back in the twenty-first century, she would while away the hours of confinement with a good book. Unfortunately, the few books Anselm possessed were written in a script she couldn't understand. Anyway, something told her they weren't sizzling medieval *bonk-buster* novels, not written on precious vellum. Paper was scarce in Erde.

Only one thing prevented her from throwing herself out of the mullioned windows and onto the courtyard below, a solitary shaft of sunlight in a world of fog.

Her name was Agatha.

Two days ago, a stranger had accompanied the surly guard when he came to deliver lunch.

"I have come to check your measurements, m'lady," a middle-aged woman announced, by way of an introduction. "The seamstress needs to make a few adjustments to one of your gowns."

Over the last couple of days, Martha had been constantly measured and re-measured. At first, she'd kicked up a stink, not wanting Anselm to buy her anything. Then it dawned on her. Here was the perfect risk-free way in which to hurt him. So from then on, she began inflicting grievous bodily harm on his purse.

Suddenly, she began demanding the finest materials for her gowns, and the most exquisite embroidery. The poor seamstress and her team must have been sewing around the clock to keep up with all her extravagant requests.

Anselm had better have very deep pockets. Martha smiled to herself as she stared deep into the fire's flames. She liked fire watching; it sedated her mind, and stopped her stressing. It was almost as good as a TV.

She was vaguely aware of the strange woman sending Effie away.

"Have your luncheon in the kitchen today, child. You deserve a reprieve. I will tend m'lady until you return."

The changeover was marked by a sudden scurrying of feet and the clatter of plates. Then the door slammed, and the key turned twice in the lock as always. A heavy silence descended on the room.

"Shall we begin, m'lady?"

Martha jumped. The short, plump woman was standing beside her chair, looking her over with a familiarity she found unsettling. It was almost as if the woman knew her. Which was, of course, ridiculous.

"Whatever." Martha rose from her chair and held out her arms like an obedient tailor's dummy, waiting for the woman to take out her length of string and start measuring.

"A whole new wardrobe, hmm?" The woman stretched her arms around Martha's body in order to measure her waist. "Lord Anselm has certainly fallen hard this time." She chuckled softly to herself.

"Mmm." Martha made a small, non-committal sound and turned her head to watch the fat, white clouds drifting past the window. She wished the woman would just hurry up and go. She wasn't in the mood for silly chitchat.

"Are you happy here, Martha?"

That grabbed her attention. Jerking her head about, Martha stared at the weird woman. *She didn't call me "m'lady".* Even though she was sick to the back teeth of hearing *m'lady* by now, its absence suddenly seemed very odd.

"Am I happy?" Martha lowered her arms. *Sod the measurements.* "Ooh, I don't know. Let's think about that for a moment, shall we? Tell me, would you be happy, stuck in these effing rooms night and day with that treacherous snake of a man as your live-in jailer?"

Her snarky tone only increased the other woman's amusement. She actually laughed out loud, making no effort to disguise it.

"You know what?" Martha said. "We're done here." Thoroughly pissed off, she stalked away in the direction of her bedroom. "See yourself out, won't you."

"Vadim said you could be blunt."

Martha slammed on the brakes and stopped walking. "What did you say?" She stood rigid, not daring to turn around in case the expression on her face gave her away.

"You heard me well enough, I think." The woman's slippers slapped softly against the wooden floor as she approached. "He sent a message for you if you care to hear it."

Martha clenched her hands into fists. "Is that so?" She spun about to face her tormentor, her lips curved into a thin smile. "And how did he manage that, eh? Vadim's dead. Or are you in the habit of communicating with ghosts?"

What kind of twisted trick was this? Did the earl really think she was stupid enough to fall for something so obvious?

"He said you would be suspicious." The woman grinned, exposing her crooked yellow teeth.

"Oh? He said quite a lot, didn't he?" Martha stared the woman down from her slightly superior height. "I never realized the spirits were quite so chatty. Heaven can't be all it's cracked up to be, huh?"

The woman laughed. She stood so close that Martha caught an unpleasant waft of her onion breath.

"He also mentioned the peculiarity of your speech."

"Look, whatever your name is—"

"Agatha," the woman supplied helpfully.

"Fine. Agatha." Martha planted her hands on her hips. "Let's not waste one another's time, hmm? Say whatever it is the Evil Earl or Anselm paid you to say, and then go. I'm not in the mood for fun and games."

"Very well." Agatha's smile faded. She looked into Martha straight in her eyes. "Then listen to your husband's words: *I love you, my Martha. Forgive me for the manner in which we parted. I was not myself—*"

Martha closed her eyes, shutting Agatha out. Could it be him? She so desperately wanted to believe it. Hugging her arms about herself, she listened.

"*I am coming for you. Try to curb your tongue, my love. Smile at those you would rather curse. Do whatever it takes to survive until the day I find you again. If you still suspect the integrity of your message bearer, remember this: I am not Tony. Perhaps your Aunt Lulu might approve of me?*"

Her legs crumbled beneath her, and she sank to the floor, sobbing into her hands. It was him all right. She might have mentioned Aunt Lulu to a couple of people, but only Vadim knew about Tony, her cheating, scumbag of an ex. Agatha's words swept away the veil in her mind, and suddenly she could see Vadim's eyes again, black and brooding.

"There is one thing more," Agatha said, patting Martha's shoulder.

Martha looked up at her. "W-what's that?"

Agatha knelt on the floor beside her, grimacing as though the movement caused her discomfort. "Bad hips," she muttered. "Curse this damp-infested castle."

Martha sniffed and wiped her sleeve over her eyes. "That's the rest of the message?"

"No. That is my affliction."

"Oh." Despite herself, Martha smiled. "Sorry. So what is it?"

"Forge sends his love—"

How she missed that dog and his ever-cheerful face, but at least he was safe with Vadim.

"And then, there's this." Agatha put her hand in a deep pocket of her gown and pulled out a small dagger, its blade covered by a plain leather sheath. She handed it to Martha. "To be used only if your life is in the gravest peril."

Martha recognized the dagger. It was the blade Vadim had

used to cut her free from her stays on their wedding day. That man of hers certainly loved his sharp and pointy things. Turning the sheath over, she saw he'd attached two thin strips of leather to the back of it.

"He thought you could wear it somewhere... inconspicuous."

Martha frowned. As much as she despised the earl, she couldn't imagine plunging cold, deadly steel into his body. The thought revolted her as much as he did.

"I c-can't." Martha shook her head and held out the dagger for Agatha to take. "I know you'll think I'm crazy, but I just—"

"Hush. I know." Agatha smiled. Curving her hand around Martha's, she gently folded her fingers around the dagger's leather sheath. "I told him as much myself. Hold onto the blade, m'lady. Tuck it beneath your bed and draw comfort from knowing it is there, just as Vadim takes heart from knowing you have it."

Put like that, how could she refuse?

Martha stuffed the dagger into her skirt pocket. Taking a deep breath she got up from the floor and extended her hand down to Agatha.

"Most kind."

With Martha's aid, and several pained grunts, the older woman was finally back on her feet.

"When did you see him?" Martha asked. "Is he all right? When is he coming for me?" There was so much she wanted to know, now that she believed Agatha was a friend.

"Ask me no questions, and I shall not be forced to lie to you, my dear. Know only this: I never saw a man so intent on re-claiming his woman." She chuckled, and this time Martha didn't recoil from the close proximity of her onion breath.

Until the guard returned, they sat beside the fire and talked. Now that the barrier of mistrust was gone, Martha enjoyed Agatha's company. She was part of Vadim's world. Part of him.

Speaking in low, hurried voices, always fearful of being overheard, Martha learned that Agatha was a member of one of the deposed noble families. Now she worked in the kitchens of one of the very castles where she'd once been received as an honored guest.

Her husband was dead, and her sons had been overseas for the past few years, accompanying Rodmar, the wannabe king.

No matter how much she tried, Martha couldn't share Agatha's enthusiasm for the uprising that lay ahead. Instead, she smiled politely and said nothing. What was the point? No matter how long she lived here, she'd always be a woman of the twenty-first century. She'd never share their love of battle.

"I think Vadim has done well for himself," Agatha said at last, helping herself to some of the ale that the guard had delivered. She looked Martha up and down. "You suit him nicely. Tell me, do you still have that old dress of mine?"

Martha blinked. "Not the gray one? That was yours?" She almost laughed. *So this is Vadim's mystery woman!* The femme fatale of her imagination who had driven her half crazy with jealousy. "I still have it," she said, "back in Darumvale though it's a little... weathered now."

"It matters not. I donated it to the cause long ago, but it amused me to learn who was wearing it. I doubt it will fit you now though, m'lady."

It was true. Martha was much slimmer than she'd been on her arrival in this world. The simple diet and hard lifestyle had played havoc with her womanly curves, which wasn't a bad thing.

The sound of heavy bootsteps and men's voices approached the door. Martha and Agatha exchanged glances.

"I am not certain when I shall next see your man," Agatha whispered, "but do you have a message for him?"

A message? Enough words to write a novel tumbled around in Martha's head, but all she could manage was: "Tell him I love him, that I'm waiting for him, and I miss him so much." Her eyes welled with more hot tears. A key turned in the door lock. "Oh, and tell him not to get himself killed again. I couldn't bear it."

Agatha smiled and squeezed Martha's hand. "Courage, m'lady," she murmured as the door swung open. "You have more friends here than you know." With that, she got up and glared at the surly guard. "About time too. I do have other duties this day." She inclined her head respectfully toward Martha. "Your silk gown will be ready in a few days. Farewell for now, m'lady."

chapter four

A SERIES OF TIMID TAPS AT the door of her bedchamber roused Martha from her thoughts. She knew who this was.

"Hang on, Effie." Sliding the bolt, Martha opened the door to admit her maid. "Come on in."

A neat, elfin-faced young woman bustled into the room. "Oh, what a beautiful gown!" she cried, heading straight for the beautiful ghost on the bed.

Why do I even need a maid? Not that Anselm had given her any choice in the matter. Martha still wasn't sure whether the girl was his spy or not.

Effie picked up the dress, her touch almost reverent.

"You like it?" Martha asked.

"I never saw anything so exquisite," Effie replied, a little breathlessly.

"Tell you what, when I finally leave this place, you can have it as a present."

"Oh, m'lady." Effie's cheeks flushed. "What would Sir Anselm say?"

Martha shrugged and sat down on a wooden chest at the foot of the bed. *Sir Anselm's* views no longer interested her.

"He is most devoted to you." With a sigh, the maid carefully laid the gown back on the bed, the silk whispering as the air escaped its voluminous folds. "And so very handsome too."

"Oh, please." Martha rolled her eyes skyward. She couldn't help it. The girl was barely out of her teens. It was time someone put her right about men. "Buying me a dress... a gown doesn't make Anselm any less of a snake."

Effie gaped at her. "B-but he is in love with you, m'lady."

Martha snorted. "No, he isn't! And this... thing." She reached over to grab a careless fistful of the dress, "is nothing more than a cheap bribe. It's an insult, if you really want to know." She threw the dress down as if contaminated by its touch.

Effie glanced toward the door. "An insult, m'lady?" The girl looked distinctly nervous.

Martha sighed. "I'm sorry, hon," she said with a little less heat. "You've caught me at a bad time. The Evil Earl's supper invitation has rattled me, that's all."

"I do not understand, m'lady."

"No." Martha smiled. "I don't expect you do. And please, won't you just call me Martha? I'm a prisoner here, Effie, not a guest." She looked around the bedchamber, taking in the elaborately embroidered wall hangings. "This comfortable cage is only an illusion of freedom."

Still, it was better than the alternative. Anselm's rooms were a damn sight better than the dungeon. At least she had clean clothes here, daylight, decent food, and the occasional visitor Anselm didn't know about. Out of the two, she much preferred her upgraded prison cell.

"May I ask you something, m'lady?" Effie asked.

Martha arched her eyebrows.

"I mean... M-Martha?"

"Shoot. I mean, go ahead."

The maid sat on the wooden box beside her, perching like a nervous sparrow. "Is it true you are Lord Hemlock's bride?" Her voice was barely above a whisper.

"Say who now?" She pretended not to understand. It was safest that way.

Effie leaned closer. "Your husband? At least, that is what the townspeople call him. My mother always calls him The Outlaw king." The girl smiled. "Although it is forbidden to speak of him, my brothers and I used to pretend we were his masked knights, fighting to rid this land of..." the girl cast another glance at the bedroom door, "wrongdoers."

Martha stared at the young maid. More and more, it seemed to her as if this world was morphing into a Robin Hood film, with

Vadim playing the role of The Outlaw king. *Hmm.* She had to admit, it did have a certain ring to it. Instead, she said, "I don't know what you're talking about, Effie."

"I speak of Vadim." Effie's eyes sparkled. "He *is* your husband, is he not?"

Great. My maid is a rabid fan-girl.

"He was." She carefully smoothing non-existent creases from her skirt. "Right up until the earl's men killed him." No matter how genuine young Effie appeared to be, Martha daren't let down her guard. Anselm had taught her a valuable lesson about trust.

"What was he like?" The maid lowered her voice to a conspiratorial whisper. "Was he as fearsome as they say?"

"Vadim?" She almost laughed. "Not with me, he wasn't. He was beautiful, inside and out."

"Did he really kill thirty soldiers before he... died?"

Thirty? Talk about Chinese whispers. Still, she might as well gild the legend her husband had become. "That sounds about right," she said with as straight a face as she could manage. "Though, I wasn't there at the time."

Bang. Bang. Bang.

Both women leapt at the sudden fierce hammering on the bedchamber door.

"Martha?"

Fecking Anselm!

"I will return shortly. Kindly ensure you are ready, or I vow I will dress you myself!"

Martha scowled and made a rude one-handed gesture at the door. "Yes, Sir Anselm," she answered in a sweet, singsong voice. "Anything you wish, Sir Anselm."

His muttered expletive was clearly audible. So were his departing bootsteps.

The earl descended the moment they entered the banqueting hall. Smiling broadly, he wove his way through the throng toward them.

Martha shuddered. She would have backed off if Anselm hadn't held her arm so tightly.

"How wonderful to see you again, Martha, my dear." The

warmth of the earl's smile was about as sincere as his greeting. His eyes lingered on her exposed cleavage a beat too long, making her squirm with discomfort. "Your fair companion does you credit this night, Anselm."

"Thank you, m'lord." The two men shook hands and began chatting with the familiarity of old friends.

Martha tugged discretely on the neckline of her gown. Effie had laced her into it so tightly, her boobs looked as if they were about to make a break for freedom. She looked around the banqueting hall and was unsettled to find so many pairs of eyes trained in her direction. Some of them were distinctly unfriendly. Envious most likely, thanks to the syrupy sweetness of the earl's greeting. Not that she wanted to be in his favor. She looked away, still pulling at her gown and wishing it wasn't cut quite so low.

If Martha had harbored any hope of skulking away in the shadows, she was to be disappointed. Hundreds of expensive beeswax candles burned brightly in branching candelabras, banishing the gloom from every corner of the hall. With its vaulted roof and legions of candles, the Great Hall reminded her of a church.

She had to admit, the whole place looked fabulous. Every stick of furniture had been polished to within an inch of its life, the brilliant candlelight reflecting on the mirrored surface of the wood.

As she moved her foot, the sweet scent of herbs and flowers rose up from the fresh floor rushes. Either the earl was an extraordinarily tidy man, or an army of cleaners had been at work here. Nothing had been overlooked.

The centerpiece of the Great Hall was a vast table, which stretched the full length of the room, groaning beneath the weight of its many elaborate floral displays and sparkling tableware.

On the way to the banquet, Anselm informed her that each place at the table held a subtle meaning. Those innocent-looking benches were a public announcement of who was *in* and who was *out*. Those highest in their lord's favor sat closest to him at the head of the table. The seating plan must have been a nightmare.

And where would she be sitting, as if she couldn't guess?

The splendor of the earl's guests rivaled that of the room.

Men and women stood around in small groups, their muted conversations accompanied by the gentle notes of harp music. Everyone was decked out in their shiniest bling and most colorful finery, as if to advertise their wealth. They reminded her of a flock of displaying peacocks.

She sighed, suddenly feeling very lonely and far from home. All of this was a far cry from the Great Hall back in Darumvale. There were no cows or poultry living here, no underlying stink of poop. The fire didn't smoke, and there were no children running around, shrieking as they played around Seth's barrels of ale.

It wasn't a difficult choice. She knew which of the two halls she preferred.

"Little wonder you are so impressed, my dear." The earl must have heard her sigh. "You cannot be much accustomed to such luxury, not living as the wife of a wolfshead."

Although she wasn't entirely sure what that meant, it was definitely derogatory. But as she met the earl's arctic eyes, the insult she'd been about to deliver suddenly died on her lips. An undefinable something in their expression warned her against speaking. Despite the heat of the room, a shiver rippled up her spine. Barely conscious of doing so, she shuffled half a step closer to Anselm.

"You should thank me, really," the earl continued, his eyes dropping to Martha's muffin-top cleavage again. "I have vastly improved your prospects, and almost overnight, too. What say you, Anselm?"

Anselm glanced at Martha's unsmiling face and chuckled. "I quite agree, m'lord. Although I fear my lady does not yet view her fortune in the same light."

Knots of fear twisted in her stomach, but Martha tried to play it cool. "Let's cut the crap, all right? Just tell me why I'm here."

Anselm's grip on her elbow tightened. "Behave, sweeting," he murmured against her ear.

But the earl only threw back his golden head and laughed. He looked resplendently evil tonight, dressed in a long burgundy tunic with gold edging. Taking Martha's hand, he lowered his head and planted a wet kiss upon it. "Your sour wit is a taste I have begun to appreciate," he said, his words vibrating against her skin. "I must admit, I find your candor most refreshing."

"Yeah?" She pulled her hand free and immediately wiped it

down her dress. "What a pity you didn't think so back in Darumvale before you hit me, m'lord."

He broke into peals of loud, braying laughter, drawing the attention of all the other guests. Although the earl's eyes glistened with amusement, Martha wasn't fooled. They were the coldest eyes she'd ever seen on a person—dead looking, almost like a shark's. And who trusted a grinning shark?

The earl's laughter went on and on, echoing about the room. Even the harpist stopped playing and looked over. No wonder. Talk about a fake laugh. It sounded more than a little psychotic. Whatever medication His Evilness was taking, he definitely needed to up his dosage.

She tried to back away, but Anselm wouldn't let go of her arm.

"Is she not priceless?" the earl demanded at last, turning to look at the other guests as if seeking their approval. There was a murmuring ripple of agreement.

Martha rolled her eyes. What a bunch of brown-tongues.

The earl gestured toward the table with a gracious sweep of his arm. "Come, my friends," he announced in a loud voice. "Let us sit down and feast before the entertainment arrives." He darted a glance at Martha. "This will prove to be, I think, a most interesting evening."

What the feck is he up to, I wonder?

While His Evilness settled himself on his cushioned seat at the head of the table, Martha found herself pushed down onto the seat to his right—the most coveted chair at the earl's table—Anselm's regular seat, or so he informed her as he sat at her other side.

To her disgust, she was trapped between the two men, the *meat* in their evil sandwich. Their close proximity, and the overwhelming scent of violets coming from the earl, killed off what little appetite she had.

The envy-laden stares she was receiving from some of the other guests made her uncomfortable. Oh, if they only knew.

Less than impressed with the honor the earl had bestowed upon her, Martha sought the liquid courage contained within her silver goblet. It was quite magical really. No matter how many times she emptied the drinking vessel, moments later it was full to the brim with wine.

As soon as the first course arrived—jellied eels, or something equally revolting—the earl and Anselm turned to speak to their neighbors, leaving Martha free to get smashed in peace.

Slumping back in her chair, her goblet balanced precariously on the mountainous swell of her breasts, Martha listened to the young harpist who sat playing in an unobtrusive corner of the room. He was good. The heavenly string music eased the tension from her bunched-up muscles, and little by little she felt herself begin to relax.

Or maybe it was the effects of the wine? Her head was at that nice fuzzy stage. She took another sip from her goblet. Thank God for the invisible wine pixies. *Wine pixies?* She snort-giggled into her goblet, getting wine up her nose. Neither of her jailers noticed. She sat up and reached for a napkin. Immediately, one of the servants appeared, refilling her goblet when she set it down on the table, quite ruining her wine-pixie fantasy.

What a shame. Better to be a pixie than a servant. What a horrible word that was. *Servant. Ugh!* She dabbed her nose again with the napkin then slumped back in her chair.

Course after interminable course was set before her, only to be taken away untouched minutes later. It was the strangest food Martha had ever seen—although some dishes, such as the swan, hedgehog, and peacock were instantly recognizable.

The earl's wine did a marvelous job of anesthetizing her, and now the room swayed, ever so slightly. She reached for a chunk of dry bread to nibble on. The flour had been finely milled, giving the bread a less crunchy texture than she was accustomed to.

"Are you not hungry, my dear?" the earl asked, turning to her during a lull in the conversation when his neighbor went to pee in a corner of the room. "You have barely eaten a thing."

"I'm good with this, thanks," she said, waving her bread at him. By now, she was so loaded with alcohol that her smile was almost genuine. "I feel a bit sick for some reason. I can't imagine why." With that, she dissolved into helpless giggles.

Anselm turned and glared at her. "How much wine have you taken?" he demanded, attempting to wrench the silver goblet from her hand. "Give that to me!"

But Martha wouldn't let go. "No, it's mine!"

They wrestled for the goblet for a few moments, but Anselm was too strong. With a tiny smile, Martha suddenly let go of the goblet's stem, sending a crimson wave splashing all over Anselm's immaculate yellow tunic.

With a dismayed cry, he leaped to his feet, arms extended, wine dripping from his fingers.

"Oops!" Martha's grin widened as she watched the crimson stain blossoming on his chest. "That'll be a bugger to get out, Anselm. I think you're going to need another tunic. Hang on. Let me help you."

Before Martha could scrub at the stain, he snatched the napkin from her hands, glaring at her with a rage that made her recoil. "You little bi—"

"Anselm." The earl's soft voice carried a heavy note of warning.

One word from his master, Anselm's temper was back under control. He took a deep breath and then forced his mouth into an unconvincing smile. "It is of no consequence," he said. "The fault was all my own." But the anger in his eyes remained.

The other guests seemed oblivious to the tension at the head of the table. The merry rumbling of conversation went on. Martha heard bright tinkles of female laughter, and she envied the other women their amusement.

Suddenly, the wine's warm, fuzzy stage wore off, and stage two hit her with the force of a truck. The need to be with Vadim crashed over her like a huge rogue wave. Hot tears scalded her eyes. In an instant, all the alcohol she'd consumed seemed to evaporate from her blood. Without the aid of her temporary crutch, Martha felt naked and vulnerable. She longed for the sanctuary of her bedchamber, to be alone.

Taking a deep breath, she turned to speak to the earl. "Anselm said you have a surprise for me. Can I have it now please? I don't feel well." For once her tone was civil, such was her desperation to be gone.

"Of course, my dear." The earl's smile was almost compassionate. He beckoned to one of the soldiers who stood guard by the doors of the Great Hall. As the man leaned over, the earl muttered something in his ear. The guard straightened up and nodded. Without speaking, he strode swiftly from the hall.

The earl returned his attention to Martha. "I wonder if you

are in the mood to scratch an itch that has been troubling me for quite some time, m'lady?"

Jesus, Mary, and Joseph. Martha stared at him, open-mouthed. He wanted her to scratch his itch? What a disgusting thought. "I-I'm n-not sure what you mean."

Her revulsion must have shown. "Not that kind of itch." He glanced at her breasts again. "Although I am certain I should enjoy the feel of your sharp little claws. No. 'Tis your origin, I speak of."

"My origin?" Martha exhaled with relief. "What about it?"

"Despite extensive inquiries, I have uncovered no trace of your existence." The earl propped his elbow on the table, resting his chin on his upturned hand. "Does that not strike you as odd?"

The hairs at the back of Martha's neck prickled. "Not at all." She tried to smile. "You obviously haven't looked in the right places."

"And then, of course, there is the peculiarity of your speech and manner," the earl continued, as if she hadn't spoken. "Most singular indeed." He regarded her like a cat watching a mouse. "How do you account for those, I wonder?"

Martha shrugged, battling to stay calm. How could she tell him she was from another fecking world? If he learned the truth, he'd probably have her burnt at the stake. So what else could she do but lie? She cursed herself for having drunk so much. Her head still felt thick and stupid.

Maybe if she gave His Evilness a few answers, he might loosen his grip on her leash. "Okay, fine. I come from a far-off land." She smiled at the manservant standing behind the earl's chair. "Could I have some water, please?" The man bowed and walked away.

"How far off?" Anselm demanded.

Martha turned to look at him. "Very far off. A place way beyond... the Great Sea." That sounded convincing, right? They couldn't have mapped out the whole world yet. She returned her attention to the earl. "I daren't name my country for fear of discovery." His face revealed none of his thoughts. Did he believe her?

"I see." The earl picked up his goblet, staring into its depths as though he might find the answers he sought there. "Then, how did you get here?"

"Well, I didn't swim!" Her laughter died when she met the earl's eyes. "All right, I stowed away on a boat. My family was going to marry me off to a revolting toad of a man." *This is good. All those romance novels can't be wrong. Keep it going.* "The night before the wedding, I stole my brother's clothes and assumed a man's identity."

A little historical romance cliché with a garnish of Shakespeare. That should do nicely.

"I find that difficult to imagine, m'lady." The earl glanced pointedly at her chest. "Your... c*harms* are not what I would call subtle. Eh, Anselm?"

"As you say, m'lord."

Martha's cheeks burned, but she resisted the urge to cover her chest with her hands. "Believe me, it's amazing what you can do with a strip of linen. It certainly brought these puppies to heel."

"If your story is true, why did you choose to come to the Norlands? Were you already intimate with your future mate?" He leaned closer. "Why were you out in the hills with Lord Hemlock on the day we first met, hmm?"

Oh, why had she drunk so much? The earl was too sharp for her wooly head.

"I didn't choose to come here. I stowed away in the first boat I came across; I could have ended up anywhere. When I came ashore, I picked a direction and set off walking. Vadim happened across me when I collapsed in the hills."

The earl and Anselm exchanged glances. *What does that mean?* She wasn't sure whether they believed her or not.

"So you claim my outlaw *brother* was a stranger to you back then?" The sneer in Anselm's voice was apparent. "How quickly you must have fallen in *love*."

"Not that it's any of your business," Martha said, turning back to look at him, "but it's true. We did."

Anselm's smug expression worried her. *What does he know that I don't?*

"I understand you were married by a holy man," the earl said, diverting her attention.

"That's right." But her confidence wobbled. She heard Aunt

Lulu speaking within her mind: *You need a good memory to be a good liar, child.*

Perhaps she ought to shut up for a bit? Any minute now, she was going to trip herself up.

"Do you happen to recall his name?" The earl's eyes glittered as he leaned closer.

"No. Sorry." Martha sat back in her chair and folded her hands on her lap. Unfortunately, this new position allowed her to see both Anselm and the earl. They were definitely gloating about something.

The noise of the banquet continued, soft music accompanying the hum of conversation and bright laughter. But at the head of the table, the three of them seemed to be protected by an invisible bubble. Only the red-headed harpist caught Martha's eye, but he swiftly looked away.

"Shall I tell you what I think, my sweet?" Anselm reached out and touched a ringlet that had escaped from her elegant raised hairdo, twirling it about his index finger.

Martha tried to jerk away but she was trapped by the high back of her chair. There was nowhere to escape to anyway. She glanced at the earl, who watched the scene with obvious enjoyment.

"I think your husband is alive and well," Anselm said softly, releasing her hair in order to trace his finger down her cheek. "So why has he not come to claim his pretty little wife, hmm?"

"Why don't you enlighten me, fuckwit?" At times, Anselm looked so much like Seth and Sylvie, Martha found it difficult to deal with him. How had such sweet people managed to produce... this? Anselm was the polar opposite of his parents.

"I do not think you are Vadim's wife at all. My poor Martha. How little he must think of you. Were you even lovers?" He touched her burning cheek. "Ah, yes. Of course you were. That much is clear to me."

Martha sat rigid in her seat, staring off into the distance. She refused to give him a reaction. Fear was food to sickos like him. The young harp player met her eyes again. There was something vaguely familiar about him, but as he looked away, the feeling vanished.

"How long will you wait for him, Martha?" Anselm continued to attack her with his gentle words. "Hemlock does not love you, not as you love him. He has used you terribly." He took her limp hand in his and clasped it tightly. She didn't attempt to pull away.

That's your fantasy, not my reality.

Anselm could go to hell. Even though the rest of her world was crumbling, she was secure in this: Vadim loved her.

"Why do you smile, m'lady?" the earl inquired. "It seems to me you have little cause to do so."

She kept her eyes on the harpist and didn't reply. Not verbally, anyhow. Suddenly, Anselm released her hand, his eyes trained on the doors of the Great Hall.

"He has come, m'lord." There was an unmistakable note of awe in his hushed voice.

Martha turned to see who he was looking at.

The soldier had returned. Walking beside him was the tall, lean figure of a man. The stranger's simple brown robe dragged on the floor rushes as he moved, and a deep cowl covered his head, concealing his face. He clutched a tall wooden staff, which thumped upon the floor as he walked, rather like an unwieldy trekking-pole.

This is my surprise? Martha frowned. *What is he, a monk?*

Loud whispers traveled down the table, and one by one, the many conversations petered out. Silence descended on the room. The banquet lay forgotten; everyone stared at the monk. Even the harpist had stopped playing. His hands lay flat on the strings of his instrument, stifling its final, plaintive note.

Every pair of eyes stared at the new arrival. The room seemed to hold its collective breath as the stranger advanced. The steady thud of his staff on the floor sounded deafening.

Martha slithered lower in her seat, wishing she were invisible. Who the hell was this guy? And was the silence out of respect or fear?

Anselm and the earl rose from their seats, smiling as their guest approached.

"Thank you for coming, Learned One." The earl swept an elegant low bow before the raggedy monk, and Anselm followed suit. "You honor my hall with your presence."

"Let us forgo the meaningless courtesies, m'lord," came a stern voice from within the hood. Deep shadows hid the stranger's face. "Where is she then, this woman who vexes you so?"

The earl stepped aside, indicating Martha with a graceful sweep of his hand. "M'lady," he grinned broadly at her, "allow me to present Madoc the Seer."

chapter five

MARTHA'S JAW DROPPED. EYES BUGGING, she looked rapidly from the cowled figure to Anselm and back again, desperately trying to articulate some coherent words.

This was him? The man who might know the way back to twenty-first-century Earth? She clasped her trembling hands together on her lap.

This couldn't be a coincidence. How had the earl known she'd been looking for this elusive seer?

Anselm must have read the question in her wide, staring eyes.

"I overheard you one day at the market in Edgeway," he said with a smirk. "Do you remember? You were asking the stallholders for news of Darumvale, and you happened to ask after our friend Madoc during one of your conversations. I thought it rather strange, so I mentioned it to Lord Edgeway."

Anger fizzled in Martha's blood. Yet another reminder of just how stupid and trusting she'd been back then. "You're nothing but a worthless piece of—"

"Come now." The earl lay a warning hand on her exposed shoulder, his clammy touch making her flesh creep. "We are all friends tonight, are we not?" The ruby on his pinkie finger glittered with a fire to match her temper.

"No, we are most definitely not fecking fr—" She gasped, squirming with pain as the earl squeezed her shoulder. His cruel fingers dug deep into her soft skin, effectively silencing her.

"The guards will escort you back to your chambers, my dear," the earl said in a kindly voice, as if causing her pain was a weird sign of affection. "Do speak freely with the good seer. Ask him what you will. I will ensure you are left undisturbed." Mercifully, he let go of her shoulder and stepped away.

Martha slumped back in her chair, gasping and clutching her aching shoulder, but there was no time to catch her breath, for Anselm pulled her to her feet.

"Come along, sweeting," he said. Keeping hold of her arm, he escorted her from the banqueting hall. The rhythmic clunk of the seer's staff followed close behind them.

The iron key grated in the lock, two full turns as always, locking her in with the mysterious Madoc the Seer, the man who might be able to shed light on her accidental slip across time. Unfortunately for her, at that moment, Martha's fear of the man far outweighed her curiosity.

"Make yourself at home while I change," she said before fleeing to her bedchamber.

Breathing hard, she leaned back against the securely bolted door. Effie had left a candle burning. Combined with the firelight, it gave her little room a cozy feel. She exhaled, forcing the tension from her body.

After enduring the banquet from hell, she needed a couple of minutes to get her head together—and to shed her slut-suit, as she'd taken to calling her beautiful, expensive gown. Horrible thing! Sod giving it to Effie as a parting gift; the maid could have it now. Martha certainly had no intention of wearing it again.

She walked to the window, absently pulling out the pins that secured her elegant piled-up hairdo. What was His Evilness up to? Why was he allowing her a private audience with Madoc the snarky monk? Certainly not out of the goodness of his heart—if he even possessed such a thing. No. This was definitely all for his benefit.

The last hair pin tinkled to the floor, and Martha's hair cascaded down about her shoulders. She massaged her throbbing scalp, groaning with bliss. Whatever the earl was up to, as sure as Anselm was a two-faced weasel, it wouldn't be anything good. In the meantime, she had to go out there, to talk to the scary monk. Some primal instinct warned her that facing him half cut wasn't a good idea.

Oh, why had she drunk so much? The first sign of the hangover to come pulsed beneath her right eyebrow. She spied the jug of water on the chest beside her bed. She needed to rehydrate, and fast.

Almost ten minutes later, Martha reopened the door of her bedchamber. Without Effie's help, she'd struggled to get free of the loathsome dress. The back lacing had posed quite a challenge, but as it turned out, the expensive material tore very easily. Who knew?

The plain blue gown she wore in its place had a far more modest scooped neckline, keeping her puppies well concealed, and her hair hung about her shoulders in loose waves. Much better. She felt almost human again.

"Sorry I was so long," she said with a forced smile. "I had a spot of dress trouble."

Madoc sat by the fire, his booted feet resting on the hearth, and a tankard of ale clasped in his hand. "Yes. I heard your profanities. Most... original." He didn't turn to look at her, his gaze fixed on the red glow before him. "Now that you are here, come and sit beside me."

Inexplicably, Martha's fear of him vanished. Despite his gruffness, somehow she knew that he wouldn't hurt her. She sidled up and took the chair beside his.

"Aren't you hot with your hood up?" she asked. Immediately, she wanted to kick herself. What if he was disfigured in some way and preferred to keep his face hidden? "But you can keep it on if you like... I don't mind."

"How gracious of you, m'lady."

Hot color flooded her cheeks. "Sorry. That came out all wrong."

"An all-too-frequent occurrence for you, I imagine. Your mouth has the unfortunate habit of speaking too soon." Madoc flung back his hood and turned to look at her. "Am I so horribly disfigured, then?"

How had he known what she'd been thinking?

The seer wasn't what she expected. A pair of serious-looking hazel eyes regarded her from a thin and clean-shaven face. His close-cropped brown hair made him look like a convict. But it was his age that shocked her most of all.

"You-you're..." Martha floundered, wary of offending him again.

The man arched an eyebrow. "Let me guess: young?"

She nodded. "I imagined you'd be much older." This guy was barely out of his teens.

"Most people do. The title of Madoc the Seer is more of an... occupation than an actual person."

"Really?" Martha leaned in closer. "It's funny, in my head, you were always old with a long beard. Maybe with a pointy hat." She giggled. "At least I got the staff part right." *Oh, just stop talking. You're being rude.* "I'm sorry. I had a lot to drink tonight."

"Indeed?" Madoc's stern mouth twitched. "Sober or drunk, I suspect in essentials you are always much the same, m'lady."

He's as rude as I am. She grinned. It was comforting somehow. "That's true."

Brusque as he was, Martha felt more at ease with the seer than she had with any man during her stay at the castle.

"Tell me," Madoc said, returning his gaze to the fire. "Why did you first seek my guidance?"

Martha exhaled. Here it was at last. How many times had she longed to meet this man? How often had she prayed for a way to return home, to leave this medieval world and resume her comfortable twenty-first-century life? Madoc the Seer might just have the power to make her dreams a reality.

Mentally salivating, she recalled the bliss of indoor plumbing, the miracle of electricity, and the comfort of central heating. *Imagine it: medicine and feminine-hygiene products. Do you remember the taste of chocolate? How about the hot, cheesy indulgence of pizza delivered hot and fresh straight to your door?* And then, more importantly, there was Aunt Lulu.

It might be possible. All she had to do was ask.

There was just one problem. Despite the lure of so many incentives, she no longer wanted to go. For better or worse, she wanted to stay in Vadim's world. Admittedly, she might not ever see him again. But if she left, "might not" would become an absolute "never".

I made my choice when I married him. Leaving was no longer an option.

"It doesn't matter anymore," Martha said quietly, stifling the pang of regret for Aunt Lulu. "I finally worked it out for myself. Thanks anyhow."

Madoc slowly turned his head, studying her face through narrowed eyes. "There is nothing you wish to ask of us?"

By the sound of it, this was something new for him. Hold on. Had he just said *us*? Martha shook her head and shrugged. She must have imagined it.

"You are quite certain?" he asked.

She nodded. "Why? Was there something in particular you wanted me to ask?" Since he was here at the earl's command, it wouldn't hurt to try and find out why. No doubt the seer would be reporting back to him as soon as he left.

To her surprise, the grim line of Madoc's mouth curved into a full, beaming smile, transforming his features from granite into sunshine. More than ever, he seemed impossibly young for the role he'd assumed.

"Well said, m'lady. Your caution was gleaned from a true master."

Does he mean Vadim?

"For sure." Madoc replied.

"Excuse me?" Martha blinked. *Did I say just that out loud?* She massaged her aching temples. Two mugs of water obviously wasn't enough.

"No. My role comes with... certain abilities, you might say. Each one passes from seer to seer."

"Oh?" *He's reading my fecking mind?* "Oh!" Suddenly Martha felt horribly exposed. Naked, in fact. She rapidly replayed any thoughts she'd had that might have betrayed her... them.

Madoc chuckled and reached for the jug of ale that sat beside his feet. He refilled his tankard and poured one for Martha.

"Be at peace, Martha," he said, handing her the ale. "I will not reveal your secrets."

She wasn't reassured. "So if you're not spying for His Evilness, why *are* you here?" She took the drink he offered her and nursed it between her hands. "What's in it for you?"

Madoc took a sip from his tankard before answering. "You have seen, I suppose, how the people of these lands already struggle to pay the earl's heavy tax demands? My meeting with you tonight means there will be no further increases this year."

Martha snorted. "And you believed him? God, and I thought I was gullible."

Her remark made Madoc smile again. "Ah. But the Lord Edgeway fears our wrath, m'lady. Unlike you, he has witnessed it before."

Our? Perhaps there's an army of seers out there?

"So, why didn't you just threaten him with your *wrath* when he mentioned raising the taxes, hmm? You didn't need to come and see me at all."

"You are right," Madoc agreed. "But in truth, I wanted to meet you. My earlier bluster was all for the earl's benefit."

This was unexpected. "You wanted to meet me? Why? Before His Evilness approached you, I doubt you knew I existed."

Madoc nodded. "Although I did not know you personally, Martha, we have been aware of your presence here for some time."

This is crazy talk.

Madoc might be harmless, but the weird way he referred to himself unsettled her. She put down her ale and went to throw another log on the fire.

Instead of sitting back down, she began pacing the room, pausing to move a book or to adjust the position of a wall hanging, giving herself time to gather her thoughts.

How could he have been *aware of her*? Who could have mentioned her to him?

Madoc watched her, the shadows cast by the fire flickering over the thin angles of his face. "You are not the first to pass through the veil between the worlds, Martha. There have been others."

His words sent a ripple of ice through her blood. *There have been others like me?* Her knees wobbled. Reaching out her hand, she sank down onto the nearest chair. *How can he know this?* Even so, she believed him.

"W-what happened to them... the others?" she asked.

"Some stayed. A few attempted the journey home."

"Attempted?" That didn't sound good. "Did they make it back?"

Madoc shrugged. "Who can tell? We cannot see through the veil, and no one ever returned to tell us. Those who chose to stay lived out their lives as the rest of us. Or so I am told. Their bones have been dust for many years now. You are the first traveler to cross over in generations."

"But how is this even possible? How did I end up here?" Her headache was getting worse.

"Most accounts mention the traveler crossing a river or stream. At certain times, and if the stars are favorably aligned, the veil between the gateways is thin. The river seems to act as a pathway." Madoc leaned forward suddenly, fixing her with his piercing eyes. "Is that what happened to you? Did you cross the water, Martha?"

She nodded. "I crossed over the stepping stones." The Lake District now seemed so very far away. "Then I fell into the river, and woke up... here." She rubbed her eyes, suddenly feeling very sleepy.

Madoc sat back in his chair with a satisfied smile. "Just as we thought."

"I've heard people refer to you as a *traveler* before." Her voice sounded a little slurred. "Are you like me? Did you come from... my world?"

"Alas, no." Madoc replied. "That name is an echo of another time—a time when we gave our aid to the true travelers. Nothing more."

"Have you ever tried? To cross the river, I mean?"

"Yes, we tried, but never with any success. The portal chooses the traveler, it seems. Not the other way about."

"We?" Martha yawned and covered her mouth with the back of her hand. "You keep saying *we* and *our*. Who are *we*?"

"Madoc the Seer, of course." Her lack of understanding seemed to amuse him. "When one host dies, we move on to the next. This..." he glanced down at his body, "is a recent acquisition. It takes time to... settle in, you might say. The quality of host candidates is not what it once was. The thirst for the Old Wisdom is being quenched by the desire for wealth and position."

A finger of cold fear caressed Martha's spine. This was incredible, and more than a little creepy. *How many people are there, living inside of him?*

As if controlled by the will of another, she got up and began walking toward the seer, swaying across the wooden floor, an unwilling puppet, dancing to an invisible pull on her strings.

"Sit beside... me." Madoc took her limp hand and drew her

down onto the seat next to his. "Now," he said as she settled back in her chair, "let me see you, m'lady."

Although her mind remained active, Martha couldn't move. The seer kept hold of her hand and closed his eyes. What had he done? Had he hypnotized her without her knowing it? Or maybe he'd slipped something into her ale. No. She hadn't had so much as a sip from the tankard he'd given her. Her heart pounded wildly in her throat, and perhaps he sensed that too.

"Hush now," he said softly, as if she were a nervous horse. "I will not harm you, child. Let us in."

And because he commanded it, she relaxed. Her head felt heavy, and her neck wilted with the strain of supporting it. She couldn't resist his will. Leaning back in her chair, she closed her eyes.

"Good."

She heard the smile in his voice.

"Show us your mind."

Suddenly, she was home walking around Aunt Lulu's home, back in the Lake District.

The cluttered lounge was just as she remembered it. Books leaned in precarious towers, propped against the back wall. Her aunt's collection of Lladro figurines still battled for space on the crowded mantelpiece, obscuring the ticking clock that always displayed the wrong time.

She reached out to touch an ornament depicting a young girl in a pensive mood. *When did she buy this one?* To her astonishment, her hand passed straight through. She tried again. Same result.

Okay, now I'm officially spooked. Or perhaps I am a spook?

She went over to the window—only she didn't actually walk there, it was more of a wispy glide—and looked out into the small, well-tended garden. What she saw made her heart leap with joy.

There was Aunt Lulu, sitting beneath her parasol, sheltering from the bright autumn sun. The old lady's hand stilled on her sketch pad, her frown emphasizing some new lines on her pink-scrubbed face.

No sooner had she thought it than Martha found herself

outside, leaning over her aunt's shoulder. Although she stood in the sun, she neither felt its warmth, nor cast a shadow. She studied Lulu's drawing of a craggy hill that she was attempting to commit to paper.

"Your shading is all to cock, old love."

"Martha?" The stub of charcoal slipped from Lulu's fingers and fell onto the grass, but the old lady made no move to retrieve it. Instead, she continued to stare straight ahead at the hill, her pale blue eyes welling with glittering tears. "Am I asleep?" The soft Irish lilt of Lulu's voice almost broke Martha's heart. "I've dreamed of you so many times!"

"It is me, love. I'm back." Martha crouched down beside her aunt's chair. "Can you see me?"

Slowly, Lulu turned, gasping when she saw Martha. "Jesus, Mary, and Joseph!" Her liver-spotted hands flew up to cover her mouth. "It is you! My dear, sweet Martha!"

It must have looked almost comical as they repeatedly tried—and failed—to hug one another. But each woman found the other as impossible to grasp as mist. Panting slightly, Lulu was the first to give up.

"Oh, my precious girl. Are you truly dead, then?" Tears streamed down Lulu's rouged cheeks, cutting white runnels into her makeup. "Have you come down from Heaven to tell me it's my time?"

Martha grinned. "Don't be daft. A fine angel I'd make!" She stroked her ghostly hand over Lulu's hair, admiring the vivid color of her aunt's latest lilac rinse. "I'm not dead. At least, I don't think I am. Please don't worry about me. I'm happy."

Time was against her. Already, Martha felt a peculiar "pulling" sensation in her head and stomach.

She took a deep breath and started talking, rapidly relating the edited highlights of her own disappearance. Another two big inhalations got her to the end of the story so far—though she left out anything pertaining to Anselm, His Evilness, or dungeons.

There was no need to worry Lulu, even if she was only a lovely hallucination.

With her mouth slightly open, Aunt Lulu listened, her eyes fixed on her ghostly niece. "Another world?" she said at last. "You went for a walk and ended up in another world? I-I don't understand, sweetheart."

"That makes two of us, hon." Martha sighed. Now that she was here—home again—it was hard to let go. She'd probably never see Lulu again after today. Insubstantial tears filled her wraith-like eyes.

Aunt Lulu obviously understood. "So this is goodbye?" Fresh tears shone in her eyes while her knobbly fingers clung to the wooden arm of her deckchair. "Well if this is a dream, I'm not sorry for it." Her aunt smiled and raised her hand to touch Martha's cheek. "I love you, my Martha. Raising you is the best thing I ever did."

"I love you too, Lulu." The "tugging" on her body increased, and it took all of her strength to resist it. "I wish I could stay, but Vadim is so—"

Too late. Lulu extended her hand to Martha as an unseen force pulled them apart. Even then, their eyes remained locked, relaying all the unspoken regrets of their hearts before a howling white vortex swept Martha away at an impossible speed.

Silence.

Gradually Martha became conscious of the physical world again. Which one, though?

The chair felt hard against her back. She heard the crackle and pop of an open fire and, from a distance away, the laughter of soldiers, their armor clanking as they passed by. A wave of sorrow washed over her for what she'd lost.

Her eyes flickered open, and there was Madoc, staring at her, shadows filling the hollows of his gaunt face.

"I thought I had lost you," he said in place of a hello. "You have more strength than you realize, m'lady. How do you feel?" He handed her a tankard filled to the brim with ale.

"Tired." Martha shuffled in her chair and sat up, grimacing slightly. "Sore." Her body ached as though she'd taken a high-impact step class the previous day. Raising the tankard to her lips, she chugged the ale back in one go.

"And thirsty too?" A brief smile softened the seer's features. "Tell me, have you ever considered studying the Old Wisdom? You have considerable potential."

Martha sighed and wiped away her ale mustache with her fingers. "You don't say?" Well, if he wanted to assimilate her into the Madoc collective, he could go whistle. But, of course, she'd forgotten about his funky mind-reading ability.

"Women are quite unsuitable for the role," he said, staring down his thin nose at her, as if the fact should be common knowledge.

But Martha was more interested in what had just happened. "Was I really home just now?" she asked softly. "Did it really happen?"

Madoc nodded. "As payment, you might say, for allowing me to read your memories."

Allowing? But she let it go. She stared into the fire, absently rolling the empty tankard between her hands.

I was actually home again.

Grief and longing gnawed painfully at her heart. After seeing Lulu again, Martha was more homesick than ever. The craving to be home rose up and overwhelmed her.

She turned to look at Madoc. "I-If I wanted to go back—for good, I mean—would you help me?"

chapter six

"**Y**OU HAVE CHANGED YOUR MIND?" Madoc asked with a frown. He looked almost disappointed. "What about the man you call husband, m'lady? Will you abandon him now and deny him his family?"

"Yes... no." Oh, what did it matter? She couldn't leave this room, let alone the castle. And what about Vadim? There was still a flicker of hope. She mustn't forget the message he'd sent through Agatha.

I am coming for you.

The words calmed her, warming her aching heart and soothing the desperate urge to go home. Aunt Lulu would be fine. As for Martha, her place was here now, in Vadim's world. Of course she'd see him again. No one could keep them apart. Not forever.

Madoc nodded. He'd obviously been mentally dropping more eaves. "I thought as much." He reached for his staff and stood up. "Thank you for your company, m'lady. Tonight has proved most illuminating."

"Huh?" Martha got up too, still holding her empty tankard. "You're not leaving already, are you?" Her stomach lurched. Why was it whenever she started liking someone, they left, abandoning her to Anselm and the four walls of his chambers? It had been so nice, sharing the fire and a jug of ale with someone she didn't actively despise.

"You... like us?" Madoc's raised his eyebrows. "What a singular person you are, Martha." He pulled up his hood, covering his head and wreathing his face in shadows once more.

"What will you tell His Evilness?" she asked as she accompanied him to the door.

"Whatever it suits me to tell him." Madoc reached out, briefly touching her hand. Coming from him, the gesture was as good as a hug. "Keep to your story. Lord Edgeway will hear nothing to challenge it from me."

She believed him. "Thanks, Madoc—all of you. I appreciate it. Are you sure you can't stay just a little longer?"

The seer shook his young, ancient, head. "I am afraid not. Anselm is already on his way."

He bashed on outer the door three times with his staff to summon the guard. Then he turned to look at Martha, who still hovered by his side. "You would be wise to retire to your chamber before your jailer returns," he said. "Oh, and do ensure you bolt the door behind you, unless, of course, you particularly desire Anselm's company in your bed." She didn't need to see Madoc's face to hear him smiling. "I fear your young friend has imbibed a rather large quantity of wine this night."

Martha rolled her eyes. *Great. That's all I need.* "I will. And thanks for the heads-up. You're a good person, Madoc, a little bit weird perhaps, but you're all right."

"Indeed." Madoc was back to his sneering self. "I hardly know whether to be flattered or insulted. However, I wish you well, m'lady, and I will do whatever I can to aid you."

The guard turned the key in the lock and opened the door. With a brief nod of farewell, Madoc left her alone with her thoughts.

When Martha woke, for a moment, she thought she'd gone blind. Then she realized she was clutching a thick pillow over her head. She chucked the pillow aside and sat up, breathing a heavy sigh of relief. Morning at last. Weak daylight entered through the window, slowly lightening the room.

It was a good thing Madoc had warned her about Anselm. As predicted, he'd been completely rat-faced when he returned to his chambers last night.

When Martha ignored his gentle knockings at the door of her bedchamber, he'd set up camp outside her firmly bolted door and begun singing at her. She grimaced at the memory of his loud, tuneless wailings. Love songs, no less. And all for her. *Ugh! In his dreams.*

When his serenading failed to magically open her door, Anselm tried sweet talking her instead. But the lack of a positive response made him violent. That's when she'd buried her head beneath the pillow, trying to block out the vile curses and endless pounding of his fists on her door. Thankfully, the oak timbers held firm.

Martha shuddered, imagining what might have happened if it had been a modern flimsy door that separated them. Drunk or not, she suspected Anselm would have been physically capable of carrying out all of his terrible threats.

One thing was certain. She needed to escape. And soon. She couldn't wait for Vadim to rescue her, not any longer. Last night, Anselm had crossed an invisible line. His professed affection and friendship were no longer a guarantee of her continuing safety here.

She sat up in bed and pulled the cover to her chin. Even on fine mornings, the castle was usually cold. Her blanket smelt damp and slightly fusty. What would it be like here in winter? Not that she had any intention of finding out.

Straining her ears, she listened for sounds in the room beyond her bedchamber. Silence. Was he still there? She daren't open the door and find out. No. She'd wait until Effie delivered her breakfast. It wouldn't be long now.

Drawing her knees up to her chest, Martha closed her eyes and thought of Vadim, blotting out the misery of her current situation. She smiled as she relived their wedding night, the first she'd spent in his bed. Butterflies danced in her stomach. Suddenly, she wasn't cold anymore.

Tap-tap.

"Martha? Are you awake, sweeting?"

Her eyes snapped open. Anselm. *Oh, God. No.* All the loved-up heat leached from her body. It was way too early to be dealing with him. She stared at the door, willing him away.

Tap-tap-tap.

Her temper flashed to supernova. "Get lost!" she yelled at the door. "Just leave me alone, dickhead." He'd kept her awake half the night as it was. Did he have to torment her at the crack of dawn too?

"Please, Martha." His voice was soft and wheedling. "I must apologize for my ungallant behavior last night."

"Fine. You've apologized. Now feck off!" Grabbing the metal candleholder that sat on a table beside her bed, she hurled it at the door with all her strength. The heavy thump and ensuing clatter silenced Anselm for a few moments. She hoped he had a hell of a hangover.

"Very well," he said at last. "I shall return later when you are perhaps a little calmer, my dear."

Martha closed her eyes and ground her teeth together. *Sweet baby Jesus!* Her fingers positively itched to use the knife she kept beneath her mattress. Anselm was seriously doing her head in.

She heard the outer door close. Presumably, Anselm had left for the day. She stayed where she was, not prepared to take any chances. *God damn it!* She couldn't hide from him forever.

Suddenly, Martha heard Aunt Lulu's gentle voice, echoing inside her head, spouting another of those cryptic sayings she was so fond of.

If you do what you've always done, you'll get what you've always got.

Yes, she definitely needed a new approach. But what?

Imaginary Aunt Lulu was full of ideas this morning: *A carrot often works better than a stick.*

"Not if the stick beats Anselm to death first, it doesn't," she muttered as she threw back the covers, swinging her legs out of bed.

Imaginary Lulu frowned at her niece's levity.

Okay. She definitely needed new tactics. And preferably before her mind unraveled completely.

Going over to the window, she leaned on the stone sill and watched the world wake up. A skinny stable lad yawned as he crossed the cobbles, two empty buckets swinging in his hands.

Returning from the ramparts, a line of soldiers marched wearily back to barracks, leaving the castle's defense in the care of the day shift.

Martha frowned, her mind still fixed on the Anselm situation. She definitely needed a carrot. But what? Hostility hadn't got her anywhere.

Down in the courtyard, a dog raised its leg against the wheel of a hay-laden wagon, and a thin trickle of liquid darkened the cobbles.

She recalled the words of Vadim's secret message. *Smile at those you would rather curse.*

A carrot. Even Vadim had advised her to use one. Sort of. She grinned to herself. Come to think of it, that sounded more than a little pervy.

Her amusement soon faded. Although Anselm and the earl would surely suspect her motives, she didn't have a choice. Martha gave a sigh. There was nothing else for it. Like it or not— God help her—she would have to start being nice.

chapter seven

"**R**IDING?" VADIM GLARED SO HARD at Fergus the poor lad visibly wilted. "Martha went out riding with Anselm? Alone and willingly?"

Two weeks had passed since Martha was snatched from his side, two weeks filled with terrible imaginings and unyielding torment.

"Tha-that she did, m'lord." Fergus glanced over his shoulder. The tension in his young face relaxed when he saw Reynard walking down the trail toward them, a brace of pheasants swinging in his hand. "Greetings, Father!" he cried, raising his arm in greeting.

"Fergus!" Reynard broke into a jog, quickly closing the distance between them. Then he gathered his son in a rough, one-armed embrace. "It does my heart good to see you again, boy. I was not expecting you so soon. Tell me, how is life in the castle suiting you?" He looked Fergus over with a critical eye. "Whatever else he is guilty of, Lord Edgeway has not starved you, I see."

Always intuitive, Reynard must have sensed the tension between Vadim and his son, for his smile soon faded. He took a backward step and regarded the two of them through narrowed eyes. "Would one of you be so kind as to tell me what I have missed?"

With an impatient snort, Vadim raked back his hair and turned away, staring blindly into the hills as Fergus retold the news from Edgeway in a low and hurried voice.

For the past week, Reynard's son had been working as a

musician in the castle. Not only was the lad a fine harpist, more importantly, he was a reliable informant. His role there was to keep a careful watch on Martha and to provide her with assistance if she urgently required any.

Vadim ground his teeth. By all accounts, she seemed to be doing rather well on her own.

Before Martha entered his life, he had never known real jealousy. Perhaps he had experienced a flare of envy on occasion—if someone owned a weapon he admired, for instance—but certainly nothing more. Nowadays, however, he was on intimate terms with this bitterest of emotions. It dwelt coiled up within his breast, snarling and ugly.

The rational half of his mind understood that Martha was merely making the best of her bleak circumstances. But the jealous half of him would not be pacified by reason. It bayed for Anselm's blood, urging him to reckless action.

His fingers tightened upon the hilt of his sword, and the urge to hit something, or someone, overwhelmed him.

"Vadim?"

He leapt as Reynard's hand rested upon his shoulder. Spinning about, he eyed his friend with naked rage. "I should be at her side, not skulking here, hiding away in the hills like a beaten cur!"

Reynard glanced back at Fergus, dismissing him with a pointed look. Taking the pheasants from his father's outstretched hand, the lad skirted around Vadim and fled away up the trail.

Once Fergus was out of sight, Reynard returned his attention to Vadim. "We have discussed this before, m'lord," he said softly. "Edgeway castle cannot be stormed by the meager army we have at our disposal, however willing their hearts may be."

"I was a fool to heed your counsel." Vadim battled to slow his breathing. With effort, he forced his fingers to relax their grip on the hilt of his sword. "I need no army to gain access to my old home."

"True enough." Reynard nodded, rubbing his neat gray beard. "But you might wish for one on the way out, especially with your lady wife by your side. Put aside your grief and see reason, man!" The older man turned away shaking his head.

Vadim blinked, shocked by Reynard's uncharacteristic outburst. Of course, he knew the reason for it. Even after all these long years, Reynard still felt the loss of his wife.

Eleanor. The one weakness in his friend's otherwise impenetrable armor of unruffled calm.

During the first turmoil, back when Erik the Bastard seized power, Eleanor was taken hostage. Reynard had made a valiant, if ill-advised, rescue attempt, which resulted in the death of his beloved wife.

Remorse swiftly cooled the raging fires in Vadim's heart. "Forgive me, my friend. I spoke without thinking." He placed a gentle hand on Reynard's shoulder. "As always, you see the road ahead more clearly than I."

"Only because love does not fog my eyesight." Reynard turned back to face Vadim. His smile was in place but it did not reach his eyes. Their gray depths reflected the mortal wound to his heart, an injury that would never heal.

"Believe me, I understand your urgency, m'lord, but rushing might ruin all of our hopes. You cannot hope to rescue Martha alone. Trust in her. For all that she is spirited, your lady is no fool. In a certain light, her riding out with Anselm might be considered a good omen."

"Indeed?" Vadim remained unconvinced. "Then, pray, be so good as to enlighten me, my friend, for I fail to see anything positive in it."

"Is it not apparent? Not only is your lady shielded by Anselm's protection, but she is obviously using this favor to her advantage. He is gradually loosening his hold on her leash." Reynard tilted his head to one side. "Can you not see it?"

"Perhaps." Vadim scuffed the earth with the toe of his boot, kicking up a small dust cloud. He had not considered it in that way. Even so, he liked it not. What had Martha had to do to secure Anselm's dubious protection? The thought made his stomach turn.

"Your lady is safe enough for now, m'lord. Save your strength for a battle we can surely win. Concentrate on the task before us, Vadim. The men need you." Reynard was seldom so serious as this. "And so do I."

Vadim forced himself to smile, though the weight of such responsibility was a heavy burden. By common accord, they turned and began walking back up the trail that lead to the encampment in silence.

For good or evil, the long wait was almost at an end.

The outlaws had recently intercepted a messenger en route to the castle, and the contents of the rider's missive had the potential to change this land forever. At that very moment, King Erik and his entourage were journeying toward Edgeway, staying at the castle for an indefinite period as the earl's house-guests.

Messenger birds were immediately dispatched, carrying word over the sea to Rodmar.

The would-be king's reply came as speedily as Vadim hoped it would. This was too great an opportunity to miss. When King Erik reached the home of his favored cousin, the doors of the trap would begin to close about them. Far away from the well-armed capital to the south, the most dangerous snakes in the land would finally be confined, trapped together in one small basket.

If the Spirits smiled upon his bid to take the throne, Rodmar's ships would reach the east coast within the next two days. And if his army marched as quickly as they sailed, they would muster at the rally point two days after that.

As much as it pained Vadim to admit it, Reynard was right. He could not leave. Not now.

As they drew nearer to the camp, Vadim caught the sharp tang of wood smoke on the light evening breeze. Camp-fires. No one troubled to conceal them anymore. The time for concealment had passed. Each night, the number of fires only increased as more men answered the call to arms. Some traveled alone, but many brought their wives and children with them.

Vadim and Reynard rounded the final bend in the track and paused, looking down onto the hidden valley.

The sullen autumn sky reflected on the dark waters of the lake. Suddenly, the wind stirred the water, and the image was gone, vanished beneath the rippling surface. Around the edge of the tarn, a village of tents had sprung up. Brightly-colored canvases billowed and snapped in the freshening breeze.

Despite the chill, several children stood ankle deep in the water, kicking and splashing one another with high-pitched squeals of excitement. Their mothers stood close by, huddled in a group as they conversed but ever mindful of their offspring. Suddenly, one of the women broke away and hurried to retrieve a small girl who had slipped and fallen into the lake. The mother removed her own shawl and swaddled the child within its woolen folds, scolding her even as she embraced her.

So many young fugitives. What kind of world was this in which to raise a child?

Vadim had never known what compelled an otherwise sane man to marry, not until Martha entered his life. He had long regarded marriage as a foolish, and slightly selfish, act. An outlaw's grip on life was particularly tenuous, after all. But Martha had come along and, albeit unwittingly, she had begun rectifying the many omissions in his education.

Now he understood all those men who had fallen before him, casting themselves beneath love's merciless wheels. However painful it was to love, he would not go back even if he could.

Even now, his child might be growing within Martha's belly. The thought thrilled and terrified him in equal measure. For her sake, he prayed it was not so.

If he fell in battle, what would become of her? Of them? He shivered and drew his cloak about himself, blaming the autumnal wind. Without question, Seth and Rodmar would ensure Martha wanted for nothing. But the small voice within his heart would not be silenced.

If all your plans come to nothing, what will happen to Martha then?

He shook his head to dispel the unpleasant visions. If he could not motivate himself, how could he hope to put heart into his men? The battle was too close at hand. He could not allow such morbid thoughts as these to take root.

"Come, Reynard." Vadim slapped his companion on the back and attempted to smile. "Let us see if young Fergus has made a start on supper. I am hungry enough to face even his rabbit stew."

***

"Good, Martha." Anselm's breath brushed warm against her cheek. "Just a little further—"

"I can't," she moaned. "It hurts."

"Yes, you can." Anselm's fingers lightly rested on hers, guiding her into position. "Take it all the way back."

"Like this?" She glanced at him, the muscles in her arms trembling with exertion.

"Perfect. Now release."

Martha gasped in disbelief as her arrow whizzed through the air and embedded itself in the target, a swinging straw representation of a human body. Thanks to Anselm, she'd managed to hit the straw man in the approximate neighborhood of his heart. Perhaps imagining the straw man was His Evilness had helped improve her aim.

"Yes!" she cried, punching the air in delight. "I did it! I did it!" Her fingers burned, and her arms felt weak and wobbly, but she experienced a definite buzz from nailing her intended target. She executed a miniature happy-dance and tripped over the end of her long bow, still grinning like a fool.

"That was very well done indeed, m'lady," Anselm said with a smile. "We shall make an archer of you yet."

"Oh?" Martha stopped dancing and cocked her head to one side. "Aren't you scared I might use my new found skill against you? I am still your prisoner, after all." But she added a smile to take the sting from her words.

Anselm laughed then took the bow from her hands. "*Guest* is a much more pleasant word, would you not agree?" Propping one end of the bow against his boot, while firmly holding onto the other end, he pulled the wood back into a tight curve, which allowed him to flick the string loose. The weapon instantly snapped into a more staff-like shape.

"And since you can neither string a bow nor hit a target without my instruction," he added, gently taking her arm, "I think I need not fear for my life quite yet. Shall we return to the castle, sweeting? There are one or two errands I must perform for my master."

"Sure. Why not?"

To Martha's surprise, Anselm appeared to have accepted her personality transplant without question. Either he was much more stupid than she thought, or he was just playing along. Whatever it was, for the past week, she'd reaped the benefits of *being nice,* and she couldn't deny that they were very welcome.

She thought back to the morning following Anselm's drunken tirade, the day she'd changed her tactics.

When Anselm returned to his chambers, he found a very sub-dued Martha waiting for him, sitting in her regular spot by the fire.

Before he could speak, she burst into tears and covered her face with her hands. Switching on the water-works wasn't difficult. Since parting from Vadim, tears were never far away.

"What is it, sweeting?" Anselm hurried over and crouched beside her chair. "Are you ill?" He touched her arm. "Tell me."

"You scared me last night," she sniveled, allowing him to remove her hands from her face so that he could see her tears. "Oh, Anselm. What's happened to us? We used to be such good friends, but now—" She gave another sob.

Anselm rested his chin on the wooden armrest of her chair, concern clouding his gray eyes. "I am sorry, Martha. For all of it." He used his index finger to hook a tendril of hair from her tear-stained face then tucked it behind her ear. "Shall we try again?"

"How can we?" she asked, looking deeply into his eyes. Her face was swollen and blotchy, but she wanted him to see her unhappiness. "Too much has happened, and Vadim—"

"Is dead. That awful fellow Madoc confirmed it." Anselm frisked his pockets and produced a square of clean linen which he offered to Martha. "It wounds me to see you so wretched, sweeting. You may call me *fuckwit* again if it will make you smile."

Martha dabbed her eyes and tried not to smile at Anselm's apparent distress on her behalf. Good old—or young—Madoc. He'd made them believe Vadim was dead after all.

"A woman so young and fair should not waste her life in pointless mourning," Anselm continued gently. "That would be a terrible fate."

Although Martha had every intention of being coaxed, she couldn't give in too easily or he might be suspicious. "Vadim was my husband, Anselm. I miss him so much, and I love him still." With satisfaction, she watched his jaw tighten. "How can you and I be friends again?" she asked. "You won't even let me mourn him. You hate him, even now."

To his credit, Anselm didn't attempt to deny it.

"Then, let us call a truce, my sweet," he said, clasping her hand with his. His eyes burned silver as he looked at her and, just for a second, she almost believed he felt something for her. "The past is dead," he said. "In time, I hope we might bury it forever. Until then, I am content to wait for you, my sweet. Perhaps when you forget about hating me, you might—"

"Who can say?" She couldn't bear to let him finish. From Anselm's lips, words of love would sound like the worst possible profanity. "But I am willing to meet you halfway. Is that good enough?"

From then on, Martha found life slightly more bearable. Instead of keeping her locked away, Anselm began allowing her to accompany him on his business around the castle. When Martha showed no signs of misbehaving, not even whilst in the presence of His Evilness, he loosened her bonds even further.

"Perhaps we might ride out again this afternoon?" Anselm asked. They'd arrived at the door that led to Anselm's chambers. "It would be a pity to waste this fine spell of weather. Unless, of course, you are weary?"

Martha roused herself enough to smile at him. "Not at all. I'd love to go out."

Seemingly satisfied, he opened the door and escorted Martha into the living room. A solitary tray of cold food sat waiting for her on a table set by the window.

"I will return as soon as I may, my dear," he said, raising her hand to his lips. "Enjoy your meal."

With that, he was gone, locking the door behind him as always. Although she had more freedom than before, she was still a prisoner.

Grimacing, Martha wiped the hand he'd kissed down the skirt of her moss-green dress. Her face muscles ached with the effort of keeping her fake smile in place for so long. Why were fake smiles so painful?

She paced the room several times, pausing to uncover her lunch tray. Cold mutton, congealed in its own fat, and a slab of dark, heavy bread. *Oh, that's just grim.* She recovered the meal with the linen cloth.

The watery ale, however, was always welcome—though it wasn't a patch on Seth's home brew. Sipping her ale, she went over to the window, kneeling on the seat to look outside. She stared at the people in the courtyard below without really seeing them, her mind occupied with the news Agatha had given her earlier that day.

While trailing Anselm around the castle, Martha had noticed Agatha hovering on the periphery of her vision. The older woman stared at her so hard it was obvious she had something she wanted Martha to hear.

Anselm was engrossed in conversation with a group of soldiers, so Martha tugged on his sleeve.

"Is it okay if I go and have a word with Agatha about my gown? I think it needs a little extra something along the—"

"Forgive me, my dear," Anselm said with a delicate shudder. "But there are some things a man should never be exposed to. Just show me the magic. Never explain the spell. Now run along. But stay where I can see you."

Patronizing arse! Martha turned away, but not without noticing that Anselm's soldier pals all wore matching smirks.

As Martha approached, Agatha smiled her gap-toothed smile. "What excuse did you give him?"

"We're meant to be discussing dress necklines," Martha replied, casting a quick glance back at Anselm. He wasn't looking, but no doubt the soldiers would tell him if she wandered off. Martha took Agatha's rough hands and gave them a squeeze. "How are you? It's so good to see you again."

The older woman's plump cheeks flushed crimson, but she looked pleased. "My joints are more than a little painful than usual; otherwise, I cannot complain."

Somehow, Martha managed to keep a straight face.

Taking Martha's arm, Agatha led her to a quieter part of the courtyard where there was less chance of being overheard. "I have no message, but I do have some news to impart," she said in a low voice. Her eyes constantly scanned the area in case anyone wandered too near. "The king and his court will arrive in Edgeway by the end of the week."

Martha shrugged. "So?" She scuffed the toe of her slipper against the cobbles. Why should she give a damn about the earl's visitors? They were probably all as vile as he was.

"Rodmar and his great army follow close behind—"

"What?" She felt her eyes bulge. *Rodmar? The wannabe king,*

Rodmar? "B-but it's too soon! Vadim said they wouldn't set sail until the next full moon—"

"This is too great an opportunity to miss, m'lady. Do you not see it? In one fell stroke, Rodmar may rid this land of its greatest parasites." She gripped Martha's shoulders, her gray eyes shining. "There will never be a more favorable time than this." Suddenly, Agatha seemed to recall where she was. "Forgive me," she said, releasing Martha. "The excitement of seeing my sons again overcame me."

"It's fine." Martha cast a quick glance over her shoulder. "I don't think anyone noticed." As much as she wanted to ask Agatha about her sons, this wasn't the best time to discuss them, not with Anselm so near.

But at least now she knew why Vadim hadn't come to rescue her already. He was too busy preparing for Rodmar's return. Honoring the oath of his dead father was apparently more important to him than she was. A flame of anger flared within her heart. *So much for fecking love!*

"Now, Martha. Do not make yourself uneasy," Agatha said kindly. "Your lord is delayed, but he will come for you."

Was her expression so transparent? "I'm sure he will," she muttered, "if he doesn't get himself killed first." Her smile felt more like a snarl. "And I wonder how my hosts will react when they see my dead husband heading the attack? Then again, they're both reasonable men. Perhaps they won't be too angry with me for lying to them all this time."

But her snarkasm was wasted on Agatha.

"That is what I wanted to tell you, m'lady. When trouble comes, find the young harp player. Fergus is my nephew, you see. He will keep you safe."

"*He's* one of Vadim's men?" Of course he was. She'd always thought the red-haired musician looked familiar. But how the hell was she meant to get to Fergus when Anselm kept her locked up in his rooms? *What am I supposed to do, walk through the fecking wall?*

Agatha's eyes flashed in warning. "Yes, I think extra lace would be a fine idea, m'lady. The modern lower necklines are not to everyone's taste. When shall I call to collect the gown?"

"This evening will be fine." Martha answered quietly, suddenly feeling as flat as week-old roadkill. "I don't have any other plans." She felt the sudden pressure of a firm hand splayed upon her lower back. She shuddered and rolled her eyes. Anselm.

"Have you finished discussing gowns, my dear?" he asked. Martha turned to look at him, her smile firmly fixed in place. "Yes. For now. Thank you, Agatha." She dismissed the other woman with a careless glance, mimicking the regal elegance she witnessed so often amongst the castle's ruling class.

Agatha lowered her eyes and, bobbing a curtsey, departed.

chapter eight

SOMETIMES SHE DIDN'T HAVE TO fake it. On rare, sweet moments like this, her smile was real.

Martha's horse thundered alongside Anselm's, kicking up dust on the hard dirt track. Her headscarf had long since gone, and her hair streamed behind her like the tail of a kite. A bubble of happiness expanded inside her chest. Unable to hold it back, she laughed out loud, although the sound was whipped away by the wind.

She felt wild. Euphoric. Like a bird released from its cage after a lifetime of imprisonment. She would have burst into song if she wasn't so breathless.

Freedom. Well, sort of.

Anselm's gray palfrey changed gear and surged away at a gallop.

Oh, no, you don't! Leaning forward over her horse's glistening neck, Martha set off after him.

Mistral—her little bay mare—needed little encouragement. Flattening back her ears, she went turbo, grunting with the exertion, her hooves flying over the ground to catch up with her larger stablemate.

They were side by side again, Mistral ahead by just a nose. Anselm turned to grin at her, and Martha smiled back, unable to contain her delight, intoxicated by the sense of freedom. For what seemed like the first time in forever, she was herself again.

Anselm sat up in his saddle and gradually slowed his horse to a walk. Reluctantly, Martha followed his lead.

They came to a stop at the bottom of a grassy hill. The horses snorted for breath, bits jangling in their mouths as they tossed their heads, sending long strings of foamy saliva flying through the air.

Anselm flung one long leg over his horse's neck and leaped to the ground. "I need not trouble to ask if you enjoyed your ride, sweeting," he said, coming around to help Martha dismount. "I have seldom seen eyes that radiate such brilliance."

"Yeah. Right." Anselm's compliments were always way over-cooked for her taste. Even so, she let go of the reins and allowed him to lift her from the saddle. Somehow, he managed not to drop her although he did grimace a bit before he set her down, which made her smile.

But she was too happy to hate him. Her heart still galloped on, lighter than air. "Thanks for today, Anselm. It's been great."

"Your smile is thanks enough," he said touching her cheek with his gloved hand. "But the day is not over yet. Will you walk with me while our worthy animals take a well-deserved rest?"

At that moment, Martha fully appreciated why Anselm was such a hit with the ladies of the castle. With his intense, silvery eyes and wind-tousled hair, he looked like a handsome young Viking. Fortunately, she was immune to his charms. Vadim was an impossible act to follow.

"Sure," she replied. "Why not?"

They saw their horses comfortable then left them to graze—loosely tethered so they didn't wander away—and by common accord, set off up the hill.

Martha was eager to get to the top. On the ride in, she'd noticed a jumble of fallen masonry up there. The remains of an ancient hill fort, perhaps?

The incline became steeper halfway up. Her smooth-soled riding boots made heavy work of the steep, grassy slope. She kept slipping and cursing beneath her breath. It was like skating along a polished wood floor with dusters on her feet, only vertically.

"Here," Anselm said, offering his arm. "Hold on to me."

Martha was only too happy to accept his offer. "What is... this... place?" she asked, panting a little, as they went on.

"No one knows for certain. There are no accounts of it ever being anything other than a ruin."

They clambered upward in silence, saving their breath to tackle the steepest part of the hill.

The birdsong, and the gentle sighing of the wind as it stirred the sun-bleached grass, provided a lovely soundtrack to the afternoon. Only Martha's gasps and frequent muttered curses spoiled the tranquility. But she struggled on, puffing and panting her way uphill like a foul-mouthed little train that could. All the while, she maintained her tight deathgrip on Anselm's arm.

Anselm wasn't even slightly out of breath, but he wasn't hampered with long woolen skirts and flowing undergarments like she was. *Lucky devil.* He did have his hands full, though. Keeping Martha upright was proving to be a full-time job.

To Martha's relief, Anselm paused to survey the swaying grassy plain they had so recently traveled. "When I was a child, this was one of my favorite places. Whenever I ran away from home, this is always where my father would find me." He sounded wistful as he recalled the past. "Our folklore is rich with tales of this hill." The hardness of his features softened as he spoke. It suited him. He swept aside his wind-mussed hair with one hand, the action reminding her of Vadim.

"Oh? Such as?" If she kept him talking, she could get her breath back a bit. Shielding her eyes, Martha followed the path of dark ribbon that wound its way through the rolling countryside. The road home. If she followed it far enough south, it would take her back to Darumvale. To Vadim. She gave a shuddering sigh. God, she missed him.

"Some say this was once a palace of a terrible Elf king." Anselm continued, still lost in his memories. "Others claim it was the stronghold of a long-forgotten warrior tribe." His chuckle sounded bitter, "Of course, 'tis naught but childish nonsense—tales fit only for the shacks of grubbing peasants."

"I take it you don't believe in fairytales then?" Martha felt him staring at her, but she kept her eyes on the horizon. She was glad he'd spoken so derisively just now. He'd reminded her of what he actually was, the polar opposite of what she wished him to be. Anselm was Lord Edgeway's man to the bone. On the infrequent occasions when he wasn't occupied with being an utter arse, it was too easy to forget that.

Anselm gave a snort of disdain. "I never believed such dross, not even as a child. It would hardly be fitting for the son of the earl's steward..."

Hold on. What? She turned to look at him. Seth was the old earl's steward? That was a really big deal, wasn't it? How little she still knew. Did Vadim have a weird pathological aversion to telling her the plain truth? If he were an artist, he'd definitely be of the abstract variety.

"Unlike your husba—" Anselm scowled, obviously angry with himself for slipping up and mentioning his arch nemesis.

"What? So Vadim believed the stories?"

"Of course he did. He drove the elders to distraction with his thirst for the tales buried in their wizened old heads. Shall we continue?" He stalked away, abandoning her in his haste to be gone. Not that she cared.

It wasn't much further to the top of the hill. Besides, she wanted to think. Suddenly the numerous threads of Anselm's weirdness began knitting together, forming one long skein. His parents' simple honesty disgusted him, that much was clear. He'd yearned to be a man of consequence, she suspected, even as a boy.

Was that why he'd treated his parents so badly? Did he blame them for their fall from grace?

A mental light bulb flashed on in her head. Suddenly, she saw Anselm clearly for the very first time. That's why he hated Vadim so much. It wasn't about his parents taking in the old earl's orphaned son. Not really.

When the earl fell, his followers had gone down with him, and Anselm had lost the things he held dear: wealth, position, and power. Not only that, but because of Seth's loyal heart, the young Anselm had then been forced to share his family with the son of the man who had ruined them. Talk about rubbing salt in the wound.

The true, twisted root of his hatred was not actually buried in Vadim, she realized, but in the old earl, his father.

Anselm's family had fallen from grace, and Vadim was a constant reminder of it.

She was right; she knew she was. But like a female, medieval Columbo, there was just one thing she didn't understand.

Anselm was waiting for her on the hilltop, leaning against a lichen-encrusted column of rock. As their eyes met, she didn't look away. He did.

I have you now, my friend.

The ruins on the hilltop were definitely man-made, but Martha was too fixed on her quarry to appreciate their tumble-down splendor. Instead, she stalked over to where Anselm stood. "What made you ask the Evil Earl for a job in the first place?"

"I beg your pardon?" Her question had apparently taken him by surprise. Anselm stood upright, scowling at her. His body language radiated hostility.

Martha wasn't fazed one bit. "You heard me." She planted her hands on her hips and stared him down. "If we're to have any chance of a real friendship, you'll give me an honest answer."

"You have been thinking about me a good deal, have you not, sweeting?" He reached out to touch her face, countering her surprise attack with a charm offensive.

"Yes, I have," she said, swatting his hand away. "But I wouldn't get too excited about it. Not until you've heard what I have to say."

A smile twitched at the corners of his mouth. "What new game is this?"

"It's called honesty. Maybe you have some vague recollection of it?" Martha mentally crossed herself for being so two-faced. "And don't try charming me. I'm wise to your tactics by now. Unfortunately for you, I'm not one of your giggling harem of serving girls, *Sir Anselm*."

His easy smile faded. "No. That you most certainly are not." Something new flashed in his eyes. If she didn't know better, she'd swear it was approval.

"So?" She arched her eyebrows. "Are you going to answer my question or not?"

Anselm sighed. "Why does it matter? Ask me something else, m'lady."

"No." Martha shook her head, impatiently dashing away her hair as the breeze billowed it into her face. "It's the one thing I don't understand. Why do you serve the king and your master when they're the ones ultimately responsible for what happened to your family?"

Shaking his head, Anselm glanced away. "You could not possibly understand."

"Try me."

"Very well." His eyes met hers in a silent challenge. "I wish to see my bloodline restored to greatness, not left festering for eternity, housed in a stinking barn with only simpletons and animals for company."

The venom of his words made her flinch, but she didn't look away. Ugly as this was to hear, Anselm was finally being honest.

"The path I now walk," he continued, "is the only route left to me."

"And what of your honor?" *Damn. I can't believe I just said that.* "Your self-respect?"

"I used them to pay the tallyman."

If Anselm had only known that his faint smile affected Martha far more than any of his expensive gifts. At that moment, she actually experienced a twinge of pity for him, and for the man he'd become.

"And has your choice made you happy?" The softness of her voice mirrored her feelings. "Really?"

Anselm shrugged and kicked a small stone over the edge of the hill. "Would I be any more content living as my father does, buried alive in that outlaw-infested village, scraping a living from the earth? Taking orders from those he used to command?"

Anger flared in her heart. How could he speak of Seth in that way? "Your father is one of the most noble men I've ever met—"

"He lives like a peasant, Martha! He brews his own ale and shares his home with a cow! Very noble indeed." His sneering tone was worse than his shouting. "Oh, what a dash he would cut at court, all dressed up in his filthy, home-spun smock. King Erik must curse himself a fool for overlooking such a fine and splendid fellow as my beloved father." Anselm gave a grim smile. "Hardly the kind of life I would choose for myself, m'lady. In fact, I could hardly imagine a more terrible fate."

"Yeah?" Martha held his flashing eyes without flinching. "Well at least your father can sleep at night; his conscience is clean. Tell me something: how do you sleep, Anselm?"

His lips curved in a seductive smile. "Well, if you ever care to visit my bedchamber, you might judge that for yourself."

Martha gave a tut of exasperation. "Oh, for f..." Without another word, she spun on her heels and stormed away, irritated beyond reason. Just when they were getting somewhere, he'd hidden behind his mask of sleaze and reverted to pervy Sir Anselm. *Sod him!* She wasn't in the mood to hear him spouting more crap. For the briefest moment there, she'd seen a chink in his armor, the faintest spark of humanity, but now it was gone.

"Martha?" Anselm's hand closed gently about her arm, preventing her escape. "Forgive me."

She turned around. If the tone of his voice had surprised her, the sight of him came as an even bigger shock. Not a trace of his former arrogance remained. His gray eyes glittered. He seemed... naked. Vulnerable.

"I should not have spoken to you so. The fact is, you make me see things I would rather forget." He released her arm and sighed, raking one hand through his golden hair. "It is too late for me, Martha. For better or worse, my course is set. Never fear, in the veil beyond death, I will doubtless be forced to repay all my debts in full. Until then, I must enjoy the life I have remaining and taste all of its trimmings."

Martha sat down on a granite slab. *He really is unbelievable.*

"What vexes you now, my dear?" Anselm sat beside her. "Why do your eyes reproach me so?"

"I was thinking about Sylvie, if you really want to know." She glared at him. "She killed herself, Anselm, and you pushed her to it. Doesn't that mean anything to you?"

"Ah." Anselm looked solemn. "I admit, that was regrettable."

"Regrettable?" Martha raised her eyebrows. "That's the best you can do? She was your mother, for heaven's sake."

Anger flashed in his eyes. "What do you want from me? What would you have me do? Shall I wail and tear out my hair in grief? Will that bring her back?"

The carrot. What happened to the damn carrot, Bigalow?

Martha reined herself in. *Be nice.* Making Anselm angry served no good purpose.

"I-I'm sorry." She faked a timid smile. "I had no right to question you in this way. How you mourn your mother is your own affair."

Anselm exhaled hard, and the rage behind his eyes faded. "Be assured, my grief for her is very real. But you still have not told me why it matters so much to you, m'lady."

Martha shrugged and stood up. "I just wanted to know you better; that's all. To try and remove some of the obstacles to our... friendship." She drew her cloak about her. A chilly mist had begun to descend, obscuring the falling sun. Fine particles of moisture clung to her hair and clothing, making her shiver.

"And have we? Removed some of them?"

For some reason, she couldn't lie. "Let's just say we've made a start."

"That will do for now." Anselm took her arm. "Shall we depart before the mist worsens?"

Martha cast a last look at the ruins she'd so wanted to see and suddenly felt depressed. This was no fairy castle. It was just a heap of old stones. No handsome prince was coming to save her.

And suppose she did manage to escape from Anselm, where could she go? If she went back to Darumvale, she wouldn't find Vadim there; he was too busy planning his damned war. And returning to the village would only bring further pain to the villagers—her friends. They'd already suffered more than enough. No. For the time being, she was stuck with Anselm.

And where was Vadim? Her well of excuses for him was starting to dry up. War would reach her before her husband did.

In the meantime, if there was any dragon-slaying to be done, she'd just have to do it herself.

chapter nine

THEY TOOK THE SCENIC ROUTE back to the castle, riding through the busy town of Edgeway. It was just as noisy as Martha remembered it. Although it was almost dusk, the streets were still packed with people and livestock. The constant hum of human voices competed with the various *moos* and grunts of the animals.

As they rode by, a donkey brayed and hurriedly backed away from the woman attempting to lead it, and toppled a basket of hens as its hooves slipped on the wet cobbles. The outraged birds squawked in fury, adding another level to the wall of sound.

"I had forgotten it was market day." Anselm raised his voice in order be heard. "Perhaps, if you are willing, we might attend the next one together?"

Martha smiled. "Yes. I'd like that."

Just then, a large wagon full of turnips moved off, the driver not bothering to check if anything was coming up behind him. As the cart swung into the middle of the narrow street, Mistral executed a hasty step sideways and barged into Anselm's horse, who was walking alongside her.

Momentarily unbalanced, Martha reached out her hand and braced herself upon Anselm's hard thigh.

"Have a care, man!" Anselm bellowed at the driver as he helped Martha to sit upright in her saddle. "The road is ours. Give way at once."

"Ssh, Anselm. It's fine—"

"Irresponsible halfwit!"

The sound of Anselm's voice had a curious effect on the bustling street. Everyone stopped what they were doing and stared, whispering to one another from behind their hands. Martha distinctly heard the words *Lord Edgeway's man,* and an unnatural hush descended.

The reins felt slippery in her clammy hands. This silence wasn't out of respect. The fear in the people's eyes was unmistakable. She squirmed in her saddle feeling as conspicuous as a hairy facial wart.

What do they make of me? Did they think she was like Anselm? Of course they did. Why wouldn't they? Not only was she dressed as a noblewoman, she was in the company of the earl's favorite henchman.

"Come along, dearest." Anselm grabbed Martha's reins and forced his horse into a trot. Mistral followed suit. "Imbecile!" he snarled at the cart driver as they passed.

Red with embarrassment, Martha smiled at the poor man, but he wouldn't look at her. He kept his eyes low, fixing his gaze on his filthy hands.

The whispers must have spread. It was the same all along the road. The crowds magically parted as they approached, and a sea of expressionless faces watched them go by. Then the cloying silence dissipated, and life returned to the street.

Once they were clear of the crowd, Anselm slowed his horse to walk and then gave Martha her reins. "Forgive me, sweeting. I should not have brought you this way."

"Does that happen to you a lot?"

"What? Getting rammed by unruly peasants?" He laughed. "Hardly!"

"No. I meant the silence, the staring."

Anselm shrugged and didn't bother to reply. "Shall we quicken our pace? We have been out much longer than I intended."

And there she had her answer. The incident obviously meant nothing to him. If only she could put it from her mind so easily.

The moment their horses crossed the drawbridge, the earl swooped down on them like an agitated, purple-clad bat.

"Where have you been for so long?" he demanded, striding

over the cobbled courtyard toward them. "I do not employ you to go gallivanting about the countryside with your favorite doxy!"

Martha flinched. *Doxy?* Charming.

"My apology, m'lord." Anselm flung his leg over his horse's neck and dismounted, wordlessly thrusting his reins into the waiting hands of a hovering stable lad. "We took the road back through Edgeway. I had forgotten it—"

The earl grabbed the sleeve of Anselm's tunic and didn't let go. "The king is on his way."

"M'lord?"

"Erik? The king? Your liege-lord?" The earl's voice rose to a shriek. "He will be here in two days. Two days! How can I hope to be ready to receive him in time?" He released Anselm and cast his hands skyward, muttering to himself.

Anselm frowned. "At such short notice?"

The earl pursed his lips. "Not as short as you might believe. It appears the first dispatch rider was lost somewhere in outlaw country." He glared at Martha, pointing a swift, accusing finger at her. "The work of your dead husband's friends, no doubt."

"Or perhaps he met with some other unfortunate accident, m'lord?" Martha replied calmly.

The earl looked as if he were sucking on a particularly bitter lemon. "Oh, do shut up!" he snapped.

Martha hurriedly dismounted, waving away the stable lad who was waiting to take Mistral back to her stable. Hidden by her horse—safely out of sight of Anselm and the earl—her carefully neutral mask cracked. Unable to help herself, she leaned against Mistral's side and dissolved into fits of soundless giggles. As scary and dangerous as the earl was, his fits of rage were too funny. He reminded her of an overwound clockwork clown.

Still snort-giggling, she patted her horse and loosened its girth. She had to get herself back under control.

The stable boy frowned. "Are you unwell, m'lady?"

"I'm fine." She handed him Mistral's reins. "I think I must have got a piece of grit in my eye or something." Still grinning, she swiped her sleeve over her damp cheeks. "Thank you."

The lad shook his head and lead Mistral away.

Anselm beckoned to her from where he stood, visibly bristling as he listened to his master's continuing bitter tirade. He couldn't get a word in sideways.

Serves him right.

The men set off toward the keep with Martha dawdling behind.

"You must return to town at once!" the earl cried. "I need an army of servants. Take as many men as you need to coerce the townspeople. Use whatever threats you must, but get them here. Do you understand? Come what may, I want this castle gleaming and its larders full by this time tomorrow..."

Martha smiled another secret smile. *Wait until you see what's coming, you pompous old arse. Today is only the start.*

By "this time tomorrow", the press-ganged army of cleaning women, cooks, and servants had almost achieved the earl's goal.

Martha asked Anselm if she could help, and much to her amazement, he agreed.

"It is hardly fitting," he said. "But no doubt an extra pair of hands would be useful. Go down to the kitchens and help as you may. Oh, and take your maid with you."

She didn't need telling twice. Anywhere was better than being stuck in here.

The moment she and Effie entered the hot and crowded kitchen, they saw Agatha, waving to them over the heads of the scurrying scullery maids. She looked pleased to see Martha again. Leaving Effie to help one of the pastry cooks, the older woman dragged Martha off to assist with the massive task of airing and cleaning the castle's guest chambers.

The majority of the visiting knights and soldiers were to be put up in the great hall. The rest would share the barracks of the castle garrison. The remainder of the king's extensive entourage had a smaller, lesser-used hall within the shadow of the curtain wall.

Only the highest ranking nobles would have a bedchamber, but even they would have little privacy, what with having to share the space with their personal servants, who usually slept in the same room on a straw pallet. Despite Edgeway Castle's impressive size, accommodating the king and his court was, according to Agatha, proving to be quite a challenge.

The moment they were alone, carting their buckets and cleaning equipment along the second floor corridor, Martha raised the subject that had been bugging her ever since she'd learned of Rodmar's advancing army.

"When the time comes, how the hell am I supposed to get out of Anselm's rooms? Do you happen to have a spare key?"

"Hush!" Agatha glanced over her shoulder, but the echoing corridor was empty. Several seconds elapsed before she gave Martha an answer. "No," she said. "I am afraid not."

Oh, that's just great. "So, what am I supposed to do?" Martha demanded, almost dropping the bucket she carried. "It's just my life we're talking about here. No big deal."

"You have so much more freedom of late. Perhaps you will not need a key?"

"*Perhaps?*" Martha's eyebrows almost hit her hairline. "Sorry, Ags, but I'm going to need a little more insurance than that."

Agatha frowned, apparently giving some thought to the matter. "There is nothing else for it," she said at last. "The next time the guard takes lunch in the kitchen, I will attempt to steal his keys. In the event I am unsuccessful, however," her gray eyes twinkled, "it might be prudent for you try and liberate Anselm's set of keys."

"How? He never puts them down for a second. Trust me, I've had plenty of time to study him."

A grin of pure wickedness curved Agatha's lips, and her eyes shone brighter than ever. There was no mistaking her meaning.

Is she suggesting that I...? Hot color flooded Martha's cheeks. *That's exactly what she's suggesting.* "No! Absolutely not." She marched down the corridor, sloshing water from her bucket in her haste to put some distance between herself and the mental image Agatha had just given her. "Eww!" *Sleep with Anselm? No fecking way!* Her skin prickled as though a thousand tiny spiders were creeping over her.

"We are but women, m'lady." Agatha's mop scraped along the stone floor as she hurried to catch up. "We must use whatever means we can to secure our safety in these dangerous times."

Martha stopped walking and wheeled around. "You mean to say that you'd..." God, she couldn't even say it. "With Anselm?" She felt herself grimace.

"Me?" Agatha shrugged. "Why, yes. I suppose I would, if I had to." She ignored Martha's disgusted little '*ugh*'. "And you need not look at me like that. I may be an old woman, but even

I can see Anselm is not wholly without appeal. Besides," she added with a lecherous grin, "it has been a long time since I last had a man to warm my bed. And from what I have learned, as untrustworthy as Sir Anselm undoubtedly is, he would not leave me disappointed."

Holy Mother of God! This was way too much information.

"And what about Vadim?" Martha demanded in a heated whisper. "Even if I could get myself drunk enough to sleep with Anselm, how do you think he'd feel if he learned I'd bumped uglies with his evil foster brother?"

Agatha shrugged. "Is there any reason he would find out? Would you tell him?"

No. She wouldn't have to. Anselm would take great pleasure in doing that himself the very moment he learned Vadim was still alive.

"There are fates far worse than a night in Sir Anselm's bed," Agatha continued in a wheedling tone. "He is reputed to be a very generous lover. Come, m'lady. You cannot deny that he is very attractive."

Martha wrinkled her nose in disgust. "Oh, please. Enough! Gentlemen might prefer blondes, but I certainly don't." She stalked away, muttering beneath her breath. "Remind me never to play Shag, Kill or Marry with you." Something told her she wouldn't like any of Agatha's answers.

"What did you say, my dear?" Agatha called after her.

Martha ground her teeth and kept walking. "I said, I'll find another way."

The hours spent preparing for King Erik's visit were amongst the happiest Martha had spent at the castle. To be away from Anselm's watchful eyes, to be able to laugh and talk freely again, was an exquisite luxury. Okay, so she wasn't free yet, but at least Anselm had loosened her leash.

Trailing Agatha from room to room, Martha listened to the older woman's stories as they washed, swept, and polished away the dust of long neglect. For the best part of the day, no one disturbed them. Even so, they spoke in hushed tones, just in case the stone walls were listening.

In great depth, Agatha described her former life, the days

she'd lived as a noblewoman. She spoke affectionately of her dead husband, a man many years her senior. Martha thought he sounded a kindly chap, a nice husband and an indulgent father to his two young sons. It was clear Agatha still missed him dearly.

Inevitably, the conversation drifted to Vadim.

"I know you are angry with him, child." Agatha held up her hand to ward off the protest Martha was about to make. "Yes, you are. It is there in your eyes whenever I mention him, a brittleness that was not there before."

Martha shut her mouth. There was no point denying it. Was there any wonder she was so pissed off? In all the time she'd been here, Vadim had made no attempt to rescue her. So much for love. What else was she supposed to think?

She swept the floor so vigorously that a great cloud of dust engulfed the bedchamber, making them cough and sneeze.

"Wait!" Agatha hobbled over to the window and pushed it open as wide as it would go.

A cool breeze swirled through the room, cutting a swathe of freshness through the stale and dusty air. Martha leaned on her broom and inhaled, filling her lungs with the unmistakable scent of autumn: bonfires, ripe fruit, and rich, loamy earth.

Agatha withdrew her head from the window and glared at her. "At least let me dampen down the dust before you and your broom punish the floor for the supposed failings of your husband."

Hah! She'd been at the mercy of His Evilness and his mentally challenged sidekick for five fecking weeks. There was no *supposed* about it.

Taking a pitcher from the hearth, Agatha dipped her fingers into the water and began flicking it around the room, anointing every dusty corner. "*Now* you may sweep."

Martha moved the broom more slowly this time. Each stroke of her brush lifted a bright stripe of wood from the filthy floor. She found the work was strangely satisfying.

"You did not live through the dark, desperate days after the old king was murdered. Perhaps if you had, you would understand Vadim's actions better."

Martha glanced at Agatha, but continued sweeping. She wasn't in the mood to hear more excuses.

"Vadim was only a boy at the time." Agatha flicked her duster over the veil of cobwebs hanging from one of the carved wooden bed posts. "'Twas Seth who found him lying outside in the courtyard with his dead parents." She sighed. "For days, he hovered nearer death than life, but the wounds to his soul were even more severe.

"Over time, his physical wounds healed, but his hidden injuries remained unchanged. By day, the boy was little more than a living corpse. He never spoke or made a sound. Wherever Seth put him, he would still be there hours later, staring at nothing with those dark, empty eyes. Oh, but at night! That was a different tale." Agatha closed her eyes for a second and shuddered. "I will never forget that poor child's screams. Even now, recalling them gives me the chills. Awful they were. We began to think he might never recover, that death would have been a truer mercy."

Martha kept sweeping, but slowly. The thought of Vadim's suffering sickened her.

"That poor lad. To see his parents hacked—"

"I know this part." Martha couldn't stomach hearing it again. Once was plenty. "Tell me something else."

"Very well." Agatha took up a small pot of beeswax and began rubbing it in small circles onto the wooden bedpost. "Eventually, Seth brought Madoc to Darumva—"

"Madoc?" Martha stopped work and leaned on her broom. "*My* Madoc?"

"Yes... well, the old Madoc that was. May the Spirits keep his soul."

"He healed Vadim?"

"I do not know what he did, but he was shut away with the child for several days." Agatha sat down on the bed, and the straw-filled mattress rustled beneath her weight. "When he finally left, Vadim had begun speaking again. Only little words at first, you understand, but it was a start. Time completed what Madoc had begun. As the years passed and Vadim grew into a man, he began seeking out all those who had been most wounded by the new king and his noblemen and offered them a way to strike back, a chance to right the wrongs of this land."

Just like Robin Hood. Martha resumed her sweeping, absorbing Agatha's words. She still knew so little about him, the man she had married.

"As the outlaw ranks swelled," Agatha continued, "Lord Edgeway was amongst the first to taste the wrath of those he had attempted to crush. I shall never forget his rage the first time he lost the taxes that were on route to his cousin, the king. He personally beheaded two of his own captains who survived the ambush, ignoring their pleas for mercy. The other soldiers got off more lightly with a public flogging. The earl was unbearable for weeks afterward, rampaging through the castle and bellowing at anyone foolish enough to be in his path, be they knight or scullery maid."

Martha met Agatha's twinkling eyes and managed a weak smile since some response was obviously expected of her. But she had no words. It was all so barbaric.

Grabbing the bedpost, Agatha pulled herself up off the bed, giving a little grunt of exertion as she regained her feet. "And what do you think your lord and master did with all the gold he took?"

"He gave it back to the people it was taken from?" It was the only thing he could do, she supposed.

"Er... yes." Agatha looked slightly taken aback. "Has he already spoken to you of this?"

"No." Martha sighed. "But this tale is already much more famous than you know."

"Is it indeed?"

What happened at the end of *Robin Hood*, right after he got married? Did Robin get his lands back? Was the honor of his family name restored? Did he and Marion get to live out their happily ever after in peace? She couldn't remember.

I suppose I'll just have to wait and see.

chapter ten

THE MOMENT NEWS CAME THAT King Erik and his entourage were on the final approach to the castle, Anselm took to locking Martha away again.

"Forgive me, sweeting," he said. "But my master has barred you from the presence of his most illustrious relative."

"Well, I can't imagine why!" She glared at him, her hands firmly planted on her hips.

"Can you not?" Anselm smiled. "You must admit, your mood and manners are... highly changeable. I never know which way you will jump, myself."

Fair point. Instead, she said, "I'll have you know, I've been the epitome of good behavior for weeks."

"Days," Anselm corrected her with a smile.

Martha huffed. "Fine. But you don't have to lock me in again, Anselm. I'll stay put. " Widening her eyes, she worked him over with her best puppy eyes. "Haven't the last few days proved to you that I'm not about to run off?"

"No. Unfortunately for you, I am not so gullible as you might like to believe." But he didn't look annoyed. If anything, he seemed amused. "Come." Taking her arm, he led her to the window. "From your comfortable seat, you will have as good a view as any of us outside in the bailey."

Martha sat down on the folded coverlet she used to pad the window seat's rock-hard upholstery and said nothing.

"There blows a chill wind today, my dear." He gave her shoulder a gentle squeeze. "You will be far warmer in here, much more comfortable."

Despite herself, she smiled. "You're good, Anselm. I'll give you that. Tell me, have you ever considered a career in politics?"

For once, Anselm wasn't listening. Leaning forward, he peered through the mullioned window, frowning. "The outriders are already upon us. I must go at once."

With that, he turned and strode from the room, closing the door behind him. Heavy keys jangled against the metal lock. A moment later, the door flew open again, and Anselm reentered the room. "Where did I put my... Ah!" He picked up his best leather gloves from where he'd left them sitting on top of a chest. With a grin, he waved them at Martha then hurried away.

Idiot.

Resigned to her fate, she kicked off her slippers and drew her feet up beneath her, settling back to watch the show.

At first in a trickle and then in a stream, the king and his court finally arrived at the castle.

The loud clattering of hundreds of horseshoes echoed over the cobbles as the visitors rode into the courtyard. Martha had never seen so many horses in her life, manes and tails plaited to perfection, their harnesses and well-tended coats gleaming.

The riders' high status was instantly apparent, even to Martha. The panoply of gold jewelry and precious stones on display positively screamed out *wealth*. There were no paupers amongst the front riders, that much was clear.

From beneath the multitude of heavy, ornately embroidered traveling cloaks—each one voluminous enough to drape over the rump of the rider's horse—she caught glimpses of vividly colored gowns and tunics.

From what she could see, there weren't many female riders. Most of the women were confined to litters, along with their children and various ladies in waiting. They couldn't have been very comfortable, for their faces looked pinched and miserable when they finally stepped out onto the cobbled courtyard. Huddled together in their fur-lined cloaks, the noblewomen looked around them with apparent displeasure.

No wonder. After life at court, Edgeway must seem like the back of beyond. Utterly provincial.

Without a doubt, Martha liked the knights best. Sitting

astride their huge warhorses, the men talked amongst themselves, smiling often and laughing frequently, as they waited for their squires to attend them. Some wore full suits of armor, others just a few pieces, but the metal shone mirror bright in the afternoon sunshine. The men were all different. Some were fresh-faced and youthful. Many were more mature, and rather battle-scarred, but they were still handsome in their own way.

Martha knelt on the window seat to get a better look. Even from this distance, they oozed confidence and machismo. A knight for every occasion, and one to suit every taste. Magnificent.

Edgeway obviously suited the knights much better than it did the sour-faced ladies.

What was she thinking? Swords, armor, warhorses? These very men she was quietly drooling over would be going up against Rodmar and his men some time in the not-too-distant future.

She sat back down and chewed on a hang-nail. Did Vadim and his secret squirrels have any armor? It didn't seem likely. Suddenly, the knights in the courtyard seemed to lose some of their lustre. In her mind's eye, she compared the raggedy outlaws with King Erik's well-armed knights. Her stomach lurched. How could Vadim hope to defeat such men?

No doubt Rodmar would bring his own knights to even things out, but somehow she couldn't picture Vadim sitting back while other men did the fighting.

She felt sick as she imagined all that metal versus soft, living flesh. *He's going to get himself killed for sure this time.*

The parade of power and wealth went on and on. Throughout it all, Anselm and the earl stood together, individually greeting each new arrival, their fixed, matching smiles never wavering. Their face muscles must be screaming for release by now.

Welcome to my world.

His Evilness was certainly out to impress today. With the exception of his sable cloak, he was dressed from head to toe in purple and gold. In comparison, Anselm was much more modestly dressed. Even so, she preferred his more sober, dark-blue ensemble to that of his gaudy master.

From her height advantage, she noticed that the earl's golden hair was thinning on top—something he'd tried to disguise with a comb-over. Even in this world, some things never changed. The playful wind wreaked havoc with the earl's careful hair-do, repeatedly flipping the long strands into the air. Martha smiled as he smoothed his wayward locks back in place only to have to do it all over again a moment later.

It was a petty thing, but it pleased her all the same.

Suddenly, the earl abandoned his hair repairs. With a beaming smile, he set off across the yard, his arms held wide in greeting, as a corpulent horseman rode into the bailey, flanked at either side by a wall of knights.

Martha managed to read the earl's lips. *Welcome, cousin.*

That's King Erik?

While the knights helped the older man from his horse, the earl gamboled around them like an over-excited puppy.

He's going to wet himself in a minute if he's not careful.

She hadn't really wanted to meet the king, and seeing him now, watching him submit to the earl's embrace with ill-disguised impatience, Martha had no desire to see him any closer.

The king's eyes glinted like mean little pebbles from the fleshy folds of his face. A neat salt and pepper beard covered his chin, emphasizing the downward curve of his mouth.

This wasn't a man of ready smiles, fake or otherwise.

A pale, willowy woman walked up to him and slid her hand into the crook of his arm with the ease of familiarity. King Erik performed a brief mime of introduction, his pudgy hand gesturing from her to the earl. For a heartbeat, the earl's smile wavered, but he recovered quickly and took the lady's hand, raising it to his lips. After acknowledging the earl with a brief, wintry smile, the woman pulled her hand free and returned her attention to the king.

Who is she? His daughter, perhaps?

With a shudder of revulsion, Martha realized her mistake.

While King Erik appeared to be listening to the earl, all the time he groped the woman's backside, kneading it vigorously with his ring-laden fingers. The mystery beauty didn't object. If anything, she seemed to enjoy the attention, smiling down at the king from her superior height with all the signs of affection.

His wife, perhaps? Maybe they were a particularly devoted couple. But Martha didn't really believe it. Judging a book by its cover might not be wise, but as she looked at the king, she instinctively knew she'd hate his story.

A sudden thought struck her with the intensity of a halogen spotlight. Heart pounding, she sat upright on the window seat.

Two full turns. I didn't hear the two full turns.

She glanced at the door. No way. Anselm couldn't have forgotten. Could he? Hope sent her running, stumbling over her discarded slippers in her haste to find out.

She reached out, her fingers brushing the cool metal ring that lifted the door latch. *What if there's a guard out there?* She swiftly retracted her hand. Then again, it wasn't likely, not with all the new arrivals flooding into the castle. Everyone was too busy to spare Anselm's roomie any attention.

Her blood pounded loudly in her ears. Holding her breath, Martha gripped the metal ring and turned it slowly to the left. The latch lifted with a dull *thunk*. She flinched. The sound seemed deafening in the stillness of the room.

Exhaling in a long, steady stream, she pulled on the handle.

chapter eleven

O H, *PLEASE, PLEASE OPEN!*
She expected to feel a jolt of resistance, for the lock to crush all her hopes, but it didn't. Without making a sound, the door swung open. Suddenly, she was staring out into the empty passageway, her head spinning with relief. Anselm's bunch of iron keys hung forgotten in the keyhole.

Thank you!

Breathing hard, she grabbed the keys from the lock, immediately enclosing them in a tight fist to quiet their metal chinking. Then she reclosed the door and sank to the floor, quickly examining and discarding each key in turn, seeking a match to the one still clasped in her hand.

And suddenly, there it was. *You little beauty!* But there was no time to celebrate, not yet. Anselm might return at any moment.

She thrust the spare key into the lock and gave it a turn. It worked. Now, all she had to do was separate it from the others. Unfortunately, a thick metal ring held the key-bunch together, and no matter how hard she pulled, the fecking thing wouldn't budge.

Muttering and swearing to herself, Martha scanned the room for something she could use to prise the metal ring open, preferably something with a thin blade, but nothing fitted the bill. Perhaps wisely, Anselm had removed all the pointy stuff when she moved in.

What about Vadim's knife? She'd almost forgotten it.

Cursing herself for a fool, she raced to her bedroom and retrieved the little blade from where she'd stashed it beneath the mattress. She pulled it from its leather sheath and set to work, pressing the point against the joint of the stubborn metal ring. *Shit!* The blade slipped. Her hands shook too badly to hold it steady. She took a breath then tried again. *God damn it!* She almost skewered her hand this time. Almost sobbing with frustration, she wiped her sweaty palms down her skirt. Anselm might be back at any moment. She'd better check where he was.

She scrambled off the floor and ran back into the living room, to her regular spot by the window. Much to her relief, Anselm was still outside, chatting and smiling with the knights while His Evilness was deep in conversation with the king.

Good. Stay there.

She placed the keyring on the stone window sill and resumed her attempts to open it.

Several minor cuts later, after numerous attempts, the point of the blade bit into the hairline crack of the metal ring. It held firm. *Easy now!* Sweat beaded on her brow and upper lip, but Martha dared not wipe it away. Holding her breath, she gently wiggled the knife from side to side. Slowly, slowly, the crack grew wider until, at last, there was enough space to remove the key.

Exhaling hard, she wiped her face on her sleeve then slipped the six-inch lump of iron in the concealed pocket beneath her skirt.

But she wasn't done yet. Anselm might notice one of his keys were missing. He was in the habit of playing with the keys as he talked, sliding them around their ring like the beads on an abacus, although he seemed unaware of it. A miscount might attract his attention. It wasn't worth the risk.

She replaced the stolen key with one from the trunk in her bedchamber. It was a little smaller than the one she'd liberated, but it would have to do. As she closed the metal ring, several bright, obviously new, scratches on the surface of the previously dull metal caught her eye. Anselm would definitely notice those.

Oh, feck me!

She rubbed the keys with a damp facecloth to remove all trace of the dried blood her injured fingers had left behind. Although the blood-tinged water darkened the scratches, they were still noticeable. What else could she use? She looked around. The fire's glowing embers seemed to beckon her. Ashes. Yes. They'd do nicely.

Minutes later, Anselm's keys were back where he'd left them, hanging on the outside of the unlocked door.

Perhaps half an hour later, Martha heard the sound of keys jangling in the external lock. Her heart lurched.

The door swung open, and Anselm walked into the room.

"Well? How was it?" she asked from her place by the window, lowering her embroidery to her lap. "Has everyone arrived?"

"That they have. At long last." He kicked the door closed behind him and used his teeth to remove his gloves, one finger at a time. "My feet are almost numb with standing for so long. I would have much rather stayed here with you."

He looked downright perished. With his glowing red nose and cheeks, he reminded her of one of Santa's little helpers.

"Oh? Is it cold out?" The scent of fresh, cool air drifted from him, cutting through the heat of the room. "I can't say I noticed."

"That is hardly surprising." Anselm glanced at the blazing fire in the hearth. "I wager the blacksmith's shop is cooler than this room. Little wonder you look so flushed."

Martha sent him a withering smile. "Very funny, I'm sure." Thank goodness she'd built up the fire. Heat was the perfect camouflage for her guilty cheeks.

After taking off his cloak and boots, he slumped down into a chair beside the fire and rested his stockinged feet upon the hearth. He sighed and closed his eyes.

Martha picked up her embroidery and resumed her terrible needlework, not that the work gave her any pleasure. Her bleeding fingers might require some explanation, and embroidery was the perfect excuse. She'd pricked herself several times already.

"Did you watch them arrive?" Anselm asked. His voice sounded slurred and weary.

Martha looked up from her work. "Only until the king arrived, then I got bored." Her heart skipped when she recalled what she'd done afterward. "Tell me, who's the woman he was groping?"

Anselm turned his head to look at her. "Of which lady do you speak?"

Who else had the king been groping while she'd been on her key quest?

"You know. The pretty blonde one who went over to him just after he arrived?"

"Ah, yes." A slow smile curved his lips. "The fair Beatrice. I understand His Grace recently married her off to one of his knights as reward for her years of faithful *service*."

The emphasis he placed on that last word painted a very clear picture of Beatrice's duties.

"That's disgusting!" The outburst of revulsion was out before she could stop it.

"Is it?" Anselm got up and walked toward her. "I view it more of an act of kindness. What would have become of her if the king had cast her adrift? Who would marry such a woman?"

"The knight married her." Martha slammed her embroidery down on the seat beside her, her cheeks burning even hotter.

"So he did." Anselm sat beside her. "And I understand Sir Hugh was immensely pleased with the prime hunting lands he received from the king as a wedding gift."

Ugh! Beatrice was a living, breathing woman, for heaven's sake, not a bike for hire.

Anselm chuckled. "Oh, Martha. Can you really be so naive?"

Not naive, more like revolted. She wasn't entirely stupid. She'd learned enough history to know how women had been treated in the past. But reading about it was very different from seeing it up close and personal. "So why did king Pig dump her?" she asked, not that she really wanted to know.

Anselm shrugged and took her embroidery from her unresisting hands. "He desired the company of some other lady, I assume. The king only ever stables one mistress at a time."

"How considerate of him!" But her sarcasm fell on deaf ears.

Anselm raised her needlework in order to examine it better. "What is this meant to represent, sweeting?" He frowned. "Is it... a boat of some kind?"

"Actually, it's a tree."

"Is it?" Squinting slightly, he brought the embroidery closer to his nose. "I swear, I cannot make it out."

With a huff of annoyance, Martha snatched the needlework from his hands and turned it the right way up, displaying it properly. "There! See?"

"Oh." Anselm's lips twitched. He was trying not to laugh, she could tell. "That is... a vast improvement." He closed one eye. "Yes, I think I can see it now."

"Arse!" Giving him a fierce glare, Martha tossed the embroidery to the other side of the window seat. "What would you know?"

He snorted with laughter. "Forgive me, my dear. I should not mock you, but even you must admit you have little skill with a needle."

"I'm sorry you feel that way," she said coldly. "I was going to give it to you, as a present."

"Really?" His eyes bugged with the effort of containing his amusement. "And stained with your own precious blood too. How delightful!"

Unable to help herself, Martha grinned. She wasn't really offended. Her needlecraft was spectacularly crappy, there was no denying it. "Anyway, you were telling me about the king. Will I get to meet him?"

"It is not likely, sweeting. I fear my master will never really like you."

"Good," Martha replied. "I don't care for him either. Him or his royal cousin." She tilted her head to one side. "Do you like him? The king, I mean?"

He shrugged. "What does it matter if I like him or not? Erik is the most powerful man in the Norlands. Only a fool would cross him."

"Well, I'm relieved I won't be meeting him. He makes my flesh crawl."

Anselm smiled and touched her hand. "Attractive though you are, sweeting, you are hardly likely to catch King Erik's eye."

"Oh? Why's that?"

"King Erik prefers... younger flesh."

Okay, Martha was fast-approaching her thirtieth birthday, but Beatrice barely looked out of her teens, for goodness sake. *Don't ask. Please don't ask.*

"How young?" *Damn it!*

Anselm shuffled on his seat, suddenly absorbed with a loose piece of thread on his tunic. "Old enough to have had her first bleed."

"Good God!" She leapt to her feet and began pacing the

room, battling the urge to throw something. "That great fecking pervert. Ugh! The thought of him, sweating and rutting all over some poor innocent child—"

Anselm hurried over, grabbing her by the shoulders. "Hush! Calm yourself, my dear." He forced her to stand still. "Lower your voice," he hissed urgently. "Someone might hear you."

"So?" She glared up at him, breathing hard. "I don't fecking care if they—"

Anselm's mouth came down hard, effectively silencing her with his kiss. Before Martha could react, he'd wrapped his arms about, drawing her to the heat of his muscular body.

Oh hell! Martha froze, shocked into submission for several beats. Then, she began to fight. Using all her strength, she pushed against him, struggling to get free. She managed to move her head to one side, partially breaking Anselm's determined lip-lock. "Get off me, you bast—"

Speaking was a huge mistake. As she opened her mouth to curse him, Anselm's tongue slipped inside. He cupped the back of her head, tasting her more deeply.

Martha almost gagged. She pushed against at the hard wall of his chest, but he held her too firmly. There was no escape. The taste of sweet ale on his exploring tongue made her want to puke.

Anselm groaned from deep in his throat, stroking up and down her back with his free hand while his lips played upon hers, coaxing her to respond.

And Martha responded.

She bit down hard, narrowly missing his tongue, but his lower lip wasn't so lucky. The hot metallic tang of blood flooded her mouth.

Anselm hissed and drew back. "Vixen!" Although his hold on her lessened, he didn't let her go.

"Bastard!" She stamped down hard on his stockinged foot. Anselm emitted a pained yelp, and suddenly she was free.

Martha darted to the other side of the room and grabbed hold of a sturdy metal candlestick from the sideboard. "You fecking pig of a man!" She hurled it at him, her cheeks flaming with rage.

Anselm shielded his face just in time. The metal candlestick bounced off his forearm then hit the floor with a thud. "Ow! Stop, Martha."

Stop? I've only just begun! She picked up a tankard and chucked that at him too.

Anselm ducked behind a chair as the tankard struck the backrest, showering him with dregs of sticky ale. "Enough, woman!" he roared. Ale ran down the golden strands of his hair like hot wax down the sides of a candle.

"Don't you dare *woman* me!" Breathing hard, Martha snatched up another candlestick, then she waited for the opportune moment to launch it. "I'm a patient man? I can wait?" She mocked Anselm with his own words. "How dare you treat me like—"

"I wanted only to silence you." Anselm peeped out from behind the chair. He didn't look angry, only amused. "Or, do you have a particular yearning to spend more time in the dungeon?" He grinned, his hair hanging in soggy rats' tails about his face. "It was only a kiss, sweeting. Your widowly virtue remains intact."

Repulsive letch. As far as he knew, Vadim was dead. Even her *recently widowed* status was no protection from his disgusting advances.

"You have all the sensitivity of a brick." With a trembling hand, she set the candlestick back down on the sideboard. "I'm still mourning my husband, in case you've forgotten it."

The mere mention of Vadim was usually enough to wipe the smug smile from Anselm's face, and it didn't fail her now.

"A fact I am all too aware of, m'lady." Abandoning the chair's protection, Anselm stood up. He wiped the blood from his bleeding lip with the back of his hand. "Even in death, he remains to plague me," he muttered. "If I could kill his ghost, I would gladly do so."

Martha bit her lip, refusing to be provoked any further. She stood motionless while Anselm limped over to retrieve his boots from the hearth. The moment they were back on his feet, he headed for the door. Suddenly, he paused. He turned around, looking at her with eyes as cold as an arctic winter.

"Sometimes you push me too far," he said softly. "Your precious husband is dead, Martha. Gone! You cannot hide behind your widow's weeds forever."

"I—"

"Be silent!" he roared, making her jump. He held up his index finger as if daring her to defy him. "It is time you learned the truth, m'lady."

Her stomach liquified, and her knees shook. Scary Anselm was back.

"Whether you like it or not," he continued in a low, measured voice, "you *will* marry again. The earl had selected several prospective husbands before I expressed an interest in owning you. Believe this: you would gladly welcome even King Erik between your legs over any of my master's choices."

Martha felt sick. *Sweet baby Jesus.* Just how awful were these other men if King Erik was the best option?

Out in the corridor, beyond the open door, a group of knights walked by, talking and laughing as they passed. Anselm acknowledged them with a nod and a tight-lipped smile, but when he turned back to Martha, his eyes were granite-hard.

"Your wild willfulness may have suited your husband," he said, "but these are not qualities I desire my own wife to possess. Modesty and obedience are but two of the things I require."

Somehow, Martha managed to remain standing as the full impact of his words permeated her shocked brain. *Marry...him?*

"I will leave you with that thought, my sweet." Anselm flashed her a brief, glacial smile. "Think on it until I return. If my terms are unacceptable to you, I will advise my master I am no longer interested in taking you for my wife. Do I make myself clear?"

What else could she do except nod? But that wasn't enough for Anselm.

"Say it!"

"I understand," she muttered.

"Good. The morning will suffice for your answer. Until then, I bid you a good night, m'lady." He bowed his head then left, locking the door behind him.

The moment the key turned in the lock, Martha's control shattered, fracturing into a thousand tiny shards. She raced for the sanctuary of her room and bolted the door behind her, hot tears of dread and rage streaming unchecked down her cheeks.

Oh, Vadim! Just hurry up and get here.

Flinging herself face down upon the bed, she sobbed into the pillows. Suddenly, she longed for Rodmar and his army, for the war to begin. Surely, anything was better than this life of fear and uncertainty.

Although the threat of being married off to Anselm was bad enough, she had a new reason for terror, something she'd refused to acknowledge until this moment.

Her period was overdue.

At first, she'd blamed it on the upset, on the change of food and company. But a small inner voice kept on whispering the truth, no matter how many times she tried to ignore it.

The frequent waves of nausea made sense now. She could no longer blame them on Anselm's company. Well, not all of them, anyway. Not only that, but her breasts were heavier. They looked much fuller in her close-fitting gowns. She'd blamed their fevered aching on an approaching period, a period that never arrived.

Pregnant. With Vadim's baby.

If she and Anselm ever made it to the altar, that'd be a heck of a wedding gift for him, his new wife already bearing the child of his mortal enemy.

No. She stopped crying and sat up. *That'll never happen.*

She dried her face on her skirt and took several hiccuping breaths. Although she'd never considered herself particularly maternal, a new fierceness overwhelmed her. She placed a hand upon her stomach.

Don't you worry, little fella. Daddy's on his way. No matter what happens, I'll make sure we get out of this.

All she had to do was keep her cool for a few more days. And if Anselm thought he'd broken her, so much the better.

chapter twelve

I T WAS ALMOST NOON THE next day when Anselm finally staggered through the door. Martha sat in her usual place by the window, schooling her face into a neutral mask. *Let the games begin.*

"Good morning, sweeting." Anselm was all smiles, as though the events of the previous day had never happened. "Did you miss me?"

"Of course." *Like I'd miss an STD!* At least she managed to summon a genuine smile.

He closed the door and locked it behind himself, though it took him several attempts to locate the keyhole. His golden hair was mussed and frizzy, and his clothes were rumpled. His tunic hung open, his half-fastened shirt exposing the muscles of his hairless chest.

Martha sniffed then wished she hadn't. He reeked of sweat and booze and sex.

"Pardon me." Anselm patted the chair he'd stumbled against, almost knocking it over. "My fault entirely."

God, he's still absolutely bladdered. "I take it you had a good night, then?"

"Not at all." He grinned and fell sprawling onto the window seat beside her. "It was all terribly dull... matters of state and such. I should have much preferred to remain here with you." He leaned back, sitting with his legs so wide his knee brushed against hers.

"How sweet." Martha attempted another smile, adjusting her position slightly so her leg no longer touched his.

"So? Have you considered my offer, hmm?" He leaned toward her, fixing her with bleary, bloodshot eyes.

Damn. She'd hoped he'd forgotten about last night's *proposal*.

"I have." Martha scratched her nose in a vain attempt to shield herself from the blast of his toxic morning breath.

"And?"

"I accept your terms."

"Martha!" He beamed at her. "You have made me the happiest of men."

Afraid he might try and hug her, she leapt to her feet. "I would like to know why you want to marry me, though."

Anselm sat back and rubbed his face, his hands rasping over his stubbled cheeks. "I am hardly fit to be looked upon. Might my declaration of love keep until after I bathe, my dear?"

Declaration of love, indeed. "There's no need for anything like that. I was just curious about something, that's all." She went to throw another log on the fire, any excuse to put some distance between them. The smell of him was making her stomach roll.

"Oh? What might that be?"

Martha turned to look at him. "You said the king gave Beatrice's husband some land as a sweetener... to encourage him to marry her, I mean."

"So?" Anselm stretched out his arms and yawned. "How does their arrangement concern us?"

"You could marry a proper lady, Anselm, someone with a big fat dowry. Isn't that how it works amongst the nobility? I have nothing to bring to our... marriage. Even my clothes," she said, sweeping her hands down the skirt of her blue gown, "were paid for with gold from your pocket. And so my question stands; why do you want to marry me?"

Anselm chuckled. "What would you prefer to hear, sweeting? The truth, or something more palatable?"

She shrugged. "The truth usually works for me."

"Very well." Anselm seemed to sober up. "But first, pour me some ale, would you? My mouth tastes like a cesspool."

Martha did as he asked. She had no intention of making him angry—not now the end was surely so close.

"Thank you." He took the tankard from her outstretched

hand and chugged it down in one go. Then, with a contented sigh, he wiped his mouth on his grimy sleeve. "Sit down,
Martha," he said, patting the seat beside him. "I want to look
at you."

Oh God! Must I? But she obeyed, perching on the edge of the
seat with her hands clasped tightly on her lap. The feel of his
eyes on her face made her skin crawl.

"You are uncommonly pretty, my dear. I have always found
you so. Little wonder your feral husband abandoned his solitary
ways and took you for his own." A tiny smile curved his lips.
"In death, he bequeathed unto me his life's greatest treasure.
'Tis quite fitting, do you not agree, your life entrusted to his
only brother?"

"*Foster* brother." The words were out before she could stop
them, though she attempted to soften them with a smile. If
Anselm wasn't drunk, he was far more delusional than she'd
suspected. Whatever he was, arguing with him wasn't going
to help.

"I admit, I have grown rather fond of you over these past
weeks, m'lady. In time, I am convinced that our fledgling feelings
will develop into... something more permanent."

Her eyes widened. She couldn't help it. Anselm must have
interpreted their silent message.

"Yes they will, my sweet, if only you will allow it to happen."
He reached across and patted her tightly knotted fingers.
"When we are joined, the broken fragments of your heart will
finally heal—"

"So *why* do you want to marry me?" She hadn't meant to
interrupt, but she couldn't stomach much more of his purple
prose, nor his closeness. She felt ill enough already.

Anselm's gray eyes hardened. He slowly withdrew his hand
and made no further attempt to touch her. "Some things are
more valuable than gold. Despise him as I do, I cannot deny that
in life your husband was a leader of men. By claiming his wife, I
send a message to the world."

That you're a complete arsehole? She sucked in her lower lip,
trying not to smile as he continued to speak.

"With you at my side, new doors will open before me. I may
finally be able to shake Edgeway's dirt from my boots."

"Ah!" So it was all about street credibility. Of course. By that reckoning, this would make her the medieval equivalent of his dangerous dog on a leash. The flashy bling around his neck. "I see."

Anselm smiled. "How would you enjoy life at Court, m'lady? I believe the king is warming to me."

"What about His Evilness?" she asked. "You'd leave him?"

"Certainly. Ambition is its own master."

Martha got up. "Do you want more ale?" She had to move away. In the heat of the room, Anselm's sweaty stench was fast becoming unbearable.

"Wait." Before she could escape, his hand encircled her wrist. "Do not flinch away from me, Martha. I will not take your body, not until you are properly mine." He drew her closer. "Tell me one thing. When will I be able to call you wife, my sweet? Just name the day."

She stood rigid between his open thighs, taking little sips of air through her mouth. How long could she put him off? How long before Rodmar won the castle? *How long is a piece of string?* "Springtime?"

"Why not this winter?" he asked with a wicked leer, placing his hands on her hips. "Something to warm those long, cold nights?"

"Yeah, right." Martha rolled her eyes at him. She'd rather freeze to death. But how could she put him off? Maybe it was time she morphed into *Bridezilla?* "And what about my gown, the guest list, and the hundred-and-one other arrangements?"

His smile faltered. "I thought you might prefer a simple ceremony."

Ha! You wish.

"Then you thought wrong." Martha patted one of his stubbly cheeks then stepped away. "I want a proper wedding this time. No expense spared."

"Martha—"

"Don't give me that face, m'lord," she said, frowning at him with mock severity. "I thought you were ambitious. Who's going take you seriously with a hole-in-the-wall wedding? Certainly not King Erik." She smiled. He was falling for it just as she hoped he would. "If I'm your *prize*, what better time to show me off than on our wedding day?"

Anselm stood up. "You may be right, sweeting." His eyes twinkled as he looked at her.

"Of course I am." When Anselm was in good humor, she felt she could almost be herself again. "Will you do something for me, m'lord?"

"Anything you ask of me."

"Go and take a bath. You reek of serving wench."

Fortunately, her timing was perfect. Anselm burst into loud laughter.

"Are... are you not angry?" he asked when he was finally able to speak.

"Of course not." *Rather a serving wench than me.* "I understand that men have certain... needs, and spring is a long time away. Only a shrew would object to her future husband finding... relief in the meantime."

"My, Martha." Anselm walked over and planted a kiss on top of her head. "What a rare gem you are. Go and visit your friends in the kitchens. While you are there, instruct the maids to prepare me a bath."

"Really?" He was letting her out on her own?

"Really." He took the key ring from his belt and, selecting the correct key, pressed it into her hand. "Go." He gave her backside a playful slap as she turned for the door. "And if you behave yourself, I will take you to Darumvale tomorrow."

Martha stopped walking and spun around to look at him, keys clanking. "We're going to Darumvale? Why?" He was up to something. She could feel it in her bones.

"Their harvest should be in by now, and as always, they are late in delivering the Lord Edgeway's share."

"Another kind of tax?" Martha's smile slipped. "They can't afford it, Anselm."

During her stay in Darumvale, she'd come to appreciate how hard the lives of the villagers really were. The fields were their daily battleground, fighting the earth and the elements in order to grow the crops they needed for survival. The reality of starvation was only ever a harvest away. It sickened her that the earl should demand the food from the villagers' mouths in addition to all the gold he took from them throughout the year.

"The earl's larder cannot wait, not with so many extra mouths to feed. You vex yourself needlessly, sweeting. My father will complain the harvest was poor, as he always does, but his secret store will already be well stocked."

"How do you know he has a secret store?" she asked in surprise.

"Whatever he thinks of me, and I of him, Seth is still my father." Anselm shrugged. "I know him and all of his twists."

"Does the earl know?"

"What do you think?"

Of course he didn't. His Evilness would tear Darumvale apart if he thought he was being cheated of so much as a handful of grain.

"So why haven't you told him?" For the life of her, she couldn't guess the answer.

Anselm shrugged off his tunic and threw it over a chair. "That, I cannot say. Some last vestige of family loyalty, perhaps?" He unfastened the loose tie on his shirt and quickly pulled the garment over his head. "Whatever it is, I would not want to see my father dead too."

Martha's eyes widened. The image of Anselm's naked torso seemed to burn onto her retinas—pale and hairless, disfigured by the numerous scars his violent life had given him.

She hurried for the door and pushed the key into the lock. Why were Anselm's scars so repulsive to her? Vadim's body was equally disfigured, but on him the scars were nothing but sexy. Her heart fluttered as she recalled some of her favorites.

"I'll see you later." She threw the words over her shoulder as she stepped out into the corridor.

"And Martha?"

"What?" She stuck her head back inside the room, and tried not to look as Anselm reached to unfastened his trousers.

"Do not speak to any of the guests. If anyone should address you, be polite and excuse yourself just as soon as you are able to do so. Give me your word."

She rolled her eyes skyward. As if anyone would take any notice of her. But Anselm wasn't joking—she read it in the stern set of his face. "Fine." She raised the palm of her right hand. "I promise."

chapter thirteen

MARTHA SAT ASTRIDE MISTRAL, HUDDLED deep in the folds of her cloak. Despite the bright morning sunshine, she was cold. Mounted soldiers surrounded her, chatting to one another as they prepared to ride out.

Anselm pushed his gray horse through the ranks of other horses and reined in beside her. "Are you still sulking?"

He must have found his answer in the venomous look she sent him, for he muttered something beneath his breath, then turned away to talk to one of the other men.

She didn't care. Why was it whenever she vowed not to react to Anselm anymore, he always managed to ignite her temper?

That morning at breakfast, he'd informed her she'd be traveling to Darumvale as his *intended*. Not only that, but if she gave anyone reason to suspect their forthcoming union was anything but a happily anticipated event, he threatened to take an even greater share of the villagers' precious harvest.

Refusing to go wasn't an option.

Anselm wanted to flaunt his trophy wife before they were even married. *Damn him.* How would she face Seth, Bren, and the others? She cringed inwardly, imagining what they'd think when they saw her simpering and smiling at Anselm's side. Would they guess the truth?

God, I hope so.

More importantly, what would Vadim think when he heard of it? She frowned, imagining the cold glint in his dark, pirate eyes. Would he believe she'd gone over to the other side too?

"Where is your smile, m'lady?" Anselm leaned over, his warm breath brushing against her ear. "We are meant to be a happy couple, remember?"

"We're not in Darumvale yet, m'lord." She gathered up her reins, preparing to move away from him.

Anselm's gloved hand stilled hers. "I believe you would benefit from a rehearsal, my sweet."

Martha snatched her hands away and glared at him. "How's this?" She bared her teeth in a parody of a smile.

Before she knew what was happening, Anselm had reached across and pulled her to him, one arm hooked about her waist, punishing her lips with a brief and grinding kiss. Afraid of being unseated from her horse, Martha clung onto the pommel of her saddle. Lusty cheers of the onlooking soldiers rang in her ears, further heightening her humiliation.

Anselm thrust her away at last, observing her bruised lips and hot cheeks with apparent satisfaction. "Much better. Your temper is preferable to the charade of a spiritless milksop."

Martha wiped her mouth on her sleeve. "I really hate you," she hissed.

He nodded. "Good. And I wager you will hate me a good deal more before you are finally broken." Grabbing her chin, he forced her to look at him. "But make no mistake, my sweet. Eventually, you will submit."

With that, he let her go and rode away to join the captain at the head of the column, accepting the accompanying cat-calls and back-slaps with good humor.

Oh, fall and break your fecking neck, why don't you?

She tightened her hands on the reins, confusing her horse into taking several hasty backward steps. "Sorry, hon." She loosened the reins and patted Mistral's neck, ignoring the many leery grins directed her way.

When Vadim finally catches up with you, Anselm, you'll learn what submission really is. I just hope I get to watch.

The sound of fast-moving hooves thundered over the drawbridge. Martha glanced up as a rider cantered into the courtyard, his foam-flecked horse clattering and skidding over the cobbles.

On spotting Anselm, the man reined his weary mount to a standstill and leapt from its back.

"Grave tidings, m'lord," he cried, pushing through the horsemen until he reached Anselm's side. "A vast army advances on Edgeway. Even as we speak, it has reached the border of town!"

Martha's heart soared. *Finally!* She stared at Anselm, eager to see how he'd react. Even as she watched, the color drained from his face.

"Whose army?" he asked in a toneless voice.

The rider shook his head. "Although I saw the standard, I can scarce—"

"Curse you, man!" Anselm lost his rag. Swiftly dismounting from his horse, he grabbed the weary rider by the ties of his leather tunic. "Who the devil is it?" he roared.

A tense silence descended on the courtyard, every ear straining to hear the messenger's reply.

The messenger shook free of Anselm's grasp and scowled at him. "Rodmar of Weyland, *m'lord.*" The emphasis the man placed on the word 'm'lord' made it sound like 'bastard.'

Martha covered her mouth to hide her smile. But no one was paying her any attention.

The soldiers exchanged hurried glances, muttering to one another, repeating the messenger's words. Borne on a low rumble of voices, Rodmar's name soon reached every corner of the courtyard. The men looked shocked, as if they'd collectively seen a ghost.

Anselm was the first to recover himself. "That landless whelp? You must be mistaken." Despite the levity of his words, his smile looked strained.

"No, m'lord." The messenger shook his head, and spoke more forcefully. "That 'landless whelp' is now a man full grown, and a powerful one at that. It seems his years in exile have earned him many new friends."

Anselm looked poleaxed—there was no other word for it.

"'Tis true, m'lord." The messenger pulled off the tight leather cap he wore on his head. As he spoke, he wrung it between his hands. "Well do I recall the House of Weyland. Mark my words, the old king's ghost dwells in the eyes of the man leading this army."

Without speaking another word, Anselm raced for the steps leading to the castle's ramparts, taking them three at a time. Shielding his eyes, he peered over the wall for several long seconds. Whatever he saw, it was enough to kick-start him into action.

He bounded back down the steps. "Sound the alarm!" he called in a loud, clear voice. "A vast dust cloud hangs over Edgeway town. Captains! Muster your men. Enlist any peasant able to bear arms."

Martha watched the sudden reanimation taking place all around her. Men jumped from their horses, obeying the loud summons of their captains. Stable boys raced about, attempting to retrieve the wandering horses. The constant low tolling of a bell provided a soundtrack to the ensuing chaos.

Her heart fluttered with excitement. The drawbridge was down, and everyone was racing about like headless chickens. She might never get a better chance than this. Gathering up her reins, she pointed her horse toward the gatehouse. Ever obedient, Mistral set off at a slow walk, weaving her way through the crowd.

We're almost there. Keep going, Mistral. Walk casual, baby. Framed by the short arching tunnel that led to the drawbridge, the distant hills beckoned her on. Freedom.

"Where do you think you are going?" Anselm appeared, grabbing Mistral's bridle just beneath her bit and turning her about.

Damn it!

"Keep the gate open until the last possible moment," Anselm called over his shoulder to the gatekeeper of the barbican, shouting to be heard above the melee. "The serfs have left their fields and are headed this way. Let them enter. We may have use for them in what is to come. I must hasten to break the news to the king and my master."

Frustrated beyond belief, Martha sent a last look at the open gateway. *So close. So fecking close!*

Anselm led Mistral back toward the keep. Once there, he helped her dismount. "Go back inside," he said curtly. "Stay with the other women." Wordlessly, he thrust the horse's reins into the hands of a passing stable hand. Then, taking her by the arm, he steered her toward the looming hulk of the keep.

"I take it the trip to Darumvale is off, then?" she asked in a voice laced with saccharine.

The look Anselm sent her made her wish she'd kept quiet. "Now is not the time to bait me, Martha. Do as I command, or must I lock you in the dungeon?" Without waiting to hear her reply, he turned and collared a loitering man-at-arms. "You, man! Escort my lady back to our chambers." With that, he strode away and was quickly swallowed up by the crowd.

Though it pained her to do so, when they reached Anselm's rooms, she thanked her guard before dismissing him. *Yeah, thanks for nothing, pal!* But good manners, it seemed, weren't an easy thing to override.

Tugging at the front lacing of her gown, she lifted the latch and went inside. She couldn't wait to get out of the fecking thing. The dress was yet another of Anselm's choices. He'd insisted she wear it for the trip to Darumvale, probably to make some kind of statement to the villagers.

With its billowing skirt and flowing sleeves, the gold-embroidered garment was certainly impressive, but it was bloody uncomfortable to wear, and it made her itch too. Time to change into something a little less dazzling, something sober and serviceable. Her blue woolen gown would do nicely.

On entering the room, she found Effie sitting on the window seat with her apron held up to her face. Martha frowned when she heard the girl's sobs.

"Effie? What's happened?" Martha hurried over and crouched down beside her. "Are you hurt?"

"N-no." With a loud sniff, Effie dropped her apron. Her eyes were red-rimmed and teary. "Oh, m'lady, what is to become of us all? Will they spare us, do you think?"

"Who, love?" She took Effie's trembling hand and gave it a squeeze.

"The army, of course. They say it is led by Rodmar, the nephew of the old king—the one King Erik had murdered." Her lower lip wobbled. "Surely he will not rest until we are all dead and the debt of blood repaid." She set off weeping again.

"Effie? Effie!" Martha was forced to speak sternly to her. "Stop it. You're frightening yourself over nothing. Listen to me. I've heard that Rodmar is a good man. If he's looking to avenge his uncle, he certainly has no quarrel with anyone other than King Erik and his followers."

Effie stopped sobbing. "You truly think so?" She sucked on her lower lip.

"I do." Despite the firmness of her words, a shiver of apprehension rushed down Martha's spine. In this world, "good" was a fairly fluid concept.

"Might they... offer terms, do you think?"

"Quite possibly," she replied, although she wasn't really sure what "terms" actually meant. But Effie appeared comforted. Using her apron in lieu of a handkerchief, the maid mopped it over her eyes and swollen nose. She even managed a watery smile.

Martha glanced out of the mullioned window. Although the castle sat at the top of a steep hill, even at this height she could see a vast cloud of dust mushrooming upward, expanding like yellow fog.

Vadim was somewhere within that yellow haze. He was coming at last.

As if sensing his nearness, her blood tingled in her veins. She leapt to her feet and dragged Effie up with her. "Come on. Help me change my clothes."

By late afternoon, the front-riders of Rodmar's army had reached the castle. Martha, Agatha, and Effie hurried up to one of the tower rooms to watch events unfold, taking turns to peer through the narrow window slit onto the meadowland below the castle's hill.

The sound of thunder ripped through the air, grumbling on and on. Then Martha realized her mistake. That wasn't thunder. It was a man-made storm, the sound made by thousands of feet marching upon the dry earth; the hoof beats of countless horses; the deep rumbles and creaks of the scores of heavy, horse-drawn wagons. The thick castle walls vibrated with the advance of war.

Like a bottle of spilled ink, men flooded onto the meadow until every blade of grass was saturated, obscured by the feet of a deadly swarm—thousands of men, all armed and ready to die for their cause.

She should have been glad to see them, but as she looked down on the vast army, a shudder of dread rippled along Martha's spine. When the fighting began, the innocent residents of the castle would die alongside the guilty. From outside the thick walls, there was no way to tell anyone apart.

It was ironic, really. Those she hoped would liberate her may well be responsible for her death.

From the foot of the castle hill, Rodmar's army broke into song. That was a threat in itself.

Martha was reminded of Wembley stadium on Cup Final day, only the singing was much, much louder. The raw power and cadence of so many voices joined in song was deafening. The sound vibrated in her throat and chest until it was an effort to breathe.

Despite the merry tune, this wasn't a rowdy, harmless football crowd. These men wanted blood—literally. They began setting up camp only spitting distance away from the castle—or so it seemed to Martha. They worked quickly, unloading the wagons and pitching their city of tents. But throughout it all, although the songs changed, the singing continued until night.

"Why are they camped so close?" Martha asked Agatha, their resident warfare expert. "Aren't they afraid of getting hit by arrows and stuff?"

"They are not so close as your eyes would have you believe, m'lady. They are well out of arrow and trebuchet range."

"Treboo... What?"

Agatha tutted at Martha's ignorance. "Trebuchet. The castle has three. Surely you must have seen them? They resemble giant slings?"

"Oh, right." Martha was none the wiser, although she didn't admit it. From outside, a familiar metallic *ticking* sound reclaimed her attention. "They're raising the portcullis." The narrow window afforded them with a very narrow view of the world. Pressing her cheek against the cold, rough stone, Martha strained to see the barbican. Several riders trotted toward the gate, one without armor or helm, golden hair whipping about his face. As he turned his head to speak to one of the other men, she realized who it was. "Oh, my God! Anselm's riding out with some of the knights."

Agatha and Effie hurriedly crowded their faces into the long window slit to see for themselves.

"He is acting as the king's messenger, I expect." Agatha said calmly. "'Tis quite usual in circumstances such as these." She leaned back from the window and grinned. "Not that Rodmar will be swayed from the task at hand. No matter what words King Erik has sent, only his head on a platter can prevent what is to come."

A group of riders broke away from Rodmar's camp, cantering on an intercept course toward the king's men. One of them bore a standard, a bright piece of red fabric that danced and curled in the wind.

Martha screwed up her eyes, peering at the standard bearer. "Can either of you make out the picture on that flag?" Long vision had never been her thing.

"It is a fox, I think," Effie replied. "Or perhaps... a dog?"

"'Tis a wolf hunting a bear," Agatha informed them with quiet authority, not bothering to look through the window.

Martha and Effie turned to stare at her. Did she have x-ray vision or something?

"I remember the Weyland coat of arms from when the old king was still alive," Agatha said, unconsciously divesting herself of the superpowers Martha had just awarded her with.

"Oh, look!" Effie tugged on Martha's dress, her voice quivering with excitement. "Masked riders accompany Rodmar's messenger. They must be Lord Hemlock's... I mean, Lord Vadim's men, m'lady."

Or even Lord Hemlock himself? Martha's heart fluttered. Surely not? If Anselm recognized Vadim, a lot of unpleasant stuff would hit the fan and blow straight in her direction.

"Perhaps. I wouldn't really know. I never saw their faces."

Rodmar's outriders silently parted as Anselm approached, allowing him and his men to pass. Martha shivered as the ranks closed up behind him. *He has balls. I'll give him that much.*

The two groups of riders came to a halt at the center of the meadow, facing one another in their respective lines. An eerie silence descended on the field. All work stopped, and the singing died away.

Martha held her breath as Anselm and Rodmar's representative dismounted and walked toward one another, their arms outstretched—to show they weren't armed, she supposed. Well, they certainly weren't about to hug.

A few minutes elapsed. No one in the tower room spoke. The silent debate on the field below claimed all their attention.

Suddenly, things became more animated. Anselm made a series of wild gesticulations, pointing first at the castle and then toward the invading army. Rodmar's ambassador was taller than Anselm. Even from this distance, he appeared older and more restrained than his young counterpart. He didn't flail his arms or shout. If anything, he looked relaxed.

Agatha gave a wet-sounding chuckle. "Sir Anselm is not having his way this time." The sudden blast of her onion breath made Martha's stomach roll. "Then again, Reynard's placid nature can be most disagreeable on occasion."

"You know him?" Effie asked in surprise.

"I should say so. He is my brother."

The maid's blue eyes widened, "An outlaw?" she whispered. "Your own brother is a wanted man?"

Martha felt uncomfortable. As sweet as Effie was, she still wasn't sure how much she trusted the girl. "Oh, I'm sure he's not an—"

"Reynard is a defender of the realm." Agatha said, choosing to ignore the escape route Martha had tried to offer her. "When Rodmar takes back the crown, he will reward all the outlawed lords for their loyalty." She looked proud. Noble, even. "Yes, Effie, my brother included." She held her head high, and a soft bloom glowed on her cheeks. Suddenly, Martha glimpsed a younger version of Agatha, and the fine lady she must have once been.

Loud jeers from outside reclaimed them. Anselm was striding away, obviously in a proper strop. Snatching his reins from the knight who held them, he swung himself onto his horse. With a last lingering stare in Reynard's direction, he yanked his horse's head around and set off in a fast canter toward the castle, sending the enemy ranks scattering. The other knights followed in close pursuit.

Rodmar's army jeered at the retreating men and broke into another song, their voices even louder than before.

The sound of the drawbridge being raised was followed by the loud crash of the descending portcullis.

"Oh, my." Effie's hand flew up to cover her mouth. "Lord Anselm looks most distressed."

Martha looked down as Anselm clattered back into the courtyard. His mouth was set in a grim line. His whole demeanor was of one of seething rage. *Definitely not a happy bunny.*

Then again, neither was she. The castle was in lockdown. There was no way in or out. A cold ball of dread settled in the pit of her stomach.

This is it. The beginning of the end.

chapter fourteen

W HILE AGATHA AND EFFIE WENT to gather news and food, Martha remained in the tower room. She knelt before the little window and peered out, her arms resting on the sloping sill. It was almost sunset. As she looked outside, a wedge of swans flew overhead, honking sadly as they passed. The last dying rays of the sun touched the birds' snowy bellies, briefly transforming the white feathers of their undercarriages to a dazzling silver.

She envied the birds their freedom. What must it be like, to have the ability to fly away?

The shadows of day gradually lengthened, but Rodmar's army toiled, on banging and hammering in the dark. One by one, lanterns and campfires punched bright holes through the black wall of night.

A light evening breeze carried brief snatches of a hundred conversations up to her window—voices of faceless strangers she would probably never meet. Although the odds of hearing Vadim amongst them were virtually nil, she strained to hear his voice. But she didn't expect to hear him, she told herself. Not really.

Suddenly, the door of the tower room crashed open. Heart pounding, Martha leapt to her feet, half-expecting to find Anselm standing there. But it was only Agatha.

"Oops." Illuminated by the candle she carried, Agatha's grin looked slightly demon-esque. Deep-angled shadows etched her face.

"Fecking hell!" Martha clutched her chest. "You scared the crap out of me!"

"Sorry. I tripped on the last step." Agatha kicked the door closed behind her. "Here. Take this."

Martha relieved Agatha of her heavy basket and carried it over to the window. She raised the linen cover and sniffed. *Mmm!* Bread. Her stomach immediately clawed with hunger. It had been ages since her last meal. "Have I been missed yet?"

"Not at all. Anselm has been locked away with his masters for hours." She eased herself down to sit on the floor beside Martha, grunting a little with discomfort. "I doubt he will have time for anything but battle now."

"Good." Martha tore off a chunk of bread and stuffed it into her mouth, too hungry for politeness. "Have you... found out what it is they're... building out there?"

Even as they spoke, the hammering from the camp continued. The work sounded much too heavy for mere tent-pitching.

Agatha handed Martha a bladder of ale. "Lord Rodmar, it seems, has brought along some trebuchets of his own."

Martha gulped down the half-chewed bread, and it lodged like a hard ball in her chest. "The sling things?" She took a swig of ale to dislodge the painful bolus.

Agatha gave a nod. "It will soon begin, my dear. The waiting is always the hardest part." She rummaged around in the basket. "Now, where did I put that cheese? I do hope I—Ah! Here it is." She produced it with a little flourish, like a magician pulling a rabbit from a hat. "Would you like some?"

Mouth crammed full of bread, Martha nodded. How could Agatha be so calm when missiles might start raining down on them at any moment? Suddenly, the tower room didn't seem the best place in which to sit out the approaching battle.

"Aren't you scared?" she asked once her mouth was empty. "Or do you and Reynard share the same calmness of disposition?"

"Hardly." Agatha handed Martha a lump of cheese wrapped in a linen cloth. "I have waited many years for this moment, child. Why should I now fear my heart's greatest desire?"

"But we might be killed, or worse. Doesn't that bother you at all?"

Agatha shrugged then devoted her attention to a chicken leg, slurping noisily at it while fat ran unnoticed down her chin.

Munching on her bread and cheese, Martha looked out of the window again. Above everything else, what she feared most was injury. In a world with no hospitals or antibiotics, no surgeons or shiny operating theaters, a quick death had seemed a much better option. But now she had a brand new little person to consider—she touched her belly—and her perspective had changed.

Please, God. Don't let me die. Give our baby the chance to live.

Being pregnant had somehow strengthened her resolve. No matter what happened, no matter whose ass she had to kiss, she was determined to make it out of the castle, alive, healthy, and in one piece.

The fires and lanterns of the enemy camp burned brightly in the darkness. Martha gave a sight. As much as she dreaded the oncoming battle, a part of her longed for it to begin. Agatha was right; the waiting was hard to take. This was going to be a very long night.

Two days passed—endless hours of inactivity and waiting. Martha began to feel she would explode from the tension of doing nothing. And it seemed she wasn't alone in feeling this way.

The lords and ladies of King Erik's court mooched around the castle, never straying far from the windows. There was no more music or laughter. The merry conversations of only a few days ago were now sombre, huddled-in-the-corner affairs. Even the castle's fool sat pensive and still, absently stroking the strings of his lute as he sat by the fire, waiting for a summons from his master that never came.

It appeared Anselm had forgotten about her. She hadn't seen him since the day he'd ridden out to speak to Rodmar's emissary. The door to his chambers were left unlocked, leaving Martha free to roam the castle at will.

To keep herself occupied, she spent most of her time in the kitchen. It was the most "normal" place left in the entire castle. The world might be changing, but the servants' lot remained unchanged. They had no other choice but to carry on, feeding, cleaning, and satisfying the demands of the Edgeway's noble captives. But even there, Martha sensed the same shift in atmosphere.

Like rising damp, fear seemed to seep through the very

fabric of the castle, fettering its occupants in chains wrought by their own fevered imaginings. No one was spared, neither servant nor lord.

Then, she began to hear the whispers. The rumors. *Siege.*

At first, she couldn't understand why the word evoked such dread. Surely a siege was better than being blasted off the face of the planet? But as the hours dragged on, day following reluctant day, she began to feel differently.

And this was only the start. The castle larders were well stocked with food, but it wouldn't last forever. What then?

As she sat alone at a huge table in the warm and noisy kitchen, Martha shivered. From behind the heap of vegetables she was supposed to be chopping, she noticed another servant slope off outside, heading in the direction of the ramparts.

Besieged. Cut off from the outside world. How long before the cracks showed and friend turned upon friend? A siege would strip them raw, one slow and painful layer at a time.

"M'lady?"

Martha blinked and looked up, glad to be diverted from her miserable thoughts. She met the gray eyes of Fergus, the young harpist. Vadim's man. Her heart leapt at the sight of the gangly man-child with his shock of spiky red hair.

Fergus frowned. "Are you unwell?"

She forced a smile and shook her head. "I'm fine now." She reached for his hand, pulling him to sit down beside her. "Please tell me you have news?"

Fergus glanced over his shoulder, his cheeks glowing pink, but no one paid them any attention. Although lunch was over, there was still tonight's feast to prepare. The king and the earl insisted that standards were maintained.

Satisfied they weren't observed, Fergus leaned his head closer to Martha's, murmuring, "The trebuchet battery begins at first light."

Oh, dear God.

"Do you still keep to Anselm's rooms?" he asked.

Martha nodded. "Anything to keep the peace." Not that she'd seen anything of Anselm during recent days. She loosened her death-grip on Fergus's hand. "Sorry." Picking up a carrot from the table, she twirled it like a baton between her fingers.

Fergus flexed his fingers and grimaced. "Does he still lock your door?"

"Sometimes. But I have a key now. Didn't Agatha tell you?"

The lad shook his head. "I have been detained... elsewhere until only recently."

Martha stared at him. She hadn't missed the brief hesitation, nor the trove of information it concealed. "You've been with Vadim, haven't you?" Not really a question but a statement of fact. "Tell me."

Fergus blushed to his ear tips. He looked around the kitchen as though hunting for an escape.

"Give me the truth." Martha clutched at his arm, disregarding the constant flow of people about them.

Fergus sighed and reluctantly met her eyes. "I have seen him, yes."

Her heart skipped several beats. "When? Before the lockdown or..."

He shuffled on the bench beside her. Although he didn't answer, his face was as informative as a newspaper—definitely not a good character trait for an outlaw.

"Yesterday?"

Fergus fidgeted again and darted a shifty sideways glance at the kitchen door.

Martha felt lightheaded. *You have got to be kidding me!* "Today? What did he say? Do you have a message for me?" She let go of his arm and set down her carrot baton. One overriding question canceled out all of the others. "How did you get back inside the castle?"

The lad gave a wry smile. "It was no easy task, I assure you, m'lady."

"B-but I could get out the same way, right?" Even she could hear the hope that flared in her voice.

"It is still too dangerous—"

"You managed—"

"No." Fergus manned up right before her eyes. The tone of his voice brooked no argument. Not a trace of a blush stained his smooth cheeks.

Martha recognized the outlaw in him well enough now. It was there in the unrelenting set of his jaw. Arguing, she knew, would be a waste of breath. "So how do you intend to get me out?" she demanded in a heated whisper. "Or am I here for the duration?"

Fergus leaned closer. "You will leave the way I came in. Through the tunnel."

The tunnel? Images of crawling blind like a mole in the dark made her feel slightly woozy, even in the bright warmth of the kitchen. "B-but you said it was too dangerous."

"So it is. Now." Fergus smirked, seeming youthful again. "Men are shoring up the passageway even as we speak. Vadim wants you alive and whole, m'lady."

Now it was Martha's turn to blush. "Did... did he say anything else?" It embarrassed her, begging the boy for news of Vadim, but pride was no deterrent for her hungry heart.

"He... asked me to give you something."

What? Not another knife?

Fergus glanced around the kitchen then planted a quick kiss on her cheek, much to Martha's astonishment. "Forgive my impertinence, m'lady." The poor lad flushed scarlet again. "But I am sworn to carry out all of my lord's commands. Oh, and I have this to say: *Soon, my love.*"

He sent me a medieval kiss-o-gram!

For the first time in forever, butterflies of happiness fluttered inside her stomach. But not for long. Her smile faded. "Just how soon is *soon?*"

The lad tilted his hands, palms up, and shrugged his shoulders. "That, I cannot say."

Yeah. I thought as much.

"Keep to your rooms when the bombardment begins. You should be safe there." Fergus got up. "I will come to you when it is time. Farewell." With a brief touch on her shoulder, he strode out of the kitchen.

Martha couldn't sleep. The fear of impending bombardment kept her awake. Long after Anselm returned to his own bedchamber, she lay motionless in her bed, staring up into the darkness.

She'd heard him preparing for bed—the sound of his boots thudding onto the floor, and the creaking protest of his bed as he settled down to sleep. He must be exhausted. He hadn't slept in his own bed in days—nor in anyone else's, if the castle's grapevine was to be believed.

According to the servants—a regular and inexhaustible source of gossip—neither the king nor any of his advisers had taken much rest. Most of them fell asleep in their chairs, snatching a few brief minutes of oblivion while they sat at the table discussing tactics.

Anselm's deep, rhythmic snores roused a pang of guilt within Martha's lapsed-Catholic conscience—which was ridiculous. Anselm deserved all he had coming to him, and then some. The man was an utter arse! Surely she didn't care? Not after all the things he'd done?

Boom!

"Mother of God!" Sitting bolt upright in bed, Martha woke from her semi-waking dream. Heart thumping, she stared blindly into the darkness, clutching the blankets to her chest like a beloved teddy.

Boom!

But this one was followed by a distant *crump*. A hit? Her scalp prickled, and blood whooshed in her ears, keeping time with her racing pulse.

Frantic fists pounded on the external door of Anselm's rooms.

"M'lord! Anselm!" The urgency of the deep masculine voice carried a hint of panic. "Are you awake?"

At least she wasn't the only one teetering on the brink of a major freak-out.

Anselm must really have been dog-tired not to hear all the commotion. Finally, Martha heard movement from next door—a muffled curse, and a creak as Anselm finally got out of bed. His footsteps stumbled across the room. Then, there was a crash, and something heavy hit the floor. More muttered curses followed.

She heard him unlock the outer door. He flung it open with such force that it struck the wall. "This had better be import—" Another deep *boom* from outside interrupted him. "By all the Spirits! Go on, man. I will catch you up."

Moments later, the outer door slammed. Another *boom* shattered the brief silence that followed Anselm's departure.

Flinging back the covers, Martha got out of bed and padded to the window, still tightly clutching her blanket. The courtyard glowed like day, illuminated by dozens of torches. Soldiers stumbled outside, most of them still clad in their nightshirts, attempting to dress on the move. One man hopped along in just one boot while desperately attempting to pull on the other.

Hair askew, eyes puffy with sleep, the men helped one another strap on weapons and armor, and all the while, the captains strode between the ragged ranks bellowing orders, verbally whipping the men into line.

The warning bell clanged. Each toll was a dismal warning. *Doom. Doom. Doom.*

A thin sliver of light brightened the eastern horizon, slowly diluting the night into day.

A flickering red glow caught her attention. With her face pressed to the window, Martha looked in the direction of the smithy. Its roof had caved in, brought down by the tumble of masonry from a gaping breach in the ramparts.

A chain of people had formed a line between the water pump and the ill-fated smithy. They were passing buckets of water to one another to put out the blaze. Such was their haste, much of the precious water sloshed out of the buckets and onto the shining cobbles. The flames and sparks danced skyward, refusing to be tamed.

There was another deep *boom!* With a squeak of fright, Martha backed away from the window as a fine mist of plaster floated down from the ceiling. *Jesus, Mary, and Joseph! That was too close.*

A series of rapid taps sounded on the door of her bedchamber. "M'lady?" It was Effie. Her voice trembled as she spoke. "Please let me in."

Martha hurried to open the door.

The flame of Effie's candle wobbled, upset by the trembling of her hand. The girl's pallor matched that of the long nightdress and bed cap she wore.

Wordlessly, Martha stepped aside to let her enter.

Effie carefully set her candle down on a stool by the door, then flung herself into Martha's arms, sobbing against her shoulder.

Who could blame her? Martha stroked the girl's back and made soft shushing sounds. *God knows, I feel like howling myself.*

Over the cacophony of confusion coming from outside, she heard a series of deep, labored cranks and creaks. They seemed to be coming from somewhere within the castle's walls. The castle's trebuchets must be winding up, preparing to return fire. There was a single, powerful whip-like *whoosh*. Martha closed her eyes, and tightened her hold on Effie, imagining a deadly missile hurtling towards Rodmar's army. An image of Vadim flashed into her mind—his body was laid out on the field, broken beyond repair.

She gave herself a mental slap. *No—he'll be fine.* Unlike her, Vadim knew what to expect and how to take care of himself. She had to stay strong, to keep it together for their baby's sake. Now that she had Effie to support, the task was somehow easier. She had no choice. The indulgence of unraveling would have to wait.

Effie stepped back and wiped her face on the sleeve of her nightdress. "We will all burn this day, roasted alive by their accursed fireballs." She spoke quietly, as if death was inevitable.

Martha shook her head. "I don't think so. The smithy only caught fire because the wall fell on top of it."

Effie's lower lip trembled. "I miss my mother," she whispered. "I wish I had never sought work here. I should have stayed with her in Edgeway."

A return volley struck something close by, making them jump. And then the screams began—terrible, heart-rending howls of agony. Whether the victim was male or female, Martha couldn't tell, but the sound of it sent goosebumps racing up her spine. She'd never heard anything so horrific. Effie looked ready to bolt, her eyes were wide and wild like those of a skittish horse. She had to distract the girl—somehow.

"Come and sit down." Taking Effie by the arm, Martha led her to the bed. "We might as well be comfortable." She drew the down comforter over their icy feet and legs.

The screams outside reached a crescendo then stopped. They both looked toward the window, but neither woman made a move to get up. The silence was even worse than the screaming. Martha pulled a shawl about her shoulders. The castle was usually chilly in the morning, but these shivers had little to do with the cold.

A few red embers glowed in the hearth, a reminder of last night's cheerful fire, but she didn't have the heart to build another one.

"W-what does your mother do in Edgeway?" Martha asked, for want of something better to say.

"She runs a... boarding house—of sorts."

"Does she? Good for her." Martha forced a smile. It wasn't easy to sound cheerful while her stomach churned with fear. "I suppose you didn't fancy working together, huh? It must be difficult, living and working—"

"I cannot lie to you, m'lady. 'Tis a house of... ill repute."

"Oh!" *A brothel?* Martha felt her eyes bug. She couldn't help it.

"Now I have shocked you. Forgive me, I should not have spoken so freely." Effie stared down at her hands, blushing hard. But the color in her cheeks was a big improvement from her earlier ghost impression.

Although Edgeway boasted several brothels, and the chances were remote, Martha felt compelled to ask: "I don't suppose your mother's name is Wilkes, is it?" She and Mrs. Wilkes went way back. Not that they'd ever met, of course.

Now it was Effie's turn to go bug-eyed. "H-how could you know?"

Unbelievable. A bubble of laughter formed in Martha's chest. She sucked in her cheeks, and battled to keep it there. This neat, timid girl was Mrs. Wilkes' daughter?

In her mind, she traveled back to her first encounter with the Evil Earl. Newly arrived from the twenty-first century, he'd assumed she was a prostitute seeking work at the house of one Mrs. Wilkes.

"Oh, someone... once mentioned her to me."

The appalled look on Effie's elfin face further inflamed Martha's amusement. Despite the hellish sounds coming from outside, she burst into laughter. She couldn't help it.

Stop it! You're hysterical. Maybe she was. But it made no difference. Effie's lips twitched into a smile, and she began laughing too. Hysteria was infectious, apparently. Better that than crying. They laughed until they could barely sit up straight, and tears poured from their eyes.

"Whatever are you doing in here?" Agatha appeared, her stout frame filling the doorway of the bedchamber. She frowned at both Effie and Martha in turn. "I could hear you from halfway down the corridor. You do realize that the castle is under attack?"

Martha mopped her eyes on her sleeve. "S-sorry, Ags. Private joke."

"Indeed?" Agatha pulled Martha's gown from where it hung over the back of a chair and threw it to her. "Now is not the time for levity. Make haste and get dressed, both of you. There are many injured folk who need treating this day. Friends and enemies alike."

The aim of twenty-first century weapons wasn't much better. Friendly fire. Collateral damage. They sounded so innocuous on the evening news.

Quickly sobering themselves, Martha and Effie leapt to their feet and hurried to do Agatha's bidding.

chapter fifteen

A THICK WALL OF SMOKE ENVELOPED them as they stepped out into the courtyard. Reaching for their headscarves, the women covered their noses in an attempt to protect their lungs.

Martha's eyes stung with the force of a thousand onions. Coughing like a hardened smoker, she reached out to clutch the back of Agatha's shawl, but Effie's hand had beaten her to it. Like baby elephants clinging to their mother, they followed in Agatha's wake, stumbling blindly over the rubble-strewn cobbles.

A group of soldiers accidentally jostled them as they went by. One or two murmured a curt apology before continuing on their way.

In amongst the shouting and the sounds of destruction, the panicked cries of the castle's animal population pierced Martha's heart—squeals, barks, and whinnies. But what could she do? Poor innocent creatures, caught up in a war between men.

"I thought you said Rodmar's slings wouldn't reach us," she called at Agatha's back. Her voice held more than a hint of accusation.

"I said nothing of the kind." Agatha kept on walking, casting the words over her shoulder. "If you recall, I said Rodmar's camp was out of range of the castle's trebuchets."

"What fecking difference does that make?"

"Quite a lot. Rodmar's weapons are bigger."

"Oh." *Size really does matter.* Martha's lips curved into a grim smile as she imagined the earl's fury at being unmanned in this way—especially with his big cousin King Erik there to witness it.

There was another loud *boom*, this time from the direction of the main gate.

A horn blew, one long and melancholy note. "The barbican is hit!" someone cried. "Water bearers!" Lines of men ran to answer the summons, their armor and weapons clanking like pots and pans tumbling from an overstuffed cupboard.

A sudden gust of wind sent the smoke billowing in another direction. Martha let go of Agatha's shawl and inhaled deeply. It was good to breathe sweet air again. She trotted after her friends, looking around as she replaced her headscarf.

The castle's defensive wall showed evidence of the severe battering it had taken so far. Great holes had been punched through the stonework. Rubble from previous strikes littered the courtyard. The crenellations of the battlements—once so regular and even—now looked like a set of smashed-in teeth.

There was no sign of Anselm or His Evilness. Not that Martha expected to see either of them fire-fighting or loading fallen masonry onto carts. They were probably overseeing from a distance, tucked away in safety with King Erik while the lower ranks did all the grunt work.

If there was any organization within the chaos, she couldn't make it out.

Winding though the twists of the castle complex, they finally reached the infirmary. Audible signposts directed them over the final stretch—terrible, blood-chilling cries that made the hair on the back of her neck prickle.

"In here." Agatha ducked inside a narrow doorway with Effie close behind her. Taking a deep breath, Martha followed them.

Martha froze. *Holy Mother of God!* As she entered the infirmary, the sounds of suffering rocked her like a physical blow. Standing rooted on the threshold of the room, she clapped her hands over her ears to muffle the agonized shrieks.

The smells were almost as bad: body odor and excrement, the unmistakable metallic tang of blood, burned hair, and... a barbeque?

Outside the medieval hospital was bad enough, but inside was infinitely worse. A new circle of hell.

Effie and Agatha had vanished into the crowd of people milling about the long, narrow room. A small fire burned at one end, throwing out more smoke than heat. The light was so dim Martha could hardly see. The few lanterns and torches did little to penetrate the gloom.

She was still standing just inside the open doorway. *Get a grip, Bigalow.*

Removing her hands from her ears, Martha took a step forward and immediately fell over a man's outstretched legs. He sat on the floor, his back resting against the wall.

"Oh, I'm so sor—" Lifeless eyes stared back at her. "Feck me!" Her hands flew up, covering her gaping mouth. Why the hell had she come? She wasn't going to be any use here. Hadn't Fergus told her she should stay in Anselm's rooms? What if he was looking for her right now?

I should go back.

The stench of the infirmary wasn't doing her rumbling morning sickness any favors. The acidic taste in her mouth was a definite early vomit warning.

With effort, she dragged her gaze away from the dead man. Big mistake. As her eyes adjusted to the darkness of the room, they gorged on images that would surely haunt them forever.

The wounded were everywhere. On the floor. On the beds. Most of them were still breathing—and screaming. For how much longer, she wouldn't like to guess. If their injuries didn't kill them, infection surely would. She wasn't the gambling type, but the odds of surviving this place didn't look good.

There was one parallel with her own world, though: There weren't enough beds. And still the wounded arrived. She edged away from the open doorway so that the new arrivals could be brought inside. Not that there was much room.

The waiting area resembled a human dumping ground. There was no triage system in operation, not so much as a fire-breathing receptionist to assess each new arrival. The patients who were able to do so sat with their backs against the wall. The more serious cases lay where they were on the cold, cobbled floor. People constantly stepped over them as they passed, almost without seeing them.

No one deserved to die this way, friend or enemy. Finally, Martha moved away from the door then stumbled into a depression on the floor. Immediately, a cold unpleasant ooze seeped through the flimsy fabric of her slipper. She glanced down. The 'depression' was actually a shallow drain containing a thick, and evil-smelling liquid, much of it trickling from the motionless bodies on the floor.

Oh, God! She wiped the side of her slipper on one of the cleaner cobbles. As she looked up, she met the eye of a burn victim.

Time slowed. The screams and cursing became low and muffled, distorting like a recording on a tangled audio cassette.

A man lay gasping on a low wooden cot. Well, she assumed he was male, going by his build. It was impossible to tell from his looks alone. He had no face.

As she looked at him, for some reason Martha was reminded of jam making—of bubbling red froth, boiling in a pan. The man's hair, nose, lips, and ears were gone, melted away like hot wax. Miraculously, one blue eye remained undamaged, and its perfection struck her as strangely obscene.

Of course, he was dying. With burns like that, he couldn't be saved—not even back in her own world. All alone, the man lay on his cot, chest heaving with the effort of dragging air into his ruined lungs.

Blinking back tears, Martha walked toward the bed, her steps slow and uncertain. Whoever this man was, whatever he'd done, he was someone's son. She thought of her own child, growing in the safety of her womb. God forbid that he should ever experience such suffering.

The blue eye watched her approach without blinking. As Martha stopped beside the bed, she realized why. His eyelid had melted away. The sickly smell of singed hair and roasted flesh hit her nostrils, and hot bile rose into her throat, but she swallowed it back down.

Somehow, she managed to smile at the man. "Are you th-thirsty?"

The man made a gargling sound, which she interpreted as "yes." She glanced around and spied a jug on a nearby table. "Hang on."

She returned with a tankard of ale and a square of clean linen. Drinking in the usual fashion was out of the question for the poor man, so she improvised. Kneeling beside the bed, she dipped the linen into the ale. Once the fabric was soaked, she held one corner of the cloth over the man's blackened mouth, drip-feeding him the ale. The man swallowed a few times, making appreciative gurgles.

He turned his head to the side, indicating he'd had enough. The way he looked at her reminded her of Forge. There was no mistaking the silent gratitude in the stranger's solitary blue eye.

"You're welcome," she replied softly.

Suddenly, his breathing worsened, bubbling and rasping in his heaving chest. He sounded as if he was drowning. Martha wanted to run, but she forced herself to stay where she was, crouched down beside the bed. She covered one of the man's claw-like hands with the wet piece of linen and clasped it. He made no protest. All his pain receptors had likely burned away too.

"Shh." What else could she say? One final flash of panic in his eye, and mercifully, the man's body relaxed. The sounds of his labored breathing ended, exhaled on a last gurgling breath.

Martha covered his face with the linen square. Tears slid down her cheeks, but not of sorrow. She was only grateful that the unknown man's suffering was over. Although she wasn't an overly religious person, she closed her eyes and muttered a silent prayer.

Effie's voice interrupted her. "What are you doing, m'lady?"

Martha wiped her eyes and got up off her knees. "I'm just having a quiet word with the Big G."

Effie frowned. "Who?"

"The Great Spirit."

"Ah!" She took Martha's arm and led her away. "Come. We have need of another pair of hands."

With her mind full of the man who'd died, Martha allowed Effie tow her through the crowd. They stopped between a pair of long tables. It only took a second for her to register what was about to happen.

"Oh, you've got to be kidding me!"

An unconscious man lay stretched out on one of the tables. Martha grimaced. His right arm was crushed and mangled below the elbow. Several people, Agatha amongst them, stood around the blood-smeared table, obviously awaiting the instructions of the knife-wielding surgeon. Dressed in his filthy leather apron, he looked more like a butcher.

The surgeon seemed less than impressed at the delay to his procedure. "Might I proceed now?" He gave Martha a frosty look as if she were the one responsible.

"No. Way." She backed off, shaking her head. This was far beyond the call of duty. She'd tried to fit into this world. God knows she had. But assisting in an amputation? *I think not.*

Agatha grabbed Martha's arm. "If you are going to be squeamish, take my place at the foot of the table. I will hold his head."

She felt everyone glaring at her.

"But wh-what if he wakes up?" Despite her objections, she found herself steered to a place beside one of the man's outstretched legs.

"If you delay me any longer, he may well do so," the surgeon said with a superior sneer.

Martha clutched the man's leg—more to steady herself than for any other reason—burying her fingers in the fabric of his woolen leggings. His leg muscles felt warm. Alive.

The surgeon nodded to a young boy beside him. Immediately, the lad handed him a steaming jug of water. But it wasn't for sterilization purposes. The surgeon dribbled a little water over a sponge then held it in place over the patient's nose and mouth.

Martha leaned on the unconscious man's boot, straining to see. She caught the faint scent of herbs coming off the sponge. *Anesthetic?*

She must have spoken aloud.

"Well done, m'lady." The surgeon's lips formed a thin smile as he glanced at the people standing about his table. "Not quite so ignorant as I assumed, it appears."

There were several sniggers from Dr. Death's sycophantic helpers.

You think I'm the ignorant one, you pompous arse? Martha bit her lip. *Rise above it, Bigalow.*

She tried. But when she saw how filthy the surgeon's knife was, her mouth refused to stay shut. "Have you washed that thing recently?" Surely he wasn't about to use that dirty, blood-smeared thing on the unconscious man?

The surgeon didn't bother to look up. "'Tis hardly necessary." He ran a dirty finger over the man's arm, probably decided where to cut first.

"What about infection? Gangrene?" Martha ignored the chorus of groans from the surgeon's devoted disciples. *Tough.* Her conscience wouldn't allow her to stand by and say nothing.

"You speak of putrefaction?" The surgeon glanced up at her. "Unlikely. Would my learned assistant object terribly if we deferred this conversation on experimental medicine to a more appropriate time?"

Before Martha could protest, the surgeon's blade descended, slicing through the mangled flesh of the patient's arm.

The surgeon dropped the knife then held out his hand. "Saw." His young assistant was quick to respond.

Martha tried to look away but couldn't. Wide-eyed, she watched the surgeon saw through the glistening bone of the man's arm. In a few deft strokes, it was over. The patient hadn't moved at all.

After dropping the amputated limb into a basket at his feet, the surgeon reached for the bladder of wine his assistant held out to him.

He's drinking? At a time like this?

But, no. Instead, he poured the wine all over the stump before handing the bladder back to the boy. "Brand."

"Holy Mother of God!" Martha gagged and clung onto the patient's leg. No wonder the infirmary smelled like a dodgy barbeque.

The surgeon pressed something resembling a hot metal poker to the naked stump. The raw flesh hissed, sizzled, and steamed. Fat and loose bits of skin spattered everywhere. The stump was cooked in seconds.

Martha held her breath for as long as she could then turned her head away. She took several shallow breaths over her shoulder, trying to avoid the smell of toxic Sunday roast.

It was no good. *I'm gonna barf.* Bile flooded her mouth, hot and bitter. She swallowed it down. The last thing the poor patient needed was her vomit adding more contamination to this most un-sterile of theaters.

The surgeon handed the brand to his assistant, then untied the leather tourniquet from his patient's upper arm, loosening it gradually. He bent down to examine the stump.

"Perfect. No ooze at all." The man's stern face relaxed into a smile. "Thank you, everyone." He took a swig from the wine bladder and then turned to Agatha. "If you would apply a light dressing of..."

Martha just stared, unable to believe what she'd just witnessed. She glanced at the patient. His chest barely moved. It would be a miracle if he survived.

Her stomach rebelled again, and this time she couldn't fight the urge to vomit. She managed to turn her head aside before emptying the sparse contents of her stomach into the floor gutter. Thank God, she hadn't had any breakfast. She closed her eyes and leaned against the table, waiting for the room to stop spinning and for the buzzing in her ears to subside.

A gentle hand rested against her lower back. The same someone pressed a piece of linen into her hand so she could wipe her sour mouth. No words. Just silent compassion.

The surgeon wasn't so kind. "For the love of the Great Spirit. Will someone please take that woman outside?"

Her head felt as heavy as a chunk of masonry. She managed to focus her bleary eyes on the surgeon as he sat perched on the table's edge, alternately swigging from the wine bladder and then tapping at his unconscious patient's face.

A gentle angel held onto Martha's arm. Effie. Right then and there, she dismissed every doubt she'd ever harbored about the girl.

The surgeon smirked at Martha. Agatha was occupied with bandaging the patient's stump, but she happened to look up and witness it.

"Now, Alric. Do not mock her. M'lady is untested in the trials of war."

"Hmm." The nostrils of the surgeon's hooked nose flared, and he regarded Martha as if she was an unpleasant insect. "Then let her remain untested. Take her away, young Effie. I think m'lady's charity work is over for today."

Martha took a deep breath. His sneering sarcasm was just what she needed. Her temper flared, calming her stomach and slowing the whirling pit inside her head.

"Come." Effie slid her arm about Martha's waist. "Can you walk, m'lady?"

She nodded and drew herself upright, dabbing at her sour

mouth with the linen cloth. She took a few tentative steps away from the table.

"Thank you." The surgeon launched a parting shot. "Your assistance has been... invaluable, dear lady."

"Oh, go and boil your tools, why don't you?" Martha snapped. She had the satisfaction of seeing the surgeon's brown eyes widen before she walked away.

chapter sixteen

A S THEY MADE THEIR WAY back to the keep, they saw Anselm up one of the wall-walks, overseeing makeshift repairs to the battlements.

With luck, they'd manage to sneak by without him noticing.

"Martha!"

Uh-oh. Busted!

Anselm bounded down the steps and across the ruined courtyard, closing the distance between them in a few quick strides. "Erde! What are you doing out here?" he demanded. "Death stalks those who are foolish enough to poke at it."

Lovely. Just what she needed, a little bit of weird homespun wisdom to properly round off her morning. Aunt Lulu would love that particular little gem.

Before she could reply, there came a loud collective shout of warning, "Beware!" A second later, a large missile flew over the castle wall at terrifying speed.

"Get down!" Anselm dragged Martha and Effie to their knees and pulled them close to him, sheltering them against his body.

Boom! Chunks of wood and masonry rained down about them, clattering and crashing in a deafening shower of sound.

Terrified and trembling, Martha burrowed her face beneath the arm of Anselm's leather hauberk, breathing in the scent of sweat and leather. She closed her eyes tightly as a light hail of falling debris pelted her exposed back. She heard Effie whimpering at Anselm's other side, the sounds of the maid's terror echoing through his chest.

Then, there was silence.

Cautiously, Anselm raised his head and looked about.

Martha followed suit, forcing her fingers to release their death-grip on his belt. The danger had passed. For now.

Without speaking, Anselm helped them to their feet.

Martha raised her arm and used it to shield her mouth and nose from the worst of the billowing dust. Suddenly, the wind changed direction and the dust cloud parted. Moments ago, an empty wagon had stood by the wall of the keep. Now, only a crushed wheel and a few large splinters of wood remained.

One by one, figures rose from out of the haze, coughing and dusting themselves down.

"You there!" Anselm bellowed at a soldier who emerged from the shelter of a nearby outbuilding. "Yes, you man! Take a message to those imbeciles on the slings. Tell them if they want to keep their worthless heads on their necks, they had best find a way to increase our range. Make haste!"

The soldier raced away up the ramp leading to the castle's trebuchet platforms. As he did so, he stumbled over a plank of wood.

Anselm scowled and shook his head. "Useless dolt." Then he turned his angry gaze on Martha. "So, where were you today?"

"The infirmary." Martha reached for Effie's hand and clasped it tightly.

Anselm's jaw dropped. "For the love of Erde! Why?" He looked horrified.

A good question. Martha still wasn't sure how she'd ended up there. "I-I wanted to help—"

"Help? Little wonder you are so pale." His eyes narrowed. "Did that old witch Agatha force you into it?"

Yes. "No. It was my idea."

He didn't look convinced. "Is this true, girl?" Anselm demanded, targeting Effie with a cold, hard glare.

"Yes, m'lord," she squeaked, before casting her gaze downward.

Thankfully, he said no more on the subject.

Instead, he offered Martha his arm. She was glad to accept it. The loan of his strength had never been more welcome. The trials of the morning had definitely taken their toll. Her legs felt like jelly, and her head was still woozy.

With Effie trailing silently behind them, Anselm escorted Martha across the perilous courtyard, weaving a careful path through the rubble.

"I do not much care for the influence of your chosen companions, my dear," he said. At least he wasn't shouting anymore. "I would much prefer that you remained in safety with the ladies of the court."

"Oh, stop fussing, Anselm," Martha snapped. The last thing she wanted was to spend time with those superior bitches, forever gossiping and competing for the king's favor. "At least let me choose my own friends."

"M'lord!"

A knight clanked toward them on a fast intercept course, saving her from Anselm's reply.

The man removed his helmet and drew a weary hand over his grime-streaked face. "A messenger approaches bearing the white flag. What do you think it means?"

Martha's heart skipped a beat. *Rodmar's surrendering? But why? He's beating the crap out of us in here.* Even so, hope flared in her heart. Was the siege finally over?

"So soon?" Anselm clasped Martha's hand as it rested on his arm, giving her cold fingers a gentle squeeze. "'Tis a little early to be offering terms, I think. Our masters are certainly not yet ready to hear them."

So the white flag didn't necessarily mean surrender, then?

"Aye. I fear you are right there, my friend." The knight stroked his silver-streaked beard. "Though, it would hearten me a good deal if the women and children were allowed to go free."

Anselm chuckled, but not unkindly. "Ah, Hugh. The fair Beatrice has transformed you from a warrior into a husband."

Beatrice. King Erik's discarded mistress?

Martha studied the knight with fresh interest. He was older than many of the knights she'd seen about the castle. Perhaps he wasn't quite so dashing, nor so swaggering, but his eyes were kind. Instinctively, she knew this wasn't a man who would ever ill-treat his wife.

"That she has." Hugh smiled. "And I am not sorry for it." He nodded, indicating Martha. "I wager you will feel much the same way after you and your good lady are wed."

Anselm tightened his grip on her hand. "I am quite certain I shall," he replied.

Hugh exhaled. "I had better go and inform the king of developments." The prospect didn't seem to thrill him. "M'lady." Giving Martha a brief bow, he headed away in the direction of the keep.

As she watched Hugh depart, Martha felt Anselm staring at her. She turned to look at him, and the expression in his eyes made her cheeks burn. For once, his look was unguarded, vulnerable.

Vadim used to look at her in a similar way. If they were ever reunited, would he still do so? She dared not consider the alternative.

Was Anselm in love with her? For his sake, she hoped it was only a mild dose of lust. She wouldn't wish unrequited love on anyone, not even him.

Suddenly, Martha noticed a thin trickle of blood running down the side of his face. "You're hurt." She pulled a linen handkerchief from its hiding place down the front of her gown and offered it to him.

"'Tis nothing." But all the same, Anselm took the handkerchief and applied it to the top of his head, wincing a little. His fair hair was dark and matted with blood.

"It doesn't look like nothing to me," she said with a frown. "Here, let me take a look."

He ducked away when she tried to examine him. "Stop fussing," he said with a smile, using the very words she'd so recently used on him. He dabbed the wound one final time then tucked the bloody hanky inside his hauberk.

"Effie?" Anselm addressed the maid, but his eyes never strayed from Martha's. "Take your mistress back to our rooms. See that she is fed and well rested."

"Yes, m'lord."

He raised Martha's hand to his lips and pressed a light kiss on it. "You are a good deal too pale, sweeting."

He's twitching about me? I'm not the one with a head wound. "I really think that—"

"Go. I must seek out my master." He gave her a small bow then walked away.

As she watched him leave, Martha shivered. The gray folds

of his cloak swirled about him like the wings of a huge, dark bird. She felt as if a shadow had blocked out the sun. "Anselm?"

He paused and looked back. "What is it, sweeting?"

"Be careful." The words were out before she realized she was saying them.

When did I start giving a damn?

Anselm swept a low theatrical bow and grinned. "As always, my dear." Then he departed.

The arrival of Rodmar's flag-bearing messenger bought the castle a welcome respite from the constant bombardment.

Taking advantage of the unexpected ceasefire, Martha bathed, washing away every trace of the infirmary from her skin. If only her memory could be cleaned so easily. Once dressed in fresh clothes, she consumed every bite of the substantial breakfast that Effie had brought for her—surprisingly, the horrors of the morning hadn't managed to kill off her appetite.

Clean and well fed, she sat on the hearth, drying her hair by the heat of the fire. She ought to have been content, but she couldn't shake her bleak mood.

For once, thoughts of Anselm, not Vadim, claimed her attention. How had the lines become so blurred without her noticing? There was no black or white anymore. No wrong or right. Just a sludgy, uniform, gray color.

What the feck is happening to me?

Anselm was still a complete arse, but she found she no longer hated him. When had that happened, she wondered. It wasn't love. Not on her side, anyway. But she couldn't deny a grudging fondness for the man. *Why, though?* Were his occasional kindnesses enough to cancel out all the terrible things he'd done? Apparently so.

She groaned and covered her face with her hands. Vadim wouldn't be happy if he ever learned she cared about his foster-brother—however grudgingly.

But Vadim isn't here, said a small voice inside her head—not that she needed a reminder.

She was so angry with him. Rationally, she understood the choices he'd made, but the fact remained, he'd let her go, abandoning her to Anselm and His Evilness. The small voice inside her was bitter and unforgiving.

You'll always come second to his noble causes. In this world, there will always be another war for him to fight. And now you're carrying his child? How will you cope? In case you've forgotten, this isn't the twenty-first century.

If she had any sense, she'd find Madoc the Seer again and beg him to find her a way home. Problem was, she still loved Vadim as much now as on the day they'd spoken their vows. Love trumped anger. Just.

A headache rumbled behind her right eye, the pain knifing to the back of her skull. She got up from the hearth and lowered herself into her fireside chair then leaned back. She was tired of thinking. Closing her eyes, she let the blissful silence to wash over her.

chapter seventeen

"THE KNIGHTS ARE RETURNING."

Effie's excited voice jolted Martha from her catnap, shattering Vadim's face within her dream. She staggered to the window seat and knelt beside the young maid, staring toward the gate.

She'd been asleep longer than she thought. Now, vivid pinks and purples stained the sky as the sun set on another day.

Anselm and the knights had been gone for hours this time.

The first meeting between the opposing factions had taken place early that morning, and it had been worryingly brief. But not half an hour after arriving back at the castle, Anselm and his men had ridden out a second time—presumably carrying fresh orders from King Erik.

Time slowed to a drunken crawl after they'd gone. Men lined the wall-walks, looking from the battlements into the enemy camp below. The war machines stood still and silent. Somehow, the peace seemed too loud.

All around the keep, people pressed their faces to the windows, waiting and watching for the messengers to return.

Even the servants—that last bastion of normality—gave up all pretense of work. They stood together in the courtyard, huddled in little groups, seldom speaking, constantly glancing at the gate.

What had happened inside the luxurious folds of Rodmar's purple tent? Had they hammered out terms? Would they all soon be free?

Effie touched Martha's arm, but there was no need. She'd already seen the riders trotting through the gate.

As the men rode into the yard, her eyes zoomed in on Anselm. *Oh dear!* The grim line of his mouth told her he wasn't bringing good news. He pushed through the crowds who swarmed to greet them then dismounted without speaking a word.

Martha exhaled a shaky breath. If anything, he looked angry.

"Shall we go down and hear the news, m'lad—Martha? I long to know what has happened."

Shaking her head, Martha withdrew from the window. "You go if you want. I think I might lie on the bed for a bit."

"If you are certain." Effie looked worried, no doubt remembering Anselm's orders to take care of her mistress. "You still look a little pale."

Martha waved away her concern. "I'm fine. Stop fretting and just go."

Effie bustled out of the room, closing the door behind her. Martha sighed. The quiet was a welcome companion.

Lord, I'm so tired.

Dragging her feet, she walked to her bedchamber. Her bones ached with weariness. The urge to sleep was irresistible. It must be the effects of her pregnancy. She remembered reading that exhaustion was common during the first trimester.

She closed the door and then lay down on the bed. The mattress sagged beneath her, cradling her like a chick in a nest. With a blissful sigh, she snuggled her face into the soft pillow. The moment her eyes closed, she felt sleep stealing over her.

It seemed only seconds had passed when an urgent voice roused her again.

"Martha? Martha! Where are you?"

Sleep-fuddled and confused, she sat up. For a moment, she thought the voice was Vadim's. "In here," she called.

The door of her bedchamber flew open, and there stood Anselm, glowering at her from the doorway. The look in his eyes was nothing short of murderous.

Shit! Why didn't I lock it?

The violence in his eyes made her blood run cold. His chest heaved beneath his armor plate as he battled to control his breathing. What could have happened?

"Wh-what is it?" She resisted the urge to hide beneath the bedcovers. "Why are you looking at me like that?"

"Did you know?" He spoke so quietly she barely heard him.

"Huh?"

"Did. You. Know?" His hands clenched into fists at his sides, his knuckles showing white beneath his tanned skin.

Oh, crap! With a flash of intuition, Martha knew exactly what he was talking about. And who. Her stomach lurched. *Play dumb.*

"Know? Know what?" She swung her legs out of bed and stood up. "Are you all right? Tell me, Anselm." The concern in her voice was real. She didn't have to fake it.

Anselm remained motionless in the doorway, dissecting her with glacial eyes.

She'd need an Oscar-winning performance to pull this off. "Anselm?" Her spine prickled with fear, but she forced herself to walk toward him. "What is it? You're scaring me." That last part was true, at least.

"I will ask you one more time. Did you know?" The quietness of his tone was worse than any ranting.

"I don't know what you're—"

He moved with frightening speed. Grabbing the tops of her arms, his cruel fingers dug painfully into her soft flesh. He dragged her up onto her tiptoes, her feet almost leaving the ground.

Unable to speak for pain, she looked pleadingly at him. But his eyes were as warm as a Siberian winter.

"Forgive my impatience, sweeting," he murmured against her gasping mouth. "But I have passed a most vexing day."

"Anselm. P-please!" Her knees buckled. She would have fallen if he had not held her so tightly. "You're... h-hurting me."

"Good." He dragged her close, crushing her chest against the cold metal of his breast-plate. "You deserve a little ill treatment for the way you have—"

"M'lord?" A man's voice interrupted them.

Oh, thank God. Martha could hear her own panicked breaths.

Sir Hugh was hovering in the doorway of her bedchamber, a frown in his eyes. "The king demands your presence."

Anselm didn't look at his friend. His attention was fixed

wholly on Martha. "Not. Now." The quiet warning in his voice was unmistakable.

"But, Anselm—"

"I said, not now!" He spun around to face Hugh, taking Martha with him. The pressure of his painful hold didn't let up for a second.

To his credit, Sir Hugh didn't flinch. "What would you have me say?" he asked mildly. "You know how His Grace hates to be kept waiting."

"Say what you will," Anselm muttered. "I neither know nor care. Lie to him if you must." He held Martha away from him, but he didn't release her, only looking deeper into her eyes. "I am sure you can lie well enough at need."

The last few words weren't meant for Sir Hugh, but her. Perhaps playing the role of Anselm's concerned fiancée might help?

"Anselm, you m-mustn't anger the king. If you ever hope to join his Court, we must keep him happy." Her voice trembled, but it sounded convincing.

"Well said, my dear." The venom in his softly spoken words made her flinch. He obviously wasn't buying it. "I can hardly disregard such fine counsel. Hugh?" He glanced at the knight. "Be good enough to inform His Grace and Lord Edgeway that whilst at the enemy camp, I must have imbibed something disharmonious to my health."

"M'lord?"

Anselm rolled his eyes at his friend's lack of understanding. "Tell him I am on the privy suffering from a bout of explosive bowels, man!"

"As you wish."

The knight ignored the despairing looks Martha was sending him. "Do not delay for too long," he said. "Your domestic concerns will keep."

After Hugh departed, Anselm finally let Martha go. She stood her ground, rubbing her aching arms.

He stroked a strand of hair away from her face with a gentle finger. "Shall I tell you how I have spent this day, sweeting?"

"I wish you would," she muttered through gritted teeth. "I can't imagine why you're in such a foul mood." Playing ignorant was keeping her fear in check. But only just.

"I have been bartering for our lives, m'lady. Smiling, and

speaking words of friendship to win the favor of that upstart dog Rodmar and his followers." His eyes hardened. "When in truth, I longed to draw my sword and cut them all down where they stood."

Tingles prickled up her spine. Martha didn't doubt him. Unable to stop herself, she took a couple of steps backward. Hearing him speak so calmly of violence ramped up her panic by several notches.

"Can you imagine the humiliation of having to woo that insolent cur?" Anselm sneered, his eyes following her as she moved toward the window. "Of being forced to accept the hospitality of his table? Can you imagine what it cost me, Martha? They may as well have cut off my balls and forced me to eat them."

Martha shuddered at that particular mental image. "Th-that must have been very difficult for you."

Why had she ever imagined she was fond of him? She'd forgotten just how scary Anselm could be, but it was fast coming back to her.

"Feigning friendship where one feels only loathing is no easy task." In one long stride, he closed the distance she'd managed to put between them. He stroked her cheek with the back of his gloved hand. "I think," he said softly, "you understand that better than anyone, my sweet."

Martha remained still, rigid beneath his touch, though her legs wanted to carry her in the opposite direction. "I d-don't know what you mean."

Oh, but she did. And no matter what she said, he knew it too. It was there in the bitter accusation of his eyes.

A ghost of a smile played about his lips. "My poisonous little dove." His tone was that of a kindly parent reproaching a naughty child. "No more lies. The time for pretense is over though your tenacity does you credit. Were I not so vexed, I might even admire you for it."

Martha flinched as he suddenly extended his hand, half expecting to feel the sting of a blow.

Instead, Anselm entwined his fingers with hers. "Come. Let us speak honestly together for a while."

She sensed her fear amused him. He was getting off on it. *Sick bastard!*

He led her out of the bedchamber and into the sitting room,

away from the temptation of her bed. Not that Anselm would need a bed if he decided to use sex as a form of punishment, but she didn't want him to get any ideas. The sight of her rumpled bed linen was much too intimate, especially with him in this mood.

Perched on her chair beside the fire, Martha watched as Anselm poured two tankards of ale. She craved a drink so badly she could almost taste the bitter-sweet brew.

Without speaking, Anselm handed a tankard to her. Then he slumped down in his chair, sipping at his drink, scowling deeply into the depths of the fire.

What's he thinking? How best to kill me?

Martha held the tankard between her hands. Her mouth was as dry as moon dust, but she dared not drink it. Death by poison wasn't in her top three of ways she wanted to shuffle off the mortal coil.

Anselm looked up. "You are not drinking." He must have guessed her thoughts because he took a couple more sips from his own tankard then handed it to her. "How little you must think of me, my sweet." He took her own untouched drink from her hand.

"I don't know what to think anymore," she muttered. In several quick gulps, she drained Anselm's tankard. The ale was warm and flat, but it tasted as good as any fine wine. She dried her lips with the back of her hand. The ale had restored her courage. She was ready to hear the worst.

"What's going on, Anselm?" she asked quietly. "Just tell me."

Anselm's sigh was a very weary sound. "You are right. The time has come for me to speak plainly, my dear. I wonder, do you have the courage to return the favor?"

Do I? Oh, what the hell. Decision made, Martha nodded. "Okay. But you go first."

"Very well." Anselm took a sip of ale then set the tankard down on the floor. "Whilst suffering Rodmar's hospitality, I noticed several masked men amongst those he counts as his advisers. I paid them little heed at first. The business at hand kept me distracted. However, during a pause for refreshments, I happened to notice a man lurking by the tent entrance. Although he was hooded and masked, I recognized something familiar in his stance." He leaned forward in his chair, regarding Martha through narrowed eyes.

Keeping a poker face wasn't easy. Not when her heart beat so fast. When she didn't speak, Anselm resumed his tale.

"The negotiations reclaimed my attention for a time, but I repeatedly felt the weight of the unknown man's stare. It felt... personal." He reached for the key ring he kept on his belt, absently flicking through the keys.

Martha held her breath. Would he realize she'd replaced one of his keys with a dud?

But Anselm kept on talking. "I knew several of the assembled men—none that I would call friend—but no one paid me the same attention the masked man did. Naturally, I did not think of your husband at first. After all, why would a ghost be haunting Rodmar's tent?"

Why indeed? Martha tried not to frown. Vadim was usually so cautious. What was he thinking? Of course Anselm would recognize him. They'd grown up together, for fecksake!

"It suddenly came to me that I knew the man." Anselm looked grim. "There was no longer any doubt in my mind. And even better, I had a name for him too."

Martha daren't look away from him. Her fingers pleated hurried folds in the material of her skirt.

"Shall I reveal how I unmasked him, sweeting?"

"Please do." With effort, her voice was steady.

"I called to him by name." Anselm looked smug, pleased by his own cunning. "I waited until we were mounted and ready to return to the castle. The man stood lurking at the back of the crowd that had come to see us off. As I shortened my rein for departure, I called out to him. He had half turned away, but the name of a ghost brought him back round again."

Martha's hand flew to her mouth. *Game over.* Anselm's chuckles sounded like a death knell to her ears.

"Little wonder you are so shocked, my dear. Your beloved husband, raised from the dead. Are you not pleased?" His smile broadened as he leaned back in his chair. "Of course, I sent him your warmest regards."

He looked like the cat that had got not only the cream, but the whole damn dairy too.

"I informed him you were being well... taken care of. Though for some reason, my assurances did not please him." Another chuckle. "Perhaps he inferred some other interpretation from my kindly meant words? That might explain why one of his companions grasped his arm and held on to him so tightly."

That's just great. It was Martha's turn to slump back in her chair. *Now Vadim thinks Anselm and I have been bumping uglies all this time.* Looks definitely couldn't kill. Anselm would've been dead on the floor right now if that were possible. But instead of keeling over, he just sat there, grinning at her with that infuriatingly smug expression on his face.

"Your turn, m'lady." His smile faded. "Although your lack of reaction only confirms my suspicions, I should still like to hear you admit it out loud. Did you know he still lived?"

Caution be damned. Anselm knew the truth anyway. She was already a dead woman walking. Taking a deep breath, Martha answered him. "Yes. I knew."

Anselm exhaled a long and hard breath, the sound an evil apparition might make. The keys in his hand were silenced as closed his hand about them.

Several long seconds elapsed before he spoke again. "Well played, m'lady. Your game was faultless. Though in my defense, I suspect I was blinded by my partiality for you."

Damn it. This was no time for guilt pangs. Anselm was probably going to break her neck any minute. But what she felt wasn't about him. For the sake of her own conscience, she needed to say it:

"I'm sorry if I hurt you, Anselm." She clasped her hands together in her lap, willing him to understand. "But what else could I do? I didn't want this—not any of it."

"You deceived me without mercy," he snarled. "There is a name for women like you."

"Yeah? I guess you should know since you've slept with so many of them."

To her surprise, his expression softened and his smile returned. Even more shocking, it looked genuine.

"Oh, Martha. You cunning and treacherous vixen." He touched her cheek with a tender hand. "How well you understand me. A nature such as yours is wasted on... *him.* You and I would be a much better fit."

Would we? She gave herself a mental shake. No matter how

high Anselm turned his charm dial, he wasn't Vadim. "I don't think so." The only time Anselm made her blood simmer was because of anger, not passion. "Unlike you, I take no pleasure in inflicting pain on anyone."

Anselm's jaw tightened. "Insolent wretch. Have you no shame then for treating me with such despicable cruelty?"

"At least I said I was sorry." Martha scrambled to her feet, a flash of temper evaporating her fear. "Anyway, why are you acting like you're the victim here? You kidnapped and imprisoned me, remember? I'd say that makes us about even, wouldn't—"

He leapt up, encircling her throat with a rough hand. "I protected you, you ungrateful wretch," he hissed as he dragged her toward him, his fingers pressing upon her windpipe. "Without me, you would have died weeks ago."

Black dots danced before her eyes. *Oh, Jesus!* Heart hammering, she clutched his wrist with both hands and pulled. The pressure on her throat eased a little, enough for her to snatch a few ragged gasps of air. But she wasn't about to waste her final moments begging for mercy. He'd just love that.

"Without you, none... of this would have... happened," she gasped. Her fingernails dug into his wrist, gouging at his skin, but Anselm didn't flinch. He loosened his hold enough so that she could speak properly. "Vadim and I were happy," she cried. "And you ruined it. The only thing you ever gave me was a comfortable prison."

"Have a care, Martha."

She was too angry to heed the quiet warning of his voice. He could only kill her once.

"You and His Evilness deserve one another," she sneered. "In the end, you'll only have each other. You're both so cold and twisted, no decent person could ever want either of you—"

The pressure on her windpipe increased again. Martha gagged, her eyes bulging in their sockets. Anselm observed her suffering without expression. As her vision faded, she stopped tugging at his wrist. The oncoming blackness stole all of her strength along with the will to fight.

chapter eighteen

A N URGENT VOICE SUMMONED HER to the light. "Come back
to me, Martha."

Suddenly, she could breathe again. Coughing and
spluttering, she filled her burning lungs with heaving gulps of
air, gorging on it.

She was on the floor, the wooden planks pressing uncomfortably into her spine with each coughing spasm. As oxygen
flooded back into her body, the dark veil fell from her eyes.

Anselm was kneeling beside her, briskly chafing her trembling hands between his. With effort, she pulled away from his
touch. *Get off me, you fecking psycho!* Tears of fear and relief slid
down her cheeks and dripped into her ears. She didn't want to
cry, but the effort of holding back the tears put too much pressure on her aching throat.

"Oh, thank the Great Spirit!" Anselm's relief at seeing her revived was apparent. He looked pale, his eyes glittering with emotion. This was a very different man from the one who'd almost
strangled her. Bad Anselm was gone. For now, at least.

He leaned over and pressed his warm lips to her forehead.
"Forgive me. I did not mean to..." Shaking his head, he turned
away, muttering fiercely beneath his breath.

When her breathing leveled out, Martha swiped her sleeve
across her eyes and tried to sit up. Anselm was there at once,
lifting and guiding her with gentle hands, helping her back into
her chair. She was too wobbly to object.

"Drink this." He held a tankard to her lips. "Just a little, mind."

Her airway felt swollen, constricted to the diameter of a drinking straw. She took a tiny sip of ale and forced it down her raw throat. She gagged. Gradually, her heart stopped hammering, and her breathing slowed.

"W-what are... you going to do with me now?" she asked in a ragged whisper.

Anselm crouched beside her chair and traced the line of her shoulder with his fingers. "Do not ask me that, I beg of you."

Martha circled her shoulder to escape his touch. To hell with him. She wasn't scared anymore.

The trembling man before her seemed incapable of doing her further harm. Not by his own hand, anyway. "Will you tell the earl about Vadim... about me?"

"Should I, m'lady?" The warmth in his eyes cooled a degree. "Shall I tell him how you have lied and deceived us? Can you imagine my lord's reaction?" He leaned closer, his breath brushing her cold lips. "By the time he finally slit your throat, you would consider it an act of mercy."

Martha's scalp prickled. She knew he spoke the truth.

He stood up, looking about the room as if he'd never seen it before. "I am shackled on all sides," he muttered, raking both hands through his tangled hair. He winced, probably encountering the wound to his head he'd received earlier. "For the love of Erde, what am I to do? No matter which path I walk, I am damned." He kicked over a small table, sending it crashing into the wall.

Martha flinched. Why was he so upset? It was her life on the line, not his.

He paced the room, muttering to himself like a madman.

Watching him made her dizzy. He reminded her of a tiger penned up in a too-small enclosure. She tried to speak but couldn't make a sound. Clearing her throat, she tried again. "Anselm?" Not exactly a shout, but at least he heard.

"Hush, sweeting. Let me think."

She massaged her throat and coughed a couple of times before speaking. "What about? You've... won. King Erik... will probably give you a reward when he learns—"

"Can you truly be so blind?" Anselm crouched beside her chair again, his eyes wild and desperate. "I do not wish to see you dead, Martha."

She arched her eyebrows. *So, strangulation is just an enthusiastic form of affection, is it?*

He accurately interpreted her expression. "I was half insane before. My passion momentarily overcame me." He touched her hand as it rested on the arm of the chair, scowling when she moved it away. "I vow to you, sweeting, I will never hurt you again."

He got up and resumed his pacing, indulging in another weird muttered conversation with himself. "I could remain silent. Ah, but what if I do not speak up, and my masters learn of her treachery? My life will be forfeit too. No." He shook his head. "I cannot take that risk."

Martha listened in disbelief. Why would he even consider keeping quiet? That could only mean that he really did... Her heart sank. *Oh, surely not?* He'd just tried to kill her.

She coughed to get his attention. "You... care about me?" she whispered. One of them was crazy, and she had a sneaking suspicion it might be her.

Anselm's smile was grim. "Why else would I consider courting the wrath of my powerful masters?"

"Oh." She was too shocked to say anything more.

He knelt beside her chair. This time when he took her hand, she didn't pull away.

He raised her hand to his lips. "I must get you to safety." His urgent words warmed her icy fingers. "But how?"

She sat up a little straighter. Perhaps there was already a way. "Didn't you discuss terms with Rodmar? Are the women and children going to be set free?"

"Unfortunately not," he said with a brief shake of his golden head. "The king insists on the immediate withdrawal of Rodmar's camp, nothing less."

This was a blow. A lot of people had been banking on some kind of agreement being hammered out, herself included.

Anselm must have read her disappointment. "Perhaps when the barrage recommences, he might have a change of heart."

Despite his smile, she knew he didn't believe it.

"So, don't say anything," she said. "Did anyone else hear what you said to Vadim?"

Anselm released her hand and began stalking the room again. "The other knights were with me when I called out to...

him. Sir Hugh made some mention of it on the ride back." He froze in his tracks and stood a little taller. "Oh, but I am a fool! I must go to my masters now. If anyone mentions it, I shall say I was mistaken. Lord Hemlock is still dead."

Unexpected tears blurred her vision. He knew the truth, and he still wanted to protect her. Unbelievable. "Thank you." She held out her hand to him. "Even if everything goes to hell, I won't forget this, Anselm."

"I would rather see you with *him* than have you dead." He kissed her hand then held it against his cheek, his silvery eyes boring into hers. "But make no mistake, sweeting. I do this for you alone."

She nodded. Whatever happened, there seemed little chance of Anselm and Vadim would be sharing an emotional happily-ever-after reunion anytime soon. "I understand."

Rodmar's war machines resumed their attack, bombarding the castle with stone missiles well into the night. Anselm didn't return to his chambers.

Martha paced the room. Sleep was impossible. Since Anselm had left, she'd been wired and twitchy. But the noise of war wasn't to blame. The trebuchets' deadly song no longer bothered her. Time and repetition had somehow lowered the volume of the destructive forces beyond the window. Besides, the crashes and rumblings weren't yet close enough to be a cause for concern.

She knew the reason for her hyper-alert state. The end was coming. In her heart, she was certain of it. What kind of end remained to be seen.

With Effie's help, Martha changed into her warmest woolen gown and exchanged her flimsy slippers for a pair of sturdy boots. Her cloak hung over the back of the chair by the door, in readiness for when the summons to leave came.

Effie was kneeling on the floor packing some of Martha's things into a small linen bundle. When she looked up, her hazel eyes were serious. "You are leaving us." The statement contained no hint of a question.

Martha sighed. "Yes." She couldn't lie to her. Not now.

Sucking in her bottom lip, Effie lowered her head, suddenly intent on the task before her.

"I'm sorry." Guilt twisted Martha's heart. "I have to go. Please don't make me feel bad."

"Then take me with you." Hope glittered in Effie's eyes. "Do not abandon me to this awful place, I beg you."

"But I thought you liked it here?" Martha crouched down beside her. "This is your home."

"No." Effie shook her head. "Not without you. I wish only to serve you, m'lady."

Will she ever call me by my name?

"But I don't understand. Why would you choose service over freedom, Effie? There's a whole world out there, beyond this castle," she said, gesturing toward the window. "There is more to life than these four walls."

"True enough. But I am only a woman." Effie clasped Martha's hand. "Where would I go, all alone in this world of men? I have no husband to protect me. No. Service is the best I can hope for." She gave a smile that pricked Martha's heart. "And in serving you, I am most content with my lot."

It was the longest speech Martha had ever heard from the girl. What she said made sense. In this world, a lone woman was undeniably vulnerable. The liberation of women didn't exist here. Perhaps it never would. "What about your mother—your brothers?" Martha asked. "You aren't alone. You have a family back in Edgeway."

Effie shook her head. "My brothers are both wed, and with families of their own. My mother turned her back on me on the day I exchanged her roof for this castle; there is no going back now, she made that quite clear." Sadness radiated from the girl. "I saw Mother on the street in town only recently. I waved, but she turned away."

Oh, for fecksake. Effie was a grown woman, not a stray dog needing adoption. She decided to try another angle. Maybe the truth would work?

"What if I told you I'm about to do something Lord Edgeway won't like?" She lowered her voice. "What if I said that my friends are his enemies?"

Effie's eyes widened. "Really?" To Martha's surprise, the girl laughed, clapping her hands in apparent delight. "Oh, I hoped you would say so."

"But I thought you liked Anselm?" Martha said with a frown. "Just the sound of his name was enough to make you blush."

"Aye." Right on cue, the girl's cheeks reddened, but she seemed more embarrassed than besotted. "In the beginning, perhaps. But my infatuation lessened each time he locked the door. How could I continue to admire the man who holds my beloved mistress against her will?"

"The door's not locked now, is it?" *Damn.* That sounded like she was defending him.

"And what about these?" The maid lightly brushed her fingertips over the ripening bruises on Martha's neck. Her young eyes were suddenly so serious. "Do you imagine because I say nothing I do not see?"

Hot blood flushed Martha's cheeks. She adjusted her thin shawl, pulling it a little higher up her neck. *Hang on. Why the hell am I embarrassed?*

"How could I love any man capable of such cruelty?" Effie asked with a sad little smile.

"I-it's complicated..." *What am I saying?* Martha gave herself a much-needed mental shake.

Anselm had almost killed her. End of story. Why was she suddenly making excuses for him? She smiled, and shook her head. *What will I say next? That I pushed him to do it? I trapped my neck in a door? Fell down a flight of stairs? Wake up to yourself, woman.*

Pulling off her shawl, she threw it over a chair. "Actually, it's not complicated at all." She held her head up and met Effie's sympathetic eyes. So what if Anselm was now trying to protect her? After what he'd done, it was the very least he could do.

A series of light, hurried taps sounded at the outer door. Martha knew who it was, even as Effie reached for the latch. Fergus.

The lad's eyes widened when Effie answered the door. He raked one hand through his wild thatch of red hair, staring at Martha over the maid's shoulder. "Good evening, m'lady."

Martha's stomach flipped. The moment had finally come. "Is it time?" She sounded slightly breathless.

Fergus nodded, darting a suspicious look at Effie as she stepped away to gather Martha's belongings.

"Your maid," Fergus said in a low voice. "Can she be trusted?"

Martha retrieved her cloak from the chair by the door and swung it about her shoulders. "Fergus, meet Effie. Effie? Meet Fergus. I think you've met before?" She performed the introductions with the ease of a birthday-party hostess. "There. Now we're all properly acquainted—"

"She is not coming with us," Fergus protested. "I cannot allow it. My lord will be—"

"End of discussion, Fergus." Screw Vadim and what he wanted. "Don't worry, hon. When the time comes, I'll deal with *my lord.*"

A frisson of excitement tingled up Martha's spine. Even the thought of *dealing* with Vadim was enough to make her blood flow faster. Until that moment, she hadn't realized how much life in the castle had ground her down. The siege wasn't wholly to blame. The process had begun long before that.

Effie hovered uncertainly beside Martha, hugging the linen bundle tight to her chest.

"It seems I am outnumbered." Fergus glanced at the maid. "So be it."

However, he remained in the doorway, blocking it with his gangling body. Occasionally, he looked out into the corridor, head tilted, as though he was listening for something. The rest of the time, he studied Effie from beneath his eyelashes.

Martha enjoyed a budding romance as much as anyone, but the delay was getting unbearable. "Er, what exactly is it we're waiting for?"

A huge *boom* sounded from somewhere close by. The force of it caused one of Anselm's shields to fall from where it had been mounted on the wall. It hit the floor with a deafening clatter that made them jump.

Effie gave a squeak of fright and sidled closer to Martha.

"What the fecking hell was that?" Martha demanded, pressing a hand to her pounding chest.

"The signal." Fergus gave a gap-toothed grin. "Shall we go?"

chapter nineteen

A RANGE OF EMOTIONS WASHED OVER Martha as she left Anselm's rooms. Relief, guilt, sorrow, and joy competed within her heart. She watched Fergus close the door on a place that was now so familiar. It had been her prison, but it had been a home of sorts too. Whatever happened, she hoped she'd never see it again.

The explosion brought people running from their rooms and out into the corridor. Ladies in long nightdresses called to one another in fright. Sleepy-eyed servants hovered close to their mistresses, some attempting to console numerous bawling children. Most of the men were already outside defending the castle. The few that remained ran along the corridor, pulling on their clothes as they went, seemingly deaf to the pleas of their womenfolk to "be careful".

Another explosion. The corridor seemed to rock. *Shit!* Martha stumbled against Fergus. Several women screamed and clutched one another in alarm. Fergus set Martha back on her feet, then he strode away. Effie and Martha had to trot to keep up with his long-legged gait.

Mortar dust drifted in a thick and silent cloud, coating everything. Martha placed her hand over her mouth, but she was already crunching tiny particles of mortar between her teeth.

As they hurried along, pushing through the crowd, she caught fragments of panicked conversations:

"...there are many secret tunnels beneath the—"

"...and Robert says the devils must have undermined the walls!"

Fergus wove a swift path through the bystanders, heading for the servants' staircase at the far end of the corridor. Pausing beside the nondescript door, he waited for Martha and Effie to catch up. Without speaking, he grabbed a wall torch from its sconce then stepped inside the doorway.

The servants' staircase was much less grand than the main staircase used by the castle's noble guests. This dark and narrow passageway traveled to every floor of the castle, from basement to penthouse, transporting the servants to the rooms of the people they served.

Martha followed Effie through the doorway and closed the door behind them. The sounds of their rapid breaths echoed in the silence.

Fergus held the flickering torch aloft and looked back at them. "Take your time going down. These narrow treads can be perilous."

Martha and Effie arched their eyebrows at one another. They used this staircase every day. Had Fergus forgotten that Effie was a servant? Martha used the stairs almost as frequently, to minimize the risk of encountering His Evilness and Anselm on her jaunts around the castle. It did look different lit by torchlight. Servants usually carried candles to light the way.

Using the wall to guide her, Martha followed behind the others, carefully picking her way down the winding staircase. Fergus's torch bobbed as she walked, sinking lower in the spiraling darkness. Each breath sounded harsh and unnatural, amplified by the narrow space. They tip-tapped down the stone steps in silence. Strange shadows danced on the walls—weird, elongated figures that swayed with every step.

Effie gasped and slipped, stumbling into Fergus's back, almost knocking him over.

"Have a care!" Fortunately, he managed to steady them both before they tumbled down the remaining steps. Despite his irritated outburst, he rested a hand on Effie's shoulder, his eyes searching hers. "Are you injured?" he asked in a gentler tone.

Effie shook her head. "I f-felt a little dizzy for a moment, nothing more."

The torchlight's hypnotic effect was probably to blame. Looking directly at it made Martha's head feel strange, like a bunny in the headlights, unable to look away.

"Then take my hand, if you will," Fergus said. "I will not let you fall."

Without hesitating, Effie took his hand. Martha smiled to herself. Someone more suspicious might think Effie's "accident" was a little too well-timed, especially after Fergus's warning. Unfortunately, she couldn't see the girl's face, just the back of her head.

You'll keep until later, miss. She hadn't missed Effie's blushes back in Anselm's chambers when Fergus had been furtively checking her out.

A deep rumbling rose from the depths of the earth. From far away, distant cries and screams penetrated the tomb-like silence of the stairwell.

"What the hell is going on out there?" Martha whispered. *Why am I whispering? I haven't done anything wrong yet.*

"Rodmar's forces are undermining the wall beneath the postern gate," Fergus replied with a smile in his voice. "With any luck, it should have fallen."

"Undermining?" A memory jangled in the back of Martha's mind but she couldn't access it.

"The secret tunnels beneath the castle walls have been extended in places then packed with faggots of wood and barrels of pigs' fat." He grinned. "Then we set them ablaze." Holding Effie's hand had made Fergus uncharacteristically chatty. "When the wooden supports collapse, the walls should go down at the same time."

Martha nodded, recalling a long-ago history lesson back in the mists of her schooldays. "But how will that help? Walls or not, Rodmar's men still have a steep hill to climb before they reach the castle." To say nothing of the deep, earth-cut moat surrounding the outer wall. The archers would pick the invaders off as easily as ants from a picnic blanket. She frowned. "It's suicide."

"Perhaps." Fergus smiled, his teeth shining in the torchlight. Either he was completely heartless, or there was more going on than he was prepared to admit. "Shall we continue?"

They exited the gloom of the stairwell then hurried along the groundfloor corridor that ran the length of the keep. People in nightwear—mainly females and the elderly—clustered around the windows, staring outside with matching expressions of terrified fascination. Fires raged, flames of red and orange licking at the inky-black sky.

Only the children seemed unconcerned. They roamed the corridor in a rowdy pack, running and weaving through the milling crowd, laughing and calling to one another as they played a late-night game of tag. Martha smiled as two boys ducked behind one of the long tapestries that adorned the cold stone walls.

A woman's scream diverted her attention outside. She paused by the window just in time to see a streak of fire blaze across the night sky—like a meteor entering Earth's atmosphere. It was the stuff of an apocalyptic movie, but for real. Along with dozens of other people, she followed the fireball's trajectory and rapid descent.

Oh, dear God! A deep boom and a crescendo of shouts and screams indicated where the fiery comet had touched down.

"May the Spirits be merciful!" The old man standing beside Martha staggered back from the window, clutching his chest.

"Here." She slipped her arm about his frail, bony shoulders and guided him to a nearby bench. "Come and sit down. Catch your breath for a minute."

Fergus stalked back, scowling at her. "M'lady, we cannot afford to linger—"

"Go, then." She glared at him, not releasing her hold on the old man.

The more she saw of Rodmar's terror tactics, the less convinced she was of who the bad guys really were. *Fire-bombing kids and old people? Truly heroic.*

With a grunt of relief, the old man settled onto the bench. His face was gray and pinched with pain. Martha crouched before him, rubbing his cold hands. What if it was a heart attack? Thankfully, his face began to relax, losing its expression of contorted pain.

"Is that any better?" she asked softly. "Try and take a few slow, deep breaths." She ignored Fergus hovering beside her. "That's it." The man's breathing eased. "As you breathe out, try and imagine you're carrying a heavy basket in each hand." This visualization technique had always helped Aunt Lulu when she was suffering an asthma attack.

The old man closed his eyes and exhaled slowly. He looked

better already. Martha smiled. "That's really good. How's the pain now?"

"B-better," he muttered. "Thank you, my dear."

Fergus crouched beside her. "M'lady, we really must—"

"Father? Oh, no." A middle-aged woman pushed through the crowd. "What happened?"

Martha stood up, relinquishing her place to the old man's daughter. "The fire-bombs put the fear of God into him."

"He is not alone in that," the woman replied bitterly. She took off her cloak and flung it over the old man's shoulders then gave him a gentle hug. "Thank you for tending him." She sent Martha a tight smile. "I am grateful."

"No problem."

"Curse those devils outside. Come, Father. Let us return to our rooms."

Martha glanced at Fergus and arched her eyebrows. *Your precious Rodmar's not exactly winning any hearts and minds here tonight, is he?*

The lad's jaw tensed. Perhaps he understood. "We must go. Now," he said quietly.

After saying goodbye to the old man and his daughter, Martha got up and followed Fergus along the corridor. He stalked ahead, cloak swirling, without looking back.

"He is exceedingly vexed," Effie said, slipping her hand through Martha's arm. "I thought the two of you were friends?"

"I don't know who my friends are anymore," Martha muttered. "And that's the truth."

As they hurried across the entrance hall, past the foot of the castle's grand staircase, a loud, echoing voice froze Martha in her tracks.

"Ah! Mistress Bigalow. The very person I was seeking."

Oh, shit! His Evilness.

chapter twenty

MARTHA LOOKED UP AND SAW the earl descending the staircase, taking the steps two at a time in his haste to get to her.

Fergus wheeled around and grabbed her arm. "Go!" he said in an urgent whisper. "Make for the dungeons and find a place to hide." His young face suddenly seemed older than his years. "I will hold him at bay for as long as possible."

To her horror, he reached beneath his cloak and drew his sword, the shrill shriek of metal setting her teeth on edge. "What the hell do you think you're doing?" It was a silly question really.

Fergus stepped in front of her and faced the earl who had reached the landing of the final flight of stairs, his sword raised in challenge.

Sick with dread, Martha tugged on the back of his cloak. "Please don't do this." Oh, why hadn't she listened to him? Why the feck had she stopped to help that old man? No good deed ever went unpunished.

Fergus glanced over his shoulder. "Run," he whispered. With a last lingering look at Effie, he strode off to meet the earl.

His Evilness paused on the stairs, looking down his nose at his young challenger. "Insolent whelp. You dare to challenge me? But wait, your face is familiar." He tilted his head to one side, studying the lad more closely. "Ah! My harpist, no less. How novel." The earl chuckled and then swept the folds of his purple cloak over one shoulder, displaying the jeweled hilt of his ridiculous fancy sword. "Tell me, boy, how many other snakes lurk in the darkest corners of my hall, hmm?"

Fergus didn't answer. He stood motionless. Waiting.

"M'lady?" Effie slipped her hand into Martha's. "What shall we do?"

A small crowd had begun to gather, watching the scene unfold. Martha heard the murmurs of the people behind her, but her gaze remained fixed on Fergus. The earl might be a preening peacock, but according to Vadim he was a master swordsman. That poor lad didn't stand a chance against such an experienced opponent.

Judging by the tight set of his jaw, Fergus knew it too.

Martha let go of Effie's hand. She knew what she had to do. "Stay away from me, Effie," she said without looking at the girl. "Become my servant again. If His Evilness thinks we're friends, he'll kill you."

Without another word, she forced her trembling legs to go after Fergus.

She arrived too late. Teeth bared in a snarl, the earl drew his sword and raced raced down the last few stairs, launching himself at Fergus. "Outlaw scum."

Martha gasped and covered her face with her hands, watching the fight from between her splayed fingers. She wanted to look away, but she couldn't.

Just in time, Fergus raised his own sword and managed to deflect the vicious shower of blows raining down on him. His arm trembled beneath the savagery of the onslaught.

More spectators arrived, probably attracted by the clang and squeal of metal.

Although the earl was reputedly an expert swordsman, so far, he'd displayed little of his skill. "Accepting the gold from... my purse! Sleeping beneath... my roof..." His attack was more like a physical expression of his rage, wild and unpredictable.

Poor Fergus did well to block the flurry of frenzied cuts delivered by the earl's thinner, gaudier blade.

"Eating the food at my table..." The earl slipped on the train of his cloak, but instantly corrected his footing. "Drinking my wine..."

He took another ferocious swing at Fergus.

"Watch out!" Martha yelled, unable to stop herself.

As his enemy's sword descended, Fergus ducked behind the ornately carved upright at the bottom of the stairs. Instead of hitting him, the earl's blade embedded itself deep into the timber pillar with a dull *thunk*.

Muttering viciously beneath his breath, the earl planted his foot against the handrail and pulled, trying to free his sword. As he did so, Fergus thrust his own blade through the open balusters of the staircase. The earl gave an unmanly shriek and fell backward, sprawling onto the stairs, entangled by the folds of his voluminous purple cloak.

The spectators let out a collective, shocked, *ooh!*

Martha wanted to cheer, but instead she hurried to Fergus's side. He was breathing hard, his eyes fixed on his wounded opponent.

The earl was clutching his thigh, blood oozing between his fingers. With luck, his injury might prove fatal.

Martha placed her hand on Fergus's tense forearm. "Leave him," she murmured. "Get away while you still can."

Four knights were shouldering their way through the crowd. Swords drawn, their eyes locked on Fergus.

A faint smile flickered upon the lad's lips. "Abandoning you and my honor in the process? That I cannot do."

"Oh, screw your honor!" *I'm sick to the back teeth of fecking honor.* It was like a terrible disease in this world. No one was immune. Well, almost no one. The earl moaned feebly to himself as he secured a piece of purple cloak about his bloody thigh. Her eyes darted back to the advancing knights. "Will you just listen to me, Fergus?" she hissed. "Run. Now!"

The earl stopped whining and sat up. The look in his eyes was enough to give her the goosebumps—big ones. A shiver rippled along the length of her spine.

She tugged at Fergus's arm, but he wouldn't budge. Was he determined to die?

As the grim-faced knights came closer, His Evilness got up. Limping slightly, he had another go at freeing his sword from the staircase. This time, he was successful.

Martha's panic level spiked. In fierce whispers, she renewed her attack on Fergus, begging him to leave. She might as well have saved her breath. The stupid boy was hell-bent on his kamikaze honor mission.

"You have courage, boy. I will give you that." The earl limped down the stairs, halting the advancing knights with a brief shake of his head. "Not many living men can claim to have bloodied me." He walked toward them, stopping just short of the point of Fergus's sword.

His cold shark's smile liquefied Martha's bowels.

"How unfortunate," he continued, "you swore fealty to the wrong side."

Fergus remained calm. Not even a hint of a blush stained his cheeks. "I do not agree, m'lord." His voice never wavered. "I chose the side with honor as its standard, integrity as its sword, and truth as its shield." He smiled. "And to my promise I hold. Even now, I do not regret it."

Martha's jaw dropped. She'd seriously misjudged him—this man-child. While she trembled and quaked like a blade of grass in the wind, Fergus faced death with unimaginable bravery.

The least she could do was not make him ashamed.

She took his free hand, entwining her fingers with his. After a brief hesitation, he gave her clammy hand a gentle squeeze.

Martha raised her chin and looked directly at the earl. Maybe she could buy them some more time. "What did you want to see me about, m'lord?"

The earl's eyes narrowed, fixed on their clasped hands. "Ah, yes. *That.*" He took a step forward but retreated when Fergus raised the tip of his sword. "I understand your husband has miraculously risen from the dead."

"Really?" She kept her face neutral. Who'd told him? Despite everything, her money was still on Anselm. *Damn him.* "Are you sure?"

"The news came from a most reliable source."

"Oh." *Definitely Anselm. The two-faced tosser.*

"Well? Are you not relieved, my dear? You do not seem very heartened by my glad tidings."

"That'll be the shock—"

"Or, perhaps you already knew?" The earl examined the handle of his sword and frowned. "Perhaps you always knew?" Using his cloak, he buffed the glittering stones set in the pommel of his sword.

So maybe Anselm hadn't betrayed her. If he had, the earl would already know the full story, and he wouldn't be wasting time questioning her now.

This thought made her smile more genuinely at him. "Will you set me free so I can go to him?"

The earl chuckled, but his pale blue eyes were devoid of amusement. "I wish I could, my dear. Unfortunately, I have other plans for you."

Her smile faded, and she clutched Fergus's hand a little tighter. "S-such as?"

"Bait, or insurance? I have not yet decided which." The earl began pacing the entrance hall, swiping with his sword at imaginary foes, his wound apparently forgotten. He seemed oblivious to their ever-increasing audience.

"And what about my friend here?" Martha indicated Fergus with a jerk of her head. "What's going to happen to him?"

The earl paused to glance at Fergus. "Oh, he will die... eventually." He grinned. "And no doubt screaming for his mother, as they all do." He treated them to a dazzling display of fancy footwork before lunging at an invisible enemy. Then he straightened up, looking very pleased with himself.

Martha eyed him with disgust. *God, you're a really sick puppy.*

Fergus, bless his brave heart, only laughed. "I have no fear of death, m'lord. When I arrive at the Hall of the Ancestors, my worthy mother will be there to welcome me."

"Indeed?" The earl stopped dancing around. "Then we shall all be content with the outcome. Most satisfactory all round." Suddenly, his expression went blank. The performing clown show was over. "Lower your weapon, boy," he growled. "The time for jest has passed. Resist me any further, and I will cut you down where you stand."

Martha chewed her lip until she tasted blood. There was no way out. No matter which way they stepped, death was waiting. She glanced about the silent spectators, seeking a familiar face in the sea of strangers. She couldn't even see Effie. Not that it really made a difference.

Fergus cleared his throat. "So be it." With that, he slipped his hand from Martha's.

Her heart gave a sickening lurch. "What the feck are you doing?" she hissed. But the answer was all too obvious.

With a brief bow of his head, Fergus raised his sword and moved toward the earl.

His Evilness swept him theatrical bow then raised his own weapon. He slowly advanced, circling Fergus like a purple vulture.

Outside, the sounds of the war machines continued their soundtrack of death. Breathing fast, Martha willed Rodmar's trebuchets to hit something close by. Surely, nothing else would save Fergus now.

She could have slipped away, lost herself in the crowd. No one would notice. The knights had put away their swords. Like everyone else, their eyes were fixed on the two combatants. It would be easy to escape.

But she couldn't leave Fergus alone—not that he was aware of her. The earl claimed all of his attention. She might not be able to save him, but if death was his fate, she'd make sure he didn't die alone in a hall full of enemies.

The earl suddenly went turbo. Fergus did well to evade his opponent's rapid succession of cuts and thrusts. He retreated, beaten back by so many savage blows. The constant ringing of metal sounded oddly musical as it echoed throughout the hallway.

Fergus stumbled and almost fell. Martha gasped, certain that the end had come, but the lad regained his balance and fought on. Fought! He had yet to deliver a single blow. He was too hard pressed defending himself to have the opportunity to attack. Always in retreat, Fergus reversed toward her. She was forced to climb several steps of the staircase to avoid getting in the way of their swords.

But the earl wasn't having it all his own way. He might be the better swordsman, but his age was against him. As the fight progressed, sweat rolled down his face. At length, he lowered his sword and took a step back, obviously in need of a breather.

"Not bad, boy. Someone has obviously taken the trouble to instruct you. Come." He swiped the back of his hand over his sweaty face. "You have earned a free shot at me." He opened his arms wide, exposing his gold-embroidered tunic. "Strike me down, if you can."

The knights sniggered and nudged one another. Although they were amused, they didn't look surprised. Neither did the crowd. A loud muttering traveled the length of the hall. To Martha's disgust, she heard the jingling of money. *They're placing bets?*

Now she understood the earl's delaying tactic. This was nothing new, it was expected. A way to heighten his kicks before he delivered the killing stroke.

What could she do? She clutched the banister, her mind reeling as it searched for a way out of this godawful mess. Fergus might be brave, but even to her untrained eye he was totally outclassed.

She became aware of the weight of Vadim's knife in her pocket. Maybe if she got close enough she could stab the earl? The thought of plunging sharp metal into his soft flesh made her feel slightly sick. But if push came to shove, could she do it? If she hesitated for a second, she'd be dead before Fergus.

"Come on, my fine young fellow," the earl said, softly taunting Fergus. "Take your chance." He twirled in a slow circle, arms open wide. "No doubt your outlaw friends would leap at the invitation."

"Don't do it, Fergus!" Martha yelled from the safety of the stairs. "Don't give him what he wants."

The earl spun about, fixing her with his most toxic glare. "Be silent, you duplicitous whore! I will deal with you later."

"Is this how you get your jollies, killing children?" she demanded, leaning on the banister for support. "Ooh! Most impressive. Not!"

"I am not a child," Fergus said with a scowl.

She ignored him. Hurting the boy's feelings was preferable to seeing him dead.

The earl shrugged. "You heard his words as well as I, m'lady. Honor demands I afford him the same courtesy as any man who crosses me."

"You could try showing a little mercy for a change. Save yourself for a worthier opponent."

"Such as your husband, I assume?" The earl laughed. "Even this boy could best him," he said, nodding toward Fergus. "Your beloved Lord Hemlock lost his edge a long time ago, and now he has lost his wife too. Most careless of him."

This provoked another ripple of laughter from the crowd.

Martha, however, was far from amused. Her cheeks glowed hot. Maybe it was time they all learned the truth.

"He cut you down once, remember?" she said softly, once the merriment had died down. "Believe me, he can do it again."

That wiped the smile from the earl's arrogant face. He definitely didn't want reminding of that particular day, and certainly not in public.

"You poor deluded creature," he sneered as he moved toward the stairs. "Our paths have crossed many times since that day, and yet Hemlock has done me no further harm. Why should that be, hmm? He has certainly had the opportunity." The shark's smile was back. "I believe he has not the courage to confront me. Your husband…" He spoke so low, she had to strain to hear him. "Is a fraud and a coward."

Fergus raised his sword. "How dare you speak such—"

"Fergus!" Martha yelled. "Keep still, shut up, and listen."

The boy's eyes flashed with a rage to match her own, but he backed down, enabling her to concentrate on His Evilness.

"You're wrong, m'lord." Desperation made her break the confidence Vadim had shared with her so long ago. If he ever learned of it, she hoped he'd forgive her. "The only reason you're still alive is because of the promise Vadim gave his sister before she died."

"Lissy?" The mention of his dead wife leeched the color from the earl's face. He almost dropped his sword and fumbled to catch it before it hit the flagstone floor.

Fergus gave an irritated huff and went to lean on the banister at the bottom of the stairs.

The crowd fell silent, and a deathly hush descended on the hallway. Every pair of eyes were trained on the earl, waiting to see his reaction.

"I-I think," he said at length, "you had better explain yourself, madam."

Martha took a deep breath. She was in too deep now; she might as well tell him. "Lissy made him promise not to hurt you—"

"Liar!" The earl pointed a trembling finger at her, his eyes like splinters of blue glass. "She would never—"

"But she did! That's how much she loved you. God knows why!"

"Hold your tongue."

But she couldn't. Not now. "You butchered her family in cold blood and left Vadim for dead with your arrow wedged in his body." The mental image of his brutality made her blood boil. Caution, be damned. "He was only a little boy. What kind of man are you?" She shook her head, tears blurring her eyes. "And despite all this, Lissy loved you. Personally, I think she must have had a major problem in her attic." She tapped the side of her head with her finger to emphasize her meaning.

"How dare you besmirch her memory!" The earl's color returned. His face glowed crimson, incandescent with rage.

"Me?" Martha snort-laughed. "You do that all by yourself, every single day, you stupid man."

"M'lord?"

Anselm's voice forestalled whatever reply the earl had been about to make, which was probably a good thing, all things considered. With more than a little relief, Martha watched him walk through the crowd, Sir Hugh at his side.

"Enemy forces are massing near the postern gate..." Anselm's glance flicked from Martha, to Fergus and back to the earl. "What has happened?"

For once, His Evilness didn't look pleased to see him. "Why are you here? Your orders were to lead the charge on the enemy's castle-breakers."

"And so I will. But the breach in the back wall is too severe. It needs shoring up. The enemy force stands poised to attack and only lacks the command to do so."

"Our troop is short of men." Sir Hugh looked pointedly at the knights who'd been watching the earl's fight with Fergus. "The soldiers outside are in great want of leadership. I think your time would be better spent elsewhere, m'lords."

The knights looked at the earl, but he only shook his head, so the men remained where they were.

"Return to your duties, Anselm," the earl commanded in a cold clear voice. "Do what you can to prevent the inevitable. There is nothing for you here."

"I disagree, m'lord," Anselm replied. "Why does my future bride stand there so pale and still, and who is this boy?" He shook his head. "No, sire. Whatever this is, I am involved up to my neck."

Martha held her breath. Thank God he'd come. But what would he say when he learned she'd planned to escape with Fergus? Would he still defend her then? She wasn't hopeful. Anselm's reactions were always unpredictable. Relying on his protection was about as safe as a game of Russian roulette.

The earl gave a mocking little smile. "As you are only too aware, your future *bride* is already married, and her husband still lives and breathes. Please, let there be no more lies between us, my *friend*. I caught her ready to flee the castle in the company of this... outlaw cub." He wafted his hand in Fergus's direction. "What do you say to that, hmm?"

Anselm's jaw tightened, and his eyes sought Martha's. "Is this true?" he demanded.

She opened her mouth to speak, but the words stuck in her dry throat. Instead, she gave a noncommittal shrug.

"Answer me, damn you!" Eyes glinting dangerously, Anselm strode for the stairs, but Fergus leapt into action and stepped into his flight path, standing between him and Martha. The sword trembled in his hand in the face of the fury emanating from his new adversary.

Anselm unsheathed his own sword.

"Anselm, no!" Martha cried, her heart almost hammering through her chest.

Without slowing up, he lashed out at Fergus and knocked the weapon from his hand. The sword crashed to the flagstones, spinning and skittering wildly over the uneven surface. But before Fergus had time to react, Anselm was upon him. Grabbing the back of the lad's neck, he smashed his head against the ornately carved wooden upright at the foot of the stairs. There was a loud echoing *thunk*, and Fergus crumpled lifeless to the floor.

Another chorus of *oohs* rose from the spectators.

"You bastard!" Martha edged her way up the stairs, breathing fast. A wave of dizziness struck her, and blackness hovered at the periphery of her vision. *Don't you dare faint. Oh, poor Fergus!* Was he dead? *Please don't be dead.*

chapter twenty-one

ANSELM PAUSED AT THE FOOT of the stairs, staring up at Martha. His face was as emotionless as a shop mannequin's.

"Well played, indeed." The earl tucked his sword beneath his arm and applauded, beaming in delight. He turned to the knights. "See if the lad still breathes."

One of the knights clanked over to Fergus, bending stiffly in his metal suit. "He lives, m'lord."

Martha closed her eyes and exhaled hard.

"Excellent!" His Evilness sounded happy about it too, but probably not for the same reasons. "Take him to a cell. Oh, and treat him gently. We shall have much to discuss when he wakes."

Martha's relief at hearing Fergus was alive didn't last. Not only was the poor lad now a prisoner, by the sound of it, he was about to become the earl's new favorite plaything. Death might have been a better outcome.

A rumble of conversation rippled through the crowd. To Martha's disgust, more money changed hands. Was everyone in this fecking castle sick and twisted? Clutching her skirt in her hand, she turned and fled up the stairs.

Before she reached the first landing, Anselm roughly grabbed her arm and spun her about to face him. "Where are you off to, m'lady?"

"Let go of me!" Hampered by the heavy folds of her gown, she aimed a kick at his legs. "Ow." A pulse of hot pain flashed in her toes. His shins were protected by armor plates. Anselm dragged her up the stairs, but she continued to struggle.

"Be still, you hellion," he growled.

When they reached the second landing, Anselm paused to lean over the banister, addressing the earl who remained in the entrance hall below. "Perhaps Sir Hugh might have the honor of leading the company in my stead, m'lord?" he called in a loud voice. "I will deal with the threat at the postern gate the moment I return." He glanced at Martha and smiled. "My business with m'lady will not take long."

The earl stood at the bottom of the stairs, his hand pressed to his wounded thigh. "As you wish, my friend. But do not kill her. Not yet, at least." The sound of the dispersing crowd almost drowned out his voice. "I may have a use for her before the end comes."

Anselm inclined his head. "As you command, m'lord."

Tears slipped down Martha's face. Everything had gone to hell.

Fergus lay face down and motionless on the floor. As she watched, two knights raised him and dragged him away, red hair trailing across the flagstones. His long legs flopped in a lifeless V behind him, reminding her of a rag doll she'd had as a child.

Then she saw something else, something that ignited a spark of hope in her heart. Effie stepped out from the mass of people and looked up, meeting Martha's eyes. She gave a tiny smile then hurried after Fergus. *Good girl!*

"Go on." Anselm released his death grip on Martha's arm and gave her a rough shove. "Move!" He made her walk ahead, herding her down the corridor directly ahead of them.

What could she say to calm him? Surely there was another way out of this that didn't involve pain and dying? Her mind reeled. She was too shell-shocked to think clearly.

A smooth metallic scrape told her Anselm had replaced his sword in its sheath. That was a small comfort.

"Turn left here."

Martha obeyed his curt command, still wracking her brain for a solution. But all she could come up with were lots of graphic images of all the awful ways in which she might be tortured.

Another of Rodmar's missiles struck nearby, making the floor shudder, but Martha didn't flinch. Death by trebuchet now seemed like a soft option.

"Wait here a moment, sweeting."

Huh? Martha turned around, stunned by Anselm's gentle tone.

He walked back along the corridor they'd so recently traveled and peered around the corner. "We are safe enough now, I think," he said with a grin. "Did I frighten you, m'lady?"

What the...? Martha blinked several times. Had she misheard him? No, he was still smiling. His face bore none of its previous hardness.

He'd been acting all along? *Un-fecking-believable.* Relief flooded her body in a warm and heavy wave. Suddenly, her legs sagged, refusing to support her for another second.

She slid down the wall and slumped inelegantly to the floor. Anselm crouched down in front of her, concern shining in his eyes.

"Are you hurt?" He stroked back her tangled hair. "Answer me, sweeting."

"I'm fine." *Lord, but I'm tired though.* The urge to rest her forehead on Anselm's metal breast-plate was too tempting to resist. She closed her eyes and let her head slump forward. The metal felt cool, soothing on her skin.

Cradling the back of her head in his hand, Anselm rested his cheek against her hair. "I am sorry I was rough. My master is not an easy man to fool."

"Well, you certainly fooled me," she muttered. It felt good to surrender, to rely on the strength of another, if only for a few brief moments.

"What on Erde were you doing back there?"

"Trying to stop Fergus from being killed."

"Not very successfully." Anselm cupped her face in his hands and looked into her eyes. "Had I not intervened, you would both be dead by now. No one is allowed to mention the earl's lost wife—not even I. I am surprised your husband failed to tell you this."

"Why would he?" She summoned a bitter smile. "Neither of us planned on me becoming one of His Lordship's long-term house guests."

"Be that as it may, you and the lad were both damnably foolish. Come on." He helped her to her feet. "We must not linger here."

They set off walking again. Anselm covered her hand with his as it rested on the crook of his arm.

"Will Fergus be all right?" she asked, unable to shake the vision of the boy being dragged away.

"Apart from a very bad headache when he wakes up, I expect he will make an excellent recovery. The pity is, his plan to get you out of here failed. Now I must think of something else, and quickly."

Martha glanced at him. "You aren't angry?"

"Should I be?"

"But I left without saying goodbye."

Anselm smiled. "To my mind, our final conversation was a goodbye of sorts. Did I not tell you I would rather see you back with Vadim than dead?"

Martha pretended she hadn't noticed him use Vadim's name. "So if you didn't tell the earl about Vadim, who did?"

"How well it must have suited you to believe me guilty." He chuckled. "Anselm the demon! Tell me, sweeting, was I your *only* suspect?"

"Of course you were." She shoulder-barged him as they walked, making him stagger. "And you can drop the wounded expression, my friend. It doesn't suit you at all."

"Unfeeling witch." But his smile remained. "To answer your question, 'twas Sir Hugh who spilled his guts to the king. Hugh is a good man, but he can be a royal dunderhead on occasion. Almost as soon as we returned, the poor fool informed our masters of my ill-advised remarks whilst we were playing emissary at Rodmar's encampment. I expect it never occurred to him that I might want the truth concealed." Anselm snorted with laughter. "It certainly never occurred to me—not until I confronted you with my discovery." His face became suddenly serious. "Can you ever forgive me for what I did to you, I wonder?"

She became aware of the bruising on her throat again, like brutal ghostly fingers pressing into her skin. The moment he'd almost strangled her to death wasn't a moment she was keen to relive. Avoiding his eyes, she glanced through one of the windows. The skyline had lightened. Dawn wasn't far away.

"Your silence is eloquent enough." Anselm sighed. "I will say no more on the subject and bear my guilt as best I may."

Oh, for heaven's sake! "Let's just forget about it." Anything was better than his sackcloth-and-ashes routine. The role of St. Anselm didn't suit him at all. "If you get me out of here, we'll call it even."

Anselm squeezed her hand. "Hugh may be a fool but he is a harmless one," he said, swiftly changing the subject. "I can detect no malice in his make up. In fact, I confess to having grown rather fond of him over recent days. Thank Erde he was privy to my master's discussion with the king. Old Hugh was greatly troubled by it."

"What were they saying?"

He shrugged. "Only what you might expect. That you had turned my head and poisoned my loyalty." Suddenly, Anselm wouldn't meet her eyes. He glanced out of the window at the breaking dawn. "My master intended to deal with you whilst I was occupied with the attempt to destroy the enemy's castle-breakers."

Martha shivered. What would have happened if Anselm hadn't come back? What if he'd ridden away to do his lord's bidding? Although things were bad enough now, they might have been a hell of a lot worse.

"If Hugh had not—" He stopped walking and froze. "Hush!" He glanced behind.

Martha couldn't hear anything. She was about to say so when Anselm pressed his gloved index finger to her lips. With his head tilted to one side, listening, he put her in mind of a golden Labrador. Seconds later, they were on the move again, hurrying down another long corridor lined with more dusty, sun-faded tapestries.

"Where are we going, anyway?" She had no idea where they were.

"That, I cannot say. I had hoped our walk might inspire me."

Learning he didn't have some cunning plan or other up his sleeve didn't exactly fill her with confidence.

They paused by another small window and looked out onto the courtyard below, and Anselm fell silent. In the pre-dawn light, the devastation was apparent. The castle's outer wall contained more holes than bricks.

There would be no sun today. Menacing clouds hung in a thick, heavy drape that robbed the world of color. As they watched, a troop of mounted knights clattered toward the gate, jumping their horses over the worst of the rubble.

"May the Ancestors ride with you, my friends," Anselm said softly. "I pray Rodmar is more merciful than our own masters have been." He shook his head as if to dispel ugly images within his mind. Then, his eyes cleared, and he looked at Martha again. "The lad—Fergus? Where was he taking you before you encountered the earl?"

Should she tell him? Could Anselm really be trusted?

She wavered, but only for a second. "The dungeons. He told me to hide down there. I don't know what he planned after that."

"The dungeons?" Anselm raked back his hair with a careless hand. "They must be using another of the old tunnels to get inside." A tiny smile played upon his lips. "Clever thinking, my brother."

My brother? Who—Vadim?

"That will have to do." Anselm was himself again, brisk and full of action. "Come along, sweeting. Time nips at our heels."

For the second time that night—or morning—Martha found herself negotiating the perils of the servants' staircase. This time, Anselm was her guide. With her hand in his, she followed him down the steep steps. Flames from the torch he carried danced and reflected off his armor, dazzling her.

Anselm was actually helping. Maybe he could be trusted after all. Perhaps there was still some hope for him.

"I will hide you as best I can, then I must return to my duties, or Lord Edgeway will suspect me."

"What?" Martha stopped in her tracks, unable to believe what she was hearing. "Surely you aren't going to continue defending this castle?"

Anselm paused and turned to look at her. "I must."

"B-but why? It's going to fall soon. You've seen the size of Rodmar's army." She waved her arm in the general direction of where it could be found. "When they get in here, they'll kill you along with everyone else."

"Yes. I rather fear they will."

His calmness made her seethe. "Just let it go. Come with me, Anselm." Her voice sounded excited, breathless, in the echoing stairwell. "You could have another crack at life. Don't turn your back on it now."

"And be beholden to my *brother*?" His smile looked weary. "Would you have me abandon the little honor I have remaining?

That I cannot do, not even for you, my sweet. Come. Have a care over this step, it is a little uneven."

Martha clasped his hand and followed him down the steps again. *Honor again!* It was such a nice-sounding word, so good and wholesome. But in her experience, it left a rather nasty aftertaste.

"Who have you sworn loyalty to?" she asked. "The earl?"

"Of course. To him and, in turn, to the king."

"But by helping me, you've already broken your oath—"

"Lord Edgeway is my liege lord," Anselm answered firmly. "He took me in when everyone else turned away. In exchange for my fealty, I gained a home and position." He chuckled. "I cannot claim he is always the perfect master, but he has been a better father to me than the one who shares my blood."

In her mind, Martha pictured Seth's kindly, bearded face. How could Anselm possibly compare the earl to him? Then she recalled Vadim's account of Anselm's fall from grace, when Seth's personal honor code had driven him to disown his only son. They were all as bad as each other, if they only knew it.

A chink of light indicated the end of the stairwell, but Martha wasn't ready to leave it yet. The dark, narrow confines made an excellent confessional booth. It reminded her of the one in her church back home, small and dimly lit. Maybe truth was shy and preferred semi-darkness to reveal itself.

"Wait." She stopped walking again and tugged on Anselm's hand. "Why not give Seth another chance? He might surprise you, you know."

Shaking his head, Anselm looked away. "In his eyes, I killed my mother. That is something he will never forgive, and I cannot blame him for it." He shoved the flickering torch into a wall sconce then wheeled round to face her. "If only I had kept my mouth shut. If only I had helped her escape. If only she had not taken those accursed berries. If only." He sighed heavily. "Truly they are the saddest words."

The sorrow in his eyes tore at her heart. Martha exhaled a trembling breath and forgave him on the spot. The manner of Sylvie's death had played a large part in her antipathy toward him. Now, even that barrier was gone, and she was glad. Anselm was still an arse, but he wasn't quite so black as she'd once believed.

"Then, tell him. Tell Seth the truth; I'll back you up."

"Would you?" His teeth shone white in the torchlight. "Thank you, my sweet."

Hope flared in her chest. "So you'll do it?"

"No." He took her hand and raised it to his lips. "But your offer to stand at my side means more than you can imagine. Now, we really must go."

They hurried down the remaining steps. When they reached the bottom, Anselm pushed open the door that led to the ground floor.

He stopped so suddenly that Martha ran into the back of him. She peered around his body and saw the reason why. *Oh, shit!* Six well-armed knights were waiting for them, their eyes as steely as their shiny swords.

chapter twenty-two

NSELM PUSHED MARTHA BEHIND HIM. "What is this?" he asked brightly. "An escort? I am most honored, my friends, but it is hardly necessary."

Martha clung to the back of his cloak, peering over his shoulder. There was no answering smile from the knights. No one spoke. Her heartbeat sounded loud in the thick silence.

"Step aside at once." Anselm made a motion to walk by, but a thicket of glittering sword points herded him back towards the doorway. "By whose authority do you detain me against my will?"

"By mine." The knights parted, and Lord Edgeway limped through their midst.

"My lord? B-but why? I do not understand." Anselm sounded genuinely confused.

"Oh, Anselm." The earl shook his head as he halted before them. "You have wounded me most grievously, my friend. I fear I may never recover from the blow you have dealt me this day."

Martha rolled her eyes. *Oh, please. Someone pass me a bucket.* If the situation hadn't been so dire, she would've laughed. His words were as sincere as a politician's promise on election day.

Anselm stepped forward, hands raised in supplication. "M'lord, I cannot imagine what—"

"Be silent!" The earl shouted so loudly even the knights were startled. Their armor made a collective rattle of surprise. "No more lies, Anselm. Not from you." His voice fell to a murmur. "You, who have been my most faithful companion for so many years."

In the depths of the earl's cold, pale eyes, Martha thought she saw a glimmer of real sorrow, then it was gone again.

"And for what?" the earl continued. "The slut of your sworn enemy? A woman polluted by his touch?" He glared at Martha.

She flinched from both his words and the naked hatred in his eyes.

"I should have slit your throat back in Edgeway," he growled. "At least I might have spared myself this bitter day."

"Oh come, m'lord." Anselm used his most winning tone. "Surely you cannot think I meant to betray you? How could I even consider it after all the weary roads we have traveled together?"

Anselm might as well have saved his breath.

His Evilness turned to the captain of the knights. "Hold him," he commanded, "And bring that bitch to me."

As the knights moved in, Anselm pressed back, half crushing Martha against the door of the staircase. He tried to grab his sword, but too many hands reached for him. "Come now, Richard! Edmund? If you would only allow me to speak, the matter could be cleared up in an instant. See reason, I beseech you!"

But the knights paid no attention and dragged Anselm away from the door.

Martha trembled. She felt exposed, vulnerable. What would they do to her?

Once Anselm had been secured—shouting and struggling some distance away—the knights' captain resheathed his sword and extended a gloved hand toward Martha. "If you will, m'lady."

She shook her head, and held her hands against her chest, frantically seeking an escape route. There was only one, the door they'd so recently used. In one quick movement, she spun around and yanked the door open, but the knight grabbed her wrist before she set foot inside the doorway. It'd been a vain hope anyway.

"This way please, m'lady." The man's touch wasn't cruel.

"Martha. No!" Anselm fought against his captors in earnest, barging and struggling to escape. "Release me, you fetid dogs! The crows shall feast on your balls before this day is out!"

It was no use. The knights held him too firmly.

As she walked by, Martha met his wild eyes and held their gaze for as long as possible. Anselm represented safety now. Without him, she was screwed.

Impatient to claim his prize, the earl marched toward her.

Martha yelped as he grabbed her hair and wound a thick skein of it about his hand. Raising her hands, she pressed them upon his fist as it tightened against her scalp. She felt her hair snapping, strand by agonizing strand. Pain rendered her speechless.

"You are as slippery as a whore's undergarments, Mistress Bigalow," he hissed against her ear. "Ah! But I have you now."

"Unhand her, m'lord!" Anselm struggled so violently he managed to unbalance one of the knights. The man clattered to the ground like a set of saucepans dropped from a great height.

The earl only increased his grip on Martha's hair. She gasped, tears stinging her eyes, her guts icy with fear. This was it. She was going to die.

"Am I hurting you, my dear?" His Evilness pressed his stubbly face against her cheek. "Good." He jerked her head around, forcing her to look at Anselm. "See what you have reduced him to." He yanked her hair again, making her cry out. "Look at him, you cunning bitch!"

Whimpering, she did as the earl commanded, clutching at his hand in an attempt to ease the white-hot pain of her scalp.

Anselm fought and bellowed like a demented bull. It took all of the knights to restrain her brave defender.

"Your spell has been the ruin of him, witch. Too late did I heed the signs, and now I pay dearly for my negligence. Anselm was mine. *Mine.*" Another vicious tug on her hair. "You have robbed me of my most loyal companion. Perhaps when you are gone, his intoxication will pass."

She couldn't answer. Couldn't think. Only pain and a primal fear remained, but the earl more than made up for her gasping silence.

"I underestimated your influence, Mistress Bigalow. Be assured, it will not happen again. Come along." With that, he dragged her away down the corridor.

Martha whimpered like a dog on a too-tight leash, the unwilling puppet of a madman. She wanted to vomit. The end was drawing closer, and a terror greater than anything she'd ever known had her in its grasp. His Evilness was way beyond dangerous. He was a man with nothing left to lose.

"Damn you!" Anselm sounded desperate. Fearful even. "Where are you taking her?"

The earl kept walking. "It is time I discovered just how valuable this drab little bird of yours really is."

Panting with pain, Martha trotted alongside the earl as they swept along the corridor. His hand remained snarled in her hair. Suffering rendered her docile and biddable, quenching the hot coals of rage.

They encountered a group of chattering women. Still dressed in their nightwear, they resembled a flock of white birds. The earl slowed up.

"Pardon us, ladies." He smiled appreciatively at the women when they stepped aside to let them pass. "Although, I confess, I have never been delayed by a fairer blockade."

Sleazy git!

The women drew their shawls tighter about their bodies and fell silent, watching Martha and the earl with ill-concealed curiosity.

Martha met the eyes of a gray-haired, motherly-looking woman, perhaps the eldest of the group. *Please help me!* She mouthed. But the woman only looked away and moved closer to her companions. No one challenged him. A swell of giggles and excited whispers followed in their wake.

They left the keep by the main door and stepped out into the pale dawn. Martha shivered as the cool air touched her fevered skin. She inhaled, ridding her lungs of the earl's cloying scent—an unpleasant combination of wet dogs, body odor, and lavender.

He paused and took a deep breath. "Is there any sweeter scent than that of the morning air? What do you think of that sky?" He yanked roughly on Martha's hair, pulling her head back until her chin jutted skyward. "Not very promising, is it?"

Her breathing was a series of shallow pained gasps, and her neck felt ready to snap. Hot tears slid from the corners of her eyes and dripped into her ears. She could have begged for mercy, but that would only amuse the sick bastard. It wouldn't help her cause in the slightest.

"Would you object if we made a brief stop on the way?" The earl spoke as if they were out on some pleasure jaunt together.

"I need to see how they fare at the postern gate before our path is decided."

The path to where?

Thankfully, the brutal tension on her scalp eased, and her head was allowed to resume a more natural position. The earl dragged her across what remained of the courtyard. It now resembled a demolition site, covered with shattered masonry from the defensive wall and outbuildings.

Martha stumbled and slipped as they negotiated the shifting mounds of rubble. It was difficult to stay on her feet.

The trebuchets of both sides lay silent now—no more creaking or crashing, no more agonized screams. For what seemed the first time in forever, she heard birdsong, and the sound of it pierced her heart. Her throat constricted with the effort of holding back more tears. She couldn't recall a sweeter or sadder sound.

"It appears Sir Hugh has managed to subdue Rodmar's castle-breakers," the earl said in the same conversational tone as before. "An excellent man, that. Oh, to be sure, he can be rather dull at times, but his devotion to duty is without question."

Yeah? So why did he give Anselm the heads-up, you pompous fuckwit?

"Perhaps if my liege lord, the king, does not object, I may offer him a permanent place in my household. Might he be persuaded to accept, do you think?"

Martha stumbled over a chunk of stone and went over on her ankle. Unable to stop herself, she fell to her knees with a pained yelp. Her knees burned almost as fiercely as her scalp— she was sure she'd just lost another clump of hair.

"Whoops! Up you get." The earl yanked her back on her feet and kept walking. "But, my dear, you never expressed your thoughts on Sir Hugh," he reproached her mildly. "After all, I will need a replacement for poor Anselm."

She glanced at him. Was he actually serious? *Jesus H. Christ!* After dragging her halfway round the fecking castle by her hair roots, he wanted to hear what she thought? Martha trembled, but not with fear this time.

Some imaginary switch had flicked to the *on* position inside her brain. *Furious* didn't cover it. Neither did *livid*. A runaway train was taking her emotions for a ride, and it was accelerating. Heat bloomed in her stomach and spread, until every nerve ending tingled. She'd hit that sweet spot where pain and regret didn't exist.

His Evilness wanted to know what she thought? Fine! She was so sick and tired of being afraid all the time. Of course, her courage wouldn't last. She'd pay for it afterward, and it was going to hurt. A lot. But at that moment, she felt like a fecking gladiator.

"You want to know what I think?" Taking a deep breath, she told him. "If there's any justice in this world, you'll be dead before the day is out. Very soon, you won't be in a position to offer anyone anything, *m'lord*. Not Hugh. Not Anselm. No one. *That's* what I think, you pathetic, twisted little scrote-sac!" For her finale, she dug her fingernails into the earl's wrist as it rested on top of her head, and had the satisfaction of seeing him flinch.

"Indeed? Well, that is certainly candid enough, I grant you." The earl stopped walking, his upper lip raised in a parody of a smile. "But be that as it may, I am sure to outlive you, m'lady."

This time, the threat in his glacial eyes didn't affect her. This time, Martha stared him down. It was a small victory, but intoxicating all the same.

"Perhaps Anselm will rally once you are gone," the earl said as he looked away. "Yes. I am certain that he will."

Now it was awake, her inner demon didn't give a shit. Hearing the earl mention her death didn't faze her at all. She wanted to hurt him. Badly. And she didn't need a weapon or her freedom to do it.

"You won't get him back, you know," she taunted him softly. "Anselm is mine now, whether you kill me or not."

"Oh?" The earl's eyes narrowed, and the tension on her hair increased. "Are you so certain of his devotion to you?"

"Yes," she said quietly. "I am." Knowing she'd wounded him heightened her buzz.

Without speaking another word, the earl dragged her on. They were nearing the back of the castle complex, and a rhythmic *thump-thumping* guided them through a drifting curtain of smoke. It was much noisier here. The bailey was crammed with soldiers, calling to one another as they carried stones and lumber toward the back gate.

The earl finally disentangled his fingers from Martha's hair.

Then, giving her a shove, he sent her to walk ahead of him. Groaning with relief, she massaged her tingling, throbbing scalp.

The majority of knights and men-at-arms were attempting to brace the crumbling walls about the postern gate with whatever materials they could lay their hands on. Meanwhile, archers lined the precarious battlements, firing down on the enemy. Shrill death cries from the other side of the wall indicated when they hit their targets. Martha shivered. So much death. So much pain. And for what?

The heavy thumping sound was coming from outside the wooden gate. It could only be a battering ram. The chants of the men wielding it came regularly with every strike.

They pushed through the host of men, the earl calling out bright greetings to several of the knights. On reaching the wall, and His Evilness shoved Martha up the narrow flight of stone steps that led to the battlements. The thought of being so exposed to Rodmar's archers made her stomach flip, but she had no choice but to obey him.

She rested her hand on her belly. *My poor wee lad.* What with the events of the last couple of hours, she'd almost forgotten she was pregnant. Would the baby suffer because of her ill treatment? God, she hoped not.

As they reached the top of the steps, a battle-grimed knight clanked along the walkway toward them. "Bad tidings, m'lord Edgeway," he called with the briefest bow of his head. "The gate cannot hold for much longer; the enemy is too numerous. They are massing faster than we can kill them." He took off his battered helmet and ran his filthy fingers through his limp, dark hair. "And now we are almost out of arrows."

At that very moment, an arrow hissed past Martha's face. She dove down, heart racing, and pressed her back against the battlements. The earl and the knight didn't react at all.

"Come now, Sir Owain. Take heart." The earl's brow puckered as he frowned. "Surely our situation cannot be so dire as all that? Tip more hot oil over them. Fry them alive. Where is your courage, man?"

A muscle pulsed in Sir Owain's stubbled jaw. "I suspect it went over the wall with the last vat of oil, m'lord. We have been using boiling water since midnight."

The earl stiffened, apparently not accustomed to being addressed in such a manner. His eyes bulged in their sockets, making him resemble an angry frog. But Martha didn't smile. The thought of deliberately pouring scalding liquid over someone horrified her.

"And what news of Sir Hugh?" the earl asked, pointedly ignoring the knight's previous comment. "Has there been any word of him?"

Sir Owain shook his head. "None of his company have returned, m'lord."

"Oh? That is a great pity." The earl looked affronted by the news, as if Sir Hugh's failure to return was a personal slight. "I was about to offer him a promotion. Ah, well."

Martha and the knight exchanged a brief glance, arching their eyebrows at one another. Although she'd never met the man before, she knew he shared her revulsion. It was there in his eyes.

She moved away, edging along the wall-walk and weaving around the archers, until she found a vacant piece of wall to lean against. Weariness hit her with the force of a sledgehammer. The urge to rest her eyelids was almost irresistible. And she badly needed the privy—her bladder felt ready to burst.

While the earl was occupied with the knight, Martha decided to chance a look over the battlements to see what was happening for herself. She peeped cautiously around the block of stone. Immediately, an arrow whooshed past her face, the breeze of its flight brushing her cheek in a lethal kiss. She fell back, clutching her chest and gasping.

Fuck! That was much too close.

"Have a care, lass." A gray-haired soldier limped along the walkway towards her. "They have some decent archers amongst them. You would not look half so pretty with an arrow stuck through your face."

Martha grimaced at the mental image he'd just given her. "Sorry. I wasn't thinking."

"Then, you had better start thinking. Unless, of course, you wish to live out the remainder of your days looking like me." He gave a broad smile, displaying what remained of his long, yellow teeth.

Although he looked like a man in his sixties, the light in his eyes was that of someone much younger. The variety of scars on his craggy face told the grim tale of life as a foot soldier; a living record of places he'd been and of the battles he'd fought in. The most striking of these scars ran in a silver line from chin to ear, puckering the skin either side of it.

Martha tried not to stare, but with little success.

"A sword wound from many moons ago." The man rubbed his bristly jaw. "Why are you up here, lass? Do you want to see over the wall so badly you would risk your life?"

"No. His Lordship made me come." She nodded across to where the earl stood dwarfed by a wall of knights. Three other men had joined Sir Owain, and judging by the way the earl's arms were flailing, it wasn't for a friendly chat. Unfortunately, she wasn't close enough to eavesdrop. Had he forgotten her? Might she be able to give him the slip?

Right on cue, the earl turned to look at her. His icy glare dared her to run. Martha knew all too well how he dealt with people who ran, so she stayed where she was. An arrow in the back? No thank you.

"Ah. I see." The battle-scarred soldier placed a surprisingly light hand on her shoulder. "In that case, if you have a mind to see outside, crouch down and have a look through here." He directed her to a narrow slit in the stone wall she hadn't noticed before—probably because of all the men milling around. She thanked the man, then looked through the archer's window on the world.

The meadow below the castle was nothing like she remembered. The continuous movement of men and machines had transformed the once-lush grass to a brown and barren wasteland, pitted by a complex network of trenches. Slabs of masonry embedded into the earth at weird angles resembled a herd of gray animals that had been slaughtered then left to rot.

The trebuchets and slings sat silent. In the morning light, she could make out their ropes and moorings moving in the gentle breeze. An evil-looking thicket of sharpened stakes surrounded the precious war machines, jutting from the ground at an angle. The high-tech weapons of medieval warfare must need constant protection.

Sweet baby Jesus! Suddenly, she realized that not all the lumps on the ground were chunks of broken castle. A shaft of sunlight broke from the thick cloud and reflected off a piece of armor.

Like a juxtaposed picture, once she "got her eye in," the hidden image appeared, and a terrible scene revealed itself. Bodies of men and horses lay tangled together, united in death. Figures moved amongst the fallen, frequently pausing to check the motionless bodies. But whoever these people were, they weren't looking for signs of life.

Like vultures, they were picking their prey clean of anything of value.

Disgusted, Martha looked away, and a swift movement drew her eyes. Several riderless horses ran wild through the encampment, evading the efforts of those trying to capture them. Meanwhile, a two-wheeled cart drawn by a donkey wandered onto the killing field to load up the dead.

Poor Sir Hugh. Was he lying out there somewhere, broken beyond repair? Was Vadim? She drew her hand over her eyes and turned away.

"Here, lass." The kindly soldier pressed a bladder of ale into her hands. "Drink up. His lordship looks mad enough to burst, and I have a feeling you might be the one who pays for it."

He was right. The earl looked livid. His face was drained of color, his lips compressed into a thin, grim line. Without so much as bowing their heads, the knights turned and walked away from him.

What was that all about?

She raised the bladder and poured the sweet ale into her mouth, swallowing it in fast greedy gulps. It was best not to dwell too much on her new friend's lack of oral hygiene. Better that than having to face the earl again without some form of anesthetic.

"How on Erde have you offended him so?" the man muttered as the earl headed toward them, stuffing a wad of white fabric into his tunic as he walked.

"I'm Vadim's wife."

The man's jaw slackened slightly. "The dead outlaw? Hemlock?"

"Uh-huh. Only he's not dead." *Though he might wish he was if I ever catch up with him.*

"And Lord Edgeway knows?"

Martha nodded, managing a weak smile.

The man puffed out his cheeks and exhaled a long breath. "Aye. That would do the job all right."

As the earl came closer, he adopted the stooping walk used by all the men on the ragged battlements.

Martha wiped her mouth on her sleeve then handed back the bladder of ale. "Thanks for the drink. You've been very kind."

There wasn't time to say more.

"Carry on, man," the earl snarled. "This is no time for idle chattering."

"Very good, m'lord." Sparing her a look of sympathy, Martha's companion swiftly departed.

Although she didn't know the man's name, she already missed his friendly company.

"My, how you thrive in the company of the lower ranks." The earl pushed her to walk ahead of him on the battlements, away from the activity at the postern gate. "What can you have found to talk about with that dreadful fellow?"

"He's a nice man," she replied, flinging the words over her shoulder. "I wouldn't expect you to understand."

"I am, however, beginning to understand what a thoroughly ill-bred chit you truly are."

Martha didn't bother to reply. *Stick and stones.* Instead, she concentrated on imitating the crouching gait of the soldiers. There was nothing to hold onto, and in places the battlements were non-existent. One false step and she'd plummet from the narrow wall-walk to her death.

As the earl approached, the soldiers squashed themselves up against the walls to let him pass. Even so, Martha frequently found herself perilously close to the edge. The path disintegrated completely in places, but the earl pushed her on, forcing her to step over vertiginous drops. She tried not to look down.

The earl walked behind her, muttering darkly to himself. Martha could almost hear him mentally unraveling—not that he'd been the tightest of weaves to begin with. She tried to make out his words.

"Terms, indeed!" Mutter, mumble. "...interest is in saving their own worthless necks... pox-ridden whoresons..."

Crazy Earl FM wasn't exactly easy listening, but the ale she'd consumed helped to tune him out. She hadn't eaten in hours, and the alcohol was working its magic, numbing her with a gentle, golden glow. The sharpest spikes of fear lessened with each step she took, lending her the courage to make several more leaps of faith over the dangerous pathway.

Arrows hissed by in fast blurs. The blood chilling screams made the hairs on the back of her neck prickle. For some reason, a strangely liberating mantra took up residence in her mind. *If I'm gonna die, I'm gonna die.* Tears and terror wouldn't help her now, not if it was her time to shuffle off the mortal coil. It was a comfort of sorts.

The earl tapped her shoulder. "Go down the next flight of steps."

Martha gladly obeyed him.

They had barely touched ground level when Rodmar's trebuchets set to work again. She looked up and saw a huge shape flying overhead at great speed. A second later, it impacted, hitting the southern face of the keep with such force she felt the vibrations of it in her teeth. Immediately, she crouched down, arms around her head. Small fragments of rubble stung the exposed skin on her hands. She winced and hugged her head more tightly. Thank God they hadn't been any closer.

Gradually, the thundering crash of falling debris lessened to a soft, pattering shower. Martha cautiously lowered her arms and looked up at the keep. Tapestries flapped from a jagged hole high up on the castle wall. Through the thick dust cloud, she saw a chair teetering on the edge of the void. Moments later, it fell, toppling through the air and shattering onto the courtyard.

"I am heartily glad the repairs will not be coming from my coffers," the earl remarked cheerfully.

Martha turned her head. He was crouched directly behind her—most likely using the lee of her butt as a shelter from the flying debris. What was that about the castle repairs? Had he given up all hope of holding on to it?

He scrambled to his feet and brushed himself down, liberating a thick cloud of dust from his cloak. Then he nudged Martha's butt with the toe of his boot. "Up you get."

She scrambled to her feet. "S-so, who will be footing the repair bill, if not you?"

"Why, the next Earl of Edgeway of course, you silly goose." His eyes narrowed, glinting like shards of broken glass. "Surely even you can see that we are almost overrun? It is only a matter of time now." He grabbed her upper arm and led her toward the main gate. "Come. You may yet be of use to me."

"I don't see how." She raised her arm, trying without success to shrug from his hold. "Rodmar doesn't know me, nor I him. If you think you can use me to negotiate with him, it'll be a waste of breath. He won't care if I live or die."

"Did I mention Rodmar? What care I for that arrogant young pretender? He is nothing to me."

His chuckle made her flesh crawl. She had a very bad feeling about this.

"With you as my bait," he continued, "I am hoping to hook a very different kind of fish."

She frowned. "Then, who do..." *He means Vadim, of course.* The realization hit her so hard she stumbled. Only the earl's hand on her arm prevented her from hitting the ground.

"I see you share my mind, my dear."

"B-but why?" For the life of her, she couldn't understand the twisted workings of his mind.

Placing his hand on top of her head, he shoved her through the low wooden doorway that led inside the squat stone bulk of the barbican. Its blackened walls still smelt of smoke.

"Vadim can't save you." Her voice echoed in the darkness. "He wouldn't. Not even for me."

Amplified by the stone walls, the earl's laughter was an eerie sound. She shivered and reminded herself he was just a crazy mortal man and not a vampire.

"I have no desire to escape my fate. My bones are too weary to face fresh battle in some faraway place. But if I can be the instrument of your husband's suffering in the years to come, I shall die content." He reached up and removed a dying torch from its wall sconce.

Martha gasped in outrage as he pushed her up the narrow, spiraling stairs. "You massacred Vadim's family, and almost killed him in the process. You robbed him of his birthright and made him an outlaw. Don't you think he's suffered enough by your hand?"

"Your loyalty is most touching. I wonder how he will manage without you in all the empty years he has remaining?" He patted her backside. "Keep walking—all the way to the top, if you please."

Now she knew the true meaning of fear. She could hardly breathe. Terror constricted her throat and turned her blood to ice. She trudged up the steps, imagining herself on the way to the guillotine. This couldn't be happening.

But it was.

Vadim still hadn't appeared, and Anselm was well and truly out of play. No knight in shining armor was going to come and rescue her now. This was it. The end.

He's really going to kill me!

chapter twenty-three

THERE WAS STILL HOPE.

As Martha trudged up the stone steps, she became aware of a gently swinging weight in her pocket, bashing rhythmically against her thigh. Vadim's knife. If there was ever a time to use it, it was now.

Could she do it? Abandon the values of the twenty-first century and play by a new set of rules? If she wanted her baby to survive, she had no choice.

Decision made, she slipped her right hand into the deep pocket of her gown. Her fingers closed around the smooth, ridged handle of the knife. She faked a stumble and raised her skirt a little higher. Praying the earl wouldn't notice her sly fumbling, she worked her left hand through the bulky material of her gown and closed it around the sheath of the blade. One gentle pull and the knife slid free. She exhaled through her mouth, long and slow.

Now, all she had to do was pick the right moment to use it. If she had the courage—and stomach—to do so.

You'd better, Bigalow. His Evilness won't hesitate to kill you.

They climbed on, their panting breaths echoing in the narrow confines of the spiraling staircase. A chink of light up ahead indicated they'd reached their destination, the very top of the barbican. The earl prodded Martha's back. Clutching tightly to the knife's handle, she ducked her head and stepped through a narrow doorway.

Oh, shit!

The flat roof was horribly exposed. Only the open air separated them from the vast might of Rodmar's army as it swarmed around the bottom of the hill. The men were packed together in such tight formation it was impossible to pick out an individual soldier. Like a murmuration of starlings or a shoal of fish, the soldiers moved as one, each man forming a tiny part of the whole.

The kaleidoscopic motion made her eyes ache. At that moment, the army began singing. Hundreds of voices united in what could only be a battle song. Although she didn't understand the words, the challenge in each note was unmistakable. The blast of raw sound struck her ears in a powerful wave that vibrated into her chest.

If the song was meant to intimidate, mission accomplished. She couldn't stop shaking. Then again, that might be down to the close proximity of His Evilness.

He stood at her shoulder. "What on Erde are those savages howling about now?" He tilted his head slightly to one side, listening. The freshening breeze brought the voices closer, and the earl's mouth compressed into a grim line. What he heard obviously didn't please him.

What *were* they singing? As curious as she was, there was no way she'd ask him for a translation. Instead, she backed away, retreating to the relative safety of the stairwell. The earl reacted quickly, clamping his hand about her right wrist before she'd managed to take three steps.

"Oh, you must not leave me yet." His thin lips curved into a mocking smile. "That would ruin everything."

Reluctantly, she let go of the knife's handle. This wasn't the opportune moment anyway. Not with him standing so close, attentive to her every move. Unless she wanted to be overpowered and killed by her own blade, she needed to pick a better moment.

How many more do I have left?

"Shall we take a look over the edge?" He began dragging her toward the battlements.

Martha almost lost the fight to control her painfully swollen bladder. Icy fear balled in her chest, compressing her racing heart. She struggled furiously, her boots skidding and plowing furrows in the dirt as she skied over the rooftop. "Let me go."

She gasped for breath, desperately trying to twist free of the earl's iron grip. "I promise I won't try to escape."

One thing was certain. Given the opportunity, she'd willingly stick that knife into him now. Conscience be damned.

The earl snort-laughed. "What use have I for the promise of such a seasoned liar?"

He pushed her ahead, shoving her with such force she hit the battlements at speed. Her outstretched hands absorbed most of the impact; the pressure of it vibrated through her wrists. The earl moved behind her, his chest pressed firmly against her back, sandwiching her between himself and the wall.

Martha looked down and instantly regretted it. It was a very long drop. The ground swirled before her eyes, and she clenched them shut, but the image of the horrible ditch surrounding the castle played on behind her eyelids. Gray chunks of rubble poked up from beneath the frothy green water, breaching the surface like jagged icebergs. The bloated corpse of some unfortunate animal bobbed in the foul water. It might have once been a dog. She couldn't tell. God only knew what else the ditch contained.

The stench of decomposition combined unpleasantly with the earl's sickly scent. Her stomach finally revolted. Warm bile flooded into her mouth. Gagging and coughing she retched the meager contents of her stomach over the wall.

"Oh, are you feeling unwell, my dear?" The earl pressed his body closer to hers, his words brushing against her ear. "Never mind. You will not suffer for much longer."

His breath bore the sweet note of decay. Although unpleasant, the intimacy of their position was far worse.

Oh, please let that be his sword.

Still clinging to the wall, she turned her head to wipe her sour mouth at the top of her sleeve. Was he really going to throw her over the wall? Given the choice, she'd prefer a quick, clean stabbing. Her stomach pitched again as another wave of nausea washed over her. She forced her eyes open and tried not to imagine herself smashed on the rocks below, yet another ingredient in the ditch's vile, rotting sludge.

Her bladder screamed for release. The pressure of being squished against the wall was more than it could take. She couldn't hold on any longer.

So what are you waiting for? Go on. Do it.

Why not? It might even work to her advantage. Despite everything, the earl was only human. He should react in the same way as anyone else. She might not be able to escape, but she might buy herself her a few seconds of precious freedom.

While he was occupied—one-handedly flapping a wad of white material into a make-shift flag—Martha shuffled her knees apart and let go of her bladder.

She sighed as the stream of warm liquid gushed to the ground. Pure bliss. Tears of relief streamed down her cheeks.

"What the..." With a cry of disgust, the earl leapt back from the fast-pooling liquid. "Urgh. You revolting bitch! Do you know how much these boots cost?"

With great effort, she managed to stop peeing. Thankfully, her aim was good. Apart from a couple of splashes, she was dry. Not wearing underwear had certain advantages.

She took a few steps back, quickly distancing herself from the danger of the wall. But all the time, she kept her eyes fixed on the earl, not daring to look away for a second. The fact that he hadn't reached for any of his own weapons was strangely worrying.

They circled one another, moving warily, like hunters. Martha slipped her hand into her pocket, closing her fingers around the handle of the knife. As the earl advanced, his pristine square of fabric trailed on the ground behind him.

"What are you going to do with that?" she asked, jerking her head to indicate his now-grubby flag.

"That is none of your concern." He made a sudden lunge for her.

With a squeal of fright, Martha swerved out of his reach and danced away. The earl was limping heavily. His wounded leg was obviously paining him. Good.

He gave an exasperated *tut.* "Come back here." He made another grab for her—and missed—snarling with fury. "Do you wish to die upon my blade?" He touched the hilt of his sword. "Though it would vex me exceedingly, I will kill you here and now if you force me to it."

Martha snorted. *"You'd* be vexed?" She glanced over her shoulder, backing toward the stairwell. There was no hiding place—nowhere else to go except over the wall.

The earl kept on coming, advancing steadily, like a murderous, mad-eyed sheepdog, repeatedly blocking her escape route. "You choose death, then, m'lady?"

Since escape wasn't currently an option, maybe she could cut a deal?

"Fine. You win." She reluctantly let go of the knife and raised her hands. "I'll do what you want. Just don't touch me, okay?" She nodded at the makeshift flag in his hand again. "Are you going to parlay with Rodmar's men?"

The earl's pale eyes flashed. Whatever he was thinking, it couldn't be good because he was smiling again. Even worse, it looked genuine.

"What gave me away?" He waved the grubby flag at her. "Very well. Shall we return to the wall? I need them to see you."

Maintaining the distance between them, Martha walked back to the parapet. The earl matched her pace. She dipped her hand back into her pocket, seeking the comfort of her knife. His Evilness was going to grab her the first chance he got. And when he wasn't expecting it, that's when she'd make her move.

He made her stand between the battlements, then he waved his cloth over the wall. At length, the missile bombardment ceased, and the singing faded. Not long afterward, a group of men on horseback cantered up the hill to the castle, one of them bearing a white flag.

Martha chewed her lip. *Now what?*

To her surprise, two masked riders accompanied the three knights. Her heart skipped a beat. Was Vadim amongst them? No. But they had to be his friends. The riders reined in at the other side of the ditch, just as the first drops of rain tumbled from the swollen clouds.

The knight with the white flag took off his helmet and tilted his head back in order to look at them. "Greetings, Lord Edgeway!" he called in clear voice. "I trust you have passed a peaceful night?"

At this, the knight's companions roared with laughter.

The earl's jaw tensed. "Regrettably, I have not yet slept. But do not blame yourself, sir knight. 'Twas the serpents in my own house that kept me from peaceful repose."

The rain intensified, pattering on the knights' armor like pebbles on a tin can. Martha hunched her shoulders, longing for her cloak. When exactly had she lost it? She frowned. The previous hours had blended into a big blur.

The spokesman's smile broadened. "I am sorry to hear that, m'lord. I trust you have now dealt with your... infestation?" This drew more laughter from his friends.

"Not quite." The earl bared his teeth in a snarl-like smile. "But at least I have the majority of them under interrogation."

The men exchanged glances. Their smiles were not quite so bright now.

"Tell me, my lords." His Evilness nodded at Martha, gesturing for her to lean over the wall. "Do you recognize this woman?"

Holding back the sodden weight of her hair with one hand, Martha looked down at the men's upturned faces. A quick scan of each face left her disappointed. She didn't know any of them. Her eyes lingered on the two masked riders. Surely if they'd met before, a bell would jingle somewhere in the dark recesses of her brain? But nothing happened—not the tiniest spark of familiarity. Her heart sank. Until that moment, she hadn't known how much she'd longed to see someone familiar.

"Well?" The earl had to shout to be heard over the noise of the wind and rain. "Look closely at her now."

As the men studied her face, their smiles went out. It wasn't a trick of her weary mind. Although she didn't know them, they definitely knew her. She wanted to punch the air and sing.

But His Evilness was smiling again. Damn him. He'd obviously interpreted the men's non verbals in the same way she had.

"So, she *is* worth something to you," he muttered. "Excellent."

The men exchanged glances. Leaning on their horses' necks, they began murmuring to one another in low voices. The masked men suddenly became animated, angry. She frowned. *Why?*

Rodmar's spokesman raised his hand to silence them. The masked men stiffened in their saddles and rode off a few paces. They didn't move far, just enough to indicate some dissention in their ranks.

The rift between the knights and outlaws was apparent. Something was very wrong. She clutched the wall so hard her fingertips burned as they grated over the rough stone.

The earl leaned a little further over the parapet. "Oh, do make haste and answer, preferably before I am soaked through to my undergarments. Do you know her or not?"

The knight looked up with a solemn face. "No, m'lord." He cleared his throat. "The lady is unknown to us."

What the—?

"Very well," the earl said brightly. "Then I have no further use for her." With frightening speed, he sprang at Martha.

Shit!

She went for her knife, but as she tried to withdraw it, the point of the blade snagged on the inside of her pocket. There was no time to pull it free. The earl made a grab for her hair, but Martha jerked back and took a quick sideways step to evade him. Then panic set in, and logic flew over the parapet. Heart pounding, she turned and ran.

The earl stumbled over the thick folds of Martha's swirling skirt but managed to grab her by the shoulder. Martha squealed and pivoted round, kicking his shin with all of her strength.

With a bellow of pain, the earl let her go. "Whore!" He lashed out, the back of his right hand connecting viciously with her cheekbone.

She staggered as a galaxy of stars exploded before her eyes. Her ears buzzed as if she'd just returned from a rock concert. A brutal hand burrowed into her wet hair, and she heard the echo of desperate whimpers. Her own? The earl's voice became a slow, meaningless rumble. As her legs buckled, a black blanket put out all the stars, simultaneously sapping all the strength from her limbs. Despite her best efforts, she couldn't keep her eyes open.

chapter twenty-four

A FAMILIAR STENCH ROUSED MARTHA FROM her semi-conscious state. She forced her heavy eyelids open and found herself dangling over the edge of the battlements, looking down into the ditch and its foul green soup.

"No." Her voice was almost inaudible. Then a rush of adrenaline flooded her body. "Oh, God. No!" She clung desperately to the wall and kicked out. The earl grabbed her thrashing ankles and secured them against him. Then he lifted her, tilting her over the edge.

"Last chance," he yelled to the slack-jawed men staring up at them.

Martha stopped kicking, afraid her own struggles would send her over the brink.

Oh, please, let me wake up now.

The knights remained motionless, watching the scene with expressionless faces. But even with their masks, the outlaws feelings were easier to read. As they muttered to one another, the two men cast frequent glances at Martha as she see-sawed over the battlements. Their horses danced beneath them, probably picking up on their masters' discomfort. Suddenly, riding side by side, the men pushed their horses forward.

"Enough!" one of them cried, ignoring the scowls of the knights. "The woman is known to us."

The earl stopped lifting and hugged her legs to his chest. "Then, speak her name out loud. Tell me who she is."

The pattering rain cooled her tears and washed the blood from her ruined fingertips, turning the stonework a watery pink.

"She is Martha, wife of Vadim—the true Earl of Edgeway." The pride in the outlaw's voice was obvious.

Great. Another fecking fan boy. That's all I need.

The earl chuckled. "Tell me, where is *His Lordship* while I am abusing his wife so cruelly, hmm?"

The masked men exchanged another wordless glance.

Even coming from the earl, that was an excellent question. Would she live long enough to learn the answer? A flame of temper licked through her body.

It was over. Not just her precarious hold on life, but everything else too. She was done with making excuses for him. Through with trying to convince herself Vadim still cared. His lack of action spoke for itself. He didn't give a shit about her.

I'd divorce the handsome gobshite if I wasn't just about to die.

The earl raised Martha's ankles higher again. "Where is he?" he roared. "I will not be deprived of my rightful vengeance."

She screamed. Only her shoulders, jammed painfully between the battlements, prevented her from falling over the edge. Eyes clenched shut, she began to pray. She didn't want to see death as it rushed to claim her.

Holy Mary Mother of God. Please let it be quick!

"Put her down."

Was that... Anselm? Although she couldn't see him, her heart soared.

From the corner of her eye, she saw the earl turn to look behind him.

Over her breathy sobs, she heard the unmistakable smooth glide of a sword being pulled from its sheath.

"Do not test me, m'lord." Anselm spoke quietly, but the edge in his voice was as lethal as that of any sword.

"Anselm!" His name ripped from her throat, half scream, half plea.

Oh, thank God.

"As you wish." The earl set her down. "Let us not fight, my friend. Not over her."

Martha's jelly legs refused to hold her, and she crumpled to the floor in an inelegant heap, resisting the sudden urge to do a "pope." The ground was much too wet for kissing, no matter how grateful she was.

"What vexes you, Anselm?" the earl asked with a frown. "Surely you know I do this for you as well as for myself?"

Anselm stood only a few feet away, sword raised. His hair hung about his face in dark rats' tails, clinging to the grim line of his jaw. He didn't meet Martha's eyes. His attention was too focused on his master.

She was extremely happy not to be on the receiving end of that particular look. It was way beyond "Bad Anselm." Even so, she'd never been so glad to see anyone.

"Come here, sweeting." He spoke without looking at her, beckoning to her with his free hand.

The earl's eyes were wide and wild, darting from side to side. Two pink spots of temper flushed his cheeks. In her opinion, Anselm was wise not to look away from him.

Hampered by the heavy weight of her saturated gown, Martha scrambled to her feet. But before she'd taken three steps, the earl sprang at her. His arm snaked over her chest, his forearm an immovable weight against her neck.

Oh, for the love of God!

"Release her," Anselm growled. "At once, if you please."

"And if it does not please me? What then, my friend?"

Anselm's eyes glittered in his pale face. Tightening his grip on his sword, he took a step toward them.

Bugger this for a game of soldiers.

While the two men were occupied with staring one another down, Martha slipped her hand into her pocket and took out her knife. Taking a deep breath, she plunged deep it into the earl's thigh.

With an agonized scream, he thrust her away. Unfortunately for the earl, she still clung on to the knife's handle. It exited his leg with a nasty, meaty *slurp*. She stumbled forward into Anselm's arms, bracing herself against his metal chest plate, grinning up at him like a blood-crazed lunatic, while the earl hopped around the barbican roof bellowing and cursing.

"I really enjoyed that," she said with feeling.

"So it would seem." Anselm's stern countenance cracked into a smile. "And just how long have you owned that particular weapon, m'lady?"

"Er... how long were we cohabiting?"

His eyes widened. "As long as that? Then, I should consider myself the luckiest of men." With that, he pulled her behind him.

No. It wouldn't do to neglect the earl. A wounded animal was always the most dangerous. Clutching his leg, she watched him limp over where his filthy white flag lay floating in a puddle. Using his teeth to help him, the earl tore off a strip of fabric and quickly bound it about his leg, howling with pain as he tied it.

On the plus side, he now had a matching set of thigh wounds—a bandage on either leg. Very battle chic.

Outside the castle walls, the sound of battle resumed, but Martha didn't care. She pressed her cheek against the damp wool of Anselm's cloak. "Thank you," she murmured. If not for him, she'd be dead now.

"You are most welcome."

"Come on. Let's go." She tugged at his arm. "You can tell me how you escaped as we walk."

But Anselm remained immobile. "I cannot leave him, sweeting. Not like this."

"What?" Her eyes bugged. "Are you insane?" She swept back her sodden hair as she stepped in front of him.

Anselm continued to stare at the earl. "He is my liege lord, Martha."

"He's a fecking fruit-and-nut job. That's what he is." She watched the earl grimace as he stood upright again. Fresh blood had already soaked through the dressings of both legs. *Good.* "Please, Anselm?"

He shook his head. "I cannot. I do not expect you to understand."

No, she bloody well didn't. His Evilness would kill the pair of them, given the opportunity to do so.

"Long has he been my closest companion." Anselm's voice was almost tender. "I owe him a great deal."

The earl glared at them. "How good of you to finally remember it." He began hobbling toward them, but after only a couple of paces, he stopped, groaning feebly as he pressed his hands to his thighs.

Martha exhaled. *Bloody men.* "You've picked a hell of a time to develop a conscience, Anselm."

Anselm lowered his sword and smiled. "It is a matter of honor. Even I have some remaining."

That word. Again. She ground her teeth.

The earl directed a look of undiluted hatred her way. "I gave him everything," he snarled. "When the world turned against him, I gave him a home, employment, and more wealth than his barn rat of a father ever dreamed of."

Martha retreated behind Anselm's shoulder, cowed by the force of the poison spewing from the earl's mouth.

His eyes softened as they flicked to Anselm. "I gave you a purpose, a way to harness your ambition." His words were gentle now, coaxing. "Why do you prostrate yourself like a beaten cur before the landless whore of an outlaw? You could have wedded anyone. Why her?" He glanced at Martha. "Look at her. She is *hardly* beautiful."

Thank you very much.

Anselm turned his head and looked into Martha's eyes. "Yes she is." A half smile played on his lips. "Though, I must confess, she has looked better."

His words warmed her heart. Although she wasn't in love with him, it was hard not to feel affection for someone who saw beyond her battered and bedraggled appearance. "You old charmer." She grinned at him then planted a kiss upon his cheek. "Ma warned me about your sweet tongue."

Anselm's eyes sparkled. "So we are friends now, m'lady? Progress indeed. What would your husband say?"

Quite a lot, she imagined. *Tough. Vadim can go to—*

The earl groaned again and suddenly crumpled to the ground.

Anselm sighed and reached for her hand. "Go." He placed a gentle kiss on her bloody knuckles. "Find a place to hide and wait there. I will be with you as soon as I can, unless Vadim finds you first, of course."

Yeah. Fat chance of that happening.

There was a thunderous crash, and the roar of hundreds of voices raised in triumph.

Anselm's eyes clouded. "Erde! They have broken through the back gate. Hurry, Martha! Hide yourself well. Do not reveal yourself to any man except those you trust." With that, he replaced his sword and hurried toward the earl.

Heart racing, she turned and headed for the low doorway, the bloody knife still gripped in her hand. But as she reached the first step, a cry of agony made her look back.

Fuck. No!

What she saw almost stopped her heart.

"Anselm!"

chapter twenty-five

ANSELM HIT THE GROUND LIKE a sack of wet sand, eyes clenched tight, his face contorted with pain. He clawed at something in his side but failed to reach it. Then he lay still.

No. No. No!

Martha's jaw dropped. Her head shifted repeatedly from side to side, denying the brutal truth of her eyes. Anselm couldn't be dead. She'd just spoken to him, for heaven's sake. Her brain refused to accept it.

The earl casually withdrew a bloody dagger from Anselm's body then wiped the blade on his victim's cloak. With only the slightest grimace of discomfort, he stood upright again, looking down at the body of his former friend.

Martha clutched the door frame of the stairwell. Too late, she realized the earl had been faking the severity of his wounds.

She glanced at the knife in her hand, reassuring herself there was blood on the blade, that she'd actually stabbed him with it. Although the rain had washed away the worst of the gore, dilute pink rivulets of water dripped from the point. Then, of course, there were her hands. As Lady Macbeth was only too aware, it took more than a bit of water to remove all traces of blood.

Not that it mattered. The fact was, the earl wasn't as injured as they'd so foolishly supposed. Now Anselm had paid the price. Their stupid gullibility might have cost him his life.

After a few moments of quiet contemplation, the earl gave Anselm's body a hefty kick. "Betray me, would you?"

The hollow thud sickened her. "Leave him alone, you fucking psycho!"

"Feckless dog." The earl kicked Anselm again and again. "That will teach you to bite your master's hand."

Martha tugged at the neckline of her dress. Despite being soaked to the skin, she was suddenly much too warm. Her heart accelerated, fast and thready, pounding with a speed to rival a hummingbird's. Steaming blood thundered through her veins and roared in her ears, and a thick red mist descended inside her brain.

She squeezed the knife handle so hard it creaked in protest.

The quiet voice of caution was gone. Her common sense was lost within the murderous fog. Only a dark and primal urge remained. Every muscle throbbed, pumped with adrenaline. Her fingers curled into claws, readying themselves to tear into the earl's throat. Or to rip out his black heart. Either was acceptable.

Barely aware of having done so, she threw her knife at him. It sailed through the air in a blur of spinning silver, but her aim was off. *God damn it!* But the knife handle did make a satisfying *thunk* as it struck the earl's temple. He staggered like a drunk, struggling to stay on his feet.

Close, but no cigar. The bastard wasn't dead.

A low, feral sound of frustration grumbled from the back of her throat. Grinding her teeth, Martha glanced around, searching the top of the stairwell for another weapon. There was nothing except for a smoking wall torch. She snatched it from its sconce and hurled it at him with all her strength.

The earl recovered enough to dodge before the wall torch struck him. He touched his fingers to his temple, and they came back bloody. "Bitch!" He fumbled for his sword, his legs wobbling beneath him, as uncoordinated as a new-born lamb's.

Still surfing a huge adrenaline wave, Martha only laughed. She was much too wired to feel any fear. At that moment, she was aching for a fight. Nothing would give her greater pleasure than the chance to punch, claw, and bite at that revolting snake of a—

Her breath hitched in her throat. *Anselm?*

His eyelids flickered then slowly opened.

He's alive!

She stopped walking, her mission to kill the earl aborted.

The raging fires of insanity were put out in a heartbeat, extinguished by the pain in Anselm's eyes.

Her inner beast slunk away into the shadows of her soul, sullen and growling.

For better or worse, Martha was herself again, and the abrupt withdrawal of adrenaline left her trembling and weak. She exhaled a shaky breath. Anselm had saved her again, but this time, from herself.

As he looked at her, his pale lips mouthed a single word, "Go."

The earl regained his balance and fixed Martha with a shark-like stare. "My turn!" He stepped over Anselm, unaware that his former friend still lived and breathed.

Anselm seized the earl's leg, hugging the jerking limb to his chest, grimacing with the effort of clinging on. But he didn't let go.

With a cry of surprise, the earl toppled face-first onto the barbican roof. His sword flew from his outstretched hand and touched down with a splash in a distant puddle.

Anselm was fast losing the fight to keep his eyes open. Unable to hold on, he released the earl's leg. "Martha. Run!" he gasped.

Tears shimmered before her eyes. The thought of leaving him alone to die was unbearable. Anselm was obviously seriously wounded. But how could she stay with His Evilness on her case? He was already crawling over the roof, hunting for his sword, cursing and snarling beneath his breath.

Still she hesitated, her feet like dithering cement blocks of uncertainty. She didn't want to leave him, but when it came down to it, she had no other choice. She held his gaze for a final, lingering moment. "I'll be back as soon as I can. Just keep breathing. Do you hear me?" Her voice was fierce, as if she could scare him into living.

A shadow smile curved Anselm's lips, then his eyelids drooped and it was gone.

There was nothing else she could do except hitch up her skirt and run. She didn't look back.

The courtyard now teemed with men of both factions. A heaving mass of combatants, fighting and dying before her eyes. Rodmar's coat of arms dominated the field. Almost every shield and surcoat bore the image of the wolf hunting the bear.

Martha paused in the doorway of the barbican, steeling herself to head out into the melee. The steady shuffle of the earl's descending footsteps echoed in the stairwell behind her, urging her on. She had to go. Now.

Taking a deep breath, she dashed across the courtyard, heading for the keep. The sea of warring men ebbed and flowed, diverting her off course as she skirted around its periphery.

She squealed as a disemboweled body slumped from the living wall of men and toppled into her path. Dead eyes stared back at her, almost accusingly. Coils of glistening intestine slithered from the man's abdomen, steaming in the morning air, reaching for her like the tentacles of some hideous sea creature.

She forced herself to look away. This wasn't the time to be squeamish. Her thoughts returned to Anselm. Was he dead now? No. She took a deep breath, refusing to cry. Her tears could wait. Besides, if he had progressed to the spirit world, at this rate, she'd soon be reunited with him. She ducked as a short-sword hurtled through the air toward her, let loose by some unseen hand. Whether the act was deliberate or accidental, she didn't stick around to find out.

The reality of battle was nothing like she imagined it would be. There was little fighting skill on display. From what she could see of the scrum, brute force and stamina ruled the day—and luck, lots of it, both good and bad.

The men were packed together so tightly there wasn't room to swing a sword. Instead, they used their shortest blades and daggers, or anything else that came to hand. She witnessed several fierce head-butts that made her grimace.

From the center of the fray, a black fountain of blood spurted high into the air. Martha shivered. Was any of it Vadim's? Her stomach gave a sickening lurch as an unwelcome image flashed into her mind: Vadim lying dead and broken somewhere within that lethal scrum, trampled beneath hundreds of pairs of boots until he was unrecognizable.

Don't do this to yourself. Vadim will be just fine. He hadn't exactly rushed to get into the castle so far, had he?

She stumbled over rubble and slipped on the blood-slicked cobbles. Although she tried to switch off her emotions, the agonized screams and battle cries scarred her ears and cut into her soul.

The rain had slackened off to a light mizzle. Combined with the flying droplets of blood, it seemed as though a fine red mist hovered over the heads of the warriors, lurking like a grim specter.

Little by little, her convoluted path took her closer to the keep. For the most part, no one paid her any attention. The fighters seemed too intent on killing one another. Avoiding the falling bodies and combatants as best she could, she made her wary way toward the keep.

Risking a glance over her shoulder, she spotted the earl's fair head bobbing in the crowd a short distance away. He hadn't taken her own cautious route and, instead, had plowed straight into the battle. Teeth bared, he slashed his way through the men in his path, uncaring whether his victims were his own men or those of the enemy. Then he looked up and met her eyes. The promise in his cold stare made her heart gallop and forced her legs to move faster.

Finally, the crush of bodies eased. She stepped over a river of blood and jogged away from the main scrum. Suddenly, there was room to breathe again, and the space to use a sword. She dodged two knights who were slugging it out on the steps of the keep. The terrible clangs of their gore-slicked weapons reminded her of the smithy, of the blacksmith at work on his anvil. She ran up the steps and hurried through the open doorway, slamming the door behind her.

The thick oak muffled out the sounds of war. Unfortunately, there was no key in the lock. Panting, she reached for the bolt above her head—the lower one was missing—but it was stiff and rusted with lack of use. It posed too much of a challenge for her aching fingers. Besides, there wasn't time. His Evilness was only seconds behind her.

She looked around the empty hallway, her gasping breaths echoing harshly in the cavernous silence. With one hand, she raked back her sopping-wet hair. Where could she hide? Her complaining bladder provided her with an answer. *Of course. The privy.* No one visited those stinking, nasty places without very good cause.

Decision made, she hitched up her heavy skirt and raced up the main staircase, immediately diving into the corridor to her left. Pressed up close to the wall, Martha poked her head around the corner and looked down into the hallway. Her breath lodged in her throat and stayed there.

The door swung open with violent force, crashing into the opposite wall. The earl blundered through the open doorway, bloody sword in hand. Panting and muttering to himself, his head moved rapidly from side to side. Stringy tendrils of his wet hair lashed against his face as he searched for his prey.

"Where are you, my dove?" he called into the echoing silence. "Come along. I mean you no harm."

Yeah. Right.

Martha slid her head back around the corner, praying he hadn't seen her. Closing her eyes, she leaned against the wall, straining to hear the earl's movements, no easy task with her heartbeat thundering in her ears.

Please don't come upstairs.

Then—glory be—his footsteps hurried off in another direction. She peeped around the corner and caught a brief glimpse of his swirling purple cloak. He was gone.

She exhaled with relief then directed her trembling limbs toward the nearest privy.

The privy was an unlikely, if rather ripe-smelling, sanctuary. It was little more than a glorified cupboard, really, with a wooden seat fixed over a hole in the wall. Although Martha's nose rebelled against the stench, to her aching bladder it was heaven on earth.

Once the immediate needs of her body had been met, she leaned against the bolted door to consider her options.

Where could she go now?

Fergus was locked away somewhere in the warren of miserable dungeons that ran beneath the castle. But deranged as His Evilness was, he was no fool. That would be one of the first places he'd search. For the same reason, she couldn't return to Anselm's chambers.

Poor Fergus. Poor Anselm. She sucked in her bottom lip and tried not to think about them. After their heroics on her behalf, the least she could do was stay alive. She couldn't help either of them now, much as she longed to do so. And they couldn't help her either. She must rely on her own wits to escape this time.

Think. Think. Think. She stroked the curve of her stomach, hoping the wee lad might provide her with inspiration. Lack of food and sleep made her brain feel even woollier than usual. Nope. She had nothing.

She rested her eyelids, unable to resist their sudden, delicious weight. It was so peaceful here. The sounds of battle were muted, and the screams seemed very far away. All of the castle's privies were set well away from the main courtyard. The castle's architect had arranged it so that the human waste they generated dropped directly into the ditch via a stone gulley, the very ditch she'd almost taken a dive into earlier.

Rough splinters of wood snagged the back of her gown as she slid down the door, rousing her from a doze she hadn't planned on taking. Shivering, she hugged her arms about herself, suddenly very cold beneath the weight of her wet clothes. Her teeth chattered uncontrollably.

Maybe she should stay where she was? It was safe enough. The sturdy door only opened outward and would prove difficult to open from the outside. Anyway, who'd bother with one locked privy when there was a whole castle to plunder?

Vadim might.

She huffed in irritation, angry with herself for thinking about him. So many weeks apart had spoiled his once-beloved memory. Each fresh disappointment and hardship had smudged and tarnished the image she carried of him in her heart, blurring it into abstraction.

Edgeway and all of its concerns had somehow eclipsed him. Over time, despite her reluctance, the castle had absorbed her into its fabric. Vadim was now a shadowman who lurked on its borders. A dream. A ghost.

If it weren't for the child growing inside her, she'd doubt he ever existed at all.

New sounds from outside the privy penetrated her consciousness. She stiffened and pressed her ear to the door. Heavy footsteps thudded over the wooden floor. Loud, raucous laughter, and the sound of mail and metalware jingling. A woman cried out, and light, slippered footsteps pattered past the privy door.

"No. Please." Her breathless plea held a note of panic. "My husband is rich. He will pay whatever—"

Martha's stomach twisted at the sound of the unseen woman's desperation. She heard a deep, phlegmy chuckle.

"Get her, lads. But I volunteer for the first shift."

Heavy boots raced past the privy door, and Martha flinched back, afraid they might sense her hiding place. She stared at the door, her mind spinning. Rape? To the victor the spoils. Wasn't that how the saying went?

The woman's terrified screams mingled grotesquely with the men's booming laughter.

Martha sat on the toilet seat and clapped her hands over her ears, her eyes clenched shut. What could she do? If she went out there, they'd probably do the same thing to her.

But the screams disturbed the feral beast inside her. It pricked up its ears and growled, and another hot adrenaline rush hit her bloodstream.

"Ah, feck it." She uncovered her ears and stood up. Whatever happened to her out there, at least she wouldn't have a guilty conscience bitching at her for the rest of her life.

Her eyes rested on a long, stout stick propped up against the privy wall. Presumably its function was to unblock the outlet from the privy when it became… congested.

Martha smiled. *A shit stick?* She picked it up and gave it a couple of practice swipes. *Perfect.* Taking a deep breath, she slid the bolt and flung the door open.

chapter twenty-six

G UIDED BY THE UNKNOWN WOMAN'S screams and her terrified pleas for mercy, Martha hurried along the corridor. Her cheeks burned with rage at the callous sound of male laughter. Tightening her grip on the shit stick, she skidded around the corner.

Carelessly discarded weapons lay strewn across the wooden floor, like a trail of lethal breadcrumbs, cast aside in the men's haste to rut.

The woman lay on the ground, hidden beneath her three attackers. Only her splayed legs were visible. The men laughed and joked with one another, ignoring their victim's sobbing pleas for mercy.

One of the woman's slippers had fallen off during the struggle. The sight of her bare, clenching foot pricked Martha's heart. Alternating waves of pity and rage flash-heated her blood, goading her to violence.

Two of the men had pinioned the woman to the floor while the third—the one with his back to Martha—had positioned himself between her open legs, repeatedly attempting to guide himself into the woman's resisting body.

"Hold 'er steady, lads," the would-be rapist growled in frustration. "Give 'er a slap to quieten 'er."

One of the men knelt on the woman's arm, freeing up his hand so he could strike her across the face. Martha flinched at the sharp crack and the resulting scream.

"Now be still, whore!"

But the woman kept on fighting.

The urge to hurt someone overwhelmed her. Martha advanced at a trot, but none of the men looked up. The sounds of distant battle masked her light footsteps. Besides, they were too ravenous with lust to notice anything but their prey.

The rapist shifted position, giving Martha a glimpse of his swollen member, protruding from his meaty fist.

She grimaced. Selecting her first target was easy.

Gripping her shit stick with both hands, she raised it over her head and brought it down fast and hard. It struck the top of the man's bald head with a hollow *thunk,* and he slumped forward, falling on top of the whimpering woman. He made no attempt to get up.

The man's two companions looked up at her, slack jawed with surprise.

Martha puffed a strand of hair from her eyes. "Who's next?" She brandished the stick like a baseball bat, her chest heaving with the effort of breathing. She trembled and shook but, damn, hitting him felt good.

Maybe she was developing a taste for violence after all?

"Well, well." The younger man slowly rose to his feet, abandoning the woman on the floor. "An opponent of worth at last." He smiled, displaying a rack of blackened teeth.

The frissons of fear pricking at the back of her neck cooled the fire in her blood. Although he smiled, the man's eyes contained no warmth. There was only an unsettling wildness, an indescribable *something,* warning her that his brain wasn't firing on all of its cylinders.

The man paused and looked her up and down. Then he rubbed a spade-like hand over his rough-shorn head. Dozens of small bloody nicks covered his scalp as if he'd recently shaved with a blunt knife.

His ferret-faced companion was equally repulsive. He licked his lips, his narrow eyes raking her body hungrily, like a starving man about to feast at a banquet. Martha shivered. Cold beads of sweat prickled upon her brow.

Ferret nodded slowly. "Not bad at all, Jacob." He smoothed back several long, greasy strands of hair from his cadaverous face. "Finally, a woman with some padding on her bones." He glanced at the weeping woman on the floor then back at Martha.

Pale tongue snaking over his cracked lips, he stood up. "Would you object if I took the first bite of this one, mate?" he asked his companion.

"Just make it quick," Jacob replied, still rasping his hand over his moth-eaten scalp.

"Oh, that I will, you can be sure." Ferret's grin broadened, and he patted the bulge at the front of his trews. "The old staff of life is already salivating."

Martha almost gagged at that particular mental image. She shuffled backward, swishing the shit stick through the air in an attempt to hold the stalking men at bay. Why the hell had she left the sanctuary of the privy? The prospect of entertaining that unholy pair anywhere near her body was beyond revolting. Living with a guilty conscience now seemed a much better option.

Forgotten and abandoned, the woman on the floor wriggled beneath of the dead weight of the body on top of her. With a cry of revulsion, she pushed her unconscious attacker aside. As she leapt to her feet, she sent Martha a look of gratitude.

A name for the beaten and bedraggled noblewoman flew into Martha's head. She was Beatrice, Sir Hugh's wife—King Erik's former mistress.

Beatrice bowed her head at Martha. Although her blue silk gown was ripped and dirty, and her right eye almost swollen shut, the gesture seemed almost regal. But before Martha could admire her spirit, Beatrice hitched up her skirt and sprinted away down the corridor as though pursued by the devil and all of his minions.

So much for female solidarity. But there wasn't time to be angry.

The men were closing in, their perma-smiles never wavering as they herded her to the opposite end of the corridor.

She lashed out again with her stick. It almost flew from her sweat-slicked hands. "I-I have the pox." The lie was as feeble as her voice.

Ferret made a wet rippling sound of amusement in his throat. "So have I, pet. Who doesn't? And 'tis my firm held belief that a man and woman ought to have something in common to bind them."

Only an empty stomach prevented her from vomiting. What

would pox-contaminated fluids do to her baby? The thought sent her breathing into hyperventilation territory.

As they came nearer, the stench of stale sweat, halitosis, and long-unwashed clothes overwhelmed her, assaulting her nostrils in a putrid cloud.

"Jesus! You stink!" She hit out at them again.

Jacob pounced and grabbed the end of her stick. Yanking it from her sweat-slicked hands, he slung it over his shoulder then came after her.

Flight was her only option. She squealed and ran.

Too late. Rough hands restrained her, grabbing her about the waist. As he spun her around, she lashed out wildly with her fists, hoping to land a lucky punch, but Jacob was too fast and much too strong. He seized both her wrists and pulled her arms out at right angles, holding them away from her struggling body in a parody of a cross.

Ferret watched her struggle, a look of enjoyment etched on his goblin-like face. Only when she was secured, squirming like a worm on a hook, did he approach.

"Nice," he muttered. To Martha's disgust, he slowly ran his filthy hands over her body, exploring the curves concealed by her gown. His breathing was as rapid as hers, but for quite a different reason.

She bit her lip as his hands slid over the lacing of her dress. It took all the strength she had to remain motionless as he cupped and squeezed her breasts. Eyes clenched shut, she fought the urge to scream. It wouldn't help. Men like these got off on fear. It would only add more fuel to their lust.

Ferret exhaled. "Very nice indeed, m'lady." He slid his hands over her waist and down the back of her gown. He groaned appreciatively as he groped her buttocks.

Martha shuddered and kept her eyes tight shut. She chewed on her lip so hard she tasted blood. She was determined not to cry or plead for mercy. But this was only the start of her ordeal, and already her skin was itching with the proximity of the men and their combined filth.

How long before the urge to react overwhelmed her? What would it be like when they were taking turns at her? She recoiled from the image and tried to block it out by thinking of something more pleasant. Instantly, Vadim's face flew into her mind. He was all sexy and love-tousled, lying in bed with—

No. Her heart hardened in her chest. Not him. Not anymore. This whole situation was his fault.

"Get on with it, then." Jacob's snarling voice dragged her back to the present. "I want to get some gold before the other thieving bastards make off with it."

It was no use. The feel of their hands on her body was more than she could take. Zen-like calmness had never been her thing anyway. Taking a deep breath to bolster her failing courage, she flung her head backward with as much force as possible.

Pain flashed in her skull, white and hot, and a nasty metallic taste flooded her mouth and nose.

Jacob grunted and swore, but he didn't let go. Instead, the grip on her wrists increased. Martha whimpered with pain, her fragile bones creaking beneath the power of his fingers. The only positive aspect was that Ferret stopped groping at her.

"Be still, you bitch." Jacob hauled her back against him, his words hissing against her ear. "Or do you like it rough, hmm?" He took her earlobe into his toxic mouth and bit down on it.

Martha squealed and opened her eyes. Ferret's face was inches away, leering at her. Now he held a knife in his hand, its blade glinting in the weak daylight.

Her heart stumbled. Rape wasn't enough? They were going to kill her too? She renewed her struggles, dangling from Jacob's outstretched arms like a dancing puppet.

Ferret stroked her thrashing head. "Hush now, my filly." His bloodstained fingers snagged on the tangles in her hair. "I will not harm thee. I only desire a small token to mark our time together. Something you will have no cause to miss."

His gentle tone didn't fill her with confidence. Neither did a close-up view of his dark, soulless eyes. They screamed *serial killer*.

Panting and frantic, she could only watch as he wound a strand of her hair about his fist then cut it free. "Another lady's favor for my collection." He raised it to his lips then tucked it into the leather pouch that hung from his belt. "I thank you for your donation."

How many other *favors* did he have in that bag of his?

The distant sounds of men's voices called to one another as

the invading army battled with the castle's garrison. Clouds of plaster drifted down from the ceiling, dislodged by many hurried bootsteps on the upper levels.

Surely the invaders weren't all amoral arseholes? If only some of them would run in her direction.

Ferret lowered his head, rasping his unshaven face between her cleavage.

"Get off me!" She kicked out, but the heavy folds of her skirt foiled her attempt to wound him somewhere vital. Egged on by Jacob, Ferret molded her soft flesh with his cadaverous fingers, pressing it to his sharp-stubbled cheeks. His grunts and moans of pleasure sickened her as much as the violation of his touch.

She'd never feel clean again.

He tugged at the tie securing her shift, and the neckline of the thin linen garment slowly widened. Ferret paused to look down at what he'd uncovered.

"Ah, such a fine bosom. Perhaps the fi—"

Martha saw her chance and took it. In one swift movement, she flung her head forward, smashing it as hard as she could into Ferret's revolting face. He screamed as his nose exploded in a plume of bright blood. She turned her head away and held her breath to avoid the worst of the flying spatter. Although her head ached like hell and tears streamed down her cheeks, the satisfaction of drawing blood canceled out most of the pain.

Ferret swore violently and then staggered about the corridor with his hands cupped about his nose. "The *bish* broke *by dose*." Blood oozed from between his fingers, hitting the floor in a pattering stream.

Jacob laughed heartily at his friend's discomfort. His whole body quaked with the force of his amusement, so much that the tension on Martha's wrists eased.

Would it work a second time? She was desperate enough to try. Taking a deep breath, she launched her head backward.

There was another sharp impact and her brain collided with the inner casing of her skull for a second time. Brilliant fireworks danced before her eyes and then, for a few interminable seconds, she couldn't see anything. Dimly, she registered Jacob's pained bellows accompanying Ferret's moans.

She pressed her hands to her throbbing head and only then realized she was free. She set off down the corridor, swaying wildly. Dazed and still half blind, she stretched out her arms, hunting for the wall to guide her. When her fingers brushed over the soft wall hangings, she quickened her pace. Her ragged breaths echoed in her head, competing with every heartbeat, and black dots danced at the periphery of her limited vision. *Don't you dare faint now.*

"Come back here, slut!" The floorboards quivered with the strike of Jacob's pounding feet as he chased after her.

Martha forced her trembling legs into a drunken jog then she stumbled over a large obstacle on the ground. She fell, landing on top of a body—presumably the man she'd knocked unconscious earlier. Or maybe he was dead? She was too exhausted to care.

"Get up, wench." Brutal fingers gripped her shoulder, and she was dragged to her feet. Jacob's bloody, black-toothed grimace swam in and out of focus. "You are mine now."

Now she wanted to faint, to escape the terrible fate that awaited her at the hands of these brutal men.

"No, lad." Ferret arrived, wincing as he wiped his sleeve over his bloody face. "I told you I wanted first crack at this one."

"You had your chance. This bitch—"

"Unhand her, pig filth!" A male voice roared. "The lady is mine. Set her loose and face your deaths like men."

Vadim? It couldn't be him! Could it?

Joy surged through her veins, clearing her head and rebooting her vision. A familiar hooded figure stood at the end of the corridor, sword in one hand, a snarling, barely-restrained dog in the other.

"Vadim!" Her scream was raw and desperate, ripped from the depths of her fragile heart.

Flinging back his hood, he stalked toward them. His jaw pulsed, and his dark eyes emanated icy rage. Mad, bad, and altogether dangerous.

She'd forgotten how incredible he was. Even now, restrained by potential rapists, her body responded to his nearness. Her memory of him was like a pencil sketch when compared with the reality of him. All her love, anguish, and sorrow erupted in one massive blast. So many emotions battled for precedence. How could she hope to put them into words?

"About fecking time!" she cried. "Where the fuck have you been?"

Not exactly a Hallmark moment, but it was the best that she could do.

chapter twenty-seven

VADIM DEVOURED HER WITH HIS eyes, feasting on her presence. The long famine of her absence was finally at an end.

Although her angry words wounded him, they were not wholly unexpected. She felt abandoned. But nothing was further from the truth.

The ripening bruises on her face and neck did not mar her beauty, but his heart bayed for the blood of those who had inflicted them on her. Even her poor hands were ragged and torn. He flinched at the accusing expression in her eyes. But in that same glance, he glimpsed the heights of her suffering and the depths of her despair. Every fiber of his being burned in savage fury. Seldom had he experienced such pain—not without a physical injury to show for it.

It was as if her wounds were his own. Even so, the joy of finding her again lightened him and drove the leaden weariness from his bones. Battered and bruised as she was, he could not ever recall having seen anyone lovelier.

He glared at her attackers, but they would not meet his eyes. Cowards and rapists. They were dead men, and they knew it. The prospect of taking a life had never given him pleasure. But, by the Spirits, he would enjoy dispatching those two bastards.

Blood lust throbbed in his veins, echoing the wild rhythms of ancient war drums of the Ancestors. Unbidden by thought, his fingers tightened about the handle of his sword.

"Ah!" At last, the gaunt-faced soldier spoke. He glanced at

Martha, blood dripping from his ruined nose. "This poor fellow can only be your husband." Drawing his knife, he smiled at Vadim. "You have my sympathy, friend." He danced his blade through the air about Martha's face, a warning that he had come close enough.

Vadim stopped walking. "I would prefer to have your head," he growled.

The men laughed as if he had just made some witty jest. *Fools!*

Forge strained against his short leash, snarling at the bear of a man who restrained his precious mistress and held her to him like a shield. Vadim felt like snarling himself.

The fellow had his brawny arm draped over the gaping neckline of her gown, unintentionally preserving Martha's modesty.

Only fear for her life stilled his sword. What must she think of him?

Without words, she told him. The silent messages conveyed by her stormy-blue eyes were as easy to decipher as ink marks on parchment. Each one twisted his heart, filling it with despair. She hated him.

He drew back his shoulders and exhaled. Whether she loved him or not, he would not fail her now.

As the bear man retreated, he dragged Martha with him. Helplessly, she clung to the man's bulging forearm, silently beseeching Vadim to save her.

Forge snarled and lunged forward, almost yanking his arm from its socket. It took all his strength to haul the great beast back under control, even though he was loathe to do so. "Not yet, dog," he murmured.

"A wise choice, my friend." The scrawny man backed away, brandishing his blade to ward off any attack. "My companion here has a violent dislike of dogs." He jerked his head toward the man holding Martha. "It would not do to make him nervous. Not while his arm is about m'lady's slender neck."

Vadim ground his teeth and advanced, matching their cautious pace. Pulses of rage spiraled in his head, urging him to lunge at the men as Forge had done and rip them apart. How he longed for that luxury, the freedom to act on instinct with no regard for the consequences.

But if he fell, what would become of Martha then?

Though he was not personally acquainted with the men, he

had been a resident of Rodmar's camp long enough to know them for what they were: soldiers of fortune, two of the would-be king's precious hired swords. What they lacked in honor, they made up for on the battle field. These men excelled in the battle arts.

At best, their loyalty was transient, and it was often dearly bought. Gold was their only true master.

An idea formed within Vadim's mind. There might yet be a way to delay them. But he must act quickly. The men had already reached the turn into the next corridor.

"How much for her life?" Vadim demanded. "Name your price." He stepped over the lifeless body of their fallen comrade, and the glow of unexpected pride warmed his heart. This had to be Martha's work. His lips relaxed into a shadow smile. *Nicely done, my love.*

Forge sniffed at the unfortunate man's broken head then resumed his low, menacing growls.

"How much?" Vadim demanded, but louder this time.

"More than you can afford, outlaw." The thin man dabbed his bloody nose upon his sleeve. "What your bitch did to me cannot be repaired."

Bitch? He would pay dearly for that insult.

Despite the man's words, Vadim thought he detected a flame of interest flicker in his eyes, and in those of his burly companion. Were they hooked? If so, how securely? It was a risk, but he had to try.

Moving slowly, not wishing to goad the men into violence, Vadim put away his sword and reached for the purse dangling from his belt. "Perhaps this will make you a little more forgiving." He tossed the heavy pouch through the air.

It landed with a metallic jingle on the scrawny man's outstretched hand. He hefted the contents up and down several times, testing their weight. "Stay where you are, friend," he warned Vadim. "Let me consider the price of forgiveness." He re-sheathed his blade and peered inside the purse. Would they take the bait? He attempted to read the man's countenance as he bit down on one of the gold coins.

Forge coughed several times. Full of remorse, Vadim forced his fingers to relax their grip on the animal's collar. Poor creature. He had almost throttled him.

The younger man peered over his friend's shoulder. "What is it, Ralf? Silver?"

"No, Jacob lad. Much better than that." He flipped the coin into the air for his companion to catch. "I cannot deny," he continued, regarding Vadim with a look of wonder, "your donation has already made me feel more charitable. Tell me. How came you by such a goodly sum?"

"Release my woman, and I will tell you."

"C-can you lay your hands on more?" Avarice glinted in Ralf's narrow eyes.

Gold always proved the most reliable bait.

Wordlessly, Vadim extended his hand toward Martha, beckoning for her with his fingers. She peeped over the bulk of Jacob's arm, frowning. He could almost hear her questions. Thank Erde he need not answer her yet.

The quiet corridor echoed with the continuous rumblings of the dog's displeasure.

"Well? Can you get more?" Ralf had swallowed the bait whole.

"You have my terms." Vadim kept his hand extended. "Give me my wife. Now!"

"Bring more gold, friend, and we might consider it."

"Leaving her in your dubious care?" Vadim gave a grim smile. "I think not."

Jacob tightened his arm about Martha, making her gasp. "Fetch the gold," he snarled, baring his bloody teeth, "or I will slit her throat here and now. Is that simple enough for you to grasp, *Outlaw*?"

The very thought of it chilled the marrow in his bones.

Vadim lowered his hand and rested it upon the handle of his sword. "By all means, reach for your knife." He ignored Martha's outraged squeak of protest and fixed the big man with a stare full of hate. "Let us see who is the quickest."

Martha groaned. "Oh, for fecksake! I'll slit my own throat in a minute. Just hurry up and decide, would you? If you're not about to kill me any time soon, I desperately need to use the privy." She arched her eyebrows expressively at him, though her captors failed to see it.

Vadim could not for the life of him fathom the meaning of the pointed looks she was directing at him.

Ralf chuckled. "Your lady wife may have provided us with a

solution to our little stand-off. What if she locked herself in the privy and we stood guard outside the door until you returned with the gold. How would that appeal to you, friend?"

Friend! Vadim ground his teeth. If he heard that word again, he would—

"Yes, yes. That's fine." Martha jigged from foot to foot in a most agitated manner. "Can we just go?" She sent Vadim another indecipherable look, glancing from his belt to the scrawny man and back again. "Now?"

Curse his addled brain, of course the privy was a ruse! Martha was trying to provide him with an opportunity. An opportunity to act. All he required were a few seconds. One clear shot, and she would be free.

Vadim placed his hand on his hip, pretending to consider the offer and, just as he knew it would, the material of his cloak slid over his arm, obscuring his hand from sight. Undetected by his enemies, he eased the knife from its sheath, gently stroking the handle with his fingertips until it slid free. Then he rotated the handle and hid the blade, concealing it behind his forearm, the cold metal leeching the heat from his skin.

"Very well. It seems I have little choice," he said. "Lead on."

Responding to Martha's directions, the men reversed down the corridor, their eyes ever trained on Vadim and Forge.

They were wise to watch them so closely. Forge still strained for freedom at his side, the light *tic-tac* sounds of the dog's claws on the wooden floor matching the speed of Vadim's racing heart.

"Stop," Martha said at last and pointed to a narrow door. "This is it."

Vadim loosened his grip on the knife. The task ahead required a relaxed and steady hand. His fingers tingled, aching to use the weapon, to let it fly, but he forced himself to wait. If he timed this badly, he would not get another chance.

As if sensing his master's tension, Forge fell silent. The quiet was even more oppressive than his constant grumblings. Vadim felt the dog's neck muscles coiling beneath his fingers, quivering with his eagerness to attack.

The soldiers exchanged a wary glance. Now that the moment had come, would they release her?

"Oh, come on!" Martha cried, pulling at Jacob's immobile

arm in a futile attempt to escape. "I can't hold it for much longer. I warn you, it's about to get very messy out here."

How right she was.

Vadim stared at the men as intently as they stared at him. Revolting as they were, he dared not look away from their ill-favored faces. Their mistrust rivaled his own.

"And just so you know," Martha continued, seemingly oblivious to the deathly undercurrents swirling about her. "I'm talking solids here."

Vadim's lips twitched in amusement. How he had missed her—oftentimes unseemly—mode of discourse. This, however, was not the appropriate moment for levity. He took a firmer hold of the concealed blade, willing the men to release her.

More interminable seconds passed. The sounds of combat drew closer as Rodmar's army penetrated deep into the heart of the stricken castle. They would not be alone in the corridor for much longer.

At length, Ralf stuffed Vadim's purse into his tunic then took out his own blade. He nodded at his friend. "Do it, lad," he said. "Set her loose."

Time seemed to slow, stretching into an everlasting moment of perfect clarity.

Martha slipped from beneath Jacob's arm and hurried for the privy. At the same instant, Vadim took a deep breath and drew his knife then hurled it through the air. A heartbeat later, he released Forge.

Ralf barely had time to register surprise before the glittering knifepoint plunged deep into his right eye socket. His corpse crumpled to a heap on the ground.

Forge skittered over the slippery floor and, with a blood-chilling snarl, launched himself at Jacob. The big man staggered beneath the impact, screaming like a woman as the great beast sank his teeth deep into his fleshy forearm. He punched desperately at the furious animal with his free hand, raining thudding blows against his ribcage, but Forge clung on.

"Enough, Forge!" Vadim strode toward them, sword in hand. "Leave him!"

For once, the animal was obedient. He unclamped his great jaws from Jacob's mangled arm and dropped to the ground. Licking at his bloody muzzle and looking immensely pleased with himself, he trotted over to where Martha stood by the window, his tail thrashing the air in greeting.

Jacob sank to his knees, whimpering and clutching his injured arm to his side. His lower lip trembled as he looked up, meeting Vadim's eyes with ill-concealed terror.

Perhaps this miserable specimen of manhood could now empathize with all the fair victims he had violated now that terror was no longer a stranger to him? He was helpless and alone, subject to the will of a superior strength. Maybe Jacob finally understood.

The knowledge might be of use to him in the next life—Vadim raised his sword for the kill—it had certainly come too late to aid him in this one.

"Please... please, no!" Tears spilled from Jacob's eyes. "Have mercy, lord, I beg thee."

"Mercy?" Vadim stilled his arm and looked down at his vanquished foe. His heart beat coldly in his chest. "Were you merciful to my wife? Did you show mercy to the other lady you would have ravaged this day had my woman not intervened?" He shook his head, disgusted. "What I do now is an act of mercy, though you do not merit any such consideration."

With those words, he let his sword fall.

It *whooshed* through the air, descending in a glittering arc. One swift, bloody stroke, and Jacob's head bade a farewell to his neck. It toppled from the fast-spurting stump and bounced along the wooden floor, leaving a gory script in its wake. As it hit the wall, the head came to rest, mouth open, dead eyes staring upward.

Vadim heard Martha's horrified cry, but he did not look at her. He could not face her yet. Not until his blood frenzy had cooled. The men had died too quickly to assuage the violence thrumming through his veins.

He placed his boot against Jacob's still-kneeling torso and pushed it to the ground, being careful to avoid the red fountain that pulsed ever more slowly from the decapitated stump.

Mercy? He had been too merciful, and now he was suffering for it.

Vadim went over to the corpse of the scrawny man and reclaimed his purse of gold. Then he removed his knife from the man's ruptured eye socket, grimacing at the moist slurp as he pulled it free. He wiped the blade on his victim's tunic to remove the worst of the gore, then used the man's cloak to clean his sword.

He took his time, breathing deeply as he worked, carefully removing every speck of blood from the weapon. Gradually, the savage voices in his head diminished. Only then did he turn to look at Martha.

She was down on her knees, her arms wrapped about Forge's shaggy neck. Vadim could not see her face, for it was pressed too closely into the dog's fur. But this was not just a joyous re-union. The slight tremors of her shoulders told a different tale.

He felt something break inside of him. He rubbed his chest as if by doing so he could massage away the sudden shard of pain.

"Martha?" He went to her, closing the distance between them in a few quick strides. "What is this?" Vadim crouched at her side. Was she more wounded than he supposed? "Are you hurt?" Some inner sense warned him not to touch her.

Martha slowly unfurled and raised her face from the comfort of Forge's neck. Her glistening eyes regarded him with the wari-ness of a deer. "N-no. I'm fine." But her husky voice denied her words. "T-thank you for... rescuing me."

Politeness?

He felt a sudden chill within his heart as the painful shard moved deeper. Rage and a few well-aimed slaps he had expect-ed, but this... Their lengthy parting had altered her a good deal, much more than he had feared. Her eyes—once so warm and unguarded—were as a stranger's. Were things really so strained between them? But she was waiting, expecting a response.

"For rescuing you from those—" Vadim cleared his throat. His smile felt tight. "I need no thanks for that."

What else would I have done? You are my wife, my heart, whether you choose to remember it or not.

As much as he wanted to say them, the words would not be spoken aloud. The thick wall that separated them would first need dismantling. But how was he to set about the task of re-moving all the heavy bricks she had used in its construction?

The sound of many feet pounded up the staircase towards them. He heard the jangle of armor, and the rumble of male voices; a ribald remark followed by a quick burst of laughter.

Forge growled, and Vadim rose to his feet. "Come." He held out his hand, willing Martha to take it. "It is not safe to linger."

Martha chewed her lip. After the briefest hesitation, she offered him her trembling hand. Vadim exhaled, inwardly rejoicing at a sign so small but freely given. He clasped her cold fingers and drew her to her feet. Her very touch kindled fire in his veins.

He glanced about for a hiding place, for hide her he certainly must. By the narrowest margin, he had saved her from a terrible fate, but now the castle heaved with soldiers of both factions. Even usually mild-mannered men could act wildly with the fire of battle heating their blood.

"We could hide in the privy," Martha said softly.

She must have read his thoughts. Vadim nodded and let her lead the way.

chapter twenty-eight

W ITH THE DOOR BOLTED, THEY stood in silence in the narrow confines of the reeking privy. Vadim pressed his ear to the door, attempting to ignore Forge's wagging tail as it lashed against his legs.

He heard the group of men pause outside their hiding place, their voices abruptly stilled. He could guess the reason for it. Even for battle-hardened men, a beheading was a thing of gruesome fascination.

"Anyone know this one?" a gruff voice demanded. There came the sounds of shuffling feet and the metallic ring of weapons and armor.

"Aye," came another voice, "Yon weasly fellow is one of the hired swords. I do not recognize the headless man. An accomplice, no doubt."

As he listened to the soldiers talk, Vadim became acutely aware of Martha standing beside him. Although they did not touch, his body tingled at her nearness. He fancied he felt her life force caressing his skin, crossing the space between them.

Mercifully, the men did not linger. After all, what were two more dead men in a castle full of corpses?

Vadim exhaled his pent-up breath and turned to look at Martha. "All is well. They have gone."

She nodded but would not meet his eyes, her attention fixed on the dog. Vadim frowned as he watched Forge submit to her fussing. His puppy-like whines of ecstasy were most undignified.

Surely he was not jealous of a dog?

Although Martha's change of manner troubled him, there were other alterations that vexed him a good deal more, changes he sensed but could not yet decipher. Something hidden. Unseen.

Whatever it was would have to wait. Somehow, he must get her out of the castle.

At that moment, Martha's stomach gave a noisy grumble, so loudly that Forge jumped at the sound of it. She looked up with a shy smile and pressed her hand to her midriff as if she could muffle its loud complaints.

"Have you not yet broken your fast?" Vadim reached into the deep pocket of his cloak.

Her eyes flickered. "Not yet." Although her lips curved into a faint smile, there was no amusement in it.

No doubt she was reliving another grim memory he had yet to learn of. If only she would talk to him, he was prepared to listen, no matter how terrible the tale turned out to be.

"Here." He held out a small linen-wrapped bundle. "Try this."

"No, thanks." Wrinkling her nose, Martha moved her hands behind her back. "I feel a bit sick, actually."

Little wonder.

"All the more reason for you to eat something." Vadim unwrapped the package and offered it to her. "'Tis only a bite of rock-wafer, see?" He twisted his mouth into what he hoped was an encouraging smile.

With a sigh, Martha took the square biscuit and sniffed at it.

"Use your back teeth to bite it," he warned as she moved the biscuit to her mouth. This staple of campaign rations was aptly named. Some even named it *tooth breaker*. But bland and unappetizing as it was, the biscuit could be relied upon to move armies and keep men on their feet when all other supplies were gone.

Martha took a cautious nibble, and her eyes lit up. "It's really good," she announced then proceeded to devour the remaining wafer with noisy crunches.

Good? Not a word he would have used to describe a slab of rock. Truly, the castle's provisions must have been awful if the taste of it filled her with such rapture.

While she ate, Vadim pretended to examine his notched sword. But all the time, he studied her from beneath his eyelashes, taking in every inch of her disheveled appearance. What other trials had she suffered this day? The imagining of it sickened him. At least she had managed to secure the neckline of her gown. The ties were now pulled tight and securely knotted, concealing her flesh.

She shivered, and Vadim cursed himself for not noticing her discomfort sooner. Without waiting for permission, he put down his sword and took off his cloak, throwing it about her shoulders. Flakes of drying earth flew from the mud-encrusted garment, ricocheting off the privy walls.

"There's no need." She almost dropped her biscuit in her haste to protest. "I'm fine. Really."

"Take it." As Vadim fastened the cloak about her neck, he noticed the bruising on her skin. He swallowed hard, battling another hot flare of rage. These marks had been made by fingers. Whose? "You are soaked to the skin." He kept his voice light, suppressing his outrage. Displaying it, he suspected, would only make her retreat further from him. "Hardly surprising considering your earlier ordeal, out on the battlements."

"You heard about that?" She looked up at him then down at the filthy cloak he had wrapped her in. "Why are you so muddy, anyway? It's in your hair and everywhere."

"Ah, that." Vadim stroked the folds of the cloak, smoothing it over her shoulders. "The result of a minor mishap in one of the tunnels."

"What?" Her blue eyes widened, flashing with a little of her former spirit. "Did it collapse on you? Is that what you're telling me in your usual understated way?"

He nodded and turned away.

Twelve men buried. Only three pulled out alive.

He picked up his sword from where he had left it, propped against the door. As he slid the weapon back into its sheath, he felt the black weight of earth crushing down on him again. The screams. The dark. The utter silence. He closed his eyes and rasped his hands over his face. His last conscious thought had been of Martha. She had been his first thought on wakening too.

Her hand rested upon his arm, its touch as light and fleeting as a butterfly.

"I-I'm sorry for what I said earlier... about you taking your time, I mean."

"Why?" He turned and looked at her. "I *was* late. What did you say that I did not deserve?"

"But you were buried in a tunnel—"

"Only for a brief time. What of the other seven weeks and four days, hmm?" He took a breath to steady himself. "I listened to my head when my heart would have been the better guide." He touched her hand gently, and when she did not recoil, he clasped it and raised it to his lips. "I am sorry, Martha. 'Tis I who ought to be on my knees begging for your forgiveness."

The warmth in her eyes quickened his heart.

"Has it really been so long?" she asked. "Seven weeks—"

"And four days."

"You're right." Her lips twitched, holding back a smile. "Get down on your knees and start begging."

For the first time in weeks, laughter welled up inside of him—genuine amusement, not the forced and worthless kind. He smiled because he could not do otherwise.

He pulled her closer, slowly drawing her into the circle of his arms. She did not resist. Although she was thinner, her body felt soft and familiar. Touching his forehead to hers, Vadim closed his eyes, reacquainting himself with her scent. As he did so, heat flared within him, igniting a primitive need. He ached for her. The prospect of kissing had him trembling. But he dared not push her.

Suffering a man's unwanted lust damaged a woman. He had seen evidence of it too many times. Martha must set the pace. For now, he was content to bask in her presence like a cat in the sunshine.

She snuggled her face against his hauberk and sighed. "How did you find me? You know... before?"

"I had the good fortune to run into the noblewoman you saved from those..." Vadim cleared his throat. "When she realized I was not about to attack her, she begged me to go to your aid."

"She did? Thank God for Beatrice." She sniffed several times, her nose wrinkling in a delightful manner. "Is that me? I stink fecking awful."

Vadim chuckled. "No, love." He planted a kiss on her damp hair. "'Tis the privy, or perhaps me you smell; certainly not you."

"Liar." He heard the smile in her voice. "But just this once, I'll let it go."

Forge growled softly from his spot by the door. Ears pricked, he scrambled to his feet.

Martha tensed. "Now what?"

He kissed her brow and went reluctantly to listen at the door.

At first he heard nothing, save for Martha as she resumed munching on her rock wafer. It sounded as though she was eating a brick, not food. Closing his eyes, Vadim strained to hear outside. The gritty crunches were most distracting.

The approaching voices were familiar and welcome, men he trusted with his life and, more importantly, with Martha's.

He unbolted the privy door and flung it open. "Well met, my friends. How goes the battle?"

Seth stumbled backward, staring at him with open-mouthed surprise. At his side stood Reynard, smiling and composed as always.

"By the balls of the Great—M'lord, Vadim!" Seth clutched his chest, his cheeks glowing red beneath his beard. "What the devil are you doing hiding away in a privy?"

Vadim arched his eyebrows.

"Oh." The older man's blush deepened. "Of course. What else would you be doing in there? Forgive me."

Suddenly, Forge bolted from the privy and launched himself at Seth, whining and licking at every piece of unexposed flesh he could get to.

"Away, you vile beast of the Underworld," Seth cried as he stroked the dog's head. "I thought we might at least have had the good fortune to lose you in battle." But his affection for the animal was clear. During recent weeks, they had become fast friends.

Next, Martha emerged from the privy and stood at Vadim's side. "Are you being mean to my dog, Chief?"

"Martha... m'lady?" Seth grinned broadly and strode toward her, arms outstretched. "Oh, lass. It does my heart good to look upon you again." Enveloping her in a bear hug, he lifted her off the ground, squeezing her until she giggled for mercy.

Their easy familiarity gave Vadim a sharp pang of envy. He would give all he owned to be free to act in the same manner.

Reynard approached and shook Vadim's hand. "Your fortune seems to have improved of late, my friend." He craned his neck to look inside the privy, and his smile faded. "I had hoped to find Fergus with you." He glanced around as though he expected the lad to spring out from behind one of the many faded wall hangings. "Where has he got to?"

"Oh, shit." Martha froze in Seth's arms. She looked over at Vadim.

The distress in her eyes alarmed him. What had happened to the boy?

"Shit!" she said again, more forcefully this time.

Seth set her back on the ground. "What is it, lass?"

"It's Fergus." She fisted her hands in her hair and began to pace the corridor in obvious agitation. "He's locked in the dungeons. He had a fight with the earl, you see, and Anselm knocked him out—"

"Anselm did *what*?" Seth made a sound of disgust, deep in his throat. "Curse him for a son. I should have drowned him at birth."

Vadim silently agreed. What else had Anselm done, he wondered.

"No, you don't understand." Martha's glance flew from Seth to Vadim and back again, her eyes wide and shining. "It's not like that at all. He only did it to—"

"Forgive me." Reynard gave a brief bow of his head. "I must find my son." In only a few seconds, he seemed to have aged decades.

"We shall accompany you, my friend." Vadim clasped his shoulder, giving it a squeeze. "You may yet have need of our swords."

"And let us hope we encounter Anselm along the way," Seth muttered. "'Tis well past time I took that boy in hand."

Martha looked from one man to the other. "B-but—"

"Come." Vadim took her trembling hand. "No harm will befall you with three such doughty men as your escorts."

They set off walking, and Vadim kept a firm hold on Martha's hand.

Bringing her along was far from ideal, but the thought of leaving her again, even in a place of refuge, was intolerable.

"Will you all just stop for a second and listen to me, for fecksake?" Martha snatched her hand free. "I have something to tell you." She stood with her hands on her hips, glaring at them each in turn.

Her dander was certainly up now. Vadim smiled. He had forgotten how well anger suited her. "What is it, love?" he asked. "Make haste and speak."

She inhaled so hard her breast almost rose up to her chin. "It's Anselm," she said in a small voice.

All of Vadim's good humor evaporated. "What of him?"

"He's been hurt." Martha glanced at Seth's stony face. "Badly hurt. He might already be... d-dead."

Vadim stiffened, observing her glistening eyes with suspicion. Pity for Anselm? A cold frost attacked his heart, turning it to winter.

"You need not vex yourself on account of my feelings, m'lady," Seth answered with strained politeness. "The news does not come as a blow. I feel only a sense of relief. Now, let us go to the aid of a man worth saving."

He would have walked away had Martha not clutched his sleeve and pulled him back. "Seth, listen to me. You're wrong about Anselm. He's changed!"

Seth shook his head repeatedly as Martha attempted to convince him.

"Don't get me wrong. He's still a complete arse at times," she continued breathlessly, "but he helped me—"

"Exactly how has Anselm *helped* you, my love?" Anger goaded Vadim to speak when it might have been wiser to remain silent. He heard the poison of his words, but could not contain them. "Tell us how Anselm has managed to secure your favor so we can judge this paragon of kindliness for ourselves."

Martha turned toward him, eyes blazing. "I'll tell you, if you'd only shut up for a minute and listen!" She took a shuddering breath. "Anselm was trying to help me escape when the earl stabbed him."

"Good," Seth muttered in an aside to Reynard. "Lord Edgeway has finally done us a service."

But not quietly enough.

"Don't say that, Seth!" Martha wheeled about to face him. "Come with me," she begged. "It might not be too late. Anselm's still your s—"

"Leave this alone, love." Vadim said, willing her to obey him if only in this matter. Anselm was as a festering wound, the weakest point in Seth's armor. He would not stand by whilst Martha baited this gentlest of men into a temper.

"Don't you get it?" She backed away, regarding Vadim as though he himself were the enemy. "If it weren't for Anselm, the earl would've thrown me over the castle wall. Go and ask your men if you don't believe me." She flung out her arm, pointing toward the window. "They saw him dangling me over the barbican."

"Alas, I fear your wife has been poisoned, m'lord," Reynard said, casting Vadim a look of sympathy. "I can listen to no more of this. I must seek my son."

Without speaking, Seth followed after Reynard.

"But he's your son!" Martha yelled at their departing backs.

"No. He is *not!*" Seth turned, finally needled into anger. "The earl's brand is forever on his heart. Anselm is, and shall always be, Lord Edgeway's creature." He closed his eyes and exhaled hard, managing to master himself. "The boy I called *son* has been dead to me for many years now. I am sorry, m'lady."

Martha stared at the floor, muttering beneath her breath, as Seth and Reynard's bootsteps retreated.

Wounded though he was, Vadim could not bear to see her so down at heart. "Come. Let us follow our friends, hmm?"

But when she raised her head he realized his mistake. Defeated? Not she. With her chin held high and her cloak thrown back, her whole demeanor was bathed in the light of battle. The pale and trembling lamb he had rescued was gone. In its place stood a she-wolf—and a cornered one at that. The deadliest kind.

His heart quickened in response, sending hot blood thundering through his veins to parts of his body that had lain dormant for weeks. As discretely as he could, he turned away and, with a grimace of discomfort, adjusted himself to ease the throbbing ache.

"Friends are important, aren't they?" Martha asked in a voice so quiet he strained to hear it.

"Of... course... vitally important." Trusting his long hauberk would hide his arousal, he turned back to face her. "Especially during such dangerous times as these."

Holding him captive in her steady gaze, she advanced toward him. "I guess you must trust your friends with your life, huh?"

"Certainly. Just as they in turn entrust me with theirs."

"Remind me, what does your honor code say about promises, Vadim?" She paused, standing slightly out of his reach. "Would you ever knowingly break one?"

"Not if it was within my power to fulfill it. No." What was she up to?

A brief look of triumph flared in her eyes. "That's what I thought."

Why did he feel he had stepped into a trap and his answer had sprung the door closed behind him?

"Then you'll understand why I have to do this." She picked up a stout stick from where it lay on the floor and, gripping it in both hands, swung it several times through the air.

"Martha?" After all that had passed, she would still go to Anselm's aid?

"I'm sorry, Vadim," she said. "Whatever you think of him, the fact remains that Anselm swam an ocean for me today. The least I can do is step over a puddle for him now. If you won't help me, then I'll just have to go by myself."

With a swirl of her cloak, she set off in the direction of the stairs, with Forge trotting at her side.

"Surely, you are not serious?" He could not believe he was having such a discussion with her.

"My honor demands that I try," she called back. Her steps did not falter.

Using his own words against him? A low blow indeed.

Bravery was one thing. Foolhardiness was something else entirely. She had to be bluffing. The predators stalking this castle would eat her alive, she-wolf or not. Had she so easily dismissed her earlier attack?

In three strides, Vadim overtook her. Grasping her arm, he spun her about to face him, leaning down until he felt her warm breath upon his face. "And if I lock you away so you cannot go to him?" he hissed. "What then?"

"Do I really need to spell it out for you? Let me go!" She pulled her arm free and stepped back. "How would you feel if I'd tried to stop you doing some of the crazy things you've done recently, huh? You'd resent me and eventually hate me for it—"

That was unfair. "I have always considered your feelings!"

"I'm sure you have, but in the end you did what felt right for *you*." She jabbed her finger in his chest. "Tell me I'm wrong."

He could not answer. The snake of jealousy twisting and coiling about his heart had not yet robbed him of all reason.

Martha sighed and raked her hands through her bedraggled hair. "Just come with me," she said in a quieter voice. "You don't have to help. Be with me. That's all I ask."

"So be it." Though it was against every instinct he possessed, he would do as she asked. "But on those terms alone."

Her brief smile was his reward. It was almost worth the trial of seeing Anselm again. With luck, he might already be dead. And if not...?

Vadim drew his sword, praying she would ask no more of him.

chapter twenty-nine

THE VANGUARD HAD ADVANCED, PUSHING deeper into the castle. The clash of distant swords and the feral cries of their masters heralded the direction they had taken.

Only the dead remained to hinder them, mangled bodies piled in heaps like the detritus following a winter storm. In great number, they sprawled over the stairs, barring the way down. Mortal enemies finally reconciled, their broken limbs entwined in death's embrace.

As furrowed seeds the warriors lay, all crushed and scattered by war's great hand...

The fragment of the ancient lay revisited him, a tale learned long ago at his grandfather's knee. Long-forgotten words were now vividly recalled, ripe with meaning.

Death was a great leveler. Vadim could not distinguish friend from foe.

Martha said nothing. She took his hand when he offered it, clinging tightly to his fingers, her pallid face set in a mask of horror as they negotiated the corpses blanketing the stairs.

Though she could not know it, the feel of her small hand in his lent him strength. Such weariness as this he had seldom known. How long since he had last closed his eyes in natural repose?

It was a grim journey. The dead men's fear lingered on. Foul odors rose up, disturbed by their tentative footfalls: feces and urine, the iron stench of blood, and the sour tang of vomit. The only sound was the buzzing drone of meat flies, hungry guests at this manmade feast.

Martha tucked her stick beneath her arm and cupped her hand over her nose and mouth. Vadim was tempted to do the same. Unfortunately, he had need of both hands.

Forge was not ill at ease. He looked up from the foot of the stairs, merry eyes twinkling, and gave a sharp *yip* to hasten them. The dead were no obstacle to him. He had leapt over the bodies as if they were no more than rocks or puddles on his favorite walk. Vadim envied him.

Although the dead could not harm them, he gripped his sword tighter.

It was a relief to be out in the open air. Apart from the numerous carrion birds, this corner of the inner bailey was also devoid of life. Vadim shivered at the birds' harsh cries. Like black specters, they swooped down to peck at the dead. He swallowed and averted his eyes.

By common accord, they paused by the charred remains of a wagon. He looked up into the gray monotony of the sky. There would be no sun today. It seemed only fitting on a day of so much slaughter. He inhaled deeply. The damp air was blessedly sweet and untainted, gradually banishing the scent of death from his lungs. Cool drops of rain fell in an endless sheet, battering against his face, reviving him.

For all that they had suffered this day, together and apart, they were still alive, two of the lucky few. His heart swelled with gratitude. Did Martha feel the same way?

He looked at her. Eyes closed, her upturned face seemed to worship the sunless sky. Fast-moving rivulets of water cascaded down her face, smudging the dried specks of blood that adorned her pale skin. She still clung to his hand. His fingers tingled, such was the force of her grip.

Her lips glistened in the rain, beckoning him to kiss her. Would she welcome it, though?

Disturbed, perhaps, by the weight of his gaze, Martha's eyelids flickered open. What he read in her eyes shocked him, a look both wild and needful.

His gut tensed. Perhaps he had misread her?

She licked the rain from her lips. Whether it was an act of innocence or provocation, he could not tell. Heat coiled within him.

The stick she carried made a hollow clatter as it hit the ground, abandoned and apparently unwanted.

He held his breath as she placed her hands on the hard leather of his hauberk. Her hands slid upward, gliding over his chest. With a tiny smile, she linked her arms about the back of his neck.

He dared not move for fear of scaring her, but his self-mastery cost him dearly. It was all he could do to stifle a groan as she wantonly pressed her soft body up against his. No feather bed could be more inviting. Raindrops glistened on her slightly parted lips. He could not look away from her. The hunger in her eyes rivaled his own.

He needed to touch her. Still holding his sword in one hand, he pulled her into a clumsy embrace. Blood pounded in his ears, dispelling the last of his uncertainty. She still wanted him; that much was certain.

This woman of his changed like the weather.

Standing on her tiptoes, she strained to reach his lips. Vadim held back, determined not to let her have it all on her terms. He was still smarting from the wounds her earlier comments about Anselm had given him.

Let her earn her kiss. He could resist her... for a few seconds more.

The sudden flash of her eyes told him she understood.

Without warning, she grabbed a handful of his sodden hair, forcibly dragging him to her level. Pain seared his scalp, but it was not unwelcome. Like a warm summer breeze, her breath brushed over his lips.

"Witch," he growled softly, all thoughts of resisting her gone.

"Am I?" She arched her eyebrows. "So, burn me... if you can."

He needed no other invitation.

His lips brushed gently over hers, a slow reacquaintance following a long absence. This restrained politeness did not last. The taste of her sparked a violent need within his heart. Leaning back against the ruined wagon, he pulled her with him, crushing her to the hardness of his body as if by doing so he could assuage the ache within himself.

Without hesitation, she opened her mouth to him, countering his brutal kiss with a savageness of her own. Her small moan of satisfaction set a burst of hot need flaring in his groin.

If he was rough with her, she was much less gentle with him. Tangling her hands in his hair, she clung to him, kissing him with a frenzy that had him trembling. And he did not want her any other way.

He took what she offered, reclaiming her as his own, while her soft mewling sounds of want pushed him to the brink of control. She tasted better than all the imaginings of his fevered memory.

As Martha's hand strayed to his belt, tugging to pull it loose, several loud, lusty catcalls penetrated his love-fogged mind.

Wrenching himself from the oblivion of her kiss, he looked around. Three grinning men staggered in their direction, swigging from the squat bottles in their hands. The men had apparently discovered the earl's private store of imported wine. Despite his frustration, Vadim smiled. That would not please His Lordship at all.

He raised his hand in greeting, stifling his irritation at their untimely interruption. He knew these men. They were simple, honest folk, and as intoxicated as they were, he might have a use for them.

"Well met, m'lord!" The bearded man cried. "You have already made off with the treasure, I see."

With a disgusted little *ugh!*, Martha buried her face against Vadim's arm.

He chuckled and held her to him. 'Twas hardly the subtlest remark, but it amused him nonetheless.

"Indeed I have," he called in answer. "The greatest of all Edgeway's treasures." As he spoke, he trailed his fingers up the length of Martha's spine, unable to resist the novelty of touching her. "This rare and precious gem, gentlemen, is my own beloved wife."

Martha raised her face, her cheeks hot with color. "God! Not you as well?"

The men raised their bottles, bellowing their approval.

Vadim stroked a strand of hair back from her face. "You have an objection to compliments, my love?"

"Yes, when they're as bad as that." She grimaced. "Can we just go? My stomach is delicate enough as it is."

He tweaked her nose. "In a moment, you hard-hearted wench."

The men stood grinning before them, listing from side to

side. They were saturated—soaked through with both rain and alcohol—but their faces glowed with good humor.

"Here you are." The stout, bearded fellow thrust a bottle into Vadim's hand. "Let us drink to your nuptials, my friend."

"Aye. Drink hard, m'lord," added the youngest man. "Tupping is thirsty work."

Martha rolled her eyes, and Vadim laughed at her expression of revulsion.

"Be warned, my friends," he said. "My good lady disapproves of coarse remarks. Have a care you do not offend her delicate sensibilities too badly."

Their names were not as familiar to him as their faces. He raised the bottle to his lips, attempting to recall them. The wine washed over his tongue, rich and fruitful, bursting with the flavor of a faraway land. As he swallowed, he was transported back to the sunny slopes of the country where the grape had grown.

With regret, he handed the bottle back. The earl and Anselm still roamed free. It would not do to face them half-cut. Even wounded, they were dangerous.

The wine must have lubricated his memory, for the soldiers names suddenly came to him: Tom, Edric, and Harold.

The youngest, Tom, offered the bottle to Martha. "By way of an... apology for our ungallant be-behavior, m'lady." He spoke slowly to disguise his slurred speech.

"Oh... thanks." Martha wiped the mouth of the bottle on her skirt then took a few delicate sips. "Not bad," she said, handing the bottle back. "But I'd prefer one of those rock biscuits, if you have any."

"Rock wafer?" The bearded Edric fished about in his pocket and handed her a linen bundle. "Here. Take them all, and welcome to them." He grimaced. "Awful stuff."

Martha attacked the rock-wafer like a bear just woken from its long winter sleep. There was definitely something strange about her. The answer to the riddle hovered at the periphery of his mind, dancing away before he could catch it. Instead, Vadim returned his attention to the three merry men. "I have a boon to ask of you."

***

The killer butterflies were back. And they'd brought all their friends and relations too.

Martha clutched Vadim's hand as they hurried across the courtyard. Despite all the terrible carnage assaulting her eyes, her mouth was set in a perma-grin. She couldn't help it.

What was the collective term for butterflies, anyway? A swarm? Whatever it was, her chest fluttered as though it was crammed with dozens of tiny beating wings.

Their kiss had wiped many of the shadows of doubt from her heart. She glanced at Vadim, striding along beside her. Love welled up inside her until she felt ready to burst.

"It is most treacherous here underfoot." Vadim frowned and stopped walking. Without asking for consent, he picked her up, lifting her over a large pool of congealed blood. "Have a care you do not slip when I set you down."

Martha held onto him, her arms about his neck, staring into the depths of his dark eyes. "Yes, m'lord," she said meekly. With deliberate slowness, she slid down the hard, lean length of his body until her feet eventually touched the cobbled floor.

Vadim's eyes flared, and his mouth compressed into a harsh line. A tic pulsed rapidly in his jaw. Hands tightening about her waist, he slowly reeled her in.

She clenched her thighs together in an attempt to ease her discomfort. If she didn't get some alone time soon—

"Would you assist me too, m'lord?" a raucous voice demanded, reclaiming their attention.

Martha ground her teeth at the bellowing laughter that followed. *Damn it.* For a brief and wonderful moment, she'd forgotten all about the Chuckle Brothers. Vadim only smiled and set off walking, heading for the small doorway that led to the barbican.

Martha scowled, munching moodily on her rock wafer as she walked. Why the hell had Vadim invited those three idiots along? They were much too hammered to be useful.

"Hold me, Edric!" A deep baritone voice attempted, rather unsuccessfully, to mimic a girlish voice. "Oh, take me to your manly breast."

Casting a glance over her shoulder, she caught the disturbing image of Harold in a passionate clinch with the bald-headed Edric.

"Take your filthy hands off my bottles!" Edric cried with mock outrage.

She snort-giggled and turned away, shaking her head. *Fuck-*

wits. She crunched down hard on her rock wafer, savoring its salty goodness, and turned her thoughts to the sobering subject of Anselm.

In single file, they climbed the dark, narrow steps. Vadim led the way, leaving Martha sandwiched between him and the Chuckle Brothers. Even their voices failed to brighten the oppressive blackness of the stairwell.

Anxiety spiked in her chest as all of her previous fears returned. Was Anselm dead or alive? How long had it been since she'd left him? Half an hour? She frowned. An hour? It was impossible to tell. So much had happened since then.

Horrible things.

Ferret's leering face flashed in her mind. She flinched and shoved the image away. A graphic slo-mo replay of Jacob's beheading immediately replaced it. Even now, she could hear the gruesome thuds as his head bounced along the corridor's wooden floor.

Such terrible things.

She'd never forget the look on Vadim's face as he took the man's head: blank, and devoid of any emotion. It was difficult to reconcile the executioner with the tender man now holding her hand. She'd never seen him that way, and it had scared her. But what had she expected? That he'd rap the men over the knuckles and send them both for counseling?

She had to keep reminding herself; this wasn't the twenty-first-century world.

They exited the door at the top of the stairs and stepped out into the driving rain.

Martha glanced about the rooftop. He wasn't there. Anselm had gone.

The men stood in a huddle, watching as she hurried over to inspect the place he'd fallen. Not a trace of him remained. Even his blood had been washed away by the relentless rain. With rising agitation, she paced the empty rooftop, pointlessly hurrying from place to place. He couldn't have moved. Not by himself.

Splashing through the deep puddles, she went to look over to the battlements and peered down into the stagnant ditch. Nothing. She straightened up, raking back her sodden hair as she looked around. Where could he be?

She was about to rejoin Vadim and the others when something caught her attention. She wiped her eyes with her hands then squinted into the driving rain.

There was another doorway set deep into the hexagonal structure of the stairwell.

When she'd been up here earlier with His Evilness, the angle of the building had effectively hidden it, but from this position, the door was more obvious, especially as it now swung back and forth in the gentle breeze.

Anselm was in there. He had to be. She quickened her pace to a jog and headed for the door.

"Martha, wait!"

She ignored Vadim's warning shout and kept going.

A lump of stone on the door's threshold had prevented it from closing. Flinging it open, Martha lowered her head and stepped inside.

It opened onto a passageway. A solitary torch burned in a wall sconce, but its feeble light failed to penetrate the gloom, and cast more shadows than it banished.

Where was he? She looked around, attempting to slow her panting breaths, which sounded unnaturally loud.

As her eyes adjusted to the gloom, she spotted the sole of a boot sticking out from the deeper shadows of an alcove. Her heart lurched.

"Anselm!"

chapter thirty

MARTHA HURRIED TO WHERE ANSELM lay and dropped to her knees. Even in this poor light, he looked pale. Was he dead? She grabbed his hand. It was limp and lifeless. "Anselm?" Briskly rubbing his hand between hers, she called to him again. "Anselm, can you hear me?" No response.

Shit!

She pressed her fingers to his neck, hunting for a pulse, but her hands were too cold to feel anything so delicate; her fingertips were numb. Muttering a curse, she stuck her icy digits into her mouth and sucked on them. They tasted disgusting, but it wouldn't do to dwell on why. Instead, she stared at Anselm's chest, hoping to see it rise and fall.

A sudden thought struck her. Even if he was breathing, she wouldn't see it, not with a great chunk of metal strapped to his chest. *Duh!* Had the rain washed away all her common sense?

With slightly warmer fingers, she resumed her search for his carotid pulse. "Don't you dare give up on me now, you fecker!" she muttered, hovering over him, her ear almost touching his mouth. *Come on, damn it.*

The door creaked behind her. A pale shaft of daylight illuminated Anselm's bloody hand where it lay palm up on the stone floor. Like flakes of rust, dried blood cracked and crumbled on his fingers. Then the door closed, and the image faded into shadow.

"Is he dead?"

Vadim. Did he have to sound quite so hopeful? "Shush!"

A few seconds later, she exhaled, releasing her pent-up breath in a rush. "He's breathing!" As if to confirm it, a pulse throbbed beneath her fingers with reassuring regularity. *Thank you, God!*

"Of course he is," Vadim muttered. "The devil never dies."

She turned her head, smiling up at his dark silhouette. "I never knew you could be so snarky, love. I like it." Then she closed her eyes to focus on Anselm's pulse. It wasn't as strong as it ought to be, but at least it was there. For now.

She took off the cloak Vadim had given her and draped it over Anselm's body. The absence of its warmth made her shiver, but that couldn't be helped. He needed it more than she did. Vadim made a disapproving sound, but Martha ignored him and concentrated on tucking the garment snugly around her patient.

Anselm's breastplate moved when she touched it. She frowned, her waterlogged brain finally slipping into the right gear. Who'd unfastened it? The leather straps were undone, and the close-fitting plate hung loose on one side—his injured side. Martha gasped when she looked beneath.

A stout linen bandage swaddled his torso, and it had been in place for some time if the dark, blooming stain was anything to go by. Whoever applied the bandage had probably saved his life.

Then, why was she so uneasy? The hairs on the back of her neck tingled and stood on end as the old spidey-sense sprang to life. By now, she knew better than to ignore its warnings.

Why hadn't Anselm's mystery helper taken him to the infirmary?

If getting him out of the rain had been the motive for moving him, why hadn't they used the top of the stairwell, close to where he'd fallen? It was sheltered enough there.

Anselm was no lightweight. Why go to the trouble of lugging him here, to a dark and isolated passageway? There might be several explanations, but as far as she was concerned, none of them were good.

"Vadim..." She looked around and squealed as a man-shaped shadow emerged from the blackest end of the passageway. The wall torch flickered red on the blade of a sword—a sword aimed at the back of Vadim's head.

Before she could shout a more coherent warning, the shadow's blade fell. But Vadim had already spun about, blocking the descending blow with his sword. The horrible sound of metal screeching upon metal made her teeth buzz.

She couldn't look. Covering her face with her hands, she watched the fight from between her fingers.

Breathing hard, the opponents leaned into their locked swords. Then the shadow lunged, this time with his other hand.

"Watch out!" Her warning came too late. Vadim gave a sharp hiss of pain then smashed his fist into his assailant's face. The shadow man groaned and stumbled backward. Something metallic clattered to the floor. A dagger?

Vadim flexed his left arm, clenching and unclenching his fist. The effort made him grimace.

The shadow recovered quickly, launching himself at Vadim with a series of frenzied blows. "Outlaw scum!"

That awful voice. It would probably haunt her forever.

In the light of the wall torch, the shadow man finally revealed himself. Blood streamed from his nose, coating his bared teeth. His eyes glittered demon red in the torchlight.

The Evil Earl.

Vadim performed a hasty sidestep, shielding Martha from his deranged nemesis, and neatly wrong-footing the earl at the same time.

"Get out of here." Vadim shouted over his shoulder to her. "Now!"

Then he went on the offensive, driving his enemy further back into the shadows with each powerful swing of his sword.

She wasn't going anywhere.

Regretting the loss of her shit stick, Martha patted the ground, frantically hunting for something she could use as a weapon. The clanging of swords made it difficult to think clearly.

As she groped around for a missile, a cold hand touched hers. She jumped. *Anselm?*

He grasped her fingers, his grip so weak she barely felt it, slowly moving her hand toward his belt.

Martha's eyes bugged. What the hell was he doing? But his eyes remained closed. Was he dreaming?

He guided her hand to a small leather sheath on his belt. Then she understood. His eating knife. That would do nicely. She smiled down at him though Anselm didn't see it.

She grabbed the little knife then leaned to whisper in his

ear. "Keep breathing, d'you hear me?" A trace of a smile curved Anselm's lips before his face slackened once more. She checked his pulse again. It was still there, beating steadily beneath her fingertips.

Martha scrambled to her feet, stumbling and swearing as the wet folds of her gown snarled about her legs. How was Vadim doing?

At the far end of the passageway, he was still managing to hold His Evilness at bay though it was difficult to see them. She pushed the outside door, propping it open with a stone to let in more light.

Now she could see them better. Neither man showed any sign of tiring. The metallic clangs and screeches didn't let up though they were occasionally punctuated by panting grunts and a few choice curses.

Chewing at the inside of her lip, Martha edged nearer.

Suddenly, Vadim swept out one long leg. The earl gave a pained cry and fell, clutching his right knee. His sword clattered to the ground beside him.

A thick silence replaced the sounds of their dueling blades, in its own way, even more deafening.

Why didn't he finish him? But she already knew the answer.

She hurried to Vadim's side, her ears still ringing as if she'd just left a heavy-metal gig. Perhaps, in a way, she had.

She couldn't read his face. Without acknowledging her presence, he stared down at his vanquished foe. His blank expression was as much a mask as the strips of cloth he'd worn over his face back in his outlaw days.

From the fingers of his left hand, blood dripped silently to the ground, but Vadim seemed not to notice. His dark eyes never strayed from the earl.

Martha frowned. "Are you all right?" She moved her hand up and down his back in a gentle stroking motion.

"Why are you still here?" he asked softly. "I told you to leave, did I not?" He still didn't look at her.

What did he think she was, an obedient dog? Martha stopped stroking him and withdrew her hand. He was too prickly to touch. Instead, she followed the line of his gaze to the pathetic tangle of humanity sprawled out on the floor.

The earl was a mess, a pale shadow of his former self. Gone

was the magnificent peacock. In its place lay a rather soggy chick, wrapped in a purple cloak that now resembled a dirty rag. His once-golden mane lay in straddling rat-tails over his glistening scalp.

Still nursing his knee, the earl smiled up at Martha, displaying his bloody teeth. "You spoke... the truth earlier." He fought to catch his breath. "What you said about... my beloved Lissy."

Vadim's head snapped round. "What did you tell him?" His whole demeanor bristled as he looked at her.

Martha's stomach sank. "A-about the vow—"

"You had no right to speak of it!"

She felt herself withering beneath the look in his eyes. Unfortunately, they weren't devoid of emotion anymore. "I was trying to save Fergus's life—"

"By betraying my secrets?" His lips curved into a parody of a smile. "That was very well done indeed, my love."

"Oh, feck off!" Her own temper flashed into life. "Perhaps if you'd gotten off your arse and rescued me a bit sooner, I wouldn't have been put in that position."

The earl's laughter interrupted whatever furious reply Vadim had been about to make. "How diverting. I do so enjoy a good domestic."

"And you, Lord Gobshite," Martha wheeled around, pointing at him with a trembling finger. "You're nothing but an evil, pathetic, twisted old man. *He* might have promised not to kill you." She jerked her head, indicating Vadim. "But I certainly didn't." She brandished Anselm's knife to illustrate her point.

"And just where did you acquire that?" Vadim demanded. "You did not have it earlier."

"Anselm gave it to me."

"Of course." Vadim executed a perfect skyward eye roll. "I should have guessed it."

Did he really believe she had some kind of thing for Anselm? Was he really *that* stupid?

The earl made a grab for his sword. "Leave it!" Vadim snarled, kicking the gaudy weapon out of his reach. The sword spun away, bouncing and scraping over the rough stone floor. Then Vadim returned his attention to Martha. "What else has my *brother* given you, I wonder?"

Yes. Apparently he was that stupid.

A hot blast of rage raced from Martha's toes to her fingers, incinerating every loving feeling in its path. She clenched her hands into fists at her side and started counting. With supreme effort, she made it to eight.

"You know what?" She looked up into Vadim's smoldering eyes. "I'm done here." Her voice was steady and calm, just as she wanted it to be. "You two go right ahead and kill one another, okay?" She gestured with the knife between him and the still-snickering earl. "Enjoy yourselves. Have a nice feud."

She stomped off down the passageway.

"Where are you going?" Vadim called after her.

"Who knows? With a bit of luck, I might find a way home." She wanted to hit something, and if she stayed here, it'd probably be him. "I'm certainly not bringing a baby into this crazy fecking world—"

"Y-you are... with child?"

That stopped her. Martha froze, cringing. She'd said that out loud? *Shit!* Of all the ways she'd envisioned telling Vadim he was about to become a father, this wasn't one of them.

"Answer me."

The earl was laughing even harder now.

Slowly, Martha turned to face Vadim, her cheeks burning. This wasn't the ideal moment, but he had a right to know. "Yes," she said. "I am."

Vadim exhaled a long, slow breath. Hostility glittered from his eyes. She could feel the tension coming off him in waves. He was hardly a poster child for impending fatherhood.

His jaw tensed. "And I suppose," he said quietly, "I have Anselm to thank for this too?"

Martha gasped. *Did he*—? For once, her ready supply of insults deserted her. She had no words suitable to counter the pain now tearing at her heart. Burning tears shimmered before her eyes. They faced one another in silence.

The earl, however, had plenty to say—when he could speak without laughing. "I should have realized it sooner. Anselm's actions are finally clear to me. Now I know why he betrayed me for this drab little bird you call your wife."

At least someone was happy. Without a word, Martha turned and walked away.

chapter thirty-one

VADIM GROPED FOR THE WALL to steady him. Like a trebuchet strike, Martha's revelation rocked him to his foundations.

Anselm's babe was growing within her womb.

As if phantoms from the frozen North had ridden down on their winged steeds and cursed him, his heart chilled, a case of ice slowly enveloping it.

Though he hungered for her presence, he did not call her back.

A lesser woman might have tried to convince him he was the baby's sire. Not she. Martha had made no attempt to deny the child's paternity. One day, he might be grateful for her lack of duplicity.

Perhaps Anselm had taken her against her will? Forced himself upon her? But as he watched her, even this shameful spark of hope died.

Wiping her eyes, she crouched at Anselm's side. Was she still assessing the strength of his hold on life? Whatever had gone on before, her affection for his foster brother was apparent.

From the bitter tomb of his heart, a quiet voice mocked him as every dream he had crumbled into dust. *Even now, she lingers by his side, so loathe is she to part from him.*

Vadim clenched the handle of his sword and ground his teeth. For his own sake, Anselm had better be dead, if not—

"It is not easy, is it?" a soft voice asked.

"What?" he snapped. He had almost forgotten the serpent beneath his boot.

Taking advantage of Vadim's distraction, the earl had shuffled across the floor and reclaimed his sword. Still panting for breath, he sat with his face in shadow, leaning against the damp stone wall.

Vadim muttered a curse. As old and whipped as the earl appeared to be, he was not yet beaten. To lose sight of him now would be fatal. A wounded animal was always the most dangerous.

The earl hawked up a glob of phlegm and spat, narrowly missing Vadim's boot. "How does it feel, watching the object of your heart being so attentive to another man?"

Grimacing, Vadim moved his foot away from the froth of bloody spit. The question did not merit an answer.

As he leaned forward, the earl's eyes glittered. "You disappoint me, Hemlock. What kind of man have you become? See how tenderly your wife treats her lover, even whilst in your presence, her supposed lord and master." He pointed toward Martha, a sneer curving his mouth. "How can you stand by and do nothing? Tell me, did you surrender your balls when you spoke your marriage vows?"

"Be silent!" Vadim growled through gritted teeth. Blood thundered in his ears, urging him to violence. He quickly transferred his sword to the other hand and wiped his clammy palm upon his trousers. One way or another, he would settle the blood-debt between them. "Get up."

Using the point of his sword to aid himself, the earl struggled to his feet, gasping with effort. Vadim let him keep the weapon...for now.

Suddenly, the bell in the castle courtyard set off clanging, but not in warning. Its urgent chimes brought a message of joy to the victors. The reign of a new king had begun.

Leaning heavily on his sword, the earl tilted his head as he listened. "Rodmar took the crown, then?" He gave a sigh, perhaps in remembrance of his cousin who had worn it for so many bitter years.

"Outside." Vadim jerked his head toward the doorway. "Move." Despite his efforts on the new king's behalf, he was in no mood to partake in the celebrations. He wanted only to put some distance between this treacherous snake and Martha.

"And if I choose to remain, what will you do, Lord Hemlock? Kill me?" The earl chuckled at his own jest. "Oh, but you promised not to harm me. How unfortunate. Between them, the ladies have done an excellent job of castrating you."

Vadim smiled at this clumsy attempt to bait him. "Be that as it may, at least I had some balls to begin with. You, however—"

His words died. Further down the passageway, Martha stood up. Their eyes met in a brief glance, loaded with pain and anger on both sides. Without speaking, she turned and headed outside. Vadim exhaled. Had she abandoned her precious Anselm too?

"I should have killed you when you were a boy," the earl blustered, raking his hand through his stringy hair. "It would have been an act of mercy on my part."

Vadim nodded. "True enough." At least he would have been spared the misery of losing her. "Now, walk. Or must I kick you first? How is your knee, by the way?"

The earl sent him a look of pure loathing then set off limping down the passageway. Keeping him at sword's length, Vadim followed behind.

It was slow going. Using his own weapon as a walking implement, the earl limp-hopped with the speed and agility of an ailing slug. He stopped frequently, rubbing at his wounded legs and knee, muttering violently beneath his breath as he did so.

"What will you do with me?" he demanded on one of his rest stops.

"Nothing. Your fate lies in the king's hands now. You must trust in his mercy."

"Mercy!" The earl glared back at him from over his shoulder. "He will hang me before the sun sets on this accursed day."

"That he may." The prospect of finally being rid of him brought a smile to Vadim's lips. After so many years, at last the end was in sight. He would finally be able to bury the past. The earl was its final tether.

"What of your vow?" The earl hopped another step and stopped again. "You swore to do me no harm!"

"And to that I hold. My hands will not place the noose about your wretched neck."

"But nonetheless, they will be forever be stained with my blood."

Vadim's smile broadened. "I will deal with my guilt as best I may. But your concern for my honor does you credit, Lord Edgeway."

At that moment, Martha returned with Forge and the three soldiers in her wake. Without sparing a glance for Vadim, she instructed the men to transfer Anselm to the infirmary, threatening to smash their precious wine bottles if they dropped him along the way.

The men grinned at Vadim but did as she asked, lifting Anselm with exaggerated care and maneuvering him through the narrow doorway.

Now it was Vadim who halted. While Martha fussed over his foster brother, a tide of hot jealousy consumed him. The urge to walk over there and plunge his sword into Anselm's black heart almost overwhelmed him. Breathing hard, jaw clenched tight, he struggled to master himself.

The earl was watching. "I see your mind, *boy*." His mouth formed a sly smile. "For all your lordly ways, you are no better than I."

Without wanting to, Vadim understood. As he looked into the earl's eyes, he glimpsed the blackest reaches of his enemy's soul. All the pain and suffering he had caused lay spread out before him. "You dare to compare us?" he whispered. "I am nothing like you!"

A cold sweat pricked his brow and upper lip. He dashed it away on the sleeve of his hauberk while his heart set off galloping at a dangerous speed.

By the Great Spirit. Not now!

Unable to prevent it, the echoes of a time long gone flooded Vadim's mind, vivid in color, and terrible to behold. His stomach rolled. Boldly, the ghosts ventured into the light, the stuff of night terrors, no longer confined to the realm of dreams. Breathing quickly, he battled to push them back into the dark and close the door, but the vision was too powerful.

He was a boy again, alone and helpless, watching his parents die, cut down in the moonlight, their steaming blood glistened on the cobbled courtyard. It was real: the stench of death, the terrified screams of the castle's women as the earl's men used then slaughtered them.

The ruby ring on the little finger of his beloved father's lifeless right hand. His white night shirt transformed by a blooming patch of red as he lay shielding the corpse of his wife.

Mother?

The terror of his boyhood paralyzed him. Vadim was vaguely aware of falling to the ground, but he was helpless, shackled by the past. Panting for breath, he covered his eyes, attempting to block out the tapestry of horror.

This is not real.

The earl's laughter rang in his ears. Whether now or then, he could not tell.

"It seems a pity to end your suffering, *brother-in-law*. However—"

"What the hell have you done to him?"

The indignant female voice penetrated Vadim's drifting consciousness as nothing else could. *Martha?* He heard her light bootsteps, felt the touch of her soft hand on his brow.

A sword scraped over the stone floor. "Back off. Now!" Her growl matched Forge's in ferocity.

"Or what? You will nag me to death?" More laughter—the earl's. "Put the sword down before you do yourself an injury. Go and tend to Anselm. Vadim is mine."

"No. He's mine!"

Despite everything, she would still claim him as her own? Her very presence revived him.

"How many men do you want, you brazen whore?" the earl demanded.

"Just the two of them, thanks."

"M'lady? What are you—" Another voice echoed in the passageway. A man. Harold? Or was it Edric? Through the parting foggy strands of his mind, Vadim felt a surge of gratitude.

"Stay back, or I will kill her!" the earl warned. "Do not put me to the test, man."

Vadim heard the ringing of a sword point as it bounced on the ground. Had Martha taken up his weapon? It was much too heavy for her to wield, even if she did know how to use it. Taking several deep breaths, he clung to the present, to her, willing himself back.

"How did your wife die, by the way?" Martha's voice was friendly now, almost conversational. "Vadim never told me, but I'd like to know, what with us all being related."

"I beg your pardon?" The earl's voice was suddenly devoid of amusement.

She was deliberately baiting him. Vadim blinked several

times, and his vision cleared. He could see the earl again, wild-eyed and snarling, his sword poised to strike.

"I expect she wasn't a bundle of laughs to live with after you killed her family, was she?" Martha was saying brightly. "It's such a shame about the baby, though. Tell me, do you have any more children?"

"No." That solitary word oozed with poison.

Vadim exhaled. Martha was on such perilous ground if she only knew it. No one spoke of the earl's late wife and lived to tell the tale. Life flowed back into his limbs and left him trembling. His skull threatened to crack open like an egg, but at least he was himself again.

The past was gone. For better or worse, this woman was his present and future. If only she would accept him.

He grabbed a fistful of Martha's sodden skirt and hauled himself to a sitting position. She swayed but stood firm, shielding him from the earl with her own body.

Foolish bravery. He did not deserve such a wife. But if they managed to escape this awful place, he would spend the rest of his days endeavoring to do so.

Whatever it took.

"Ah. Here he is, back with us again." The earl grinned at Vadim. "How was your trip, m'lord? Your family were much the same as I left them, I trust?"

***

Martha glared at the earl. The *evil bastard.* Didn't he possess even the smallest shred of humanity?

By using her as a living climbing frame, Vadim managed to stand. Thank God he wasn't wearing armor, for he was no light-weight. He leaned heavily on her, an arm about her shoulders. His rapid breaths felt hot upon the sensitive skin of her ear. Martha shivered.

"You have timed your arrival perfectly," the earl said with a shark-like smile. "I was just about to dispatch your slut of a wife to the afterlife. I am so glad you are here to witness it."

Slut. The chance would be a fine thing.

Puffing a wayward lock of hair from her eyes, Martha raised the tip of the sword, grunting with effort. It was too damn heavy. The muscles in her arms burned and wobbled with the strain of keeping it steady. "Just get... on with it," she panted. Any second now, her feeble courage and her remaining strength were going to go bye-bye.

But as she spoke, Vadim's hand moved slowly down the back of her arm. His fingers cupped about her elbow, supporting her arm, keeping the sword upright. It was a relief to share the burden. The feel of his body, pressed so close to hers made her flesh tingle. His nearness boosted her flagging reserve of strength, which was just as well. She wasn't hopeful that Vadim would be switching into alpha mode anytime soon.

As the earl moved his sword backward, preparing to take a swing at her, the second hand of time switched to slo-mo. Forcing her eyes to stay open, Martha took a deep breath. Everything was sharper, more intense somehow. She was aware of Harold hovering somewhere behind her shoulder, close enough to hear his heavy breaths. He'd help them if he could. She wasn't alone anymore.

Trust them.

The earl smirked. "Farewell, you infuriating bitch." His sword swung at a terrifying speed, aimed at her head. Vadim shoved hard on her elbow, forcing the sword upward. With a deafening clang, she deflected the earl's blow. Every muscle and sinew in her arms and hands quivered, vibrating painfully with the impact.

Before she had chance to exhale, the earl took another swing, lower this time. Vadim let go of her arm, and gravity did the rest. Martha clung grimly to the sword's handle as the blade plummeted in a fast downward arc. It knocked the earl's weapon from its intended target, almost taking it from his hand at the same time.

Shit. Shit. Shit!

Harold intervened. Shoving Martha to one side, he deflected the earl's next blow, then he lashed out, forcing His Evilness to hop backward.

Martha puffed out her cheeks, expelling a huge breath.

Vadim's fingers curled around the handle of his sword and he took it from her sweaty hands. She was glad to give it back to him. Her arms still trembled with the aftershocks of using a sword. Her fingers felt numb. Never again.

She looked up at Vadim. Their earlier quarrel receded into

nothingness. They were both alive. Every problem and misunderstanding was fixable.

She held his face in her hands. "Are you all right?"

Vadim nodded. A light flickered in his dark pirate's eyes.

"Really?" She didn't believe him. His skin had an unhealthy gray tinge. "How's your arm? Is it still bleeding?" When she made to take his hand and look, he gently set her aside.

"Later." Standing unsupported, he turned to watch Harold's fight with the earl.

Both men were still beating the crap out of each other, their swords a blur of motion. But even to Martha's untutored eyes, Harold held the advantage. The earl was wounded and limping, it was all he could do to stay on his feet as he struggled to deflect his opponent's tireless sword.

She stared at Vadim's solemn profile. "W-what are you going to do?" Surely he wasn't thinking about fighting again?

"I must... finish this." Lowering his head, he placed a gentle kiss on her brow.

Martha closed her eyes, imperceptibly swaying toward him. She clutched the ties on his hauberk, inhaling his intoxicating warm man scent. It had a lethal affect on her senses. When he touched her this way, the other stuff didn't matter. Every irritation, every hurt, faded into nothing.

Vadim disentangled her fingers from his clothing then pressed a brief kiss onto the palms of each of her hands in turn. Martha shivered. The softness of his lips contrasted fiercely with the sharpness of his stubble as it moved over her skin. And all the time, his dark eyes held her captive, piercing her heart, daring her not to love him.

Without another word, he released her. Using the wall to steady himself, he headed toward Harold and the earl on an intercept course.

When Vadim arrived, Harold stepped aside, readily relinquishing his position. He backed away slowly and came to stand at Martha's side.

She glanced at his stony profile, his heaving chest, his sword still poised for battle. She'd badly misjudged this man. The bottles of wine had fooled her, but Harold was no drunken sot. He'd fought too well. Now, steely-eyed and motionless, not a trace of his former *drunkenness* remained. Perhaps the Chuckle Brothers' apparent intoxication was nothing more than a physical manifestation of euphoria at having survived battle?

Vadim stumbled, reclaiming her full attention. He almost fell, but managed to right himself at the last moment, blocking the earl's sword with a sickening screech of metal. Martha flinched. Vadim's footwork was clumsy and uncoordinated. There was no fluid grace in the strokes of his sword. Wounded in their different ways, he and the earl were now evenly matched.

It was close, too close to call. Her heart pounded in her throat as she reached into her pocket and gripped Anselm's knife, curling her fingers about the handle. If Vadim needed her, she'd be ready.

The earl attacked Vadim with renewed ferocity. With a bone-chilling cry, he lashed out, forcing his opponent into a hasty retreat.

Taking hold of Martha's arm, Harold dragged her away from the oncoming danger. "Go," he said, shoving her through the narrow doorway that led outside.

The rain had not let up. If anything, it was worse than before, hammering down in hard bullets from the lumbering black clouds. Harold took her arm again, guiding her away from the doorway. Then they stopped. Waiting.

Martha shivered, willing Vadim to appear. Her teeth set off chattering uncontrollably—a combination of cold and a bowel-clenching fear. The sound of clashing swords advanced. At any moment, he could be taken from her. One well-placed thrust of metal, and he'd be gone.

Please don't let him die. Without making a sound, her lips shaped the words of her heart's constant mantra as if by doing so she could keep him safe.

The two men stumbled out of the door, locked in a deadly embrace. Their swords were silent now, pressed together like the hands of a supplicant, pointing heavenward. Clinging to one another, they wrestled to take the advantage. Suddenly, they stumbled. Still entangled, they crashed to the ground, hitting a large puddle with a tremendous splash.

Martha sought Harold's arm, digging her scagged fingernails into his leather arm brace.

Vadim lay on his back, straining to push the earl away. The older man pressed nearer, grimacing like a gargoyle, rainwater pouring from his snarling mouth like neverending drool. While his sword hand pressed down on Vadim's throat, his free hand reached for something on his belt.

Martha gasped. Another weapon?

She pulled Anselm's knife from the pocket of her gown. She couldn't stand by and do nothing. But Harold forestalled her, seizing her arm as she made to leave.

"Let me go!" She struggled to pull free. "I have to help him."

But Harold clung on. "Be still, lass," he said without looking away from the fight. "'Tis a matter of honor. Do not interfere. He would not thank you for it."

She almost laughed. That bloody word again. "I don't give a sh—Oh!"

Vadim reared up, smashing his head into the earl's face. With an agonized howl, the older man rolled away, his free hand clamped over his bloody nose and mouth.

Martha stopped struggling and exhaled. *Oh, thank God!*

Vadim scrambled to his feet and shook his head a couple of times, strands of long black hair flying wildly about his face. Without hesitation, he advanced on his enemy.

Stooped and bent, the earl staggered for the battlements, the point of his precious sword trailing carelessly on the ground.

Martha and Harold followed after them.

"Where's he going?" Martha wasn't aware she'd spoken aloud until Harold answered:

"To his doom."

His Evilness was up against the stone ramparts. There was nowhere left to hide. Blinking against the hard rain, Martha swiped her wet sleeve over her face. Earlier today, almost in this very spot, the earl had tried to throw her from the battlements. She frowned. Had it only been today? It felt like a decade ago.

"Do you yield, m'lord?" Vadim lowered his sword and paused before the cowering figure of the earl.

"To you, pigfilth? I think not." Using the wall to support himself, the earl stood upright. Fresh blood streamed from his nose and mouth, the red dissipating to pink as the rain washed it from his face.

"'Tis over. Lay down your sword and—"

"Never!"

The earl might have been beaten physically, but there was

nothing wrong with his mouth. Well, apart from a few missing teeth, Martha noted with satisfaction.

"If you surrender, by my word I shall do you no further harm." Vadim was unruffled, a patient parent speaking to an unruly child. How could he be so calm?

"By your own admission, you would not need to," the earl sneered. "Your upstart of a king would gladly do it on your behalf." A sudden calmness transformed his wild eyes. "I would not give you the satisfaction."

Vadim made no attempt to deny it. "Then what will you do, m'lord?" he asked softly. "Shall we stand here in the rain until they come for you?"

Slowly, the earl shook his head. A curious expression of warmth entered his pale blue eyes. It almost looked like affection. "You remind me of Lissy," he said, at last. "You are not so beautiful, of course, but the resemblance has unnerved me all these long years."

A shiver raced up Martha's spine, a sudden premonition. Even Harold must have sensed it, for he resheathed his sword and clung to her arm a little more tightly.

Vadim's expression softened. "She loved you well, m'lord. Perhaps better than any of us."

Nodding, the earl wiped his hand over his face. "I know it, but all the same, I thank you for your words. They comfort me. And in return, I give you this." He twisted the ruby ring from his little finger and tossed it. "You may as well have it."

Vadim snatched the ring from the air and kept it clenched within his fist, his expression indecipherable.

The earl glanced over at Martha. "There is one thing I would ask you before the end. Why her?" His nose wrinkled in apparent disapproval. "The fair ladies of court frequently twittered over your exploits, Lord Hemlock. Any one of them was ripe for the plucking had you troubled yourself to attempt it. Why ever did you fall for this... drab little bird?"

Cheeky fecker! Indignation flared in Martha's breast. Why did he keep going on about her appearance? Granted, she wasn't exactly looking her best right now, but who would after the day—

Vadim glanced over his shoulder, silencing her with the

tender look in his eyes. "She makes me smile," he said simply. "I thought I had forgotten how."

The earl nodded. "I see." He gathered his tattered purple cloak about him. "A sound enough reason. I envy you, Hemlock." Without another word, the earl clambered onto the battlement and hurled himself over the wall.

chapter thirty-two

V ADIM RAN TO THE WALL and stared down into the ditch. Far below him, the earl lay shattered and lifeless, his head tilted at an unnatural angle. The murky waters were already claiming his body, slowly sucking it down between the jagged chunks of masonry.

After so many bloody years, their partnership, unholy as it had been, was at an end, the final tie with the past severed.

Harold looked over the parapet. "The crafty beggar escaped the noose, just as he wanted."

That he had. But Vadim experienced no joy in his enemy's passing, only a peculiar sense of melancholy.

Martha touched his arm, her lovely eyes clouded with pity as if she understood the conflicting emotions of his heart. He sheathed his sword and reached for her hand. Without a word, she entwined her cold little fingers with his and did not let go. Even without knowing it, she did him good.

In silence, they watched as the unwholesome water swallowed the earl's corpse. For a time, they continued to stare at the spot where it had vanished, each lost in a private remembrance until a loud crunching intruded on Vadim's morbid reverie.

Martha was starting on yet another piece of rock wafer.

The baby. He had almost forgotten.

A hard knot formed in his stomach, but he exhaled, forcing the tension away. Whoever had sired the child, it was innocent in all this. It had not asked to be born. He turned away from the wall and looked at Martha, studying her intently. She stood at his side, drenched to her skin, her body wracked with violent shivers. A continuous trickle of rainwater ran along the tangled strands of her hair like hot wax running down the wick of a candle. She met his gaze, and her lips curved into a smile. The sight of it drove the air from his lungs.

Despite all the hardships she had suffered these past months, both with and without him, she was still here, standing in her rightful place at his side. Their time apart had not diminished the warmth of her eyes. Her presence humbled him. What had he done to merit such loyalty?

He stroked the pad of his thumb over the fullness of her lower lip, removing the stray crumbs of wafer sticking to it. As he did so, her eyes darkened, betraying a darker, needful, emotion. In that instant, the snakes of jealousy loosened their coils about his heart and slithered away to torment some other poor fool. In their absence, he saw her clearly again.

In essentials, Martha had not changed. Except for the baby, she was remarkably unaltered by her time in Edgeway. Despite everything, her heart was constant. He knew beyond doubt that she loved him. Her valiant actions of the day had proved it.

Whether his foster brother lived or died no longer mattered. Anselm was not a threat.

If he desired a glimpse of the man with the power to ruin it all, he need only look in a mirror. His future happiness with Martha depended on his ability to make the right choice now.

The baby was not only Anselm's. It was Martha's too. He stroked back a strand of hair from her face, staring deeply into her questioning eyes. A line from their wedding vows echoed in his mind:

The storms of life shall only strengthen our bond.

Had they? Their married life thus far had been afflicted with some particularly inclement weather. Yet here they were, standing outside on a gusty rooftop, enduring some of the foulest weather imaginable, and on the bloodiest of days. But their hands were still entwined, and he had never loved her more.

The earl's death had disoriented him, temporarily robbing him of a sense of purpose. But as the fog in his mind lifted, Vadim discovered a new one, a better one. The past was gone, and the future held much more promise. In the end, it was an easy decision. Unworthy as he might prove to be as a father, the baby had secured his love and protection. One thing was certain, the child would never call Anselm *Father*. He would see to that.

"Come." Vadim squeezed Martha's hand. "Let us find you some dry garments, my love."

A small frown puckered her brow. "B-but what about... A—"

"Anselm?" Speaking his name no longer wounded him. "You commanded my men to deliver him to the infirmary, did you not?" He arched his eyebrows at Harold.

"That she did, m'lord, and with all the authority of a true captain." The bearded man grinned. "Have no fear, m'lady. Your friend will be under the leech's care by now."

"Leeches?" Martha frowned. "What good's that going to do him? The last thing he needs is to lose more blood."

Harold burst into laughter at her blunder, and it took all of Vadim's self-mastery not to do the same though, secretly, the thought of Anselm beset by blood-sucking pond life amused him a good deal.

chapter thirty-three

A S THEY APPROACHED ANSELM'S CHAMBERS, Martha's cheeks were still burning. How the hell was she supposed to know that *leech* was another name for physician? She could still hear Harold snickering to himself as he walked behind them. Vadim hadn't laughed—fortunately for him—but his shining eyes and twitching lips had given him away when he'd explained her mistake. Even now, he couldn't meet her eyes.

She wasn't cross, not really. It was good to see him more cheerful. He'd looked gutted earlier after His Evilness had jumped from the battlements. Seeing him so lost tore at her heart. At least they were finally rid of the hateful man. Maybe now Vadim's hidden wounds might have a chance to scab over. Not that they'd ever completely heal.

They reached the heavy oak door of Anselm's rooms. She couldn't wait to get out of her wet things. Although she'd lost her small bundle of possessions somewhere along the way, she still had a couple of gowns stashed away in the trunk in her bedchamber.

Vadim tried the latch. "'Tis locked. Do you happen to know if—" His perfect jaw dropped as she raised her skirt, fumbling beneath the heavy folds of wet wool.

Harold hastily averted his gaze and began studying a nearby wall hanging with a sudden rapt interest.

Ha! They weren't thinking about leeches now, or laughing at her.

Vadim cleared his throat and raked a hand through his tangled hair. "W-what are you..."

"Ta da!" She produced her stolen key on its length of ribbon, and waved it at him. "Problem solved."

"He actually gave you a key?" Vadim asked. More than a little sourly, she thought.

Martha grinned. "Not exactly, no." She stuffed the key into the lock, turning it until it gave a familiar heavy click. She lifted the latch and stepped inside, but neither man followed her. "Aren't you coming in?" she asked, sticking her head back out into the hallway.

Vadim shook his head. "I must check on the others first, love, and make sure Fergus is safe." He came closer and covered her hand with his as it rested on the door frame. "Lock the door behind you," he murmured against her ear. "Harold will stand guard outside until I return."

He was leaving her again? "Fine. Whatever." She snatched her hand away and glared up at him. Hadn't she spent enough time locked up in this room by herself?

"Forgive me." Vadim took her hand and raised it to his lips. "I cannot abandon them, not when they have risked so much on my behalf." His warm words brushed tantalizingly over her cold skin. "I owe them a—"

"But I need to tell you about the baby." She wasn't in the mood to be sweet talked just yet. "There's something you need to—"

"Shh." He placed a finger against her lips. "There is no need to vex yourself so." The tenderness in his eyes made her knees wobble. "I love you, wife, and so I must love him too. His sire is of no consequence to me. In my heart, he is my son, and the whole world will know him as such."

Martha's eyes blurred with tears, and her throat grew so tight she couldn't speak. Stupid, wonderful, infuriating bloody man! Why wouldn't he listen? And why was he so convinced the baby was a boy, for that matter?

"Then I must report to the new king," Vadim continued, his dark pirate's eyes begging for her to understand. "After that, I will return, I promise you."

"B-but he's... it's your baby." The tightness of her throat made her voice croaky, but she had to make him understand.

"I know," he said softly. Catching one of her stray tears on his fingertip, he raised it to his lips and kissed it away. "Have I not just owned him as such?"

Was he being deliberately dense? His sweetness broke her more effectively than any of the earl's brutality. Her neck wilted forward like a thirsty flower until her head rested on the chest of his leather hauberk. In a flood of hot tears, the horror of the last few hours erupted from her body. Throughout the storm, Vadim held her close, murmuring gentle words of nonsense against her hair. All the while, he stroked her back, soothing and calming her with his touch.

At last, her tears were spent. Holding her gently by her shoulders, Vadim held her away from him and placed a light kiss upon her brow. "I can hardly bear to leave you—"

"Just go." She looked up at him, forcing a weak smile for his benefit. "Do what you have to do, then hurry back." Then she'd make him understand about the baby, spelling it out for him in big letters if she had to. "While you're gone, see if you can find Effie, my maid, would you? She followed Fergus when they dragged him away to the dungeons."

"Of course." Vadim let go of her hands and leaned against the doorframe. "Is there anything more you require of me?"

Hell, yes! She had a list as long as her arm, especially when he looked at her like that. She wiped her eyes with her grimy hands. God, she must look terrible. The list would have to wait a bit longer, just until she was clean. "Yes, you might try and round up Forge. He must've gone to the infirmary with the Chuckle Brothers."

"The... who?"

"Er, Harold's friends?"

"Ah! Of course." Vadim stroked the back of his hand over her cheek. "Anything else?"

It was a pity to ruin the moment, especially when he was smoldering so nicely, but it had to be done. "Yes. Anselm." She flinched, readying herself for an angry outburst. It never came. She opened one eye and found him smiling at her.

"You require a report on his health and lodgings, I take it?"

She nodded. Why wasn't he glowering at her as he usually did when she mentioned Anselm's name? However, she wasn't one to look a gift horse in the mouth, however unexpected it was. "You'll make sure he's okay?"

"Consider it done." He took her hands and kissed each one in turn, his scratchy stubble tickling her skin. "Now, go on in. Lock the door, and get out of those wet clothes. Rest if you can. I promise to return just as soon as I am able."

And with those words, he left her.

***

It had finally stopped raining. Vadim glanced up at the heavy gray sky. 'Twas only a temporary respite but better than nothing. Splashing through the puddles, and avoiding the innumerable corpses barring his way, he hurried toward the infirmary. The quicker he performed his duties, the sooner he could return to Martha. The mere thought was enough to increase his pace and banish the chill from his bones.

As he neared the infirmary, however, his hopes of a swift retreat were dashed. A tide of men flooded the area outside the treatment rooms. Alone and in groups, on stretchers or supported by their brothers in arms, the wounded waited for the healers to attend them.

Amid the crowd, a wild thatch of red hair caught his attention. Seth. Reynard was with him, casting frequent glances toward the open door of the infirmary. Vadim's heart quickened. Were either of them wounded? Pushing through the mass of bodies, he set off through the crowd.

Reynard saw him approaching and raised his hand in greeting. As Vadim drew nearer, he saw that Forge accompanied his friends, his wandering ways curtailed by means of a length of rope attached to his collar. The other end was wrapped about Seth's fist.

The movement of the crowd sent Vadim off course, so he used his arms to swim through the strong current. At last, he reached his friends. "Are you both unscathed?"

"Not a mark on either of us, I am delighted to say," Reynard assured him.

"And the boy. How does he fare? You found him, I trust?" Nothing in Reynard's easy manner suggested he had bad news to impart.

"His Aunt Agatha is binding his head as we speak," Reynard said, jerking his head toward the open door of the infirmary.

"Though, it seems our efforts on his behalf were largely unnecessary." At this, he exchanged a secret glance with Seth.

"Oh?" Vadim looked from one man to the other. "How so?"

"When we got to the dungeon, the door to his cell was already open." Reynard's smile broadened. "Fergus was quite himself and enjoying the, shall we say, rather tender ministrations of a very comely lass named Effie."

"Martha's maid?"

"How did you guess?" Reynard asked. "Have you the gift of foresight now, my friend?"

"No." Though it would be a useful ability, especially where Martha was concerned. "Finding Effie was one of the tasks Martha set me."

"Only one of them?" Reynard arched one steel-gray eyebrow. "Dare I ask what your other commissions are?"

"Locating Forge was my next duty." He glanced at Seth, who was feeding strips of dried meat to the salivating animal, food from his own ration pack, more than likely. "But you have already accomplished that on my behalf, I see."

The older man was uncharacteristically silent, his expression strained. No matter how long Vadim stared at him, Seth would not meet his eye. Instead, he concentrated on the whining animal at his feet.

As the silence lengthened, an alarm bell tolled inside Vadim's head. Although Anselm's name had not been mentioned, it hung in the air between them like an invisible barricade. Martha's cordial relationship with his foster brother had reopened many old wounds, not least his own. But Seth suffered most by it. That might explain the sudden awkwardness between them.

Vadim was torn, his loyalty divided, and by the two people he loved best.

Reynard cleared his throat, and stroked his neat gray beard. "What of the Lord Edgeway? The last I heard, the two of you were about to settle an old debt."

"It has been repaid... in full." Vadim was glad to give his thoughts to another subject, even this one.

"In full, you say?" At last, Seth looked at him, surprise in his bright blue eyes.

With a brief nod, Vadim confirmed it. He hated being at odds with this man, especially over Anselm. The unexplained tension was sure to be about him. Guilt squirmed in his stomach. As hopeless as it seemed, he had to at least attempt to mend some of the damage Martha's friendship had caused; to make it clear that his own loyalties remained the same. "You have been my truest friend for many years, m'lord, a father to me in all but blood—"

"Vadim...no." Seth shook his head and stepped back. "Do not speak of it—"

"But I must." He grabbed Seth's arm, restraining him when he would have walked away. "This matter cannot be allowed to fester between us—"

Seth yanked his arm free. "What would you have me do, then? Forgive him?" He bared his teeth in a bitter smile. "After all he has done, you would take his part?" His voice was loud enough to still the conversations around them. Those men who stood nearest shuffled away to a safer distance, muttering quietly to one another, their eyes darting uneasy glances at Seth.

Vadim could not blame them. Although Seth was usually the most placid of men, his rare tempers were explosive enough to dilute anyone's blood into water. His own included.

"The dog could do with a drink after all that salted meat, I think," Reynard said, easing Forge's rope tether from Seth's hand. He departed swiftly, with Forge dancing along at his side.

With effort, Vadim held Seth's wild-eyed stare. The older man's flaring nostrils reminded him of an angry bull. His great hands clenched into fists at his side. He looked ready to beat something to a pulp. More than likely himself.

"There are no sides in this, Seth. I do not—"

"I saw him arrive earlier," Seth said, as if Vadim had not spoken, "swinging like a corpse in between those two men." He gave a bitter laugh. "He is probably already in the afterlife with his mother."

"Be that as it may, be assured, I would never choose Anselm over you, m'lord—"

"Yet, here you are." Seth's face drained of color, and the grim smile faded from his lips. "Have you come to visit him on his deathbed? The wonder is, you have not brought sweetmeats, or some other little delicacy that might restore him to health!" He jabbed his finger against Vadim's hauberk, punctuating each angry word with another stab. "Or would you have me believe you came here for news of Fergus alone?"

Vadim held his ground. "Of course not." Raking his hands through his tangled hair, he attempted to subdue the prickling heat of his own rising temper. He took a deep breath. It was vital he remain calm. It would not do for them both to lose control. "I did not know Fergus was here until I saw you and Reynard," he said evenly. "I am here at my lady's bidding, and for no other reason."

"Oh?" Seth leaned forward, breathing a gust of stale alcohol into Vadim's face. "'Tis Martha who wields the sword in your household now, lad? Is that what you are telling me, hmm?"

Too late, he realized Seth's rage was not solely fueled by Anselm. He should have read the signs sooner. The sickly stench of ale turned Vadim's stomach, but he struggled to conceal his revulsion. All men had a weakness. The ale barrel happened to be Seth's, and since Sylvie's death he had sought its dubious oblivion ever more frequently.

One thing was certain. This was not the opportune moment to be seeking Seth's indulgence. "Perhaps this discussion will keep until later, m'lord? Our new king has summoned me, and I am loathe to keep him waiting." 'Twas a small untruth, perhaps, but a retreat was vital. He would return to the infirmary when Seth had gone.

As Vadim turned to walk away, a heavy hand gripped his shoulder.

"What? Without first carrying out your *wife's* orders?" Seth tutted in mocking disapproval. "Whatever would she say?"

Wife? He had somehow managed to make the word sound like *slattern*. Vadim spun about and knocked away Seth's restraining arm. Despite his resolution to remain calm, hot blood thundered in his ears. "Have a care, my friend," he warned in a low voice. "This day has been long and arduous for us all. My patience is not without its limit."

"*Your* patience?" Seth shook his head and guffawed with laughter, his long red hair flying wildly about his face.

"Go and sober up." Vadim dared say no more, and strode away, heading for the infirmary. Curse him for an ale-soaked fool. Seth could go to the devil for all he cared. He would go and see Anselm, and at this very moment.

"Vadim!"

A host of outraged cries made Vadim turn. Seth was in pursuit, barging his way through the groups of waiting soldiers as if they were not there, knocking them aside like skittles.

Fearing he would follow him into the infirmary and cause trouble, Vadim waited for the older man to catch up.

"Wha—" Without warning, Seth's meaty fist slammed into his face, filling his head with a flash of brilliant stars. The force of the blow lifted Vadim off his feet and sent him sprawling through the air. He struck the outer wall of the infirmary with a hard thump, the impact driving the breath from his lungs.

Dazed and reeling, he watched Seth approach. A fleeting shaft of watery sunlight broke through the gray clouds, transforming his advancing figure into a silhouette.

"Ah, lad." Seth crouched down beside him, the rage in his eyes mellowing to something like regret. "What have you done to me? Have I been such a terrible father?"

Still gasping for breath, Vadim could only listen.

"Speak not to me of blood and lineage. On the day your own dear father died, you became my son. You were the child I should have sired, Vadim." He stroked his hair with a gentle hand. "You were the child of my heart. In truth, I loved you better than my own seed, but you knew that."

Had he known? Of course he had. Throughout his boyhood, Vadim was always aware Seth favored him over his own son. What memories of those days did Anselm carry within his heart, he wondered. Before he had come to live with them, Anselm had been an only child. What must he have felt, watching through his child's eyes as a relative stranger stole the affection of his father?

The truth held a sour taste. Over a period of years, on a daily basis, Anselm had gradually been pushed aside and ultimately discarded. If he had turned out badly, was there any doubt as to why? Perhaps the approach of fatherhood had bestowed Vadim with a new clarity of thought. Whatever the reason, he was sorry for the part he had played in ruining Seth's family, however unwittingly.

Seth was still bemoaning his fate as the liquor circulating in his blood dragged him lower: "...only to see my dearest son turn against me. I never imagined I would see this day. 'Tis a—"

"Be silent!" Vadim snarled. Using the wall to aid him, he scrambled to his feet. "My ears weary of your constant self pity." He rubbed at his aching jaw, regarding Seth with disgust.

"How dare you speak to me thus!" Seth leapt up, his simmering anger quick to the boil. "Insolent whelp." His hand balled into a fist, but this time Vadim was ready.

As Seth launched his hand, Vadim seized his wrist in a brutal grip, crushing down with his fingers until the older man yelped with pain. Then he dragged him closer until their noses almost touched. "If you strike me again, I will retaliate in kind," Vadim hissed in his face. "Consider that a fair warning, m'lord. You will get no other. Now go!" He thrust him away. "Sleep it off, and we will speak later. There is still much I have to say to you."

Seth staggered backward, his cheeks crimson with temper, but he did not attempt to take another swing. "I want nothing further to do with you, boy. From this day on, you are as dead to me as he." He spat on the ground then rubbed his hands together in a washing motion, symbolically ridding himself of both his sons.

"So be it." Vadim gave a thin smile. "Then, I will leave you in peace to wander through the empty rooms of your heart. Farewell." He turned away and ducked his head, entering the low doorway to the infirmary. He felt no remorse. Not for Seth.

chapter thirty-four

T HERE WAS BARELY ROOM TO move inside the infirmary. Bodies crushed around him, absorbing him into the mass. Every inch of space was packed with the wounded and with those attempting to treat them. Wrinkling his nose at the foul odors, Vadim looked over the heads of the crowd, seeking Anselm.

He could not see him, but he spotted Agatha and Fergus in a far corner of the room. The lad had a sturdy bandage wrapped about his head, and at his side stood a pale-faced maiden. That must be Effie. Fergus listened intently as his aunt lectured him about something or other.

Vadim moved through the crowd toward them, ignoring the moans of protest that followed him.

"M'lord!" Fergus leapt up, grinning his familiar crooked-toothed grin. "You live!"

Vadim held up his hands and smiled. "So it seems." He pulled the lad into a brief, hard hug. "How are you, boy?" He lightly touched the bandage on his head. "Does it hurt much?"

"Oh, 'tis nothing of consequence, m'lord." Blushing, Fergus glanced at the silent young woman, now perched on the edge of his cot. "In fact, I think Anselm did me a service when he brained me."

At this, the girl blushed even harder than Fergus. Casting her eyes downward, she began pleating folds into the fabric of her skirt.

"When Effie unlocked my cell, I thought the fey folk had

sent their fairest princess to rescue me." With a heartfelt sigh, Fergus sat beside her and took her hand. "I owe her a debt I can never repay."

Agatha shook her head as she looked at the young folk. "They are moonstruck, both, and in equal measure. I have barely had a sensible word from either of them since they arrived."

"I am very pleased to know you, Effie," Vadim said, disguising his amusement with a low bow. "You have my gratitude also."

The girl managed to mutter an appropriate response before returning her attention to Fergus. Sitting side by side, they continued their silent worship of one another.

Agatha sighed. "New love is truly the keenest blade, and a rather revolting one at that." But despite her words, the worthy matron looked pleased. "And how are you, lad?" She raised her cheek for Vadim's kiss then studied his face with narrowed eyes as if she could read what she sought in his expression. "You look better than at our last meeting."

That had been back in Darumvale, when he had not seen Martha for weeks. "I am much improved." He took Agatha's plump hand and raised it to his lips. "Thank you for all you have done, m'lady. I could not—"

"Oh, pish!" Waving aside his thanks, Agatha began gathering up the wads of blood-soiled fabric that lay scattered over the cot.

"You look well, m'lady. I trust the siege was not too arduous for you?"

"I cannot grumble, though all this rain has played havoc with my poor knees and hips. Still," she cast a glance around the packed infirmary, "I am a good deal better off than most of the unfortunate souls here. Poor devils."

Vadim agreed. The constant chorus of agonized screams and whimpers set his teeth on edge. "Speaking of which, have you seen Anselm?"

"Anselm?" Agatha paused in her task and looked up, surprise in her eyes. "Your litter mate, Anselm? Seth's—"

"One and the same." If he did not cut her off, she would likely ramble on in this fashion all day.

"What do you want with him?"

What did he want? He hardly knew himself. "'Tis a... delicate matter. Is he here?"

Agatha pointed to a motionless mound a few cots away. "The men who brought him in were quite insistent he be given a bed. They fairly dragged the leech over to examine him. Other than that, I cannot say how he fares."

Vadim's heart quickened. Anselm was alone—alone and unmoving. Was he already dead? Without pausing to take leave of Agatha, he hurried to his side.

"Anselm?" All he could see of his foster brother was a tangled mop of golden hair peeping out from beneath the blanket. He crouched beside the cot and gently lowered the cover. "Can you hear me?"

Someone had undressed him. He was naked apart from his trews and the fresh dressing about his chest. His armor and other effects were crammed beneath the cot in an untidy heap. With a cautious hand, he touched Anselm's shoulder, half expecting to find it cold, but his flesh was warm, and his chest rose and fell with each breath.

Vadim exhaled. His relief at finding him alive came as a surprise. "Anselm?" Suddenly, he did not know what to do. Carefully, he re-covered him, drawing the blanket up about his neck. Then he pulled up a low stool and sat beside the cot, staring at the waxy face of the man he had once called brother. He felt no hatred. That had died with the earl. Now, all he felt was pity.

In his mind, he revisited the days when they were boys. Their relationship had not always been as strained as it was now. At one time, they had been friends, getting into scrapes together as all boys will. Vadim lost himself in quiet reminiscence of the past, until a voice intruded on his silent vigil.

"M'lord? Vadim?"

"Hmm?" He looked up, his neck making a few sharp cracks of protest. Fergus stood at his side, regarding him with concern.

"Is there anything I can do for you?" he asked.

Was there? He glanced back at Anselm. He still had not moved, and his skin looked unnaturally pale. "Yes. You might ask Effie if she would be so kind as to wait on Martha? See to it she has food and drink sent up to Anselm's chambers."

"Of course, and gladly."

"If you can beg any rock wafers from anyone's rations, my lady would be most grateful to receive them. Oh, and I have posted a man outside her door. Doubtless, he would appreciate some refreshment, and a dry set of clothes, if there are any to be had."

Vadim could not look away from Anselm. His vulnerability disturbed him more than it should. Never had he seen him this way. Had Martha glimpsed this in him, he wondered. Had she seen something in his character that the rest of them had overlooked?

"M'lord?" He jumped when Fergus touched his shoulder. "I asked if there was anything more you required."

"Yes, there is one thing more." If Anselm was dying, the least he could do was ensure his foster brother's final hours were comfortable. "Have Anselm's bedchamber prepared. See that it is clean and warm for his return. Send word when it is done."

"B-but... is that seemly, m'lord?"

Fergus sounded appalled. A short while ago, he might have felt much the same. He turned to the lad with a wry smile. "He is in no condition to molest the ladies, if that is what troubles you."

"E-even so—"

"Fergus." His voice held a note of warning. "Kindly do as I ask or send me someone who will."

"As you wish, m'lord." Fergus gave a brief bow. "I shall see it done." With a final look of disapproval, he departed, his bandaged head bobbing through the crowd as he made his way to Effie.

Vadim was glad to be rid of the boy. He was in no mood for questions, particularly those he could not answer. For the first time in weeks, instinct not reason governed his actions. What felt right in his heart could not easily be put into words.

With a sigh, he looked upon Anselm. Was he unconscious or just sleeping? Whatever it was, his features had transformed into a face he remembered. The hard veneer of life's bitter experience had fallen away, softened into innocence by repose.

A heavy languor stole over him. Yawning, Vadim rubbed his hands over his gritty eyes. The warmth of the infirmary, combined with the novelty of doing nothing, was a powerful sedative. The background noise gradually receded into a hum as seductive as a lullaby. Were it not for the intermittent screams, he would have already surrendered to sleep's irresistible lure. He yawned again, the force of it making his aching jaw crack. He really should move around, but his body refused to obey him.

The urge to close his leaden eyelids was too strong. Surely it could not hurt to rest his eyes for a moment.

Was Martha already asleep? He imagined her in bed, all clean and pink cheeked, snuggled beneath the comforter, and taking up more than her fair share of space. He longed to join her there, to feel the warmth of her soft body beside him, and to wake with her in his arms. Ah, sleep. Was there any greater intimacy between two people? Vadim had never woken beside any woman except Martha. His natural mistrust forbade it. To sleep beside someone required a particular kind of closeness and an unwavering trust. Elbow propped on the bed, he rested his head on his hand, drifting between the lands of dreams and wakefulness.

A loud clang roused him. Heart pounding, he was already reaching for his sword when he realized where he was. Nearby, a red-faced old woman was apologizing to two scowling knights for dropping her kettle of hot water at their feet. Vadim relaxed and glanced at Anselm.

His lips were moving as in silent prayer.

Vadim leaned closer. "Are you awake?"

"Mmm."

"Can you open your eyes?"

Anselm's eyelids slowly flickered open as if the effort of doing so caused him great pain. "Water," he croaked.

"Of course." Vadim leapt up and snatched a pitcher and drinking horn from a nearby table. He poured the liquid into the horn and sniffed at it. Ale. It would have to do. "Anselm?" His foster brother's eyes were closing. Vadim sat on the cot beside him, the wooden frame creaking alarmingly at their combined weight. "Open your mouth."

When Anselm had drunk his fill, he turned his head aside, his dirty-gold hair splaying over the bloody pillow. Vadim got up and resumed his seat at the side of the bed.

Anselm was muttering to himself again, his lips shaping inaudible words. Vadim leaned closer until his ear was almost touching Anselm's mouth.

"Did you... find... her?"

There was no need to ask who he meant. "Martha is safe."

"May the... Spirits be praised!" He groped for Vadim's hand, clasping his fingers with a feeble grip.

Anselm's touch disturbed him. Spiraling through time, his

mind revisited the days before they were men. They had shared a bed back then, for warmth as much as from necessity. After waking from a bad dream, his young foster brother had often sought his hand in the dark.

Now, as then, Vadim squeezed Anselm's cold fingers to comfort him. How had he come to forget so much? A sharp ball of sorrow burned in his chest for all the wrong turns they had taken along life's byways. As the shadows in his mind fled, memory returned, fresh and clear, enabling him to see the truth. Although Anselm's affection for Martha was apparent, he was not a man in love. Dying or not, he would not seek comfort from his love-rival's hand.

Yesterday, back in Rodmar's tent, when Anselm had guessed his identity, his parting words had been as painful as a knife thrust to his heart: *Martha is my woman now.* Since then, terrible images had tormented him, fueling the fires of wild imagining that had afflicted him during the long weeks of separation from Martha. Now, like smoke in the wind, they were gone. Try as he might, he could no longer picture her in Anselm's bed.

What a dullard he was! The facts were plain. If Martha truly loved this man, she would be here, and if Anselm had taken her by force, she would have let him die.

Luring ladies into bed had never been a problem for Anselm. Quite the reverse, in fact. His good looks and easy charm had always ensured him a devoted following of fair admirers. He had never used force, not unless honey-coated words could be counted as such.

In the absence of another suitor, the child must be—

"How... is she?" Anselm recalled him to the present, his voice a little stronger now.

Vadim smiled into his pained gray eyes. "A little frayed, perhaps, but still in one piece." He clasped Anselm's hand tighter. "And it seems I have you to thank for it."

"Me?" Anselm snorted, half laughter, half disgust. "While she ran for... her life, I lay bleeding and useless—"

"Shh. Do not reproach yourself in this way."

For a time, Anselm lay silent, staring up at the black-beamed ceiling. "And what of my master?" he asked at last. "Do you have tidings of him?"

"I do." Vadim was reluctant to speak of it. How would Anselm react when he learned his beloved master was gone? "He is dead. By his own hand, before you ask."

"I am sorely grieved to hear that." With a heavy sigh, Anselm closed his eyes. "Had I known what he intended," he muttered, "I would have helped him on his way."

"Oh?" Vadim was both surprised and relieved. "And how should you have liked performing that final service for your master?"

"A good deal." Anselm's eyes snapped open, blazing with a touch of their former fire. "The bloody bastard stuck me like a pig! He has killed me for sure, I am certain of it."

Vadim was not convinced. Would a dying man be so easily roused to anger?

At Vadim's insistence, Anselm took a little more ale then lay back and closed his eyes, eventually lapsing into silence. Suddenly desperately thirsty, Vadim drank a little himself. His stomach growled, clawing with hunger. How long since he had last eaten? The night before the battle? It felt like a month ago. He glanced at the door, hoping to see Fergus amongst the scores of men still streaming into the infirmary. When would he return?

"W-what happened to your face?"

He found Anselm watching him. There was no reason not to tell him the truth, not when so many people had witnessed the altercation. "Seth." Being reminded of the injury caused his jaw to throb with renewed intensity. He tested it, gingerly moving his jaw from side to side. Each movement made him wince.

"He actually struck you, *golden child*?" The news heartened Anselm a good deal if the width of his smile was any measure of it. "Whatever for? You must have... transgressed very badly, I think."

Vadim smothered the flame of annoyance caused by his childhood nickname. "I am beginning to think," he said with a hint of sourness, "I might have deserved it."

"Ah! My beloved father took exception to you coming to visit me on my deathbed, did he?"

"Perhaps." Even as a boy, Anselm had been provokingly intuitive.

Anselm burst into laughter, but not for long. The exertion made him writhe and groan, and left him panting for breath, wracked with pain.

"Shh." Vadim glanced about for help. He caught Agatha's eye as she bustled past. "Can you bring something to ease his pain?"

She took a look at Anselm's pale face and nodded. "I will see what I can do."

At last, the spasm eased, and Anselm lay quiet again. Perhaps he had passed out? Vadim hoped so, for both their sakes. He prayed Agatha would return swiftly with her remedy. It was not pleasant, watching someone suffer and being unable to provide them with any relief.

He leaned on the bed and clasped Anselm's hand between both of his. "Martha is with child."

The words were out before he could halt them. Cursing himself for such folly, he checked Anselm's face to see if he had heard, but his flaccid expression did not alter. Vadim exhaled. What had possessed him to speak so freely? Incapacitated or not, Anselm was the last person he should trust with such news. Thank Erde he was unconscious.

He studied Anselm's blood-grimed hand as he held it. The shape of his fingers, each broken and bloody fingernail was so familiar to him. At one time, he had known this hand almost as well as his own.

"I suppose I must congrat...ulate you."

To his dismay, Anselm's eyes were open. Hurriedly letting go of his hand, Vadim sat upright on his stool. It was too late to retract now. But why should he? Anselm's words only served to confirm what he already knew. Had Martha not told him so herself? His rush of joy was checked by the memory of what he had said to her back at the barbican. Vadim cringed and raked back his hair. No wonder she had been so angry. "I believed, at first, that you were the father."

"M-me?" Anselm snorted. Despite his pain, his eyes widened, glittering with amusement. "I would not trust... your lady anywhere near my cock!" As he spoke, his hand fumbled beneath the blanket, resting protectively over his most vital organ. "And I suppose," he said, "you informed Martha of your... suspicion in your usual tactless manner?"

Heartily ashamed of himself, Vadim shrugged and glanced away.

"You did? Oh, you utter dolt." Anselm hugged his injured side and sucked in his lower lip, battling to restrain his laughter.

But Vadim knew this was to avoid bringing on another spasm and not due to any brotherly consideration of his own feelings.

"Subtlety was never one of your... strengths," Anselm continued, when his mirth was back under control. "Perhaps now y-you understand why I always forbade you to speak to the maidens we used to hunt?"

"A fair point." Vadim began unlacing his hauberk. He may as well get comfortable. This visit was taking much longer than he had anticipated. If Anselm *was* dying, the state suited him. Seldom had he been so reasonable or pleasant—well, apart from his insults. What else might he reveal if questioned? "Your fondness for my wife is apparent, and she is similarly struck with you. Why did you never bed her?"

"Did I say that?" Anselm gave a sigh and settled back on his filthy pillow. "Oh, it hardly matters now. Perhaps learning the truth will excite your husbandly wrath and give you cause to finish me off? I do hope so. Waiting to die is most... disagreeable."

Vadim raised his eyebrows and remained silent, steeling himself to hear whatever Anselm had to say.

"Had Martha given me but the slightest encouragement, I would have taken her to my bed. However, the kisses I stole were enough to warn me off."

"You kissed her?" Vadim's stomach lurched. Still, better a kiss than the alternative.

"I did." Anselm looked sheepish, like a child caught in an act of mischief. "But you will be glad to learn she bit me for my troubles. Very hard, I might add."

This was better news. "I hope she drew blood?" He shrugged out of his hauberk and kicked the garment beneath the bed.

"The wretch scarred me for life, however many miserable moments of it I have remaining." His voice slowed, heavy with weariness. "After that, the urge to bed her diminished somewhat. So? Am I forgiven, *brother*?"

Vadim detected more than hint of sarcasm in his tone. "No," he replied. "Not quite yet."

"Oh? I cannot think what else I might have done to offend you."

"Have you forgotten Darumvale?" Vadim leaned on the bed, glaring at Anselm as he relived that still-painful memory. "The night you first stole her from me and brought her here?"

"Oh, that!" Anselm smiled. "You really ought to be thanking me for it. My master would have killed her on the spot had I not stepped in."

"So why were you there, if not to steal my wife?"

"A source sent word that you were still alive." Anselm's eyes glittered as he spoke, over-bright with pain. "Perhaps foolishly, I imagined Martha to be safe with you. 'Tis not my fault she came blundering into the village all alone. What else could I do but take her? By doing so, I saved her life."

Vadim paused to consider his words.

"But I will not lie to you, brother," Anselm murmured. "I would have married her. In time, I hoped she would—" He grimaced, clenching his eyes tight for a moment. "—grow tamer and learn to call me dearest in lieu of *fuckwit.*" Then he was himself again. "'Tis a very strange word, that. Wherever did she learn it?"

Agatha returned, interrupting Vadim's laughter.

Between them, they helped Anselm to sit up. With Vadim sitting at his back to support him, Agatha forced a generous draught of a noxious-smelling herbal concoction into Anselm's mouth. Gagging and spluttering, he protested he would rather die naturally than be made to ingest poison, but at last it was done.

"He should sleep soon," Agatha said when Anselm was lying back on his cot. "And you ought to take some rest yourself, lad." She touched Vadim's cheek. "You look near death."

"Later. I must see Anselm settled first. Would you be good enough to ask the leech for a report on the nature of his injuries?"

With her head cocked on one side, Agatha regarded Vadim curiously. "You would save him then?"

"If I can, yes."

"Seth will not like it."

"Your warning is a little overdue, m'lady." Vadim stroked his hand over his aching jaw. "He has already expressed some of his feelings on the matter."

"So I see." Agatha chuckled and examined his jaw, turning his head this way and that with a none-too-gentle hand. "'Tis already a regal shade of purple. Do you want something for it?"

Vadim shook his head. "But if you have time to spare, I

would be grateful if you would take a look at my arm—a parting gift from the earl."

Thankfully, his leather hauberk had taken the brunt of the earl's dagger. The wound was nothing of consequence, barely a scratch; even so, it stung like fury when Agatha cleaned it. Aware of Anselm's sleepy eyes on him, Vadim somehow managed to stifle his discomfort. After applying a light dressing, Agatha hastened away to help the surgeon who was calling for her.

Vadim took up his position at Anselm's side. Nursing his wounded arm, he watched Agatha's remedy take effect on his foster brother. His breathing slowed and deepened. Slowly, the pain receded from his face, the fine lines about his eyes and mouth gradually diminishing. In the dim torchlight, Vadim watched Anselm's pupils dilate. He finally looked at peace.

"Why have you told me the truth... about you and Martha?" Vadim asked softly. "Only yesterday, you baited me with the nature of your relationship. You knew she was my weakness. Why did you not go for the kill?" Such uncharacteristic behavior must have a cause.

Anselm exhaled a long sigh. It was a very contented sound. "Has it somehow escaped your notice, brother, that *you* are my only visitor? How many friends do you see queuing up to empty my piss pot?" He waved his hand, indicating the shoals of people milling about, not one of them paying him any heed. "M-my popularity, I fear, is not what it once was."

"Your popularity only ever existed in your head."

"It certainly... appears that way, I agree."

"And," Vadim told him firmly, "I have no intention of emptying your piss pot."

"Really?" Anselm closed his eyes and grimaced. "Then would you... be so kind as to summon the old witch who just poisoned me? Have her bring me some receptacle I can use, preferably before I soil myself."

Despite his words to the contrary, it was Vadim who fetched the piss pot then positioned it for Anselm to use. Looking away, he tried not to hear his brother's deep groans of relief. When he had finished, Vadim carefully placed the warm, sloshing pot beneath the bed. Whatever else the earl's blade had damaged, Anselm's bladder appeared sound enough.

They were both drifting off to sleep, Vadim lounging against the bed, his long legs outstretched, when a voice at his shoulder roused him.

"M'lord?" Fergus was back. "I have carried out your orders. The chamber is ready." Fergus. His expression still bore a trace of disapproval. "I enlisted two men to help bear the stretcher. They will be here shortly."

"Excellent." Vadim sat up, rubbing his gritty eyes. "Thank you, Fergus."

Anselm yawned. "Are we g-going somewhere?"

"Only as far as your chambers. You are taking up valuable space here. I am sure you will be more comfortable in your own bed."

There followed a brief silence during which Anselm regarded him with incredulity. "Why would you do this?" he demanded at last.

Vadim shrugged. "Why not?"

"You owe me nothing." Anselm shook off the sapping weight of his herbal stupor, his eyes glittering dangerously. "Understand this, *brother*. What I did was for Martha's sake alone, certainly not because I harbored any residual loyalty toward you."

"I know." Why was he so vexed?

"Then, *why*?"

An unnaturally rosy flush tinged his cheeks. Vadim frowned. Was it the fever? So soon? "Do calm yourself." Perhaps a small lie might pacify him? "I am merely carrying out Martha's instructions, nothing more." He held up his hands. "You have no cause to feel beholden to me."

"Oh." Anselm sank back against his pillow, still breathing hard. "For a moment there, I feared you were about to say you loved me."

Vadim chuckled. "There is no danger of that, I assure you."

Fergus stepped closer. "Perhaps he might prefer a room in the dungeon? It is—"

Vadim silenced the lad with a glare. "Not helpful, Fergus. Go and see if you can chase up those men you promised me."

"No need, m'lord." He nodded towards the door. "Here they come."

Vadim rose from his seat and stretched, looking over to where Fergus had indicated. His heart sank. Edric and Tom—Harold's friends—were pushing through the crowd, beaming

merrily at everyone they encountered. Their appearance suggested they were more intoxicated than they had been earlier.
Vadim grimaced when Edric caught hold of Agatha's arm and
twirled her about, forcing her into an impromptu jig.

"Have a care, you drunken buffoon!" She pulled herself free,
glaring at the man with a face that would sour honey. "Find
yourself some willing maiden to cavort with. I am far too busy
for such nonsense."

"A great pity." Edric said, planting a hand on each of the
matron's generous hips. "I prefer comfort to speed."

"Take your disgusting hands off me!" Agatha shoved him so
hard he tottered backward, tripping over a carelessly discarded
lump of armor, and landing with a clatter on the cobbled floor.
"I am old enough to be your grandmother."

"But ten times fairer."

Vadim and Anselm exchanged glances. Agatha? Just how
drunk was he? To be sure, she was a fine woman, but she was
not renowned for her sweet nature. And even she would not dispute that her bloom had long since passed.

Edric, meanwhile, was walking on his knees toward Agatha,
his bald pate glistening with rain drops. He touched the hem
of her skirt, smiling up at her in the same way Fergus smiled
at Effie. "And virtuous too? Ah, the Spirits have blessed me
this day..."

"Blessed him? More like pickled him, I should say," Anselm
said in a whisper loud enough for all to hear. "You would allow
this man to bear my stretcher, brother?"

"Certainly." Vadim grinned. "For you suffered no ill effects
when Edric and his companion first brought you here."

With an impatient huff, Agatha snatched her skirt from Edric's hands. "Lecherous dolt!" She turned and marched away,
but the severity of her features melted into a secret smile that
only Vadim witnessed.

chapter thirty-five

AT THE SUMMONS OF HAROLD'S knock, Effie opened the door of Anselm's chambers. She stepped aside to let them pass. When she saw Fergus, a most becoming blush suffused her cheeks.

With a man clinging to each corner of the wobbling stretcher, they negotiated the narrow doorway and stepped into a room full of light, warmth, and comfort. Although Vadim had never set foot in his foster brother's private sanctum before, it was immediately apparent that this was a place inhabited by women.

Every candle was lit, and a welcoming fire blazed in the hearth. He sniffed, his stomach growling as he caught the mouth-watering aroma of cooking onions coming from the large black pot suspended over the fire. A basket of still-steaming flatbread sat up on the mantelpiece, out of Forge's reach. The great dog lay stretched out on a blanket before the hearth, an empty wooden bowl at his side. He raised his great head, sparing the new arrivals a brief glance before he went back to sleep.

Vadim looked about the room. "Is your mistress asleep?" he asked Effie in a low voice as they set the stretcher on a sturdy trestle table by the wall.

The pink-cheeked maid managed to wrench her eyes away from Fergus's face for a second. "No, m'lord. She is—"

"You're back!" Martha emerged from one of the smaller doors adjoining the main living area, her face alight with a smile. "Thank God." With a wonderful lack of regard for what was proper on such occasions, she hurried over and flung her arms about Vadim's neck, dragging him down to plant a kiss on his lips. "Are you alright? Fergus told me what Seth did." Frowning, she stroked her fingers over his injured jaw. "I can't believe he thumped you."

"'Tis nothing." Vadim stared into the blue depths of her eyes, entranced as always by her nearness. She looked clean and fresh, untainted by the horrors of the day. Her hair lay in glorious disarray upon the shoulders of her simple gray gown. It suited her well. The scent of warm lavender enveloped him. He drew her close and rested his chin atop her still-damp head. Briefly closing his eyes, he basked in the fragrant waves of summertime and exhaled. He felt whole again.

How had she become so vital to him? Lover. Wife. Mother. Her name was forever branded on his heart. He would not be without her again.

At length, Martha pulled back and looked toward the patient on the stretcher. "Thank you for bringing Anselm back. How is he?" Although she made no mention of her weariness, it betrayed itself in the charcoal smudges beneath her eyes.

"See for yourself, my love." Vadim could not deny that he was curious to see how she and Anselm behaved toward one another.

She moved to Anselm's side, swiftly removing the wet cloak they had used to protect him from the rain during the short journey from the infirmary. The movement showered everyone with cold droplets of water, but Martha did not heed their protests. She glanced back at Vadim, her wide eyes clouded with concern. "He's not... is he..."

"No," he assured her. "Before we set out, Agatha gave him something for his pain. She said it would likely put him to sleep."

"Oh." She exhaled a long breath then squared her shoulders. "Effie, hon?" she called to the maid, suddenly becoming all business and efficiency. "Would you dish out the food while we get Anselm into bed?"

"Of course, m'la—Martha."

"Oh, and make sure they all wash before they eat—"

"Sh-she... is keen, is she not?" Anselm's eyelids slowly opened, and a stupefied smile curved his lips.

"Hey, you." Martha took his hand. "How're you feeling?"

"All the better for seeing... you, sweeting."

Intrigued as he was by their relationship, Vadim could not

quell the stab of jealousy at seeing her tenderness directed toward another man. "Pay him no heed. He is not half so ill as he would have you believe."

This remark earned him a fierce glare from Martha. "Vadim! Have a little compassion, please." She returned her attention to Anselm. "Don't worry. You'll be back to your snarky self before you know it."

"I think not." Anselm sighed, looking truly pitiful. "I fear I am in the midst of my final hours, my sweet."

Vadim snorted. Anselm was playing her like a lute. Disgusted, he moved away, but not so far that he could not continue to listen to their intercourse. While Martha and Anselm consoled one another, he watched the other men queuing up to wash. Like a stern-faced captain, Effie presided over her bowl of steaming water, bearing fresh linen and soap in lieu of a sword. It amused him to see such battle-hardened warriors meekly yielding to the young woman's command of "scrub."

"I-is that... my h-helmet?"

Vadim caught a sudden sharp note in Anselm's voice, and turned.

"Hmm?" If guilt had a face, it was Martha's.

"Over there... by the fire." Anselm craned his neck, looking toward the hearth. "And my swords too?" He glared at her. "What on Erde did you do?"

"Well... I was filthy when I came back earlier, and I-I needed hot water." She beckoned Vadim to her side with a quick, furtive movement of her fingers. "The castle was in chaos, and all the servants were gone—"

"So you used my... best helmet to boil up water for your *toilet*?" Supporting himself on his elbow, Anselm pushed himself up, grimacing with discomfort. "Why the swords, my dear?" His honeyed voice was infused with poison. "Were you about to be attacked, perhaps?"

"No." Martha looked at her feet. "I couldn't hang the helmet on the hook over the fire, so I...I..."

"Ye-es?"

Martha seized Vadim's hand and clutched it tightly. "I-used-the-swords-to-balance-the-helmet-on-the-fire." The confession spilled from her lips in a rapid tumble of words.

She was nothing if not resourceful. Yet another of her many

admirable qualities. Vadim covered his mouth with his hand, turning his snort of laughter into a prolonged coughing fit. But he experienced a twinge of sympathy for Anselm's plight. Thank Erde his own weapons had been spared Martha's trial by fire.

Horror struck Anselm dumb. His mouth flapped wordlessly as he strove to summon an appropriate response.

"I'm really sorry, Anselm—"

"My. Swords!" His high-pitched squeak attracted the attention of the others.

"What is it?" Harold ambled over, a blanket wrapped about his shoulders. "Has his condition worsened?"

Anselm pointed to the fire and then at Martha. "My swords!" Another squeak, more high-pitched than the previous one.

"What? These swords?" Obligingly, Edric picked the blackened blades from the hearth and gave each a practice spin. "Fine weapons both," he said admiringly. "Beautifully balanced." He looked up. "Are they a pair?"

Anselm nodded his head vigorously. "Mmm."

Tom took the swords from Edric and tried them out for himself, swishing the swords through the air. "What did you want to go and put them on the fire for?" he asked with a frown. He brought the handle almost up to his nose, squinting. "The hilt is so spoiled, I can barely make out the engravings."

This was too much for Anselm. "King Erik himself presented me with those swords. The *king!*" He rounded on Martha in fury, his eyes almost popping from their sockets. "How could you?"

"I said I was sorry—"

"For ransacking my private chamber or for committing an act of wanton sacrilege? You have outdone yourself this time, m'lady."

"What else do you want?" Martha yelled back, finally needled into retaliation. "Blood?"

"'Tis no less than you deserve." Anselm fell back on his stretcher with a bitter laugh. "And to think, they called me brutal."

This had gone far enough. It was no longer amusing. "Leave this now, Anselm," Vadim said softly. "The damage is superficial. I will have the smith repair them."

But Anselm was beyond reason. "We no longer h-have a smithy thanks to the continual b-bombardment of your infernal army!" His cheeks glowed as bright as any forge, his breathing coming in ragged gasps.

This outburst was not natural, not even for him. The heat of his temper must have evaporated Agatha's sedative from his blood.

"Perhaps you might delay serving supper for a few more minutes, Effie?" Vadim turned to his men. "My brother is in need of his own bed, my friends. Would you be kind enough to take him through to his bedchamber."

Cowed by the force of Anselm's wrath, Martha had retreated behind Vadim's shoulder and now stood clinging to his arm. "Which way, love?" he asked her gently.

Sucking on her lower lip, Martha pointed to the doorway she had so recently come through, her eyes sparkling with emotion.

Had it been within his power, he would have spared her this ordeal on a day already so full of them. He ran his forefinger down the softness of her cheek. "Do not take it to heart. Anselm is not himself," he murmured. "He does not mean it."

"Oh, yes I do!" Anselm yelled as the other man carried him from the room, his stretcher wobbling violently. "Uncaring, unfeeling wench—"

The heavy slamming of the door of the bedchamber saved Martha from hearing the rest of his vitriol.

Vadim sighed and stroked back her hair which hung in a veil, hiding her face. "Look at me." He caught her chin with his finger and tilted it upward. The tears sparkling on her cheeks tore at his heart. "Oh, Martha."

"I know. I'm being stupid." She managed a shaky smile and impatiently dashed away her tears. "But I can't seem to stop crying today."

"It has been quite a day," he agreed. "And I am given to understand that pregnant women are prone to frequent bouts of tears. Is there any wonder you are so overwrought?"

Effie gasped from behind them. "P-pregnant?"

"Indeed she is." Holding Martha securely to him with one arm, they turned to face the astonished maiden. "Am I not the most fortunate of men?" He had the urge to shout their news from the highest tower.

"Oh, m'lady!" Effie abandoned the wooden bowls she was stacking and rushed to take hold of Martha's hands. "I am so glad for you... for both of you," she said, including Vadim in her shy smile.

"And so you see, we must take extra care of her until my son is born."

"Son? I'm not so sure—"

"Certainly, we must." Ignoring Martha's protest, Effie herded her to a chair beside the fire and made her sit down. "Shall I bring you more pottage? If there is anything you want, you need only ask."

"I'm fine. Really I am. I'm just a bit tired, that's all."

"I think Fergus has more rock wafer hidden in his cloak. Let me find it for you." Effie hurried away to search the pile of clothing dumped on the window seat.

Vadim sank to his knees and took Martha's hands. "Can you ever forgive me for being such a... *fuckwit?*"

She burst into peals of merry laughter. The sound of it warmed him to his heart.

"That sounded so weird," Martha said when she was able to speak once more. "Of course I forgive you." She held his face between her hands, suddenly serious. "I love you."

"Even though I believed my child was another man's?"

She nodded. "Yes."

"For abandoning you here for so many weeks?"

"Hmm." She tilted her head to one side and pretended to consider for a moment. "With certain provisos, maybe."

He smiled. "Such as?"

"Our sleeping arrangements."

"What of them?" Not that there was anything to discuss. From this day on, her bed was their bed. The look in her eyes stirred his blood; her meaning was all too clear. Despite all that had happened, she still wanted him. He could scarcely believe his good fortune.

Martha leaned over to whisper her terms in his ear. And she took her time about it. No detail was beneath her notice. The words she used and the feel of her hot breath upon his skin left him aching with need. No woman had ever spoken to him that way. He liked it.

When she had finished torturing him, she sat up, grinning wickedly. "Well? Do you think you can manage all that?"

He cleared his throat and tugged on the tie of his shirt to

loosen it, suddenly feverish himself. "You are a hard taskmaster, but I will certainly endeavor to carry out all of my husbandly duties." His stomach growled again. "Might I be permitted to eat something to sustain me?"

"Wash your hands," she said, her lips tantalizingly close to his. "I'll go and help Effie with the dishing up."

***

Vadim and the Chuckle Brothers had barely finished eating when the first visitors came knocking at the door in dribs and drabs, alone or in small groups—knights, men-at-arms, and outlaws. Vadim greeted each new arrival as a friend, shaking their hand, or pulling them into a rough hug, slapping them fiercely on the back—all men, and all of them hungry. Martha and Effie were hard pressed to find enough food to go round. When their supplies ran low, they sent Fergus downstairs to find whatever remained in the kitchen's pantries.

The main living chamber fast assumed a party atmosphere, and the guests kept on arriving. Most still wore their battle-soiled clothes, and the stench of ripe body odor soon pervaded the room. The heat of the fire made it worse, intensifying the many unique aromas of their guests. So many people, and all of them wanted to talk to Vadim.

For a time, Martha stood at his side, breathing through her teeth and her perma-smile. Eventually, the urge to puke overwhelmed her. If she didn't move away, she'd throw up on someone. Gently disentangling her hand from Vadim's, she slipped away. He barely noticed, busy as he was reviewing the day's battle tactics and other such boring man-stuff.

She didn't mind. After surviving such an awful day, he deserved to let his hair down, especially when so many people hadn't.

The noise level increased with the lateness of the hour and the amount of alcohol consumed. Edric and Tom presided over a pair of seemingly bottomless ale barrels, their noses glowing a matching red in the candlelight. No guest would go thirsty on their watch, though they tended to drink more than they served, not that it mattered. Most visitors had brought their own drink, courtesy of the late-earl's wine cellar.

At length, Fergus sent for his harp. He set it up in a corner, coaxing exquisite melodies from its strings that only Effie really heard. The maid sat on a low stool at his feet, watching his skillful fingers, her eyes wide with wonder, oblivious to the talk and laughter of the other guests.

Weary beyond the need for sleep, and in no mood to party, Martha wandered aimlessly through the crowd of merrymakers, casting frequent glances at the door of Anselm's bedchamber. Their earlier quarrel still preyed on her mind. How was he now? She daren't visit in case the sight of her set him off raging again. But at least he wasn't alone. Vadim had arranged a rota of volunteers to sit by his foster brother's bedside, ensuring he was never left unattended.

The slight thawing between Anselm and Vadim had come as a bit of a shock. Whatever the reasons for their ceasefire, it was also a huge relief. Being cast in the role of the rope in their tug-of-war hadn't been fun. Being pulled in two directions was every bit as bad as it sounded. *One down, one to go.* Now, the only thing standing between her and Mission Accomplished was Seth. She frowned. Drawing him back into the fold wouldn't be easy, if it was even possible.

Beaten back by the stench of the unwashed, she retreated to the window seat and pressed her face close to a cracked, diamond-shaped pane of glass, slowly breathing in a cold sliver of sweet night air. She felt Vadim's gaze on her as distinctly as a tap on the shoulder. She turned and met his frowning eyes with a smile. His concern was almost audible. *I'm fine*, she mouthed. Reassured, he sent her a wink and returned to his conversation with the man next to him.

Fine? If only she could convince herself so easily.

Despite scrubbing herself from head to toe, the ghostly hands of Jacob and Ferret still lingered on her body. She shuddered, splaying her fingers over the gentle curve of her belly. Poor baby. If Vadim hadn't intervened when he had—No. She wouldn't think about it.

She watched as Vadim demonstrated an imaginary sword stroke for his circle of disciples. *My beautiful man.* He wouldn't be flattered by her secret name for him, but that's what he was, inside her heart. Her eyes feasted on the sight of him, gorging themselves. Unlike many of their party guests, Vadim was now squeaky clean. He'd even had a shave. It was a very good look for him.

In the short time they'd been here, Rodmar's men had made repairs to the public bathhouse and got it functioning again. Going by the smell in this room, the need for hot water was something of a priority. As soon as word reached Vadim, he drew lots with his men to see which of them would visit the bathhouse first. They went in twos, leaving Effie and Martha under the protection of their resident armed guard. Cute, but the precaution was hardly necessary, not now the earl was dead.

Vadim's hair lay in a black tangle down his back, contrasting sharply with the pale fabric of the loose linen shirt. Her gaze slipped lower, pausing to appreciate just how well his close-fitting trews suited him, defining the perfection of his hard thighs and butt. A delicious tingle flipped her stomach and made her catch her breath. *Sweet baby Jesus.* If only they were alone right now. She gnawed on her lower lip. Only Vadim's touch, his possession, could erase the memory of Ferret and Jacob from her skin. Maybe that's why she craved him so badly?

Hugging her knees to her chest, she wiped the condensation from a small diamond in the window, the thick glass squeaking beneath her finger. Through the small peephole, she saw several orbs of torchlight bobbing around in the darkness outside, floating like will o' the wisps. It was impossible to see who carried them, for the wind constantly gutted and dimmed the flames. Why would anyone be outside on such a foul night?

"Martha?"

Vadim's call diverted her. She turned, meeting his eyes over the heads of the crowd.

"Look who has come."

Seth, perhaps? Hope bubbling in her chest, she scrambled from the window seat and hurried through the crowd.

To her disappointment, it was Agatha and her brother, Reynard. Summoning a smile, Martha extended her hand to Reynard. He was nothing like Agatha. In fact, now she saw them together, it was hard to believe the two of them were related at all. The only similarity they shared was their hair color. Reynard was tall and slim with steel-gray hair and a matching beard, his distinguished air set him apart from most of the other guests.

When she'd met him earlier on that day, just after the incident with Ferret and Jacob, there hadn't been time for a proper introduction. Reynard more than made up for it now, greeting her quietly and pressing a light kiss on her hand. Martha fully understood why the new king had chosen Reynard as his emissary. He had a very calming vibe about him. She rather liked him and his old-fashioned courtesy.

Releasing her hand, Reynard glanced over to where Fergus and Effie sat in their private bubble of music. "My son is quite smitten with your maid, it seems. Tell me, what do you know of her, m'lady? Of her background and family, I mean?"

Martha's smile flickered. It didn't feel right to tell him that his son was involved with the daughter of a local brothel-keeper. "Oh... er, I'm not really sure. Her mother is a local... businesswoman, I think."

"Is she indeed?" Reynard stroked his neat gray beard, watching the young lovers with a thoughtful look in his eyes.

Something told her that Effie and Fergus's fledgling romance was about to encounter its first obstacle. Poor things. Although she felt Vadim staring at her, Martha daren't meet his eyes.

Agatha must have been of the same mind. Her plump face was fixed in an expression of determined blankness. "How fares your patient?" she asked at last. "I trust Lord Anselm is still breathing?"

Martha could have kissed her for changing the subject. "I don't know. He's a bit cross with me at the moment, so I'm giving him some space."

"Oh?" Reynard tilted his head slightly. "Cross with the woman responsible for saving his wretched life? I find that hard to believe."

Vadim gave a crooked grin. "He took exception to my lady using his best swords and helmet to prepare her bath."

"Did she indeed?" Reynard regarded Martha with a frown. "I am sure she intended no harm."

"Hardly." Edric had apparently been eavesdropping. "She stuck them on the bloody fire," he said cheerfully, leaning over Agatha's shoulder as he spoke. "Oh! Hello again, my queen. Erde! You are even lovelier by candlelight."

Grimacing in unison, Agatha and Martha stepped away from the huddle of men. Martha linked arms with her friend. "Sorry about that."

"You actually know that... person?" Agatha asked, wrinkling her nose.

"Not really. He's a friend of Vadim's... sort of. Anyway, I don't want to talk about Edric," she said, wafting her hand to dismiss the subject. "Will you go and check on Anselm for me?"

"Whatever for? The leech says there is little to be done. He will live, or he will die. His fate lies with the Great Spirit now."

Martha tutted. "Forgive me for not placing all my faith in the judgment of a surgeon who won't even sterilize his instruments. Please, Agatha?" She widened her eyes. "Humor the pregnant woman?"

"Oh, very well," she said with a huff, and allowed Martha to steer her toward Anselm's door. "I heard about the baby, by the way. You might have told me about it. The gossips say 'tis a parting gift from Sir Anselm. Should I congratulate you, or would commiserations be more appropriate?"

"Don't you start. The baby's Vadim's, not that I expect the gossips will believe it." Martha tapped on Anselm's door and lifted the latch, half-shoving Agatha inside. "Now, go on in."

Agatha turned back when she had taken only a couple of steps over the threshold. "There is a man in here."

"Yes, that'll be Harold. Don't worry. He's mainly harmless."

"Well, leave the door open. I do not wish to hear my good name being bandied around by the gossipmongers."

"Fine. Whatever." Gossipmongers? Martha shook her head. If Edgeway had a newspaper, Agatha would certainly be the head of current affairs.

With her head wedged between the door and the wall, she strained to hear what Harold was saying to Agatha. His deep voice rumbled in response to Agatha's clipped questions. It was impossible to hear them properly, what with all the raucous laughter and conversations going on behind her.

Martha turned to scowl at the party guests, but no one noticed her. Over by the window, Tom and Edric were setting up a long line of tankards. A drinking game? *Oh, great.*

The door swung open again. "You can come in." Agatha looked grave, not herself at all.

Martha's heart sank. Was Anselm as ill as all that? She stepped into the room and quietly closed the door behind her, the thick oak efficiently muffling out the revelry outside. In comparison, the bedchamber was as silent as a church. Walking on her tiptoes, she followed Agatha and stopped at the foot of the bed.

Anselm's hands rested motionless on the ornately embroidered coverlet. His eyes were closed. Harold rose from the chair at the side of the bed, rubbing his hands wearily over his black beard.

"M'lady." He stepped back so Martha could take his place.

Beneath the grime, Anselm's skin looked unnaturally pale. Martha leaned on the bed and took one of his cold hands between hers, gently stroking it with her thumb. He was bound to be pale after all the blood he'd lost. "Is he still bleeding?" she whispered, glancing at Harold.

The big man shrugged.

Just as she was steeling herself to pull back the bedcovers, Agatha hurriedly pushed her aside. "Let me do that," she said, briskly. "He might be naked under there for all we know."

"No, lady. He still wears his undergarments," Harold assured them. "Lord Vadim insisted on it."

Agatha looked rather put out. "Whatever for?" she demanded, hands on hips. "The sight of another naked man is hardly likely to shock me."

Harold cleared his throat. "I believe he was more concerned with..." he darted a pointed look at Martha, "wounding the delicate sensibilities of his lady wife."

Martha snorted. *Yeah. Right. That'll be it.*

Shaking her head, she helped Agatha fold back the coverlet. Sensibilities indeed.

There was no fresh blood on his dressing, only a large brown stain marking the site of his injury. Agatha exhaled. "Well, that is something, at least."

"So, he'll be all right?" Hope flared in Martha's heart. "You must've treated hundreds of stab wounds like this one."

"Aye." Agatha replaced the coverlet and smoothed the creases out. "And of those men, barely half survived."

"What?" Martha's legs wobbled. She sank into the chair Harold had so recently vacated. "B-but, he's stopped bleeding. That's a good sign, isn't it?"

"Only a minor victory in the battle. We cannot yet know the damage the earl's blade has inflicted." Agatha touched her hand to Anselm's forehead and hissed. "Already he burns." Perching her ample backside on the bed, she regarded Martha sternly. "And what of infection and putrefaction? You lectured the leech long enough on the subject earlier today, did you not? Anselm is as likely to succumb to it as any man. Your friendship cannot shield him from all of life's arrows."

Infection? Martha stared at Anselm's unmoving form. What was she thinking? She'd watched all the medical dramas on TV back home. She knew the risks, perhaps better than anyone in this world. Without the benefits of a modern hospital or antibiotics, what chance did Anselm really have?

The miracle was that anyone ever survived here. Suddenly she recalled Vadim's recent—near-fatal—wound. She'd gotten through those awful days by surfing on a Pollyanna wave of positivity. But now she understood just how close she'd come to losing him, and the truth packed a hard punch.

She leaned back in her chair like a balloon with a slow puncture, her optimism tank flashing on empty.

"Are you unwell, m'lady?" Harold crouched beside the chair, concern wrinkling his brow. "Shall I fetch Vadim?"

Martha quickly shook her head. "There's no need to drag him away. I'm tired, that's all. I think I'll sit here in the quiet for a bit. You go on back to your friends, Harold." She gave his hand a reassuring pat. "They're setting up a drinking game in there, I believe."

"If you are certain." He straightened up, seeking Agatha's eyes for confirmation. "I will gladly stay."

"Oh, get on with you." Agatha got off the bed, flapping her handkerchief at Harold as though he were some irritating insect, shooing him toward the door. "If you want to do me a real service, you can tell your lecherous friend to keep his hands off me. I despise being mauled of all things."

Harold looked over his shoulder and grinned at Martha. "I will, though I am not sure it will help. Edric is a determined man when roused."

"But I am well past the age of rousing. Farewell." She shoved Harold through the door and slammed it behind him. "Men. Governed by their groins, every last one of them." She rolled up her sleeves. "Very well. Since Anselm means so much to you, let us see if we can delay your worthless friend's death. He has not yet earned the right to sit in his ancestors' hallowed hall."

chapter thirty-six

MARTHA WOKE IN HER OWN bed, neck deep in blankets. The sun was already up, bathing her room in a golden glow. The clear blue sky beyond her window held no memory of yesterday's relentless rain.

Warm and deliciously comfortable, she stretched like a contented cat, her muscles protesting over their extended use and abuse on the previous day. Sounds drifted in from outside in the courtyard; men's voices, squeaking hand-carts, and the intermittent thuds and clangs of cargo being loaded. She didn't need to look outside to guess what it was. Bodies. So many bodies. Nameless corpses, but each one would be mourned by someone. Somewhere.

She shoved the thought aside. Selfish or not, she couldn't deal with any more death. Not today. Intending to snatch a few more minutes sleep before the demands of her bladder became too urgent to ignore, she rolled onto her side.

Her heart slammed into her ribs. Vadim lay on the neighboring pillow.

"Good morning, mistress sluggard," he said, hooking a strand of hair from her eyes with his index finger. "I trust you slept well?" His slightly husky voice kick-started her hormones. He was wearing his sexiest smile, and not much else from the look of him.

Oh, dear God. Her breath hitched in her throat. "I-I... Fine, thanks." Her cheeks pricked and burned. Vadim might be her husband, but she'd forgotten just how beautiful he was. Which was probably a good thing.

He slid his arm from beneath her pillow and flexed it several times. As he did so, the runic band tattoo at the top of his arm appeared to shift and dance. "I began to think you would sleep all day," he said with a grimace, probably due to pins and needles.

"Hmm?" As his blanket slipped lower, it exposed more of him for her eyes to devour. The silvery scars on the perfect musculature of his torso were familiar friends. Unable to stop herself, Martha trailed her fingers over the heat of his golden skin, up over his chest and journeying upward to his neck.

Vadim leaned on his elbow, watching her. He didn't move, but his eyes darkened.

Holding her breath, she glided her fingers over the hard bulk of his bicep and down to the tense muscles of his forearm. His sword arm. Truth was, she'd always had a bit of a thing about that particular part of his anatomy. Amongst other things.

What a fine start to the day. But how had she gotten back to her bedchamber? The last thing she remembered was sitting beside Anselm's bed. She must have fallen asleep there.

Or had she?

"Oh!" Surely she'd remember if they'd—? Quickly grabbing a handful of the bedcovers, Martha peeked beneath them. No. She exhaled. Her shift was still in place though it had ridden up in the night and now lay bunched about her waist in an uncomfortable roll.

Vadim chuckled. He leaned over, his hair spilling about her face in a black waterfall, blocking out everything but him. "You imagine I would slake my desire on a sleeping woman?" He traced his finger down her burning cheek. "No, love. When that moment comes, I will require your full participation."

"S-so, how did I get here?" She blushed even harder, suddenly a little shy of him and the intense scrutiny of those chocolate eyes. It was difficult to think straight when he was smoldering at her like that. *Oh, damn!* She sniffed, then hurriedly covered her mouth with her hands.

"I carried you. You fell asleep while..." A frown creased Vadim's brow. "What are you doing?"

"Morning breath," she squeaked from behind her hands.

"Yours?" He moved nearer, gently prizing away her hands away from her mouth one digit at a time. "Or mine?"

Definitely not his. Her stomach somersaulted. God, he looked good, hovering over her like a predatory bird. The dark scruff of his five-o'clock-shadow enhanced the sharp angles of his face, and that lush lower lip was tantalizingly close. Bite-ably so.

Vadim sighed as he looked at her neck. "So many bruises." Lowering his head, he kissed each one in turn. "My poor love. I should have taken my time killing those bastards. They died much too cleanly."

She didn't doubt that he meant it. Pleasure wasn't the only reason for the shiver racing up her spine. The subtle edge to his voice reminded her that beneath his handsome façade, Vadim was not just her gentle husband. He was many other things besides. The man in her bed was an outlaw and a warrior. A defender of the weak. A killer.

Yesterday was the first time she'd seen him in action. She certainly didn't mourn the passing of either Jacob or Ferret, but Vadim's cold brutality at the time had shocked her. It wasn't easy to reconcile the darker facets of his character with the tender man in her bed. But if she truly loved him, she'd find a way. And she did love him. Just looking at him made her heart ache. She must accept him as he was and hope that he accepted her in the same way.

Thank God Anselm's contribution to her little collection of bruises remained a secret. If Vadim ever learned of it, the tiny embers of brotherly love would be extinguished forever.

Vadim's hot breath brushed against her ear and banished Anselm from her mind. She closed her eyes and relaxed, slowly trailing her fingers up and down his back. Each movement of his lips raised a thousand goosebumps. He smelt so good. The leather he habitually wore had permeated his skin. Combined with the scent of fresh man-flesh, its effect was as effective as female Viagra, albeit a very medieval version.

His calloused hand grazed lightly over her thigh, and she arched towards him, her body responding with a will of its own. If he didn't kiss her soon she'd explode. She squirmed, hitching her shoulder and forcing his attention away from her neck.

"Kiss me," she said, holding his face between her hands.

"But what about your morning breath?" Vadim asked with a smile.

"Feck it," she growled as their lips met.

Fireworks replaced the butterflies in her stomach. Without

words, she used her mouth to express just how much she'd missed him, a deep and drugging kiss that had only one conclusion. Vadim groaned from the depths of his throat. In one fluid movement he pulled her to lie on top of him, cupping the back of her head to kiss her more thoroughly, while his free hand roamed her body, stroking and kneading at will.

Martha tangled her hands in the silken weight of his hair, reveling in the taste of him and the feel of the powerful body beneath hers. With each gentle stroke of his fingers, he gradually erased the memory of other, less welcome, hands.

His heart thundered beneath hers, matching the wild rhythm in her breast. The heat of his naked chest burned her, absorbed her. She felt herself melting into him.

With trembling fingers, she reached for the fastening of his trews and tugged impatiently at the ties. She wanted him. All of him. Now.

Vadim clamped his hand about her wrist and wrenched his mouth from hers. "'Tis too soon, love." His breath came in ragged gasps. "Yesterday, when those bastards..." The fire in his eyes flared. He shook his head. "What I mean to say is, I can wait—"

"Tough. I can't."

Despite his noble words, she could feel how much he wanted her. Taking his lower lip between her teeth, Martha sucked on it while gently pressing her hips to the hardness of his body. His resulting groan made her smile. She let go of his lip and looked down at him. "I've waited quite long enough, don't you think?"

"What about the baby?" he asked. "Might he be harmed if we—"

She tried not to laugh, for he looked so serious. Instead, she smiled, smoothing away his frown with her finger. "You're big, sweetheart, it's true. But you're not *that* big."

It was the snort-giggle that gave her away.

"You dare to mock me, *wife*?" Vadim rolled and took her with him, imprisoning her between him and the mattress.

All control gone, Martha dissolved into helpless laughter until tears blurred her vision.

Vadim's lips twitched. "I should punish you for such disrespectful talk."

Punishment? Martha stopped laughing. "Really?" she asked,

hopefully. This day kept on getting better and better. "Did you... er... have anything particular in mind?"

"Oh, yes." Taking her unresisting wrists in one hand, Vadim held them over her head, and pushed them down into the soft pillow. "Several things." His breath caressed her lips as he murmured against them. "Be assured, wife, I will have you pleading for mercy before the sun sets on this day."

"Promises, promises." A surge of excitement rippled through her body. The vulnerability of her position was strangely empowering. In her own way, she knew she possessed a strength to match his. Brute strength and swords weren't the only weapons in life. Her only concern was that she might beg for mercy too soon.

Their smiles faded. Vadim transferred her wrists to one hand and tugged at the lacing of her shift, jerking it with his index finger. "Have a care, love," he said softly, never looking away from her face. "You know I never break my vows."

A rush of excitement rippled through her body. "I'm not afraid of you."

The neckline of her shift loosened and sagged, revealing what the thin linen fabric concealed. Vadim glanced down, and the breath hitched in his throat. "Erde!"

Ah! He'd seen the gift from the Boob Fairy. No wonder he was staring. Her breasts were much fuller than the last time he'd seen them. Martha smiled and gave a little wriggle, quite unembarrassed. "You think you can make me beg? Then, go right ahead and try. Do your worst, *Lord Hemlock*."

Hunger finally drove them from their bed. Well, that and her refusal to use the chamber pot while Vadim was in the room. Chuckling at her modesty, he went out to forage for food, leaving Martha to perform her ablutions in peace.

Humming to herself, she washed and dressed, mentally reliving some of the highlights of the past couple of hours. There were plenty to choose from. Overwhelmed with happiness, she laughed out loud, unable to hold back the geyser of joy inside of her. Vadim loved her. Any lingering doubts she'd had were gone, vanishing like smoke in the wind.

Sitting before the sheet of polished metal that served as her mirror, she gazed at her reflection. A stranger stared back at her, bright blue eyes sparkling in her bruised but smiling face. Despite all that had happened, she felt beautiful, and Vadim was responsible for it. She liked the way he made her feel. Sudden tears misted her eyes as she remembered how he'd spoken to the baby, with his face pressed against her stomach, murmuring to it in the Old Tongue.

"What are you saying?" she'd asked as she lay back in bed, lazily sifting the weight of his silken hair through her fingers.

Vadim looked up, smiling. "I am telling him how much I love you—both of you." The tenderness in his eyes struck her like a physical blow, and almost ripped her heart from her chest. She cried so hard, she thought she'd never stop.

He'd held her close, cradling her and murmuring soft words of nonsense into her hair until her sobs subsided into hiccups. Then he cupped her face gently between his hands. "Harken to me, Martha. Hear me well." His dark eyes glittered, burning into her soul. He wiped away her tears with his thumbs. "The past is dead, for both of us. Our new world begins this very day. Here. Now. In this bed. The time of doubt and uncertainty is gone."

He looked so grave, she wondered what was coming.

"I have been the worst of husbands, but no more. You are my life... my love... my heart's ease." He punctuated his words with tiny kisses pressed to her brow and cheeks. "You are my woman, and no one shall part us again. From this day on, come what may, your place is at my side. Do you understand?"

Her nodded reply wasn't enough for him. "Say it!" he growled against her lips.

"Yes, I understand." But even as she'd spoken, somewhere deep inside the loved-up mush of her brain, a tiny bell had jingled in warning.

Martha frowned at herself in the mirror. How had she forgotten that?

Now that Vadim was out of the room, her raging hormones had settled down to a low simmer, allowing her brain the chance to reboot. His closeness had always affected her ability to think clearly. But feral hormones combined with Vadim naked in her bed equaled a complete sensory overload.

Picking up her hair brush, she moved it gently through her tangled hair, trying to avoid the most painful areas of her scalp.

Even at the time, she'd sensed a hidden subtext behind his words, but now she was sure of it. As sure as God made little green apples, something was definitely "off."

She hit a knot, and winced at the pressure on her tender scalp. *Sod it.* She threw down the hairbrush and scowled at her reflection. What wasn't Vadim telling her? From past experience, she knew he wouldn't talk about it until he was good and ready—just one of the perils of being married to the Lord of the Secret Squirrels.

Her stomach grumbled, focusing her mind on more mundane matters. God, she was ravenous. If she didn't eat soon she might resort to gnawing on the furniture.

Vadim's cloak hung on the peg behind the door. A quick rummage through his pockets rewarded her with a large, slightly damp, chunk of rock wafer. She flicked off a couple of dead weevils and took a sniff. Women with hormonal cravings, she'd discovered, weren't overly fussy when it came to getting their fix. Or perhaps that was just her? She took a bite. Perfect. The wafer was still crunchy in the middle.

Maybe she ought to go and see how Anselm was doing. She opened the door and looked out into the main reception room. It was empty, apart from Forge, who lay stretched out on his blanket before the glowing fire. Not a trace of last night's party remained; everything was neat and clean. Effie must have been busy. Where was she now? Probably trailing Fergus about the castle.

At the sound of her footsteps, the dog scrambled to his feet, swaying toward her, his long tail lashing in lazy sweeps.

"Hello, sweetie." Martha scratched the base of his ear. "Where did everyone go?"

If he knew, he certainly wasn't telling. He leaned against her legs, groaning with doggy bliss. She fussed him for a couple of minutes then went toward Anselm's room.

She hovered outside the door, suddenly reluctant to go in. Watching someone die slowly and painfully was horrible. Then again, it wasn't exactly a bucket of laughs for Anselm either right now. Giving herself a mental slap, she took a deep breath and opened the door. "It's only me."

"M'lady?" Edric stood up as she entered the room. "Is anything wrong?"

"No, no. I just wanted to see how Anselm's doing today." Just one look at him told her more than she wanted to know. Red cheeked, his hair slick with sweat, Anselm twitched and writhed on the bed, mumbling to himself in words too low to decipher. Martha's smile faded. "How long has he been like this?"

"Several hours."

She leaned on the bed, gently pressing her hand to Anselm's brow—much too hot. He moaned and flinched away from her touch as though it hurt him. "Where's Agatha?" she asked, glancing at Edric over her shoulder.

"I sent her to find some rest. The poor lass was almost swooning with fatigue." He handed Martha a cold damp cloth to place on Anselm's brow.

She experienced a sharp pang of guilt. Poor Agatha. She'd spent the night nursing a man she loathed while she herself had passed the hours much more pleasurably. "Have you been here all night too, Edric?" He must have. Dark bags hung in heavy drapes beneath his bloodshot eyes. "You look exhausted. Go and get some sleep. I'll watch him now."

"With your leave, I will stay." Edric lowered himself back into his chair. "I cannot desert my post."

"Why not?" She perched on the edge of the bad. "I'm more than capable of looking after him for a while." For a man so universally disliked, Anselm had certainly acquired a devoted band of people willing to care for him recently.

"I meant you no insult." A pink flush spread over Edric's face, banishing the weary tinge from his complexion. "What I meant was, I should prefer to stay until my lady returns and gives me leave to depart."

"Ah!" Now she understood. "Agatha, huh? She asked you to sit with him?"

Edric nodded, the movement dislodging a strand of hair from where it had been slicked over the shining dome of his head. "I would rather endure another battle than face the wrath of Lady Agatha." Despite his words, he smiled, and a dreamy expression glazed his eyes.

He'd got it bad all right. "You really are fond of her, aren't you?"

"What man would not be moved by such a woman?" He sighed, handing Martha a bowl of water to wring out Anselm's head cloth. "Of course, she would never consider such an ill-bred buffoon as I for a suitor."

"She might." Martha couldn't believe she was encouraging him, especially since Edric was more or less quoting Agatha's exact words on the subject.

"There is no need to humor me, girl. I know what I am better than anyone." With a sad little smile, Edric settled back in his chair and stretched out his legs. "Still, it is enough to be in her company and earn her favor. That is why I will not relinquish my post, not even to you, Lady Edgeway."

"Huh?" What had he just called her? "Lady who now?"

Edric flushed. "Have I spoken prematurely? Forgive me. I thought the matter resolved. 'Tis common knowledge King Rodmar has restored the titles of his most faithful servants."

"Not to me it isn't." *I don't fecking believe this.* Martha wrung out the wet cloth with unnecessary force and placed it upon Anselm's waxen brow. She struggled to keep her voice calm. "You're telling me King Rodmar has made Vadim the new Earl of Edgeway?"

"So I believe, yes."

"And I suppose this castle comes with the title?"

Edric nodded. "Certainly, and all the lands attached to it. A most profitable and satisfactory outcome all round."

Satisfactory? That was one word for it.

"I fear I have said too much. Speak to your husband, m'lady."

"Oh, I fully intend to." Unbelievable. How could Vadim agree to something like this without discussing it with her first? No wonder he'd given her that talk last night. *Your place is forever by my side.* Yeah, right. Well, if he thought she'd be living in Edgeway castle anytime soon, he had another think coming.

She slid off the bed and thrust the bowl of water into Edric's hands. "I can see Anselm's in good hands. I'll leave you to it." She forced her mouth into a smile. "Sorry, Edric." It wasn't fair to take her bad mood out on the messenger. "None of this is your fault. Excuse me."

She marched out of the bedchamber and began pacing the living room. How could Vadim possibly imagine she'd agree to live in this... this... abattoir? The castle was nothing but a prison full of bloody memories. No amount of scrubbing would wash the dreadful stains from her mind. She wouldn't raise their child here. No way.

If Vadim wanted to live out his dead father's dream, so be it. But she wouldn't be doing it with him.

She smiled bitterly. What else had she expected? That they'd go back to Darumvale and live out their happily ever after there? Yeah, right. That was her dream, not his. Vadim had always seemed too big for the tiny village, and now she knew why. Darumvale wasn't his real home, and it never would be.

Her anger increased with every step until she could hardly breathe. The walls of the castle seemed to press down on her, oppressive and cold.

Vadim had his own plans. Reclaiming his rightful home and restoring his precious family honor was all he cared about. The question was, where did she fit into his grand designs? What was she, part of the fixtures and fittings?

She stumbled over Forge's outstretched paws, making the dog yelp in surprise. He looked up, regarding her with an accusing stare.

Martha stroked his shaggy gray head. "Sorry, boy." She needed to get out of here, to walk off her anger somewhere. But until the castle was properly secured, Vadim had forbidden her to go anywhere unescorted. "Come on, Forge. Let's go." She wasn't breaking her word. Forge could be classed as an escort, couldn't he?

Four-legged company was the only kind Martha wanted right now. She'd had enough of people. But as they left Anselm's chambers, she grabbed one of Vadim's spare daggers and attached it to her belt. Just in case.

chapter thirty-seven

S HE STEPPED INTO THE CORRIDOR and closed the outer door quietly so Edric wouldn't hear. She didn't need him on her case. A pack of armored soldiers clanked by, talking loudly as they passed. Martha gripped onto Forge's collar a little tighter. Although none of the men had so much as glanced at her, she felt a ball of unease forming in her chest.

She hurried down the stone steps of the servant's staircase and encountered no one apart from two maidservants running errands for their mistresses. She hoped to escape outside through the kitchen, but she was out of luck. Dozens of men sat around the long kitchen table, noisily harassing the cook and her young assistants to bring them more food and drink.

Great. No way was she going in there. There was nothing else for it, she'd have to chance the main door. "Come on, boy," she whispered and led Forge back up the steps.

Eyes cast down to avoid making any unwelcome eye contact, she wove through the clusters of loitering soldiers in the entrance hall of the keep. No one stopped her though she suspected she had Forge to thank for that. The big dog dragged her through the crowd at trot, rumbling a warning if anyone came too near. He did look scary though, with his hackles raised like a huge gray wolf.

Although the bodies were gone, their stench remained. The foul reek of death and decay lingering in the vaulted entrance hall. Martha covered her nose with her hand as the smell of un-refrigerated meat assaulted her nostrils.

Squadrons of meat flies buzzed everywhere, filling the air with their constant, heavy drone, and dive-bombing the poor servants who were scrubbing at the stained woodwork and floors.

Vadim expected her to live here? No thank you.

She let go of Forge's collar in order to wipe her sweaty hand on the skirt of her gown. The moment she did so, the dog pricked up his ears and bolted for the open doorway.

"Forge! Wait." Without his protection, Martha felt far too conspicuous. Alarmed, she hurried after him.

A group of men stood laughing together at the foot of the great staircase. None of them wore armor, each one dressed in everyday clothes: tight-fitting trousers, shirts and tunics. But they exuded a air of machismo and arrogance that put every other soldier in the shade.

Martha grimaced. *Ugh. Knights.* She could smell their egos from here.

As she attempted to scuttle past them, one of the men broke free of the group and stepped in front of her. "Are you looking for someone, m'lady?" He smiled down at her from his superior height.

With a huff of annoyance, Martha looked up at him. Tall, dark, and far too full of himself for her liking. Yep. Definitely a knight. "I'm in a hurry."

"That much is apparent." The man blocked her as she tried to sidestep round, darting a grin at his group of cronies who were obviously egging him on. "Come. Tarry with us a while, fair lady."

She circled her shoulder when he tried to touch her. "Don't!"

The man's smile faded a degree. "What? You fear I would do you harm?"

The rational part of her mind instinctively knew that this man wasn't a sexual predator, unlike Jacob and Ferret, even so, she couldn't fight the rising panic that robbed her of breath and stabbed fear through her heart.

Her breaths became shallow rasps, laboring in her constricted throat. *Breathe, damn it.* Not all flirtations were a prelude to rape, for goodness sake. But it was no good. Cold sweat pricked her brow and upper lip, and blackness swirled in a fog around the periphery of her vision. And underlying everything was that awful cloying stench of death, suffocating her.

Neither the knight nor his friends were smiling now. The young man's eyes softened with concern. "You look most ill, m'lady. If I cannot aid you, perhaps I might fetch some—"

"No need, son." A familiar, and oh-so-welcome male voice cut in. "I have her now."

Tears of relief pricked Martha's eyes as Seth's strong arm slid about her trembling shoulders. If she hadn't been gasping like a landed trout, she might have kissed him.

"Come away, lass," he said gently, half carrying her toward the door. "Let us take a turn together out of doors."

It was bliss to be outside. Clinging to Seth's arm, she took heaving lungfuls of fresh, sweet air, gorging on it, banishing the scent of decay from her lungs. Little by little, her heart rate slowed and her vision returned. Martha exhaled a long slow breath.

"Th–thank you." Although her voice quavered, she felt much better.

"Think nothing of it." Seth guided her to a step and helped her sit down. "Hugo is a dolt but a harmless one."

"I know." She managed a weak smile as Seth sat on the step beside her. "I don't know what came over me back there."

"I think I have an idea." There was no mistaking the pity in his bloodshot eyes.

Seth looked terrible. The stains of battle still smeared his face, but beneath the blood spatter, his skin was pale, drawn too tight over the bone beneath. His hair and beard had always had a tendency to run wild, but now he looked utterly unkempt: a red, woolly tangle, held together with dried gore.

She sniffed and wrinkled her nose. The heady combination of sweat, blood, and alcohol made her sensitive stomach churn. "Did you hear they managed to fix up the bath house yesterday?"

Seth snorted in amusement. "I am glad to see Edgeway has not robbed you of your delicate manner, m'lady." His smile faded. "Unfortunately, soap and water cannot help me."

A surge of pity welled up in her breast for what Seth had become. Without Sylvie, he was lost, as directionless as a boat without a rudder, helpless and drifting in life's turbulent sea. Despite the fact that he'd punched Vadim yesterday, she couldn't stay angry with him. Besides, at that moment, she felt like giving Vadim a slap herself.

The stonemasons were already hard at work making repairs to the battered keep. Balanced high up on a perilous web of wooden scaffolding, they labored in the sunshine. The constant *tink-tink* of their tools accompanied the men's talk and laughter.

Far below them, the courtyard lay in ruins. The inner curtain wall had been reduced to a heap of pulverized rubble. An army of shirt-sleeved workers cleared a track through the carnage, carelessly throwing tangled corpses onto horse-drawn carts. Once full, the cart turned about, rumbling over the cleared cobble track. Instantly, another empty cart took its place, the bored horse scraping at the cobbles with its hoof as it waited.

"Where are they taking them?" Martha asked Seth. "The bodies, I mean."

"To a great pit beyond the castle walls," he replied. "'Tis unwholesome for the dead to dwell with the living."

She watched a loaded cart crawl toward the main gate. A hand hung over the side of the cart, bloody and motionless.

So many lives lost. Each mangled corpse had once been someone's son or daughter, a baby. Martha placed a protective hand over her stomach. Closing her eyes, she blocked out the awful images and tilted her face toward the sun, enjoying its warm caress. She wouldn't think about it. Not now.

"I expect he hates me now."

Seth's voice drew Martha from her reverie.

"Still," he continued, "'tis no more than I deserve. Not after what I did."

Martha opened her eyes and fixed them on Seth's bowed head. "So why did you hit him? We *are* talking about Vadim here, aren't we?"

Seth nodded, but he didn't look up. "The fault is all mine. I drank too deeply from the earl's cellar. Wine has never agreed with me, you see." He darted a glance at her. "Sylvie warned me off it often enough." He scrubbed a filthy hand over his matted beard. "I shall regret striking Vadim until the day I draw my final breath."

"He'll forgive you." Martha watched three small boys cross the courtyard, laden with armfuls of glittering armor. They laughed together as if untouched by the death all around them.

"Aye." Seth looked up, his eyes glittering suspiciously. "And that will be the worst punishment of all. I would much rather he knocked me down and paid me back in kind."

"Okay, enough." If she didn't stop him, he'd be back at the ale barrel, wallowing in his misery. Sometimes, Martha thought he enjoyed it. Maybe it was time Seth experienced a little tough love. It might not help, but she owed it to Sylvie to at least try. "If you want punishing, then hear me out. There are things you need to—"

"Not Anselm. No!" Seth held up his hands to ward her off, his head turned away. "I will not listen to—"

"Yes. Anselm. Your son." Martha scrambled to her feet and glared down at him, hands on her hips. "God damn it, Seth. If you don't listen to me, I swear I'll follow you about this castle until you do!" She would too. This had gone on long enough. "You don't have to say anything, just listen. If you want to keep on hating Anselm afterward, that's your business. I promise I'll never mention his name to you again. Deal?"

Seth got up too, his eyes bugging from his crimson face. He was livid. Hostility pulsed off him in waves, but Martha wasn't fazed.

"Well?" She arched her eyebrows. "Do we have a deal?" Unblinking, she met his angry stare. She wouldn't back down. Not this time. She sensed him crumbling, wilting beneath her determined gaze.

"So be it," he said at last. "Say your piece and have done with it." He sank back down onto the step like an old man and folded his arms about his knees. "Speak. But I will not change my mind."

"Fine." That would do for starters. She sat down on the step beside him. "But I warn you now, some of things I have to say won't make easy listening."

She didn't hold back. With her eyes fixed unseeing on the activity in the courtyard, Martha spoke about Sylvie and her secret meetings with her son. Then she told him about Anselm's distress at the death of his mother and of how he'd intended to save her.

Seth remained silent.

Sensing his growing tension, Martha moved on to safer topics. She told him how Anselm had known about Darumvale's secret grain store and how he'd never disclosed its location to his master.

Spin doctoring Anselm wasn't easy. His decent moments were few and far between. Even so, Martha hunted out each rare gem, buffing it until it sparkled in the retelling, hoping that Seth might thaw.

Recent events were much easier to relay. Here, Anselm's heroics spoke for themselves and required little enhancement. Martha described how he'd tried to help her escape, even after learning how she'd deceived him over Vadim's death. Then she spoke of those terrible last moments on the roof of the barbican, how the earl had turned on him, stabbing him for defending her.

When the words ran out, Martha glanced at Seth. He stared at a far point on the horizon. Although his profile was granite-hard, she sensed he was listening.

"He's dying, Seth," she said in a low voice. "Oh, I keep telling myself that he'll be all right and that Agatha can fix him." She sighed and looked up at the clouds. "But I know I'm fooling myself." Without Anselm, the world would be a much duller place. She'd miss him. "I know he's no angel, Seth. God knows, I've hated him myself at times, but he came good in the end. Isn't that what really matters? Anselm sacrificed his life to save me. No matter what he's done in the past, that's got to count for something, don't you think? He's been bad, but he's not beyond hope."

Seth cleared his throat. "You speak as though you are fond of him," he said gruffly.

Am I? "Yes. I suppose I am."

"And a little in love with him too?"

Martha snort-giggled. "Ugh! God, no." What a thought. "He's much too irritating. I pity the poor woman who..." Only, Anselm wouldn't be getting married, would he?

"What ails him?" Seth met her eyes. He wasn't angry anymore.

"He has a high fever."

"Is that all?" A small smile flickered over his lips. "You worry needlessly, m'lady. 'Tis a child's illness, nothing more."

"No," she said with a shake of her head. "It's more than that. He lost a lot of blood, and I think his wound's infected. I don't think he's strong enough to fight much more."

A shadow of emotion flickered over Seth's face. It looked like fear. "Then have Agatha make him one of her foul-tasting infusions. That will soon set him right."

He *was* afraid. Martha sensed it lurking beneath the lightness of his words. "Perhaps it would," she said, "if Agatha only had the herbs to make one."

"Oh?" Seth frowned.

"Have you visited the infirmary recently? You'd be lucky to get so much as a leaf of mint." Taking a chance, Martha laid her hand upon Seth's forearm. "Come and see him, Seth. He won't know you're there, but at least you'll have the chance to say a proper goodbye."

Seth's arm tensed beneath her fingers then he jumped to his feet, looking about the courtyard, wild eyed, as if he'd never seen it before.

Martha got up too. A sudden thought occurred to her. "What about Eslbeth, Orla's mother? She fixed Vadim up. Maybe if she came here and brought her herbs, she could fix Anselm—"

"She left Darumvale some time ago. Orla went with her."

"She left?" Martha gaped at him. "Why?"

A wry smile curved Seth's lips. "How could she stay after people learned her daughter had been Anselm's informant? Still, Orla got a gold brooch for her duplicity. Much good may it do her."

"Oh." What with recent events, Martha had forgotten all about Orla—the evil little mare. Even so, she had no quarrel with Elsbeth, and the news of her leaving came as a blow.

"Come." Seth took her hand and tucked it into the crook of his arm. "Since you are so intent on a reunion, let us get it over with."

Hardly able to believe her luck, Martha linked her arm through Seth's and followed him back inside the keep. She had nothing to fear now. None of the loitering knights and soldiers dared challenge her, not with Seth at her side.

"What were you doing earlier, wandering the castle unchaperoned?" he asked as they ascended the main staircase. "I cannot believe Vadim sanctioned such behavior."

"Oh. *Him.*"

Seth chuckled when he saw her frown. "A quarrel so soon? I suppose you have heard of the honor King Rodmar has in store for him?"

"You might say that." Did everyone know about it except for her?

"Vadim suspected you might have some opposition to him reclaiming his rightful title of earl."

Martha gave an annoyed huff. Was that why Vadim hadn't mentioned it to her? Did he imagine she'd simply roll over and accept his decision? *Ha!* He obviously hadn't banked on one of his kindly henchmen spilling the beans.

"If he thinks I'm going to raise our child in this fecking castle, he can think again."

"Congratulations on the babe, by the way." They paused on the first landing to allow a group of ladies and their escorts to pass. "Forgive me for not wishing you joy sooner."

"Thanks." She looked up at him. "Aren't you going to ask if the baby's Anselm's? Everyone else has."

"Not I." Seth grinned, his teeth bright white in his grimy face. "The fire in your eyes is enough to warn me against it."

Did Seth believe it too? Oh, let him. They'd all eat their words when the child was born.

They took the next flight of stairs.

"Why are you so opposed to the title of *countess*?" Seth wanted to know.

Martha arched her eyebrows. Was that what she'd be? Countess of Edgeway? For a fleeting moment, she imagined herself dressed in lovely gowns and bedecked with jewels. Then she dismissed the thought. She looked like a fecking Christmas tree.

"I don't want to live here, Seth. I hate this castle." She sighed. "For the longest time, it's been my prison. All I want is to go back to Darumvale and make our home there."

"Depriving your child of its inheritance?" Seth glanced at her stony face. "You cannot mean it."

"Oh, but I do," she assured him.

"You prefer him to have the uncertain life of a farmer?"

Seth had called the baby "he," but Martha was too irritated to correct him. "Better that than growing up here as a noble. No child of mine is going to be used as a pawn to secure alliances, or whatever it is these people do. Not now. Not ever." She sounded so fierce, two passing soldiers glanced at them.

Seth arched his eyebrows but made no reply, and they continued the rest of the way in silence.

Harold descended on them the second they walked through the door.

"Where have you been?" he demanded, his dark eyes flashing with concern. "Lord Vadim is frantic. He is out searching the castle for you even as we speak."

"That's nice of him." She slipped her hand from Seth's arm and pointed to the door of Anselm's bedchamber. "He's through there. Go on in, Seth."

"Where were you?" Harold persisted looking from Martha to Seth and back again.

"Out!" she snapped.

"She was with me." Seth's brisk answer took the sting from the harshness of Martha's reply. "No harm has befallen her. We sat in the sunshine for a while and kept one another company as old friends are wont to do."

Harold exhaled like a bull, apparently pacified. He sent the older man a brief smile. "Edric is sitting with your lad. I am certain he would welcome a break in his duty."

For several seconds, Seth lingered before the door of his son's bedchamber. He raised his hand to knock then seemed to think better of it. Taking a deep breath, he lifted the latch and went inside, softly closing the door behind him.

Martha went to examine the contents of a small handbasket on the sideboard. As she lifted its linen cover, the smell of fresh-baked bread enveloped her in a delicious cloud. Her stomach gurgled. At least Vadim had brought breakfast before he went out hunting for her.

"I must find Lord Vadim and assure him of your safety," Harold said, grabbing his cloak from its peg.

Martha shrugged. "If you must." She tore off a chunk of bread and began plastering it with butter.

"In the meantime, I ask that you remain here until we return. No more solitary wandering. This castle is still a dangerous place, m'lady."

Despite herself, Martha smiled. "Okay, Dad." It wasn't Harold's fault she was pissed off with Vadim. "I promise to stay put. Scout's honor." She saluted with her right hand, still clutching her buttery knife.

She was devouring her third slice of bread and honey when the door of Anselm's bedroom flew open. Seth leaned against the door frame, breathing hard, his head bowed.

Heart pounding, Martha leapt up from her seat. "Seth? What's happened? He's not..." She couldn't say it.

He raised his head. "No. Not yet, at least." If it were possible, Seth looked even worse than he had before. An unhealthy pallor lent his skin a gray tinge, and his eyes were red rimmed and swollen. He staggered to the window like a drunk, hands fisting in his wild red mane. "But death's shadow stalks him closely. He cannot outrun it for long. Oh, Sylvie!" Seth tilted his face and looked at the sky. "What am I to do, my love?" he murmured. "I have never needed you more than at this moment."

The tenderness of his voice brought tears to Martha's eyes. Deciding to give him a moment to collect himself, she went to see how Anselm was doing. But there was no need to ask. He lay twitching beneath the coverlet, mumbling to himself, lost in his own private delirium.

Edric still sat beside the bed, heavy eyed and weary. "I would have left Seth alone had he not begged me to stay." He scrubbed his hand over his bristled cheeks and shuddered. "For my part, I would have preferred not to witness such raw sorrow."

Poor Seth. He'd spent so long wishing his son dead but in truth, the reality of it had knocked him sideways. Martha moved to the bed and stroked a strand of sweaty hair back from Anselm's face. He flinched from her touch and jerked his head sideways, muttering furious words she couldn't make out.

She glanced at Edric. "Do you need a bathroom break?" Someone must have fed him in her absence, for a wooden platter sat his feet along with an empty leather tankard.

"A what?"

She arched her eyebrows. "The privy." Even after all this time, she kept forgetting this wasn't the twenty-first century. "Go on. I won't tell Agatha, I promise."

Edric nodded and rose stiffly from his chair. "Thank you, m'lady." He stretched so hard she heard the kinks popping in his back. "A walk will help keep me awake." He shuffled for the door, yawning and scratching at his private parts as he went.

Martha suppressed a grimace. "Would you ask Seth to come

back in please?" However, she had no idea what she'd say to comfort him.

Edric went out, but he returned only moments later. "'Tis Seth," he said. "He has gone."

chapter thirty-eight

VADIM STALKED THE CASTLE FROM end to end, his agitation soaring with every step. Where could she be? None of the men he'd questioned recalled seeing her. What had possessed Martha to go wandering alone?

When his search of the keep was exhausted, he hastened outside into the bright sunshine. Almost immediately he spotted Forge, licking at something on the bottom step. Vadim grimaced. It looked suspiciously like a lump of flesh. He took the stone steps two at a time and pushed the dog away from his grisly find. "Leave that alone, dog."

Forge looked up and wagged his tail in greeting, his great jaws smiling as always.

"Where is your mistress, hmm? Have you seen her?" he asked, ruffling the animal's shaggy gray head.

Forge tilted his head to one side, secret intelligence shining in his eyes.

"No, and I do not expect that you would tell me even if you could."

Shielding his eyes against the sun's glare, he scanned the courtyard, hoping to see Martha amongst the crowd. Now that the siege was over, groups of women had begun creeping from their hiding places, clutching their children as if they feared they would be snatched away at any moment.

Their fears were needless now. Almost as soon as Edgeway was taken, the king had issued a decree forbidding further rape and pillage under penalty of death. To set an example, several men were already awaiting their fate in the castle's dungeon. Rodmar was not a man to be crossed, that much was clear. The pity was he had not made his proclamation sooner, before so many innocent lives were forever ruined.

Unwillingly, he relived the moment he found Martha being ravaged by Rodmar's hired thugs. A hot rush of bitter bile rushed into his mouth at the memory of their filthy hands mauling her. He leaned over, coughing the sour contents of his mouth onto the cobbles. Thank the Spirits he had found her before it was too late.

Suddenly weary, he sank down onto the steps and concentrated on calming his roiling stomach. Perhaps it was another bout of battle sickness. If so, it was a mild dose, and with none of the violent headaches that usually accompanied it. He supposed he had Martha to thank for that. The night spent in her bed had silenced many of his ghosts.

Forge laid his head on Vadim's thigh, looking up at him with apparent concern. He stroked the dog's head absently as his eyes searched the courtyard. Where could she be? The infirmary? His stomach rolled again at the thought of revisiting that hellish place.

"M'lord!"

He turned at the sound of Harold's voice, anxiety spiking in his heart as he watched the man advance toward him. "I beg you, tell me you have found her."

"All is well. Your lady is safe. She arrived home with Seth shortly after you left."

He closed his eyes and exhaled. "Thank the Great Spirit." But puzzlement rapidly replaced his relief. "With Seth, you say?" He was the very last person he expected to find visiting Anselm's chambers.

"Aye." Harold sat beside him on the step. "How she managed to talk him around, I will never know."

"What?" Vadim's eyes widened. "He actually came to visit Anselm?"

"That he did. Who knows, perhaps he intends to hasten his worthless son's departure to the ancestors' hallowed hall?" Harold gave a snort of laughter.

Vadim sat a little straighter. He had not considered that.

"Not that it would be an easy task, not with Edric standing

guard over him night and day." Harold grinned. "I believe he would cut down any one of us if we attempted to interfere with the sacred charge Lady Agatha set for him."

The fierce matron had certainly roused a fierce kind of devotion in Edric's soul, true enough. But Vadim did not smile. Was he any different? What would he not do for Martha?

He watched distractedly as Harold fed small pieces of dried meat to Forge in exchange for his paw. The king still awaited an answer, but in his heart, Vadim had already decided. With the death of the earl, the honor of his family was restored and their souls avenged, leaving him free to do as he would. But unless he had Martha by his side, the title, the castle, and all they entailed were worthless.

He turned his head, looking up at the keep, the home of his boyhood, and the place where his parents had met their untimely end.

Martha would not willingly consent to live here, and Vadim could not reproach her for it. Her memories were tied too closely with incarceration, violence, and death. He knew full well that her heart was set on Darumvale, and he could not deny part of him would be glad to leave Edgeway for the final time.

Admittedly, their children would have a very different life from the one he might have chosen for them, but it did not follow that it would be a lesser one. Although he dressed like an outlaw, he was far from being a pauper. He had enough gold stashed away to establish a comfortable life for them back in the village, or anywhere else for that matter.

You will be bored witless before the moon turns six cycles.

Possibly. Boredom was a novelty he had yet to sample. Given a little time, he might grow to prefer a simpler existence. One thing was certain, with Martha by his side, life would never be dull.

He got up off the step and stretched, working out the kinks in his neck and shoulders, the legacy of yesterday's battle. Although he was still in his prime, his growing tally of wounds were gradually taking their toll. Yes. Perhaps it was time to settle down.

At that moment, a man hurtled by in a blur of movement. He bounded down the steps, taking them three at a time and almost falling in his haste. Forge cocked his head to one side and whined, his long tail lashing.

Harold pointed at the fleeing figure. "Is that not—?"

"Seth." His unkempt red mane was unmistakable. Where in Erde was he going with such haste?

Shielding their eyes, they tracked Seth's progress as he ran across the courtyard, moving as if the hounds of the Underworld were on his scent. He dodged a slow-moving meat wagon then barged through a loitering group of soldiers, ignoring the loud shouts of annoyance aimed at his departing back.

Despite the warmth of the day, an icy ripple raced the length of Vadim's spine as he suddenly recalled Harold's earlier jest. What if Seth had done something to Anselm? If so, what would that mean for Edric and Martha?

"Is he heading for the stables, do you think?" Harold asked.

Vadim neither knew nor cared.

Seth made a sudden change of course, heading for a knight who was ambling toward the main gate astride his gray palfrey. To the astonishment of those who witnessed it, Seth launched himself at the man and dragged him from the saddle, sending him toppling to the ground. The horse barely had a chance to flatten its ears before Seth had swung himself up into the saddle. Sawing wildly at the reins, he kicked the animal into a canter and raced for the main gate.

Harold burst into laughter. "Oh, he will be for it now! I thought you said Seth was no horseman—"

But Vadim was already running for the keep.

The journey back to Anselm's chambers seemed to last an eternity. Vadim could not later recall any of it. All the while, his mind raced with terrible blood-soaked images that became more unbearable with each step.

At long last, he reached his destination. Without pause, he kicked open the door, almost falling into the room in his haste to know the worst.

"Martha?" His eyes made a rapid sweep of the living area. Empty. There was no sign of a disturbance. Was she in her bedchamber? Was her life blood now staining the bed linen crimson? Fear rooted him to the spot. Suddenly, he dared not find out. "Martha!" Her name was a howl of anguish, a living embodiment of terror, the like of which he had not experienced since the night his family were taken from him.

Then, thank the Spirits, he heard the rapid taps of hurrying slippers coming from Anselm's bed chamber. Relief robbed his limbs of strength, forcing him to clutch at the back of a chair. Then he discerned her own sweet voice muttering crossly to her Jesus God.

Anselm's door flew open, and there she was. Hale and whole.

"What the feck are you bellowing for?" she snapped. "Yes. I'm here! What?"

The sight of her restored his strength. In two swift strides he crossed the room and, ignoring her squeak of protest, took her in his arms, crushing her tense little body to him. He pressed a kiss upon her hair. "Thank you," he murmured, raising his eyes to the heavens.

"Thank you? For what?" Martha squirmed, trying to get free, and unwittingly rousing him to passion. Unfortunately, she was not of the same mind. Not yet. "What the hell is wrong with you, Vadim? For fecksake, will you let me breathe at least?" She stamped her foot down on his boot for good measure.

The pain barely registered. Holding her away from him, he rejoiced in the stormy expression of her eyes. "I thought I had lost you."

"Lost me?" She only scowled harder. "I only went for a bloody walk!"

"You never looked lovelier than you do at this moment."

"And don't try sweet talking your way around me," she snapped, still straining to pull free. "I am so pissed off with you, right now. How could you?"

He smiled. "What have I done now?" Temper lent her a most becoming air. It suited her well.

"The *Earl of Edgeway?* Is that ringing any—"

He kissed her because he could not help himself, unable to resist the sweet allure of her lips. Martha resisted for a heartbeat then her angry resolve crumbled. As she opened her mouth to allow him entry, he felt the tension ebbing from her body. Suddenly, she was soft and pliant in his arms, and more than willing.

She stopped pushing against his chest and linked her arms about his neck, returning his fevered kisses.

Blood thundered through his heart. She tasted of honey. Of summer. Of life. *Erde!* It was all he could do not to take her here and now.

But then, Martha raised the stakes. Making mewling noises of want, she fisted her hands painfully in his hair and pressed her body even closer to his. Her kisses became more demanding, tinged with traces of her previous anger. She was rough, impatient. Greedy.

He liked her this way.

Cupping one soft buttock, Vadim held her against him. But grinding himself against the softness of her body only increased his suffering.

With a groan of surrender, his self mastery deserted him. His hunger for her was too consuming. Without breaking their kiss, he walked her backward until she against the wall. Even before they got there, her eager hands were already pulling at the fastenings of his trews.

Her breathing was as rapid as his own. He had no thoughts of resisting her.

The way she sucked on his lower lip, grazing it with her teeth, pushed him to breaking point. He grabbed a fistful of her skirt and raised it then slid his hand beneath. Her skin was warm and velvet soft. He moved higher, gliding up her thigh to the place he most needed to be.

She was already slick with need.

Martha gasped in his mouth, finally breaking their kiss. "Oh, God!" Her eyes rolled back beneath her flickering lids, and her body arched against his fingers.

She reached for him, encircling his hardness with a trembling hand, guiding him toward her body. But Vadim needed no instruction.

In one swift move, he lifted her onto him, slowly burying himself in the tight heat of her body. Martha wrapped her arms about his neck, kissing him with even fiercer passion.

The imperceptible tilt of her hips set the pace, driving him on, until he was thrusting into her, hilt deep and drowning in the bliss of her. The ending was all too swift. Her legs tightened about his waist, and suddenly she was quivering, uttering his name on breathy gasps, clinging to him as if she would never let him go. With a final thrust, Vadim joined her, journeying through the heady swirl of fulfillment.

The storm eventually passed. With a shuddering breath, Vadim cushioned his head upon her fast-rising breast and listened to the thumping of her heart. Were it not for the wall's sturdy support, he would have fallen.

Martha stroked the sensitive skin at the back of his neck, her legs still locking him within her body. She seemed as reluctant to be parted from him as he was to leave her.

"Vadim?" she murmured at length.

"Hmm?" With effort, he raised his head from its soft pillow and looked into her eyes. They were dark, languid pools, shining with the aftermath of their love. But there was something more. Amusement?

"Do you think we should, maybe, close the door?"

"Wh-what?"

Grinning, she nodded over his shoulder, and Vadim turned to see what she was looking at. To his dismay, he saw that the outer door was open, gently moving with the breeze. They were in full view of anyone who happened to be passing by.

With a muttered curse, he lowered her to the ground then began to adjust his clothing. "You should not encourage me so, wife."

"Me?" Martha's eyes widened, regarding him with an innocence that fell the wrong side of wicked. "What did I do?" She was battling to suppress her laughter, the twitching of her lips gave her away.

He stroked the pad of his thumb over her lower lip. "You surrendered when you should have fought."

"Oh?" She pushed off the wall and stepped nearer. "I think," she said, tracing her finger down his chest, "you would have liked that even better, m'lord." Her sweet breath brushed his face, tempting him to kiss her again.

"Sorceress."

"Barbarian."

Only the narrowest of margins separated their lips now. He cupped her cheek with his hand.

"How can I defend you when I am too weary to wield my sword, my love?"

"Oh, I don't think you need to worry about your sword, Lord Hemlock." She glanced down to emphasize her meaning.

Impudent witch.

Vadim hooked his arm about her waist and drew her closer. "And I think your long sojourn in Edgeway has corrupted your mind."

"I can't think what you mean," she said with the same mock innocence as before.

"Oh, I think you can, m'lady."

"So?" She arched her eyebrows. "What do you intend to do about—"

"Oh!" The unwelcome sound of Harold's voice wrenched them back to the present. "Forgive me! I shall return later."

Before he could leave, Vadim reluctantly called him back. "No need, my friend." He put a more seemly distance between himself and Martha. She was laughing again, obviously enjoying his discomposure. *Minx!* As she made to move away, he grabbed her hand and pulled her to stand at his side. "We were merely discussing... weaponry."

Martha gave a loud snort of amusement.

"Indeed?" Harold looked from one to the other, doubtless missing no detail of their disheveled appearances. Martha's flushed cheeks and love-mussed hair were very damning evidence indeed. "'Tis a subject fit enough to rouse any man to passion."

"Actually, I'm glad you're here, Harold." Martha slipped her hand from Vadim's grasp and darted away. "Maybe you can tell me why Vadim just burst in here like the castle was on fire?"

Harold closed the door and hung up his cloak. "I suspect that would be on account of Seth. Or, rather, the speedy manner of his departure."

"Seth? What? You've seen him?" She glanced over at Vadim, her smile fading. "He's left the castle?"

He nodded. "I am afraid he has."

"Aye. He dragged a knight from his horse and took off out of the gate like a gale was behind him." Harold chuckled as he settled down onto one of the fireside chairs. "Sir Clarence was none too pleased, I can tell you."

She leaned upon the back of Harold's chair. "But why would he do something like that? Didn't either of you try to stop him?"

"He moved too fast," Harold replied. "He was up and away like a hare."

"And I was too intent on discovering what had become of you," Vadim added.

"Huh?" The little crease between Martha's eyes deepened until he wanted to kiss her again. "What do you mean?"

"I feared Seth might have... done something to you and Anselm." Even as Vadim spoke the words aloud, they sounded foolish to his ears. But fear was a notoriously irrational beast.

"What?" Martha was apparently of the same mind. "Are you crazy?" She stalked toward him, eyes blazing. "We are talking about Seth here, right? The man who raised you as his own son? The man who—"

"I was concerned," Vadim said, taking her hands in his. "Surely you understand why?"

"Actually, no. I don't."

The outer door swung open again, this time admitting Edric, a platter of meat and a wine bladder balanced in his hands. As he looked about, an expression of horror stole over his face. "You left Sir Anselm unattended? Erde!" Without another word, he hastened for the bedchamber.

Harold sighed as he watched his friend's departing back, shaking his shaggy black head. "Such devotion to a woman cannot be healthy. No good will come of it, mark my words."

"Consider them marked." Although Vadim understood Edric's motives, he feared Agatha would break the simple fellow's heart. "Let us follow our friend's example and eat before we return to work." For the sake of the living, the grim task of disposing of the dead needed to be completed as soon as possible. The heat of the day would only increase the rate of putrefaction.

Martha placed her hand on his forearm, stilling him. "But I still need to talk to you about that *other* matter, remember?" She arched her eyebrows, clearly unwilling to speak more plainly in Harold's presence.

Her delicacy did her credit. Vadim smiled and placed a kiss on top of her tousled head. "Put aside your concerns, my love. Despite what you may have heard, nothing has changed."

Martha looked up at him and smiled, her eyes sparkling. "Really?"

"Really." He ran his finger down her cheek. "If your heart is set on Darumvale, so be it."

"Oh, thank you!" She flung her arms about his neck, imprisoning him in a tight embrace, showering his face with kisses. "And I'm sorry for being such an evil mare earlier, okay?"

"Were you? I hardly noticed." His body stirred again at their close proximity. With Harold watching, that would never do. Reluctantly, he set her away from him.

***

Whatever else Anselm suffered from, it wasn't from neglect. While Vadim and Harold went off to work, Martha kept Edric company.

Agatha returned shortly after noon, her doughy face creased with sleep. "You stayed then?" she said, looking at Edric. "I confess, I am amazed."

Edric had been dozing on and off for the past hour, but Agatha's appearance reanimated him. He leapt up from his seat and hurried toward her, his eyes glowing with warmth. "'Twas an easy task, m'lady. I would gladly face much greater trials if you asked it of me. Here. Let me take that from you." He relieved Agatha of the woven basket she carried hooked over her arm. "Such a fine woman should not be so encumbered."

Agatha's smile transformed her face into that of a much younger woman, but she allowed Edric to take her basket.

Martha's eyes welled up at the sweetness of Edric's words. It must be her hormones. She looked away, and wrung out Anselm's head cloth.

Agatha came over to check on her patient's wound then moved on to touch his feet and hands. "Good. His hands and feet are the same temperature as the rest of him, at least."

Edric hovered at her side. "Aye. I kept rubbing them to banish their chill, just as you instructed me to, my queen... I mean, m'lady."

For once, Agatha didn't scold him for his slip. "You make a fair nurse, master Edric, I grant you that much."

Martha's eyes bulged. From Agatha, that was almost a flowery compliment—high praise indeed. Whatever she might say to the contrary, she was definitely thawing toward Edric.

"Go and take some rest, if you can find any in this infernal castle," Agatha said, dismissing him. "Martha and I will take the next watch."

Edric stroked his hand over the shining dome of his head. He looked dead on his feet. Even so, he was reluctant to leave. "Perhaps I ought to sleep in here. I could lay my bedroll by the wall over there."

"Whatever for?" Agatha demanded, returning to her waspish self.

"Two ladies should not be left alone with only a sick man to defend them."

"To defend them against what?" Agatha exchanged an irritated glance with Martha. "Another invading army? Get on with you!"

Edric's shoulders slumped, and Martha felt a little sorry for him. But Agatha wasn't finished yet.

"Before you go, look in my basket," she added in a gentler tone. "I baked a few pies earlier. Help yourself. They should still be warm."

Smiling again, Edric took a golden pastry from Agatha's basket. He sniffed at it and exhaled with appreciation. "Truly, you are goodness itself, m'lady. Thank you." He winked at Martha and headed for the door with the bouncing steps of a schoolboy. "I will return just as soon as I may."

"Yes, yes." Agatha flapped her hand at him and returned her attention to Anselm.

The door closed with a soft click.

Martha smiled at Agatha. "I don't know whether he'll eat that pie or keep it as love token."

"Not another word, if you please, m'lady."

Agatha looked at her so fiercely, she dared not push it.

While Agatha went to rummage about in her basket, Martha pressed the cold cloth onto Anselm's forehead. He moaned and tried to turn his head aside.

"Shh." She held the cloth in place until he settled. He was still so hot, and not in a good way. She stroked back his hair, each golden strand dark with sweat. His flushed cheeks looked slightly waxy, shiny and stretched too tight over his cheekbones.

"I managed to beg a few herbs from the surgeon to make an infusion." Agatha uncorked a small ceramic bottle with her teeth then brought it over for Martha to sniff.

The scent of a summer meadow filled her nostrils. Even the smell of it made her feel good. "Mmm, lovely."

"It may help a little, but the herbs are old and less potent than I would like." She gave the bottle to Martha while she raised Anselm's head.

Despite his moans of protest, they managed to get most of the fragrant liquid into him. Then Agatha sent Martha from the room while she helped Anselm to use the bottle-shaped chamber pot.

When she returned, she found Agatha smiling as she examined a glass of decanted urine.

"His bladder is definitely undamaged, I am pleased to say." She raised the glass to the sunlight. "'Tis a shade too dark, but I can detect no blood in it. See for yourself."

Martha held up her hands and backed away, nose wrinkled in disgust. "No, that's fine, thanks. I'll take your word for it."

Agatha shrugged and set the glass on the window ledge.

"How's his wound looking?" Martha asked.

"Not as well as I hoped." Agatha's smile faded. "It might have been a kindness if Seth had finished him off."

Martha gaped at her. "You heard about that?"

"The scullery maid told me when I visited the kitchen."

The scullery maid? How the hell had she gotten wind of it? Really, the castle's grapevine was as effective as any social media platform back home.

Agatha sat in the chair Edric had so recently vacated. "What I really want to know is how you managed to persuade Seth to visit his son's death bed." Using her foot, she hooked a low stool and drew it towards her. "Sit down and tell me everything."

The older woman's lack of sensitivity appalled Martha. "Jeez, Agatha! Anselm isn't dead yet." What if he could hear them?

"No matter," Agatha replied, quite unconcerned. "Unless his fever breaks, he soon will be."

They spoke quietly as they kept vigil by Anselm's bedside. Since they'd given him the infusion, he seemed more settled and had ceased mumbling to himself.

Inevitably, the conversation turned to Vadim and the title the new king wanted to bestow upon him.

"How will you like being Lady Edgeway, do you think?" Agatha asked.

"I suppose that's also common knowledge on the castle grapevine?" Martha didn't bother to correct her mistaken assumption.

"For certain." Agatha kicked off her slippers and wriggled her toes. The horny big toe of her right foot poked out through a hole in her stocking. "The king made the offer even before the army reached Edgeway. The loyal finally restored to greatness." She gave a contented sigh. "And my own brother amongst them."

She kept forgetting that Agatha had blue blood. Reynard, however, was another matter. From what she'd seen of the man, he positively oozed with nobility. How would these changes affect Fergus? More than ever, his relationship with Effie looked ill fated.

"Mother!" Anselm's voice startled them, jolting them from their talk. He sat bolt upright in bed, his bright eyes staring into a far corner of the room. "Forgive me."

"Oh shit!" Martha got up and hurried over to him while Agatha went scurrying for her basket. "Anselm?" She leaned in close enough to smell his sweat. "Can you hear me?"

Slowly, he turned his head toward her, fixing her with his unsettling gaze. "Mother?" he whispered. He stared at Martha, seeing yet not seeing her. His pale lips twisted into a beaming smile. "It is you!" Without warning, he seized her hands and brought them to his lips, kissing each one in turn. His mouth felt hot against her hands. "Praise the Spirits! I thought you were dead." His too-bright eyes glittered with unshed tears.

Martha's stomach lurched. He thought she was Sylvie? Apparently, even the toughest men cried out for their mothers when the end was near. What should she do?

"Agatha!" She glanced over her shoulder at the older woman's back. From the sound of tinkling bottles, she was making up yet another of her witchy potions.

"Humor him while I make things ready," Agatha replied, then muttered. "With luck, this one might have a more soporific effect on him."

Martha took a deep breath. She could do this. "Why don't you lie down, Anselm?" Her smile felt like a grimace. "You must rest." She tried to disentangle her hands from his, but he gripped then too fiercely.

"I was wrong, Mother. So very—" He broke into a terrible, hacking cough that went on and on.

Martha chewed her lip, anxiety tearing at her insides. She felt so helpless. It was awful to see him this way.

When the coughing fit had passed, Anselm let go of her hands and flopped back down onto his pillow, spent and exhausted.

If only Vadim were here. She longed for him with all of her being. He'd know what to do. In the meantime, there was only one thing for it. She must pretend to be Sylvie. "Take a sip of water, son." She raised Anselm's head and held the cup to his lips. "Slowly now."

When he'd finished drinking, she put the cup aside and dabbed the moisture from his lips with a piece of clean linen. All the time, Anselm studied her face with his intent gray eyes. She stroked his hair back then drew the sheet over his bare chest.

"C-can you forgive me, Mother?" he whispered, regarding her with the hopeful expression of a child.

It tore at her heart to see him so vulnerable and weak. Tears pricked behind her eyes. "Shh." She smiled and sat on the bed beside him. "Of course I forgive you. And so does your father." *Fecking Seth.* He should be the one comforting Anselm in what might be his final moments, not her, pretending to be his dead mother. How could he run out on him this way? But Martha squashed her irritation. Now wasn't the time. "We love you, son," she said gently, trying to imagine what Sylvie might say. "We always have, and we always will."

The words seemed to give him comfort. Anselm closed his eyes and exhaled a long, slow breath. When he looked at her again, a faint smile flickered on his lips. "May I come home?"

Which home? Darumvale, or the place where the spirits of his dead relatives hung out? Did it really matter which?

Martha took his hand and rested it upon her lap, stroking it. "Of course you can, if that's what you really want." What was taking Agatha so long? Deceiving Anselm, even kindly, made her feel horribly uncomfortable. "Hurry up, would you?" she hissed at her through a gritted smile.

"Patience, girl," Agatha said, not bothering to turn around. A spoon clinked against a pot as she stirred her mystery cocktail. "'Tis almost ready."

Suddenly, the door of the bedchamber flew open and crashed against the wall.

"Erde!" Agatha fumbled, almost dropping her cocktail in her fright.

"Jesus!" Martha leapt off the bed, clutching at her pounding chest as Vadim strode into the room.

His eyes swept quickly left and right before they finally came to rest upon her. Then the grim set of his jaw relaxed and his dark eyes softened. "You are safe!" he said, his words slightly breathless. There was no mistaking his relief.

"Of course I am." Martha frowned. "Why? Shouldn't I be?" He looked delicious, all hot and bothered, his naked shoulder poking through the gaping neckline of his linen shirt. "Are you okay?"

"'Twas the strangest thing..." With a brief glance at Anselm, he came over to the bed. "I was loading a wagon when I thought I heard..." He shook his head and raked back his sweaty hair. "Folly! I must have taken too much sun," he said with a smile.

Martha cocked her head to one side, curious. "What did you think?" She tried to touch him, but he shied away.

"I am filthy, love."

"Then you should not be here, contaminating my sick room," Agatha snapped. "Come back later when you are clean."

Martha rolled her eyes. "Go on," she said softly. "Tell me."

"I thought I heard you... calling my name." He grinned. "There. Now you may mock my foolishness."

But Martha didn't smile. Hadn't she been wishing for him only a few minutes ago? Spooky! Unwilling to discuss the matter in front of Agatha, she said simply, "I'm glad you came." She glanced at Anselm who lay staring up at them, smiling to himself. "He's not looking good, Vadim. He thinks I'm Sylvie." She stroked Anselm's fingers as they lay on the coverlet, and he clasped her hand tightly again. "Ooh! I could murder Seth for bailing on him."

Anselm became animated again. "Father?" He fixed his eyes on Vadim. "I c-can scarce believe you are here, but it does my heart good to s-see you." Suddenly he grimaced, sucking in his breath in a hiss. "It h-hurts so much," he said, hugging his arm about his waist.

Vadim moved closer to his brother. "I know it does," he said gently.

At last, Agatha's potion was ready. "Here," she said, thrusting a small glass phial into Vadim's hand. "Get him to drink this if you can. It has a foul taste, but it will ease his pain a little."

Vadim moved behind Anselm and helped him to sit up. "Drink this for me." He held the phial to Anselm's lips.

Obediently, Anselm opened his mouth, but he gagged after the first sip. "Poison!" He spluttered and struggled to pull free.

But Vadim didn't let go. "No, son," he soothed. "'Tis only medicine. Bad medicine, I grant you, but it will make you feel better. Drink it down fast for me."

In a couple of swallows, Anselm drained the phial. He gagged and was almost sick, but Vadim covered his mouth. "You must keep it down, my son." He took the cup of water Martha handed him and held it to Anselm's lips. "This will help wash the taste away. Good lad."

Martha picked up the empty phial Vadim had dropped in the bed and sniffed at it. *Ugh!* The potion smelled like week-old water from the bottom of a flower vase. Poor Anselm.

With great gentleness, Vadim helped Anselm lie back on the mattress. Then he covered him with the linen sheet and pressed a kiss to his brow. "Sleep now," he murmured. "Hush."

His tenderness warmed Martha's heart. Even Agatha seemed moved, and clearing her throat rather noisily, she turned to the window and began to rearrange the contents of her basket.

Vadim knelt by the bed, stroking Anselm's hair and humming softly to him until he fell asleep. Then he got up. "What can I do, Agatha?" he asked. "What does he need?"

The matron shrugged. "A miracle? Other than that, at this moment, I would give a good deal for some dried willow bark."

Vadim nodded. "Very well." He cast another glance at Anselm's motionless body. "Make a list of your mist urgent requirements, and I will ride out and find it. But you should prepare yourself for the worst, Martha," he said gravely. "I am not sure Anselm will survive his wounds, no matter what we do."

Hadn't she already told him so? Who was Vadim trying to prepare, her or himself? But she said nothing, only nodded.

"In the meantime," he continued, fixing her with his intense dark gaze, "you must give me your oath that you will not leave these chambers, not unless you have an armed escort."

She smiled. After this morning, his warning was hardly necessary, but she gave her word anyway. "Cross my heart; hope to die."

He planted a tender kiss on her lips. "Never hope for that," he murmured fiercely. "Never."

chapter thirty-nine

A COCKEREL CROWED, HERALDING THE START of a new day. Martha was already awake, and munching on another rock wafer. She swept the crumbs off the bed then pulled the bed-covers over her cold feet. Vadim should be back soon.

He'd ridden back to Darumvale in his hunt for the medicinal herbs they needed so badly. All being well, he should be back at the castle any time now. Her ears strained to hear the approach of horse's hooves outside or bootsteps in the corridor, but apart from the birdsong, there was only silence.

She'd just started her third wafer when the sound of hammering drew her to the window. At the center of the courtyard, half a dozen workmen were erecting a platform of some kind, with steps leading up to it. They must have started work yesterday while she was sitting with Anselm. His window didn't look out on this section of the courtyard.

Nails in mouths, the workmen busily *tap-tap-tapped.*

What was that? She squinted, trying to make it out. It looked like a makeshift stage.

Then three more workers arrived, each man with a coil of rope looped over his arms. *Mother of God!* The last crumb of rock wafer stuck in her throat making her cough and splutter. Now she knew what they were building.

That wasn't a stage. It was a fecking scaffold.

Shortly before noon, someone came knocking on Anselm's door. Martha looked up from her place by the window. *Vadim?* She threw down the stocking she'd been darning and was halfway across the room before her common sense kicked in. Why the heck would Vadim knock?

"Huh? Who... what—" Edric sat up from where he'd been dozing by the fire.

"It's all right," Martha touched his shoulder as he made to get up. "I'll go." The poor man still looked exhausted.

The mystery caller knocked again, harder this time, beating at the door in an increasingly frenzied tattoo.

"Alright! I'm coming, I'm coming!" Irritated, she lifted the latch and flung the door open. "Give me a chance, why don't—Oh!"

Martha blinked, mentally trying to place the woman standing before her. She was blond, elegant, and as slender as a reed. "Beatrice?" Martha clutched at the door for support. The last time she'd seen Sir Hugh's wife was on the day they'd almost been raped.

Lady Beatrice was a little more composed although her smile was undeniably strained. "Forgive me, m'lady," she said softly, "but I did not know what else to do." Her lovely face still bore the bruising from that terrible day, and dark shadows haunted her pale blue eyes.

Martha took a deep breath and fought to control her surprise. What on earth could she want? Self-consciously, she smoothed her hands over her hair.

"Perhaps I might...?" Beatrice arched one fair eyebrow and nodded, indicating she wanted to come in.

"Oh, yes. Sorry. Where are my manners?" Martha stepped back. "Do come in." She held open the door, wracking her brain for a reason as to why Beatrice was here.

Beatrice paused at the center of the room, regarding the sleeping Edric with suspicion.

"Don't mind him. He's my husband's man." Husband! She still wasn't used to saying that. "Let's sit by the window." Martha led the way, chattering nervously to fill the silence. "Vadim isn't here at the moment, if it's him you wanted to speak to, but I'm expecting him back any time now."

"No. 'Tis you I came to see." Beatrice perched on the window seat, her hands twisting on her lap. "I wanted to thank you for saving me from those... men. I am deeply in your debt, m'lady. Were it not for your brave intervention..." She floundered, her lovely eyes clouding with unpleasant memories.

"Don't mention it." Martha had no desire to revisit that dark place. "It's me who should be thanking you for sending Vadim to help me. As far as I'm concerned, that makes us quits."

"Hmm?"

"You don't owe me anything, m'lady."

"There is no need for such formality, not between us." Beatrice touched Martha's hand. Her fingers were icy cold. "I would consider it a great honor if you would call me by my given name."

How could she refuse? After the way they'd met, it seemed silly to go on *m'lady*-ing one another. "Okay, *Beatrice*. But only if you call me Martha."

"Thank you, *Martha*." Beatrice squeezed her hand. "Despite your kind words, I still consider myself deeply in your debt. I doubt that any of the women I call friends would have flown to my aid the way you did. Not that I reproach them for it. Although I am now the wife of a respectable man, my past ever taints me. I think you are well aware of my reputation." Her pointed expression dared Martha to deny it.

Martha felt heat rising in her cheeks. Beatrice had been the long-term lover of King Erik before he went and traded her in for a younger model. "What does that matter? In my book, *no* means *no* whether you're a lady or a prostitute."

Beatrice gave a soft laugh. "Even if that lady happens to be a little of both?"

"Even then." Martha said firmly. "No one has the right to take something that's not given willingly. Not even a king."

"You really believe that!" Beatrice gazed at her with wonder. "By the Great Spirit, you are unique." She sighed. "Poor Erik. Although I love my husband, a piece of my heart still mourns my king."

Love my husband? Present tense? "Sir Hugh's alive?"

Beatrice nodded. "For now." Her eyes shimmered suspiciously.

"What do you mean?" This time, it was Martha who reached out to touch the other woman's hand. "Is he wounded?" There was a lot of that going around Edgeway lately.

"A little, but not too seriously, praise be—" But before Beatrice could elaborate, Edric sat up and stretched in his chair, emitting a long, resonant fart as he got up.

Ugh! Both women wrinkled their noses in disgust.

"Edric!" Martha cried. "We have company."

"Huh?" He turned, one hand down his waistband, scratching at his privates. "Oh!" At least he stopped scratching. "My apologies, ladies."

She had to get rid of him for a while. "Would you be an angel and go and fetch some wine for Lady Beatrice? And maybe some of those sweet pastries too?" *Please let him wash his hands first, though.*

He darted a glance toward the sickroom. "What about Sir Anselm?"

"He's fine." Well, if dying could be classed as fine. "Harold and Fergus are with him. Please, Edric?" She gave him her sweetest smile.

"Oh, very well." With ill grace, he stomped for the door, Forge at his heels, muttering, "Now I am a maid-servant! A fine carry on for a fighting man."

"A little bird told me that Agatha and Effie are in the kitchens right now," Martha called after him in a sing-song voice.

"Is that so?" Edric turned, a beaming smile replacing his scowl.

She nodded. "Yep. They're having a baking day down there, apparently."

"What was it you wanted again, m'lady? Wine and pastries?"

"If it's not too much trouble?"

"No trouble at all," Edric assured her, opening the door.

"And Edric?" She called him back again. "It wouldn't hurt to call at the bathhouse on the way. You know how big Agatha is on personal cleanliness."

"An excellent notion, m'lady. Thank you." With a brief bow, he left, leaving the women free to resume their conversation.

Beatrice needed no prompting. "And now I come to the main purpose of my visit although there is no reason why you should help me any more than you already have. I hoped you might... use your influence to aid my husband." She twisted her hands in her lap, the action betraying the distress her tone did not.

What *influence*? Martha frowned. "I'd love to help you, hon, but I don't have—"

"Oh please!" Beatrice grabbed Martha's hands tightly, her eyes glistening with unshed tears. "Rodmar has incarcerated Hugh in the dungeon, along with many other valiant men whose only crime is their loyalty to King Erik." Her lower lip wobbled. "After a farce of a trial at noon, they are to be executed."

"What?" *Jesus, Mary, and Joseph!* Did the killing in this fecking world never end?

Covering her face with her hands, Beatrice broke into quiet sobs, her control gone.

Feeling sick and utterly useless, Martha stroked the other woman's arm. Poor Sir Hugh. Although she hardly knew him, he'd struck her as a nice man. Anselm liked him, and Beatrice was certainly devoted to him.

But what could she do?

Beatrice stopped crying and wiped her eyes with her hands. "Forgive me," she whispered. "I promised myself I would not weep, but here I am." She managed a watery smile.

"It's hardly surprising." She'd feel exactly the same way if their situations were reversed. What would she be like if Vadim had been locked away, condemned to death? She fished a linen hanky from her bodice and thrust it into Beatrice's hand. "Take it. It's okay, I haven't used it."

"Thank you." Beatrice blew her nose and dabbed at her tear-ravaged eyes.

"I'd love to help—I really would—but I'm not sure that I can. Who'd listen to me anyway? Being female doesn't seem to count for much in this world."

"The king would listen to you." A strange light shone in Beatrice's eyes. "Truly, he would."

"To me?" Martha snort-laughed. "To a lowly, female, ex-hostage of the Evil Earl? I don't think so."

"No." Beatrice smiled, becoming animated again. "But he might listen to the beloved wife of Edgeway's newest earl..."

Uh-oh! Martha slumped in her seat. How could she tell her that Vadim hadn't accepted the job?

"By all accounts, your husband rides high in King Rodmar's favor—"

"Stop!" Martha stood up, shaking her head violently. "You've got it all wrong—"

Beatrice got up too, her blue eyes shining with hope. "'Tis

unfortunate that your husband has been called away, but you might speak in his stead. Rodmar would hear you!"

"No, he wouldn't!"

"The prisoners would swear fealty to your husband, and to the new king if they were only given the opportunity to do so." Beatrice took Martha by the arms. "Oh, please, will you not at least try? Must I beg for your aid? Is that it? I will if I must." Suddenly, she dropped to her knees, looking up at Martha with huge puppy eyes. "I love him so very dearly, you see."

Oh, God! "Please get up." Martha felt like weeping herself. The other woman's desperation tore at her heart until she couldn't bear it.

"Not until you agree to help me."

"I can't. I just—"

"For the sake of my unborn child, please try!"

Martha's blood froze. *She's pregnant?*

The door of Anselm's bedchamber room swung open, and there was Harold. "Is there anything amiss, m'lady?" His black bows knitted together in a frown as he looked from one woman to the other.

"No, we're fine." Martha flashed a quick smile to reassure him, while her mind reeled with Beatrice's shock revelation. *A baby?* She extended her hand down to her. "Please get up."

Beatrice shook her head. "Only if you give me your word that you will try to save my husband."

"Shit!" Martha stalked away in frustration, raking her hands through her hair. "God damn it!" What should she do now? Tell Beatrice the truth and shatter her heart into even smaller pieces? And what about the poor baby?

"M'lady?" Harold wandered over, accompanying her as she paced the small confines of the room. "What vexes thee?"

She couldn't answer. The lives of Edgeway's many prisoners might now rest on Vadim becoming earl. Only he hadn't accepted the title, had he? To please her.

Feck!

Beatrice stubbornly remained on her knees, her eyes tracking Martha as she wandered about the room.

"Shall I remove this lady from your presence?" Harold asked.

Martha came to a sudden decision and stopped walking. "No." Her stomach gave a flutter. It was a weird sensation, like tiny bubbles of gas. Nerves? Or maybe her own unborn baby was trying to pressure her too. She rested her hand on her stomach. Whatever it was, she knew what she had to do.

She turned to Harold. "Can Fergus be trusted not to finish Anselm off if we leave them alone for a while?"

"Certainly. The lad's love of Vadim far outweighs any hatred of his brother. Why do you ask?"

Martha took a deep breath. "I promised Vadim I wouldn't go out without an armed escort. Lucky you, H. Get your sword, because you're it." She turned back to Beatrice. "Fine. You win. You can get off your knees now."

"Oh, bless you, my dear!" Beatrice scrambled to her feet, her face illuminated by a brilliant smile.

"Just don't hope for too much, okay?"

"Yes, yes!"

Martha sighed. Why did she have the feeling that her warning had fallen on deaf ears?

chapter forty

VADIM REACHED THE OUTSKIRTS OF Darumvale with the setting sun. The lengthening shadows bore more than a hint of autumn's chill. Shivering, he reined his horse to a walk then turned into the village.

The village dogs immediately surrounded them, barking and nipping at his horse's heels in excitement. The horse lashed out, ears flat back in displeasure.

"Easy, Tarq." Vadim ran his hand down the animal's sweat-flecked neck in an attempt to calm him. He was still unfamiliar with the black courser's temperament, having owned him for precisely one day. Tarq was a gift from the king, a costly token of Rodmar's gratitude for his loyalty.

But Vadim was cynic enough to see through the guise. Beneath his magnificent wrappings, Tarq was a bribe, a bribe to coax him into accepting the earldom, nothing more.

Perhaps when Rodmar learned he intended to refuse the title, he would take back his lavish gift and pass the courser on to a man more susceptible of the honor. Until then, Vadim intended to make the most of him.

Several village lads came to Tarq's aid, shooing off the dogs then standing open mouthed with wonder as they gazed upon this jewel amongst horses. Vadim flung his leg over the horse's neck and dismounted while the boys came to life, jostling one another in order to be the first to take the horse's reins.

Vadim fought to conceal his smile. "You will see to it that he is watered and given a stall to rest in?" The lads' babbled assurances followed him as he walked away.

Now to find Ma. If anyone possessed the herbs he sought, it was she. He marched across the street, neatly dodging the pack of strutting, hissing geese, and pushed through the doors of the Great Hall into the familiar smoky gloom.

"Ma? I am in urgent need of—"

The words died in his throat as he spied Seth sitting by the rectangular hearth with Ma at his side. They both turned as he entered, surprise registering on their faces.

"Forgive my intrusion." Vadim paused and bowed his head. *Erde!* In his haste to come here, he had all but dismissed Seth from his thoughts. It was time for a swift tactical retreat. Another violent scene with the chief was the last thing he needed. "I will return later."

There were other wise women in the village he might ask for supplies, Old Mother Galrey for one, though the thought of knocking on her door filled him with dread.

With a strained smile, he turned to leave the way he had come, but Seth called him back.

"Vadim, wait!" He sounded more desperate than angry.

Slowly, he turned, steeling himself for another confrontation. Seth was on his feet, advancing on him.

The bruise on Vadim's jaw throbbed with renewed ferocity in the presence of its maker, but he resisted the urge to touch it. "You wished to speak to me, m'lord?"

"For certain, I do." As Seth drew nearer, he extended his arms, holding them wide as if to embrace him. "But first, let us put aside the cold address of formality, I beg of you."

Vadim drew himself to his full height. "I cannot think what you mean." A better man might have been more gracious, but he still smoldered with the injustice of yesterday's altercation outside the infirmary.

"Very well." Seth stopped walking and lowered his arms. "Then save your breath and harken to me, lad. I know I have wronged you. My drunkenness is a poor excuse for my actions. Please believe that I am heartily sorry, for everything. I do not expect you to forgive me, but nonetheless you have my sincerest apology."

Not without difficulty, Vadim hardened his heart though

Seth's words moved him a good deal. "I have spent this morning deceiving Anselm, pretending to be you, his own father. Tell me, Seth, why did you run? At this very moment, your son lies dying, tended by people who, for all their kindness, are naught but strangers to him—"

"No. You have it wrong, m'lord. I did not—"

But Vadim was in no mood to listen. "The only person he can count as a friend is my wife. Not that he can currently distinguish her face from poor Sylvie's—"

"Enough!" Ma shrieked, clanging a wooden spoon on a metal cooking pot to silence him.

Wearing matching expressions of shock, both men turned to look at the frail old lady beside the hearth. Ma seldom raised her voice, but when she did, it was usually wisest to listen.

"Seth did not run away," she said. "Well, not in the way you imagine. He returned here in search of medicinal supplies."

Arching his eyebrows in disbelief, Vadim glanced at Seth's bowed head. "Then, why is he still here?"

Gripping her walking stick, Ma struggled to her feet.

Vadim flinched beneath her glare. Suddenly, he felt like a naughty child again, caught in some act of mischief.

"Have a care, lad," she said softly. "You are not earl quite yet."

"I have no intention of—"

"Come here, both of you."

Neither man moved.

"Do I have to come over there and fetch you? Believe me, neither of you mighty warriors have grown too big to feel the weight of my hand. Now, sit!"

Casting sullen glances at one another, Vadim and Seth shuffled over to the fire and sat down while Ma stood over them, flexing her gnarled fingers on her walking implement. Frail as she was, Vadim had no doubt that she would carry out her threat if either of them defied her.

"That is better." She glared at their stony faces. "I will see to the gathering of provisions. While I am gone, you boys will remain here until you find a way to smooth those ruffled feathers."

Seth raised his shaggy red head. "But, Ma—"

She silenced him with a look. "And then," she said coldly, "you will get yourself cleaned up, my son. I grow weary of seeing you wandering this village like an unkempt, ill-humored bear. It stops. Today."

Vadim bowed his head in an attempt to hide his smile, but he was not quick enough.

"As for you, *m'lord.* I suggest you direct your thoughts to ways in which you might make things right with your long-suffering wife. Martha must love you a great deal to have taken you back after all the ways you have insulted and neglected her of late. Oh, yes!" She gave a grim smile when Vadim looked up. "I have heard a full account of it."

Indeed? And only one person could have told her. Vadim darted a venomous glance at Seth.

"Now, get on with it. Make peace, both of you." With that, Ma hobbled away, muttering to herself, her feet shuffling though the dry floor rushes. The outer doors creaked then closed behind her, but neither man moved. Their eyes remained determinedly fixed on the fire's ever-shifting flames.

In the ensuing silence, Vadim became aware of the smallest sounds: the crackling of the flames as they licked over a piece of wood, the gentle creaking of the hall's roof timbers, and in the distance, his ears discerned the distant ringing of the forge. Young Will, hard at work in his dead father's shop. Poor Jared. So many good people gone, and much too soon.

Vadim sighed, his anger suddenly spent. After all that had happened, a drunken punch and a few harsh words counted for little. He did not want to be at odds with Seth. For all his failings, he loved the man.

He smiled, imagining how foolish they both must look. Two men, full grown, forced to sit on a bench at the whim of a cantankerous old lady. He looked at Seth and found the other man watching him, red faced with the effort of suppressing his amusement.

"An unkempt bear?" Seth's grin broadened, and his eyes twinkled. "Is that what people are saying about me?"

"Believe me," Vadim returned his smile. "You have been called worse."

At the same time, they exploded into laughter, the sound of it dispelling any remaining hostility between them. They exchanged a handshake then pulled one another into a brief, hard hug, talking over one another in their haste to apologize, tripping over their words. At last they were themselves again.

"Ma knew I was coming even before I even arrived," Seth said when they settled down to talk. "I would be on my way back to Edgeway were it not for her. Unfortunately, my mother has plans of her own." Seth gave a rueful smile. "She intends to accompany me back to Edgeway on the morrow. On the wagon, no less."

"What?" Vadim stared in shock. "She proposes to nurse Anselm herself?"

Seth nodded. "It looks that way."

"But we cannot afford to delay." As determined as Ma was, a swift ride by horseback was beyond her, and the wagon traveled all too slowly. "I fear Anselm will not last out the night." Vadim raked back his hair one handed. "Even if we leave at once, it might still prove too late."

"I feared the same thing, but the runes revealed a different tale."

"Oh?" Vadim sat up straighter. Ma's gift of The Sight rarely led her wrong. He would never question her ability in this matter. "What did she foretell?"

"She would not say, but she immediately commissioned young Will to make her some instrument or other. I cannot pretend to know what it is for, but Ma insists it is vital to Anselm's recovery. Until then..." Seth spread his hands in a gesture of resignation. "What else can I do?"

"Can she not send word to Agatha? When the instrument is ready, I could ride back ahead of you and—"

"I made a similar suggestion myself, but Ma would not hear of it. Agatha is a gifted nurse, no one would deny it, but Ma will not trust her to wield this mysterious tool of hers, not on her grandson."

"She has accepted him back into the fold, then?"

"Aye. Remarkably swiftly, as it happens." Seth smiled. "She thinks a lot of your lass, m'lord. When she heard of how Anselm saved your Martha, her resentment fled. Still, tomorrow feels a long time away."

It did indeed. In the meantime, they would just have to cool their heels. Vadim sighed. He longed to return to Edgeway—to Martha. Throughout the journey to Darumvale, a curious sense of unease had afflicted him, increasing with each furlong he traveled away from her. A cold rock seemed to have settled within his heart. Vadim pressed his hand to his chest, but the discomfort remained.

Martha's assurances that she would not wander the castle without an armed escort did not guarantee her safety. Never had he met any woman who courted trouble as she did. And thus far, she displayed an uncanny talent for attracting it.

"Well? Will you travel back with us, m'lord?" Seth asked. "I cannot deny that I would value your company on the road."

As much as Vadim longed to return to Martha, family duty obliged him to stay. He cursed his misfortune. Traveling by wagon! Even at full speed, a snail would easily outpace them. But with Rodmar's hired swords disbanded and roaming wild about the countryside, he could not in good heart leave Seth to defend his aged mother alone.

"Certainly, I will," Vadim replied with as much grace as he could muster.

It was only a brief delay, after all. By this hour tomorrow, they would be back at the castle. Martha was well protected. He had left her in the care of men he trusted—good men. Surely no harm would befall her in such a short period of time.

"I suppose," Seth said, getting up from his seat, "I ought to see about arranging my bath before Ma takes me to task again. Would you care to help me fetch water from the well?"

One more day. A few brief hours.

Vadim shrugged and stood up. "Of course." Anything to while away the long hours between now and then.

chapter forty-one

MARTHA ADJUSTED THE HEAD SCARF she'd put on in an attempt to look "decent" then, taking a deep breath, marched up to the two fully-armored knights who were standing guard outside the doors of the Great Hall. "I need to speak to the king, please."

"His Grace is resting," the taller of the two men informed her in a slightly accented voice. "Come back at noon," he said looking down his aquiline nose at her. "If you are fortunate, he may grant you a private audience after the trial."

"But that'll be too late!" Martha glanced over her shoulder to where Harold and Beatrice stood hovering at the foot of the staircase—the latter sending her a smile of encouragement.

She tried again. "Would you at least give him a message—?"

"Come back at noon!" The second guard growled in a voice that brooked no argument. He touched the hilt of his sword. "Now, be on your way, woman."

Great. This was going well. "And where will this *trial* be taking place?"

"In here, of course." The first guard looked at her as if she was stupid.

"Fine. In that case, I'll wait if you don't mind?" She smiled sweetly at the stony-faced duo. "I'd like to get a good seat." Preferably near the front, as close to King Rodmar as possible, although she still had no idea what she was going to say to him when she got there.

"As you will." Having dismissed her, the guards began speaking to one another in a foreign language. It sounded a bit like French, but languages had never been one of her strong points. She beckoned Harold and Beatrice over.

"Well?" Beatrice arched her fair eyebrows. "What did they say?"

"They won't let me in. We'll have to wait, I'm afraid."

Harold frowned. "Did you give them your name, m'lady?"

"Believe me, those two aren't letting anyone through." She glared at the two knights, but they pointedly ignored her and continued with their murmured conversation. "I didn't want to push my luck and end up in the dungeon myself." She couldn't help anyone from there, not that she was all that confident she'd do any better from out here. Still, for Beatrice's sake, she had to try.

They didn't have long to wait. As noon approached, more people arrived and joined the queue behind them until the spacious entrance hall was full, rumbling with the sound of excited voices. Harold did his best to prevent then from getting too jostled and kept as close to the two door guards as possible. While they were waiting, Forge emerged from the direction of the kitchens. Martha called him over, extremely glad to see him. She needed all the moral support she could get, even the four-legged variety.

Outside in the courtyard, a bell tolled, striking the hour of noon, and the knights finally opened the doors. With a collective roar of anticipation, the crowd surged forward. Martha and Beatrice clung tightly to Harold as they were swept inside on a powerful wave of humanity.

"Over there!" Beatrice pointed to a bench at the far end of the room. It was close to the dais, presumably, where Rodmar and his advisers would be sitting.

Harold wasted no time and pulled them through the crowd, roughly elbowing aside anyone who came too near.

They were lucky to find somewhere to sit. For most people, it was standing room only. Martha settled onto the bench with a sigh of relief and looked around, watching the room fill up.

Despite the open windows, the hall grew uncomfortably warm, concentrating the overpowering stench of unwashed bodies. Babies bawled and, from somewhere, a pig squealed.

Harold said the pig owner probably wanted the king to make a ruling in some dispute or other, most likely with a neighbor.

Forge had crawled beneath the bench to get away from the peril of careless feet so Martha used him as a footstool, resting her legs on the comforting bulk of his back. Her stomach quivered with nerves. The last time she'd been in here was on the night of that awful dinner, when the Evil Earl had brought Madoc the Seer to quiz her. It seemed like an age ago now.

Although King Rodmar hadn't been in residence very long, he'd already made changes to the décor of the castle's grandest hall. Vast lengths of gold silk hung in swathes from the roof beams, flapping in the breeze like the sails of a ship. Intricate tapestries ran the length of every wall, each depicting either a hunt or a battle scene in rainbow-bright hues. Whoever Rodmar was, he obviously wasn't short of money.

A long, shrill blast from a hunting horn put an end to the cacophony of voices. Silence descended, and a herald took to the raised stage.

"Citizens of Edgeway, men of Erde," he cried in a loud, clear voice. "Pray, be upstanding for your liege lord. From the mighty house of Weyland, blessed by the Spirits, and newly returned to these blessed shores, I give to you your king, the rightful King of the Norlands, Rodmar!"

The crowd erupted into cheers and surged toward the dais. Martha craned her neck, eager to catch her first glimpse of the man who had turned Edgeway on its head. And suddenly, there he was—the man himself, flanked by a flock of richly-robed advisers.

Amidst the crowd's roars of approval, Rodmar smiled and took his seat on the ornate golden throne set in the middle of the dais. He was younger than Martha had expected, somewhere in his mid-thirties, perhaps. On his head, he wore a simple gold circlet, and his hair cascaded in blond waves about the shoulders of his burgundy-colored robe. His suntanned face, contrasted with a neat golden beard.

At length, he raised his hand, a signal for the exuberant crowd to pipe down. Gradually the room fell quiet, every face looking up, straining to hear the first words of their new king.

"For too many years, I have lived in exile." Rodmar spoke softly as he looked about the faces before him. "I was a nomad, cast out by those who dubbed me an enemy of our most beloved land. To be banished from the country of one's birth..." He shook his head as if overcome with emotion. "Believe me, my friends, there is no greater injury than that."

Either he meant it, or he had the soul of a true politician. Whatever it was, a sympathetic murmur rippled through the crowd. They were lapping it up.

"I thank you, my people, for the warmth of your greeting. 'Tis balm to the wounds of my heart." His smile drew several cheers, most of them female.

Martha resisted the urge to roll her eyes. It'd take more than a handsome face and a few pretty words to convince her. Since coming to Erde, she'd learned to be suspicious of everyone. She'd reserve judgment until later. Let the king's actions speak for him.

"And so, together, let us rebuild this land of ours." Rodmar rose from his throne, his voice ringing out, increasing in strength. "Let us sweep aside the wilderness years and begin afresh. Today we make a start by removing those who oppose us." Another smile. More cheers.

Oh, please. This time Martha did roll her eyes. She couldn't help it.

With a wave of his hand, the king signaled to the door guards. "Let the prisoners be brought forth!"

From a distance came the echoing beat of a drum. Like the pulse of a heartbeat, it came nearer and nearer, loud and ominous. Every head turned, all eyes fixed on the doors. As the drumming came closer, even the pig stopped squealing. Martha wiped her clammy hands down the skirt of her gown and exhaled a pent-up breath.

Then, there they were—the prisoners. To a man, they looked utterly beaten. Dressed only in their filthy linen shirts and trousers, they shuffled into the hall, eyes fixed firmly on the ground.

"Hugh!" Suddenly, Beatrice was on her feet, running toward the line of manacled men.

Sir Hugh raised his head. The grime of battle still daubed his face, and dark shadows hung beneath his weary eyes. "Bea?"

"Get back!" One of the guards shoved Beatrice into the crowd.

With an angry roar, Sir Hugh came to life, barging into his jailers, desperately trying to reach his woman. With his hands chained behind his back, however, he didn't have a prayer. Another guard administered a swift, hard punch to his exposed stomach, and Hugh crumpled to the ground. The crowd *oh*-ed and *ah*-ed, many of them laughing and jeering the condemned men.

With a feral cry, Beatrice launched herself at her husband's assailant, clawing at him with her bare hands, cursing as she went for his eyes.

Oh, shit! Martha stood up, preparing to go to her aid, but Harold pushed her firmly back onto her seat.

"Stay put!" he growled then set off through the crowd toward her, his mouth set in a grim line.

When Harold grabbed her arm, Beatrice didn't recognize him at first. She lashed out with her fist, landing a hard blow on his bearded jaw.

Martha flinched. It was an impressive punch.

But Harold didn't react. With a nod to the guard, he tucked the madly squirming woman beneath his arm and carried her away.

The guards, meanwhile, had dragged Sir Hugh back onto his feet. As he looked up, Martha happened to meet his eyes. A look of recognition then gratitude flashed in their kindly depths, and he inclined his head toward her.

"Sit down!" Harold pushed Beatrice down onto the bench, sandwiching her between him and Martha. "Not another move or I swear, I will take you outside." He rubbed his jaw where she'd punched him.

Martha grabbed Beatrice's sleeve as she tried to get up again. "Don't, lovey. I know you're desperate, but this really isn't helping him. If we're thrown out of here, it's over. Hugh's as good as dead." And he still might be. What the hell was she supposed to say? The thought of addressing Rodmar made her long for the privy.

Beatrice stopped fighting and, with a strangled sob, she covered her face with her hands.

The guards shoved the prisoners into place, herding them into a line before the dais. There were only a dozen men—mostly knights and nobles from the looks of them.

"Where are the others?" Martha asked Harold. "You know, the men-at-arms, the ordinary soldiers?"

"The fate of their masters awaits them."

"What?" Her eyes widened. "They don't even get a trial?"

Harold shook his shaggy head then returned his attention to the unfortunate men before them. Martha clasped Beatrice's hand and glared daggers at Rodmar. Throughout the disturbance, the king's face had remained as expressionless as stone.

How could he do this? Cattle got better treatment than Edgeway's prisoners did. For all his fancy words, he was no better than King Erik had been.

As if aware of her hostile stare, Rodmar turned his head and met her eyes. She shivered and quickly looked away. Why was he looking at her? It was most unsettling.

Once order was restored, another thick blanket of silence descended, broken only by several chesty coughs and the clanking of iron manacles.

Rodmar slowly descended the wooden steps. Then he walked the line of prisoners, looking into the face of each man in turn. "The man you called king is dead. His head sits on a spike on the North Road for the crows to feast on. Which of you will flock to his banner now?" He paused before Sir Hugh. "Is there any reason I should spare you, any of you?"

Martha hissed as Beatrice's fingernails dug into her hand, but she didn't pull away. Her attention was riveted on the scene before her.

"What say you? Sir Hugh, is it not?" A mocking smile played on the king's lips. "Will you put right the sins of your treacherous father this day? Will you renounce your false king and beg your rightful heir for mercy, hmm?"

Beneath Sir Hugh's salt-and-pepper beard, a pulse ticked in his jawline. He held Rodmar's gaze, but made no response. Brave, foolish man. He probably knew that begging wouldn't do him any good.

Martha bit her lip, conscious of Beatrice quietly sobbing at her side.

Oh, where the feck was Vadim? He should have been back by now. She glanced around and saw his friend Reynard standing amongst the king's gaggle of advisers. Maybe he'd say something on the prisoners' behalf and spare her from the ordeal of what she was steeling herself to do.

"Well?" Rodmar was still staring at Sir Hugh, their faces bare inches apart. "As the senior man in this unholy rabble, will you make no attempt to save them... or yourself?"

One of the guards struck Hugh across the face with the back of his hand, the sharp crack echoing about the silent room. "Answer your king, traitor!"

Sir Hugh barely flinched.

"Oh, for the love of the Spirit. Please, Hugh!" Beatrice cried, leaping to her feet again. "If not for me, then do it for your son!" She rested her hand on her still-flat belly.

Hugh whipped round to look at his wife, his jaw sagging slightly. If possible, he looked even paler than he had before.

Beatrice's pregnancy had obviously come as a shock.

"Congratulations," Rodmar said softly. "How unfortunate though that your son will never know you."

He moved on, traveling the line of prisoners, pausing occasionally to ask a question, but the other men appeared to have taken a leaf from Sir Hugh's book of courage and remained stubbornly mute.

Martha couldn't help but admire them.

In the end, Rodmar gave up. With a heavy sigh, he ascended the wooden steps and slumped down onto his golden throne. "Will no one speak for these wretched men before I pass judgement?"

"You cannot do this!" Beatrice screamed. "My husband is a *good* man!"

Harold kept a firm hold on her arm, but made no attempt to silence her.

"Someone other than wives and sweethearts, perhaps?" Rodmar continued, sounding rather bored.

This is it. Stomach churning, Martha got up and smoothed her hands over her skirt. How the hell was she supposed to address a medieval king, let alone talk to one in a respectful manner? Her breath shuddered as she tried to inhale.

Ah, feck it! All she could do was be herself.

"I will," she announced in a loud voice. "I'll speak for them."

With a collective gasp, hundreds of pairs of eyes turned in her direction—including Rodmar's. Martha blushed, wilting beneath the sudden weight of the crowd's scrutiny.

"What are you doing?" Harold hissed through his stage smile. "Please reconsider. Your husband—"

"Vadim isn't here, is he?" She glanced at Beatrice. "I'll do my best, okay? Just don't expect too much." The new king didn't seem like he was big on clemency.

Beatrice nodded furiously, the force of her tears rendering her speechless.

She approached the dais with the faithful Forge at her side. She clung tightly to his collar, her legs wobbling like jelly. As one of the guards stepped into her path Rodmar waved him away.

"Let her speak!" He beckoned her closer. "Will you give us your name, my good woman?"

"M-Martha." She clung tighter to Forge's collar. "Martha... Bigalow." Damn it. What was Vadim's surname? Did he even have one?

Fortunately, Reynard came to her aid, muttering in a quiet aside to the king, "Lord Vadim's wife, sire."

"Indeed?" Rodmar arched his eyebrows then glanced at Forge. "I thought I recognized his hound. A very fine animal, that."

Martha stood at the foot of the steps trying not to think about how many people were staring at her.

"Very well." Rodmar said. "Speak up, m'lady. I trust you have come to beg for the life of your infamous brother-in-law?"

Anselm was scheduled for execution too? *Shit!*

"I'm af-afraid you might have to forgo the pleasure of executing Anselm, m'lord." *Be polite. Be nice. Smile.*

"Oh?" Rodmar leaned his elbow on the arm of his throne then rested his chin on his hand. "And why is that?"

"He's already d-dying, sire."

"Then, let us hope he makes a miraculous recovery. I had especially looked forward to his execution."

A ripple of laughter traveled through the crowd.

"Yes, I can certainly understand why." Martha forced a smile. Humor might be her best form of defense.

"Oh? You are not very loyal to him, m'lady."

"I know." She gave an exaggerated sigh. "He is a bit of black sheep, but for all his sins he's still family. I wouldn't want to see Anselm dead. Nor any of these men, for that matter."

The merriment faded from the king's eyes. "The fate of these men is not your concern. A lady ought not to wade into water that might prove to be too deep for her."

She blinked. What the hell did that mean? Had he just called her stupid?

"I beg to differ, m'lord... sire." *Damn it.* "Your decisions today will ultimately affect us all."

Rodmar's eyes narrowed. "I have heard tell," he said, "that you are a woman who favors plain speech. Pray, would you be so good as to indulge me now? The hours of daylight are all too finite."

More muted laughter from the crowd.

A flash of heat burned in Martha's stomach. "Fine. Then, I will." If Rodmar wanted plain speech, he could have it. With effort, she reined in her temper. "Apart from backing the wrong horse, what have these men actually done that's so unforgivable?" She waved her hand to indicate the prisoners behind her. "I mean, from what I can see, their only crime is loyalty. You can't execute someone for the mistakes their fathers made. It's... it's just plain wrong."

A shocked *ooh* rose up from the crowd. At the same moment, one of the guards stepped nearer as if to grab her, but Forge growled, teeth bared in warning.

Rodmar stood up. "Leave her be. I asked her to speak plainly and so she has." He walked back down the steps. "What would you have me do then, m'lady? Set them free?"

"Yes," Martha replied. "With certain conditions, why not?"

The king's eyes flashed. "Such as?"

"I don't know... you could take away their lands until they swore loyalty to you. Or have them bound over to keep the peace or something?"

"Indeed I could," Rodmar agreed. "But why would I trouble myself with the taming of malcontents when I can so easily deal with them today?"

Martha swallowed hard, her mouth suddenly as dry as dust. "B-because loyalty is a rare commodity. You need men like this around you—decent men, not like the thugs and rapists who attacked this castle."

There were more shocked gasps from the onlookers.

"Serious accusations, indeed." Rodmar moved closer until Martha could see his weird violet eyes. "Tell me, where does your loyalty lie, m'lady?"

"What? You don't believe me, so you question my loyalty?" She almost laughed. Instead, she pulled away her shawl to display the dark bruising on her neck and then rolled up her sleeves so he could see the marks Jacob and Ferret had left on her arms. "Where do you think I got these? Or take a look at Sir Hugh's wife. The bruises on her face didn't come from her husband, I can tell you that."

Rodmar remained silent for several long moments as he glanced at each woman in turn. It was impossible to read his face. "And these men who attacked you?" he said at last. "Where are they? Can you point them out to me?"

"There's no need, sire. My husband... dealt with them." Or executed them. *Potato, pot-hato.* She raised her chin and looked into Rodmar's eyes. "Believe me, they got what they deserved."

"A punishment befitting their crime?"

She nodded, suddenly tired of it all. "There's been so much killing. Too much. The imposter king is dead, along with his evil cousin, and you've got your throne back. Can't you leave it at that? Don't you see? You've won already. Whatever else they are, these men," she said, pointing to the prisoners, "are noblemen, and I'm sure they still have some powerful friends. Wouldn't the start of your reign go a lot smoother if you weren't having to permanently look over your shoulder for people set on revenge?"

Rodmar stroked his golden beard, apparently considering her words. "Is it your sincere belief that these men deserve another chance at life?"

"It is... I mean, I do, sire."

"And if these men refuse to swear allegiance to the House of Weyland? What then?"

Would they refuse? Martha blushed. Damn. She hadn't considered that.

"Shall we ask them?" The king pointed to Sir Hugh. "What about you, m'lord? Are you prepared to swear fealty to me in exchange for your life, for the chance to look upon your unborn son?"

Hugh remained silent, his eyes locked on Beatrice.

"You see?" Rodmar turned back to Martha with a smile. "It is quite hopeless. They are either too stubborn or stupid to seize the chance of life. Indeed, hanging them might be considered an act of mercy."

She ignored the chuckles of the king's advisors. "But what if someone acted as their... oh, I don't know... their custodian for a while?" Surely in a few months, Hugh and the others would have cooled down enough to see the sense of kissing Rodmar's regal butt?

"A custodian, you say?" The king glanced at his friends, a smile playing about his lips. "Did you have anyone in particular in mind for the role, m'lady?"

Martha wracked her brains for a suitable candidate. What about Reynard? He was a reasonable bloke. But she was out of luck there. Reynard was showing a sudden rapt interest in the floor. Was he deliberately avoiding her eyes? It certainly seemed that way.

Rodmar followed her gaze. "You seek aid from my closest advisers?" He laughed. "I doubt you will have much luck there. Come, m'lady, surely you can do better than that. Might I suggest that you look a little closer to home?"

"I-I don't know what you mean, sire." But she did—or, at least, she was beginning to.

"No?" Rodmar's violet eyes glittered. "Then, allow me to speak plainer: perhaps the new Earl of Edgeway might vouch for the behavior of the prisoners."

"The new earl?" The back of Martha's neck prickled. "I wasn't aware you'd f-found a replacement, sire."

"Oh, indeed I have. Unfortunately, the man I wanted for the role had certain... insurmountable obstacles which prevented him from accepting it." Rodmar grinned at her. "But now, having spoken with your good self, I feel confident those obstacles are about to be removed."

Unable to formulate a response, Martha just stared at him. If she'd walked into a trap, it was her own stupid fault.

A sudden commotion at the back of the room diverted their attention. The people standing nearest to the doors were grumbling loudly as a latecomer forced a path through their midst, fighting his way into the overcrowded hall.

Vadim.

Martha's heart soared. *Oh, thank God!*

He looked tired and a little travel worn, but the sight of him buoyed her flagging spirits. His dark eyes immediately locked on hers, and she had no problem interpreting the unspoken questions lurking in their fathomless depths.

What have you done?

"Ah! Lord Vadim." Rodmar smiled in greeting. "A timely arrival as always. Pray, do come and join us. Your good lady and I were just discussing crime and punishment. I think we can all agree her views on the subject have been most illuminating."

Vadim finally broke free of the crowd and hurried to Martha's side, immediately seeking her hand, clasping it with his strong, warm fingers. He bowed to the king. "I hope she was not too forthright in stating her opinion, my liege?" Pulling Martha to his side, Vadim tucked her protectively beneath the shelter of his arm. "What have you been saying, my love?" he murmured against her headscarf.

For the life of her, she couldn't remember—her mind was much too scrambled. God! It was good to have him back, though. Already, she felt the tension easing from her bunched-up muscles. She shrank closer to the comforting heat of his body, and the scent of horse and leather enveloped her. *Mmm.* He smelled so good. However, this wasn't the appropriate moment to be lusting after him.

"Not at all." Rodmar was saying, smiling as he shook Vadim's hand. "After the initial shock, I found her candor most refreshing. Almost like taking a dip in a freezing lake on a summer day, in fact."

Oh dear. She grimaced. That didn't sound too good at all.

Vadim obviously thought the same way. "I feared as much," he said with a sigh. "Tell me the worst, sire. I take full responsibility for anything—"

"Peace, m'lord. Although your lady was passionate in her defense of the accused she has done me no real harm." The king glanced at the miserable line of prisoners. "In fact, when viewed in another light, her words might have done me a great service. Let us put it to the test and see." Suddenly deadly serious, he said. "For the final time, my friend, do you want the position of earl or not?"

Time seemed to slow. Each second, every heartbeat, felt like a decade. The walls of the Great Hall seemed to press in until Martha could hardly breathe. In a blinding flash of insight, she suddenly understood just how much the title of earl meant to Vadim. There was no mistaking the hungry glitter in his eyes. Oh, it wasn't his fault; becoming the Earl of Edgeway was in his blood, hard-wired into his DNA, an inextricable part of who he was. The earl and the outlaw were forever intertwined. Where one ended, the other began. There was no parting them.

She knew he loved her. If she asked him to walk away now, he'd do it. For her. All she had to do was shake her head and the uncertainty would be over.

The thing was, when it came down to it, she couldn't ask him to. If she made him give up his dream, he'd eventually resent her for it. Oh, not now, perhaps, but some day.

And what about the prisoners—Sir Hugh and the others? Giving the wrong answer would send them to their deaths. She frowned. Could she live with such a terrible stain on her conscience?

Vadim raised her hand to his lips. "Have no fear, my love. Just answer with your heart. We will make it work, whatever it is you decide, I promise."

His softly murmured words warmed her fingers and sent a bolt of electricity racing down her arm. When he put it like that, how could she refuse?

"Well?" Rodmar arched his eyebrows, obviously growing tired of waiting.

Taking a deep breath, Martha nodded. "Fine. Let's do it." Vadim's joyful smile was ample reward for any sacrifice on her part.

He kissed her hand then turned to face Rodmar. "I thank you for your most generous offer, my liege. I gladly, and most humbly, accept."

Rodmar positively beamed, reminding Martha of a grinning golden lion. "In that case, all that remains is for me to congratulate you, Lord Edgeway and," his eyes sparkled when he looked at Martha, "the lovely countess, of course."

Oh, feck! What have I done?

But at that moment, Vadim turned, submitting her to his sexiest crooked smile. Her stomach flipped. The promise in his eyes restored her faith. It didn't really matter where they lived. She'd always miss Aunt Lulu, but Vadim was her future now—him and their baby. As for the fancy title, so what? Beneath their borrowed finery, they'd still be themselves. She smiled as he pulled Reynard into a bear hug, almost lifting the older man off his feet—everyone was getting a happily ever after today, whether they wanted one or not.

No. Learning to love the Earl of Edgeway wouldn't be so difficult. After all, she already loved the outlaw, didn't she? How hard could it be?

acknowledgments

So many people have helped me get 'Wolfsbane' out into the world. Here are just a few of them:

Thank you to all the fabulous people at 'Critique Circle' who toiled through the earliest versions of my manuscript. Your help was, as always, invaluable. Special thanks go to Belfast Larry, Highlander Jill, and 'Gina G' Chris for their tenacity. I promise I'll be back critiquing you guys very soon!

To Jamie, Cristin, Sharon, Rox, and last, but by no means least, Claudia—my Facebook 'Sexy' crew—thank you for your advice, your encouragement, and your friendship. You brighten the darkest of days.

To Krissie and Andrea—my golden girls. Thank you for for being such wonderful beta-readers. Your beady eyes didn't miss a trick! I'm so proud to call you my friends.

Thank you to all the wonderful people who reviewed 'Hemlock' and those who gave it space on their fabulous blogs. You guys truly are the unsung heroes of the self-pubbing world. I'm so grateful for all the great work you do.

Lastly, I want to thank my long-suffering family for their continuing encouragement and patience. You're my safety net, and I love you all. Special thanks go to my wonderful hubby and our two darling kids for putting up with 'Momma' while in 'crazy-author' mode! All done now, my lovelies. Until next time...

other titles by n.j. layouni

Tales of a Traveler Book One: Hemlock

about the author

N.J. Layouni has been weaving stories all of her life—even before she could actually write. For many years, she was a dedicated 'closet writer'. As a result, the attic space of her home is stuffed to the rafters with piles of aging manuscripts depicting fantastical romantic adventures. Tales of daring sword-wielding heroes and strong, feisty damsels who aren't too tough to accept a helping hand sometimes.

As well as being a mouthpiece for the various characters living inside her head, N.J. is a wife, and mother of two children. She lives in Lancashire, UK.

Connect with the NJ Layouni:

Goodreads:
https://www.goodreads.com/author/
show/8107337.N_J_Layouni

Twitter:
https://twitter.com/NJLayouni

Website:
http://njlayouni.blogspot.co.uk/

Facebook:
https://www.facebook.com/pages/
NJ-Layouni/405255156236485?ref=hl

CPSIA information can be obtained
at www.ICGtesting.com
Printed in the USA
LVHW090812270119
605398LV00001BB/147/P